THE WHITE MISTS OF POWER

THE WHITE MISTS OF POWER

KRISTINE KATHRYN RUSCH

MILLENNIUM
An Orion Book
LONDON

First published by
Roc/NAL, USA, 1991

First published in Great Britain in 1992 by
Millennium,
An imprint of Orion Books Ltd
Orion House, 5 Upper St Martin's Lane,
London, WC2H 9EA

A CIP catalogue record for this book is available from the British Library

ISBN (csd): 1 85798 000 x
(Ppr): 1 85798 001 8

Millennium
Book Two

Typeset at The Spartan Press Ltd,
Lymington, Hants
Printed in Great Britain by
Bath Press Ltd, Avon

This book survived two distinct stages in my life. In the first stage, Randy and Jeff Thompson provided valuable criticism; Paul Higginbotham and Kevin J. Anderson provided support and good advice. In the second stage, Nina Kiriki Hoffman added her affection and proofreading skills to theirs. But most of all, I could not have done this without the love and understanding of Dean Wesley Smith. Thanks, partner. I promise the next one will be easier.

Prologue

The wind blew cold off the hills, rustling branches and making the whistle-wood trees moan. Adric shuddered and wrapped his cloak tightly around his shoulders. He glanced back at the great stone palace and, beyond it, the spires of the city. No one had seen him leave. He let out a small sigh. His father would be so angry if he found out where Adric was going.

He turned and faced the grove of whistle-wood trees. The trees bent and huddled together like old men. The pitted bark caught the wind, sent it through with a tone that changed in pitch with the wind speed. Some said the Old Ones lived in the whistle-wood trees. Adric believed it. He thought he saw faces shifting in the black wood.

The moans grew into shrieks. Adric put his hand in his pocket and gripped the bell. The Enos wouldn't hear him, not on an afternoon like this. They would think the bell chime was the cry of a tree. He stared at the hint of the cave opening that he could see through the trees. He might never get another chance to approach the Enos Cache.

He closed his eyes and swallowed heavily. The tree shrieks sounded almost like laughter. He wondered what the Old Ones thought of him, a ten-year-old boy shivering at the edge of the grove. They knew his future. And so, said the legends, did the Enos. He had to know if he would be a strong leader like Gerusha, or if he would become as useless as his father.

The wind rustled his hair and then died. The shrieking laughter faded. Adric pulled the bell from his pocket. He gripped the handle when a hand covered his own.

'No need, Highness.' The voice was soft, raspy, as pitted as the whistle-wood trees.

Adric made himself turn, although his heart thudded against his ribs. An old woman stood beside him. Her skin was dark, wrinkled, and cracked. Her wispy white hair hung to her shoulders. She wore a long gray robe belted at the waist. She looked normal except for her eyes – eyes with no whites, eyes as black and deep as the mouth of the cave.

Her hand tightened on his. 'You have come to find out if you will be loved.'

He shook his head. His heart had moved into his throat. 'I – ' His voice broke and he cleared his throat. 'I came to find out my future.'

Her smile was slow. 'A ruler is loved differently than any other, Highness.'

'I didn't come here to find out about love,' he said. He had never been this close to an Enos before. He didn't realize how spooky the black eyes were, how alien they made a face. 'I came to find out what will happen to me.'

'And love is not a part of that?'

The wind began again. The trees let out a soft, deep hum. When Adric didn't answer her question, the Enos sighed. 'Very well, then. Come with me.'

She led him through the whistle-wood trees to a small clearing. No grass covered the floor, only dirt and the stumps of trees. A small stone hut with a ridged roof sat in the center of the clearing. Adric stopped. 'Aren't we going to the cave?'

The Enos looked at him. A clear point of light radiated from her eyes. 'Do they teach you nothing at the palace?'

Adric frowned.

The Enos shook her head. 'Humans are not allowed into the halls of the Cache Enos, Highness. It is our agreement.'

'Oh,' Adric said, feeling a familiar frustration. He wanted to know so much and they allowed him so little. The ballads said nothing about pacts with the Cache Enos. He followed her across the soft dirt and into the hut.

The hut was chill and damp, even though Kilot had not seen rain for many months. The Enos lit three candles, casting a soft light about the room. A wooden table sat in the center of the room, surrounded by four chairs. A cot rested off to one side, near the fireplace. In the half-light the Enos seemed to have no eyes at all.

'Sit,' she said.

Adric pulled out a chair and sat at the table. He ran a hand along the pitted surface, feeling the ridges and bumps. The table was made of whistle-wood. He tried to stop his hands from shaking. Carving whistle-wood was forbidden.

The Enos sat across from him. 'Place your hands flat on the table,' she said.

Adric did as he was told.

'You wish to see your future,' she said, and he could hear the question in her tone. He nodded. She moved a candle onto the table. 'I will do my best, but remember: time travels in circles through the mind. All future, all past, all present, is a living entity that exists on its own plane.'

She covered his hands with her own. Her palms were cool and work-roughened. A sharp pulling, almost a pain, traveled through him and out his fingers. The wooden surface of the table turned hot, and the Enos flung her head back. For a moment Adric thought she was going to faint. Then she brought herself upright, her eyes empty.

'I see a man running through a forest, a pack of hounds at his heels,' she said, her voice flat. 'He wears rags, but carries the white mists of power within his heart. The same man sits on a dais, hearing petitions. The people believe him to be their protector, but the one he protects is you.'

The whistle-wood burned into his palms, but the Enos's hands froze Adric's fingers and wrist. His eyes stung and a throbbing began in the back of his head.

'A boy's mind may be molded like soft clay, but a man's mind has the strength of granite. A child cowers in the corner while his brother dies. The brother mourns for the child pressed against the cold stone wall, the child who must have the strength of ten men and is too young to have the strength of one.'

Her grip tightened.

'They train you to be ruled as your father is ruled, as your grandfather was ruled before him. A knife glistens in the darkness. A simple silver ring adorns the hand that guides the weapon on its deadly path, the path that seals the darkness forever.'

She released him. He yanked his hands off the table and held them against his chest. The pain had grown worse.

The Enos bowed her head, took a deep breath, and then looked at him.

'What does it mean?' Adric asked.

Her eyes were a faint point of candlelight reflecting in the darkness. 'I do not know, child,' she said. 'I never know.'

'But you said you would tell me what my future is.' Adric rubbed his hands. His palms were reddening, blistering.

'And so I have,' she said. 'I did not tell you I would interpret the meaning, for I cannot. I can see the present, Highness, perhaps only a bit more clearly than you can.'

'What you told me can't help me!' he said.

The Enos smiled, extinguishing the candlelight in her eyes. 'The Old Ones think it can. You wanted me to tell you a bright, beautiful future, to wipe away your sadness. Yet you want to be a great leader like Gerusha. Great leaders are born of hardship, Highness. No one loved Gerusha either.'

'My father loves me.' Adric held his sore hands together, wishing he had some ointment.

The Enos pinched out the candle on the table. 'That is not what your heart tells me.'

Adric extended his blistering palms to her. 'You burned me.'

She extinguished the second candle. The near darkness made her seem younger. 'Pain is the price we pay for knowledge, Highness,' she said softly.

PART ONE

Chapter 1

i

White swirls of mist blanketed the trees, hiding the river that flowed along the edge of Dakin's land. Dakin shivered, wishing he had worn a heavier coat.

The sharp edges of the crumpled letter bit into his palm. Damned bard. He had looked so trustworthy when he approached the great house. He had been too thin and his gaze had been too bright, but his music had been beautiful. Dakin had always loved beautiful music.

The damp grass chilled Dakin's feet. He stared ahead at the forest. The moss-covered trees seemed greener against the fog's whiteness, making the forest itself appear impenetrable. The bard had nowhere to go. The man would die, screaming, screaming until the hounds ripped his voice from his throat.

'I hear of another hunt, Lord.'

Dakin whirled. His Enos stood behind him, dressed in a white robe that matched the fog. Her wizened face, half hidden by the cowl, seemed more foreboding than usual.

'The bard,' he said.

The Enos let the cowl down. 'Do you think that is wise?'

'Have you any objections?'

The Enos shook her head. Water beaded her hair, making her look as if her skull were covered with dewy spiderwebs. 'I guard the land, not its inhabitants.'

She walked away, leaving no impression on the damp grass. Dakin watched her go, feeling slightly unsettled. If she wanted to warn him, she should have come out and said something. Kensington had. In fact, Kensington had been the one who started this whole thing.

A month ago, Dakin had entertained Kensington in the garden just off the great hall. They sat at a table among the sculptured trees and ate pheasant with wild rice while the bard played for them. After dinner, the servants left, the bard finished his last song, and Dakin and Kensington turned to business.

Dakin had never liked Kensington. The man was slender to the point of gauntness. The bones of his face stood out prominently against the hollows of his cheeks, and his dark eyes seemed to miss nothing.

'I am surprised you let that bard serve you,' Kensington said as he leaned back in his chair.

'Indeed?' Dakin gripped the ridged stem of his glass so hard that his fingers turned white. Kensington was a distant relation of the royal family and ranked above Dakin. Dakin didn't dare be rude, even if Kensington had no right to discuss Dakin's household affairs. 'And what should my objections be?'

Kensington shrugged and stared off into the garden. 'I can't believe that you would knowingly harbor a murderer.'

Dakin took a sip of wine, letting the deep, rich flavor caress the back of his throat before he spoke. He hoped that the liquid would wash the sarcasm from his tongue. 'And who is my bard supposed to have killed?'

'The Ladylee Diana of Kerry.'

Dakin set his wineglass down. He had heard a hundred stories about the murderer of the ladylee and had believed none of them. 'That was over a decade ago. Someone would have caught him by now.'

'The bard keeps himself hidden. Your lands are about as far from Lady Kerry's as possible.'

'The bard served Lord Lafa last. If he did indeed murder the ladylee, I'm sure someone would have recognized him there.' Dakin let the boredom seep into his voice. Shadows crept across the clipped hedges, and the garden was growing cool.

Kensington glanced at Dakin. The patch of remaining light painted Kensington's face, darkening the hollows of his cheeks and adding a wildness to his eyes. 'I was there that night. I was with the Lady Kerry. I had planned to ask Diana to be my wife.'

Dakin suddenly understood why Kensington had mentioned the bard. Kensington meant no critique of Dakin's household. Kensington had an old vendetta against the bard. 'This is your vengeance,' Dakin said.

Kensington shook his head. 'It is the Lady Kerry's as well. If you don't believe me, write her. She'll be happy to know the bard has surfaced.'

After Kensington left, Dakin did write to the Lady Kerry. He had her response crumpled in his hand. She knew that the bard had murdered her daughter. She asked Dakin to kill the bard or to extradite him. Dakin would have done neither if it hadn't been for the uprising, and those insulting, hateful songs the bard had sung the night of the great banquet.

Footsteps crunched the grass behind him. Dakin turned. The bard stood behind him, held in place by two of Dakin's manservants. They looked short and fat next to the bard. It almost seemed as if the bard were leading them. He stood tall, the mist shrouding him like a cloak. Chains were wrapped around his waist, holding his hands behind his back. His black hair curled over his collar, and his face, though pale, was darker than the mist.

In the distance hounds bayed, an eerie, undulating sound that told Dakin they knew of the upcoming hunt. They would be down the trail soon.

'One last time, bard,' Dakin said. 'Who do you work for?'

The bard lifted his chin so that his eyes were level with Dakin's. 'I work for you, milord.'

'And not with Rury?'

'No, milord. If I worked with Rury, I never would have tried to stop the uprising.'

Dakin slapped the bard across the mouth. The sound echoed through the glen. Dakin's hand stung. 'I don't appreciate sarcasm from one of my servants, bard.'

Blood trickled from a corner of the bard's mouth. He licked at the blood as if to see if it were there, then tilted his head, and rubbed his lips against his shoulder. The blood smeared on the black cloth. 'It seems to me, Lord,' he said, 'that as soon as I am unshackled, I am a free man.'

Dakin permitted himself a small smile. 'You will be free,' he said.

He turned. The hounds emerged from the mist, straining at their leashes. The droplets of water on their dark fur made them appear even sleeker and stronger than they were. The four hound masters had three hounds each bound to leashes wrapped in their hands. They were big men, and rough, but they all bore scars from the hounds. The hounds seemed to pull their masters along. A tangy odor filled the air, and Dakin wondered if it was the smell of the hound masters' sweat.

They brought the hounds to the edge of the clearing. The animals stood still, waiting. They watched Dakin. Their eyes were beaded and flat. If he made one threatening movement, they would break their leashes and be on him. He had watched those long, yellow teeth tear into Rury. He didn't want them to touch him.

Dakin grabbed the collar of the bard's shirt and ripped off the bloody shoulder. The bard never looked at the hounds. His gaze stayed on Dakin. Dakin looked into the bard's eyes. Dakin had never before realized how cold and blue they were.

Finally Dakin made himself look away. He handed the cloth to one of the manservants, who walked to the hound masters. The hounds, recognizing the ritual, strained toward the manservant. They snuffled at the air, their tongues lolling. A thin thread of drool trickled from one of the hounds' mouths. The manservant's hand shook as he reached over the hounds to hand a hound master the cloth.

The hound master let his three hounds sniff the cloth. They scratched the ground, then tilted their heads back, and howled. Goose bumps ran up Dakin's spine and a shiver of excitement tickled his groin. He thought of the kitchen wench he had brought up to his rooms the last two nights, and wondered if the violence shimmering in the hounds would excite her too.

The hound master handed the cloth to the next master, who let his hounds sniff it. The hounds howled in turn, and the others danced around them. The air tingled with suppressed rage and anticipation. When the hounds were loose, they would shred the bard.

When the last dog howled, Dakin turned to the bard. 'They know your scent now,' he said. 'They know they are supposed to kill you. And they will kill you. No one has survived my hounds, although I'm sure that each who faced them thought he would be the first.'

The hounds pointed their noses at the bard. They all stood still, their gazes on him. Their mouths were open, and saliva trickled from more than one. The bard still hadn't looked at them.

Dakin waved his hand. The manservants let go of the bard. They unlocked his chains and unshackled his feet. He didn't move but continued to stare at Dakin until they were done.

'You have one hour,' Dakin said. 'Use it well.'

The bard nodded once. He rubbed his wrists and walked toward the forest. The hounds strained toward him, yipping as he passed. Some snapped their jaws on the empty air. He stared straight ahead, his stride sure. As he reached the trees, the white mist enshrouded his black-clad frame like an aura. He stepped behind some long green moss and disappeared.

The hounds howled. The hound masters' muscles bulged as they fought to keep the hounds steady. Dakin took a step away from them, their fervor making him nervous. *Do you think that is wise?* the Enos had asked. Dakin shook the voice from his head. The hunts had worked before. They would continue to work.

He stared at the forest, wondering why the mist seemed less opaque.

ii

Seymour leaned against a tree, gathering his luck around him. All morning he had heard the baying of the hounds, the mournful wailing that meant someone was about to die. The hounds had never before come so deeply into the forest. Either someone had run far, which Seymour doubted, or Lord Dakin finally realized that Seymour was alive.

The cold ground dug into his backside. He had been shaking for hours. He had survived the hounds once, through luck and some careful preparation. Usually, though, his luck was poor. He couldn't count on his magic saving him again.

Seymour stood. He had a set of traps scattered a few yards away. He would try a spell once he was certain the hounds were after him. When that spell failed, he would run for the traps. He could catch at least two dozen hounds in those traps; that would stall them for a time and at least give him a lead. He hoped to get enough of a lead to make it to the city safely.

A twig snapped. Seymour swallowed. Branches to his left rustled. He had heard the hounds. They hadn't been that close, he was sure of it. Still, he grabbed his ebony walking stick and finished placing his luck web. He remembered what the hounds were like, their mouths dripping, teeth sharp and pointed. He had seen them come back from a hunt once, bloody froth on their lips. He stood, clutched the stick to his chest, prepared to shove the stick into the ground and begin a chant should he see a hound.

A man burst through the thick blackberry brambles and stumbled on the dirt. His long black hair was matted and tangled with leaves and twigs, his face bloody and dirt-covered. His clothes hung in tatters, and he had lost one shoe. He wouldn't survive much longer.

Seymour took a deep breath. The hounds were chasing someone else, not him. He was safe.

A hound howled. The sound rang through the trees. The man glanced over his shoulder, the fear on his face clear. He was heading toward Seymour's hiding place. Another hound howled. They had found his scent. Seymour bit his lower lip. If he helped the man, he might have Lord Dakin after him again. But if he didn't help, the hounds would tackle the man and tear his skin off while he still lived.

Seymour's hands shook as he lowered his staff to shin level. The man turned forward just before he reached the staff. He tried to jump, but his left foot caught on the round black surface and he tripped, sprawling on the pine needles at Seymour's feet. The man rolled over and started to push himself up, but Seymour grabbed his arm and raised a single finger to his lips.

He moved his staff, checked to see if it was unmarked. The ebony was as smooth as it had been the day Lord Dakin had given the stick to him. Seymour ripped a piece of bloodied cloth from the man's pants. The man was still on his knees, panting, as if he were trying to catch his breath before running again.

'Wait,' Seymour whispered. He tied the bloody cloth to the staff. He could barely breathe. He had been prepared to do this spell, but he had hoped he wouldn't have to. He had never done it successfully. He had hoped that he would have enough luck, but as he stood at the edge of the clearing, traps on one side, hounds on the other, he knew that he would fail.

The underbrush thrashed. Seymour thought he could hear the hounds snuffing forward. The man was getting to his feet slowly, as if he were in great pain. Seymour shoved the staff into the hard dirt. He closed his eyes, picturing his luck web rising from his shoulders and wrapping itself around the staff. He shaped the web into the form of the man behind him. Then Seymour opened his eyes and snapped his fingers.

He could see nothing different. Panic rose in his stomach. The man had gotten to his feet and was swaying as if he were going to fall again. Seymour grabbed the man by the waist and propelled him forward. They had to get out of there, get behind the traps.

They stumbled forward, between the tall, moss-covered trees. Seymour stopped and reached into the undergrowth, setting the traps. They had to work. If they didn't he would be in trouble. As it stood, he figured that he could take the man home for at least a short time. Lord Dakin didn't know that Seymour still lived, which meant that he didn't know about the cabin, as Seymour had feared all morning.

He led the man down the dirt-covered bank into the brook. It was a dying tributary of the river that bordered Dakin's land – barely enough water to get their feet wet – but enough to stall the hounds after they escaped the traps. Seymour helped the man through the water and up the other bank to the small clearing where his hut stood.

A howl echoed through the forest, followed by several more. Seymour had heard that sound from a distance four times in the past three weeks. The hounds had found their quarry. The man turned, his entire body trembling. Seymour felt his own shoulders relax. The Old Ones were smiling on him. The spell had worked.

'We have a little time now,' he said. 'The hounds think they have found you.'

The man glanced once at Seymour and then looked away. The man's reaction – or lack of reaction – stifled some of Seymour's pleasure at his success. The man should have been surprised that a magician had helped him. Instead he seemed to accept it. Seymour shrugged inwardly, wondering who the man was and why Lord Dakin wanted to kill him.

They walked across the path leading to the hut. Grass almost as tall as Seymour brushed them, tickling his skin and making him itch. He was glad that he hadn't cut the grass away from the path. It would be hidden to anyone who didn't know it was there.

The hut was made of stone and smelled damp. Seymour stepped ahead of the man and pushed open the heavy wooden door. Inside, the hut was dark and chilly. The fire had gone out. Seymour had to squint to see the furniture. He helped the man into a chair beside the fireplace, then stacked fresh wood inside the hearth, and started a new fire. When he had come here the first time, he had used the last of his luck to do a simple child's spell on the fires made in the hearth. Any smoke rising from the fire would be colorless and odorless. He was glad that spell had succeeded.

As soon as small flames licked at the logs, Seymour rose. The man hunched in the chair, his hands to his face, breathing heavily. Seymour found his water bucket, dipped a cup in it, and touched the man gently on the shoulder. The man raised his head and opened his eyes.

He took the cup from Seymour and drank. The man's gulping noises were loud in the quiet room. When the man finished, he leaned back and closed his eyes. Within seconds his breathing was easy and steady.

Seymour stared at the man for a moment. His mother had taught him healings for burns, mostly as a protection from his own mangled spell-casting, but she had never taught him how to treat cuts and lacerations. Seymour had watched her, though, when she worked in Lord Dakin's house. She always cleaned the wounds first.

He brought the water bucket over to the chair. The fire was burning brightly now. Shadows danced across the walls. Light caressed the chairs, the bed, and the table that made up most of Seymour's possessions. The man's face was haggard in sleep. His mouth was slightly open, and his features had sunken into his face. His body was covered with cuts, and his skin hung raggedly around several wounds. In the forest he had been moving. Here he seemed almost dead.

Seymour dipped several clean cloths into the water. He wrung out one and dabbed the man's face. The man twisted and moaned, but did not wake up. Seymour gripped the man's chin to keep his head from moving. Much of the blood was old and encrusted, and most of it came from scratches, probably caused by thorns. As Seymour cleaned away the blood, he saw how the scratches were layered: a scratch near a scratch near a scratch. The man had been running for days. He must have been very fit when he started.

Seymour ripped back the man's shirt and cleaned his chest. Here the skin was covered with bruises as well as scratches. One thick red area wouldn't come off, and it took Seymour a moment to realize that the man had an old, blurring tattoo.

Seymour continued cleaning and tending, working his way down to the man's legs. His thighs were scratched, but his knees were in tatters. The man had to have fallen a lot. The skin had almost scraped off, and the knees themselves were swollen. Even after wiping the dirt and blood away, Seymour couldn't tell if there were other injuries. The scraping looked similar enough to a burn that Seymour called an herb witch ice spell his mother had taught him. Seymour could feel the power running through his hands, coating the man's kneecaps with ice. The man shivered once, and sighed deeper into sleep.

Seymour folded the dirty rags and set them in a corner. Then he grabbed the bucket, took it outside, and walked through the grass to the brook. He could hear the hounds baying, the cries of the retainers as they tried to urge the dogs forward. The retainers would have to get Dakin – and they would have to replace these hounds. By then, Seymour hoped, the trail would be cold.

He poured out the water on the side of the brook, crouched, and filled the bucket again. The water here wasn't deep, but it was cool and fresh. Without it he wouldn't have been able to survive as long as he had in the hut. He didn't know what he would have done if there had been a drought, like the one the land had suffered through 20 years before.

He glanced back at his home. The hut still looked abandoned. The grass was tall and, except for the worn area near the side where he usually walked, looked undisturbed. No smoke rose from the chimney, and the place appeared dark. He would have to leave it soon. Once Lord Dakin realized who had tricked him, he would begin a search for Seymour and the man. Within a few days the lord would find the hut. Seymour sighed. He didn't want to go to the city, but he didn't know where else to go.

When he went back inside, the man was still sleeping. Seymour set the water bucket in its place beside the door. He took the carrots, peas, and beans he had set aside for his dinner, mixed them with herbs and a few potatoes, added water, and poured them into the pot that hung over the fire. He puttered around the hut as the stew cooked, preparing the bed and cleaning a few dishes so that he could share his meal with his guest.

As the scent of herbs and cooking vegetables filled the hut, Seymour heard a groan. The man had raised his head and was rubbing the back of his neck.

'How long was I asleep?' he asked.

'Not long.' Seymour stirred the stew. He added a little of his precious store of flour to thicken the broth. 'Are you hungry?'

'Ravenous.' The man stretched and winced. 'I'm also very stiff.'

'You will be for a few days.' Seymour ladled some stew into two bowls. Steam rose from the mixture, and in the half-light the vegetables looked very bright. He brought the bowls over to the man, pulled up a chair, and sat across from him.

The man took his bowl and ate quickly. Seymour did not offer him more, knowing that a stomach that had been empty and stressed for several days could take only a little nourishment at a time. When the man had finished, he flexed one leg and then the other, but did not flinch, although the movements had to have been very painful. 'You bandaged me.'

Seymour nodded, pleased at the simple acknowledgment.

'Thank you for helping me,' the man said. 'I don't think I would have survived another half day.'

'I know.' Seymour took a bite of his stew. The gravy was too thick and had too much basil, but the food still tasted good.

'You took an awful risk. Dakin's hounds – ' The man stopped himself. He gazed into the fire and shuddered once. Finally he faced Seymour again. 'I'm Byron, late of Lord Dakin's service.'

Seymour smiled. 'I'm Seymour. Also a former member of Lord Dakin's household.'

'You're a wizard?'

'A magician.' Seymour took another bite of stew. 'My father was a wizard, but a great talent like his comes once in a century. I survive on a little talent and a handful of luck. This is the second time I've outwitted Dakin's hounds.'

Byron laughed. The sound was deep and warm. Seymour felt as if he had just found a fire on a cold and rainy day. 'And Lord Dakin would have us believe his hounds are invincible,' Byron said. 'He'll be furious to see they've been beaten by a stick and a piece of bloody cloth.'

'He'll know whose stick that is.' Seymour took a final spoonful of stew. The food had lost its rich flavor. 'He gave it to me a long time ago and let me take it with me as a "goodwill" gesture when he sent me to the hounds.'

Byron shifted in his chair. His movements seemed pain-filled. 'Does he know where you are?'

'No. And I don't want him to find out.' Seymour sighed. 'I was hoping that he would forget about me.'

'Lord Dakin forgets nothing.'

'I know.'

They sat in silence for a moment, then Byron gripped the armrests on his chair. He slowly pulled himself up, putting some of his weight on his legs. Seymour hurried to his side, planning to catch him if he fell. Byron grabbed Seymour's arm and stood completely. Gradually, Byron released his hold on Seymour, tottered for a moment, and then steadied himself.

'You shouldn't be doing this,' Seymour said.

'I wanted to see if anything was broken. I fell more times than I'd like to remember.' Byron glanced at Seymour. 'In fact, you tripped me.'

Seymour shrugged. 'I didn't think you'd stop if I yelled.'

'I wouldn't have.' Byron swayed again.

'You need to get back down,' Seymour said. 'Take the bed.'

Byron looked at the bed in the corner of the room. Seymour had restuffed the pallet to make it thick and covered it with two heavy blankets he had found in the hut. 'It's yours, I couldn't.'

Seymour put his arm around Byron's waist. Seymour could feel the ridges of Byron's spine. 'Let's go slowly.'

'No, Seymour, I – '

'No arguments. You're taking the bed.' Together they moved across the room. Byron used Seymour's shoulder to steady himself. His grip tightened with each step they took. By the time they reached the bed, Seymour knew that his shoulder would be bruised.

Byron collapsed on the blankets. 'This is soft.'

'My one luxury. Someday I'm going to have a whole room full of luxuries.' Seymour bent over to help Byron under the blankets, but the younger man had already fallen asleep.

Seymour sighed. Byron had said very little about himself. And now they seemed to be linked somehow. A hound bayed, the sound faraway and melancholy. Seymour shivered. He wished that he would wake up with the dawn and discover that the whole day had been a long, crazy dream.

iii

The Enos stood at the edge of the forest. Green tendrils of moss caressed her shoulders, touched her back. A moment before, something had pierced the earth and drawn magic. Weak magic, poor magic. She closed her eyes and reached for the source of the earth's pain. The magician, the young one, the bad one. And beside him, the white mists of power. She could feel the hounds' paws scrape the dirt, move toward them. The land remembered the blood, the violence from the last death.

Time circles traveled across her mind. The magic would not hold the hounds. The white mists would die, pollute her land. The land would know even more violence, would come to love it. She felt the weight of blood pour over her shoulders, seep into her skin as blood would seep into the dry earth. She would change, no longer steady, no longer constant, seeking to fulfill a hunger that came from the outside: the sweetness of blood.

With an apology to the Old Ones, she reached into the earth, grabbed the tip of the magician's staff, and filled it with the image of the white mists. His scent coated the land, every pine needle, every bramble, every blade of grass. She wiped the real trail clean and then clutched the tree for support.

She sent a silent apology to the Old Ones. They would understand. They would have to. She was guarding her land. They couldn't punish her for guarding her land.

The tree bark scratched her skin. She felt old, older than the land itself. She was guarding her land, but she was also helping a human, doing the forbidden. She hoped that her simple action had not caused the final time to begin.

iv

Seymour twitched in his sleep. He knew he was dreaming, but he couldn't free himself from the images. He was running, running as fast as he could, his feet slipping in the fresh spring mud along the river, the hounds baying behind him. He had to get deep into the forest – deep enough that they wouldn't find him – before he could cast his spell. Branches hit his face, his arms, causing the skin to sting. More than once he got a mouthful of bitter leaves and had to spit them out. Behind him, the hounds wailed, a long, thin sound that turned into a high, sustained note that cascaded into song. A song. Someone was singing. Seymour grabbed the sound as if it were a rope and pulled himself into wakefulness.

His back ached from the thin pallet he had placed in front of the hearth. Sometime during the night he had covered himself with a cloak, but he was still cold. He rubbed the sleep out of his eyes and sat up.

The singing continued. A tall, thin man was setting a bowl on the table. He tilted his head from side to side as he worked, his voice running up and down in scales. He looked so different from the man who had crashed through the brambles the day before that Seymour hesitated before speaking.

'Byron?'

The man looked up. His dark hair fell across his forehead and his eyes sparkled. 'Good morning, Seymour. Did you sleep well?'

'Not as well as you, I think.' Seymour stood slowly. His limbs felt stiff, aching from the hardness of his bed. Byron was moving easily as if he hadn't been injured at all. 'Last night you could barely walk.'

Byron sat down at the table and pulled a bowl in front of himself. 'I'm still sore, but I figure the more I move, the quicker I'll heal.' He ate a berry from his bowl. 'The food's good. Come on and sit down.'

'In a minute.' Seymour walked to the water bucket, poured some water into his basin, and splashed his face. The coolness felt good and wiped the last trace of sleep from his mind. He had never seen anyone heal so fast. Even his mother's advanced herb-witching spells couldn't cause such rapid healing. He patted his face dry and pulled a stool over to the table. Byron had filled Seymour's cup with water, and had filled the bowls with berries from the back of the hut. Seymour took one and let the sharp sweetness roll over his tongue.

'You were very lucky to find this place,' Byron said. 'Obviously someone had a garden out back.'

'How long have you been awake?' Seymour asked.

Byron shrugged. 'With the sun, I think. I couldn't sleep any more.'

'And you got up – healed?'

Byron laughed. Seymour remembered the warmth of the sound from the night before, but then he hadn't heard the music. The deep rills of Byron's laugh had the same richness the scales had had a moment earlier. 'No. I'm probably in more pain now than I have been in years.' He took a breath, and for an instant his skin seemed to turn pale. 'It's all in the mind, though.'

He gazed down at his food and swayed a little. 'In the mind,' he repeated, as if to himself. Then he looked up at Seymour. 'Years ago, I worked with an Enos who taught me that the best way to overcome illness was to believe that you're well. If I concentrate on how badly I feel, I'll be useless.'

Seymour remembered the tattoo on Byron's chest and wondered if it was Enos-made. 'Well, it's good to see you moving around,' Seymour said. He wondered what else Byron had learned, if he had learned Enos tricks for healing or Enos magic. He would ask on the trip. Somehow he had to tell Byron that they had to leave. The magic wouldn't hold forever, and Lord Dakin would discover the hut. Seymour wanted to be in the city by then.

'More water, Seymour?'

Seymour nodded. Byron reached behind himself and grabbed the pitcher. As he poured the water, sunlight glinted off a slender silver band on his right hand. Seymour hadn't noticed the ring the night before. 'Gift from Lord Dakin?'

Byron set the pitcher down. 'What?'

'The ring. Is it a gift from Lord Dakin?'

Byron twisted the ring slightly. His expression was somber. 'No.'

Seymour felt a chill in the word. He ate a few more berries, unable to taste them. His father had often used that cool, dismissive tone, especially in later years when he had realized that Seymour would never be a great magician. His father had never believed that Seymour could do spells more complicated than the hearth spell he had used when he arrived in the hut. And yet he had made his staff into Byron and fooled the hounds. Seymour's father would have been surprised.

'You must really have offended Dakin,' Seymour said, then stopped. Byron looked up and his expression seemed as warm as it had when Seymour awoke. 'He usually calls his hounds off when they get this deep into the forest.'

'I was his bard,' Byron said. He smiled. 'I was supposed to praise him.'

'And you didn't.'

'In the beginning, perhaps. But not after I saw who he really was.'

Seymour understood. He had grown up in Lord Dakin's service, following his father. His father had never allowed Seymour to associate with any of the other servants. Seymour only gained friends – and knowledge of Lord Dakin – after his father had died.

'You met Rury.'

Byron leaned back in his chair. 'I met Rury. He's dead now.'

The words made Seymour's hands cold. He had always known that Rury would face the hounds. Seymour hadn't realized that one of the hunts he had heard had marked the death of one of the most courageous people he had ever known. 'Hounds.'

'Yes.' Byron's fists clenched and unclenched. Seymour could see the anger, still fresh. 'Dakin raised the rents again, shortly after I arrived. Rury decided he had had enough. He convinced others in the village not to pay the additional fee. Dakin was having a quiet dinner one night, and I was getting ready to perform, when one of the retainers reported the problem. Dakin didn't move. He was extremely calm. He had no idea who was behind it all, so he punished everyone. He imprisoned the head of each household that refused to pay tribute. Of course, no one was able to pay then, and a lot of families backed down. Someone betrayed Rury.'

Seymour pushed his bowl away. It clattered along the tabletop. 'I always knew something would happen. Rury said things had to change. He said if they didn't, there would be war, and war would bring down the wrath of the Enos.'

'It's the Old Ones we have to guard against,' Byron said.

'You believe in the Old Ones?'

Byron shrugged. 'The Enos who trained me did. That's enough for me. For now. I suppose the time will come when I have to test that belief.'

'Did Rury?'

'No. No one stood up for him. Except me, in my own ineffectual way. I begged Dakin to examine his policies and make a compromise with the villagers. After all, he needs them as much as they need him. Without their labor, he has no wealth. But he doesn't see it that way. I made him angrier. And he decided to go after Rury's sister, Nica.'

'The herb witch,' Seymour said. He remembered her kindnesses. She had taken over the job after his mother died, even though she lacked formal training. Nica had always felt inferior, rather like Seymour. They shared that, at least.

'I hid her, found her a horse, and sent her to a friend of mine south of here. When Dakin discovered that Nica had disappeared, he decided to kill Rury. I think Dakin had other plans for Nica, or – I don't know. I just know that he was infuriated. Rury died the next morning. He was no match for the hounds. He had been imprisoned nearly a month, and he could barely stand when they brought him out to the riverbank. Dakin made me watch the whole thing, and I could do nothing. He expected me to write a song about it, and I did. I sang it that night at the banquet. It was a rollicking tale, about the lord of the manor developing a taste for blood. I compared him to his hounds, I laid all those deaths at his hands. I kept singing until he grabbed my lute and smashed it against the table, and even then I didn't quit. He knocked me out. When I woke up, I was in his dungeon, waiting for my turn with the hounds.'

Seymour clasped his hands together to prevent them from shaking. Dakin would never forgive the man. He wanted the bard's blood. Dakin hated a personal insult, and Byron had insulted him more deeply than anyone had before. 'Other gentry overtax their peasants,' Seymour said, wishing that he had never heard the hounds bay the day before.

'I know.' Byron shot Seymour a quick glance. 'I get into trouble a lot. But I have a lot of friends. I can find someone to help you once we're out of the woods.'

Seymour sensed that Byron was apologizing. 'Once we're off Dakin's land, what you did won't matter,' Seymour said. Unless it happened again. Seymour would have to make his own way in the city.

'Dakin's hounds will find us soon, won't they?' Byron asked.

Seymour nodded. 'This hut is pretty visible.'

'This afternoon, then.' As Byron stood up, his movements were a little shaky. 'Will you be able to get everything together by then?'

Seymour glanced around the hut. Almost everything belonged to the place. A few of the items he had made, but nothing that he wanted to keep. He would leave everything for the next needy person. 'There's nothing to take.'

'Except provisions.' Byron lifted the cloths Seymour kept near the door, probably looking for one large enough to carry things in.

'Byron?'

He looked up.

Seymour's stomach was jumping. 'I've never been away from these lands. We need to go to the city, but we can't stay there too long. Lord Dakin's land surrounds it. We might have to go somewhere else.'

Byron smiled, slowly and easily. 'You know,' he said, 'I've always fancied being bard to the king . . . '

V

Lord Dakin dismounted outside the stable. As his feet hit the soft ground, his legs quivered. He had been riding for over three days. He leaned against the stallion for a moment, smelling the sweet odor of horseflesh and feeling the sweat on the animal's side. He had ridden the horse too hard. The grooms would have to give it a good rubdown and feed it well. He needed a bath and a meal himself.

He walked up the path to the great house. He was so tired that his body felt heavy. Damn the bard. So few escaped the hounds. He should have known that the bard would be one of them.

But the magician – who would have thought that Byron the bard would have found Seymour the incompetent? The incompetent who had twice deceived the hounds. That magician had been faking his poor performances all along. Dakin remembered the feel of the ebony stick beneath his hands, the sheer force he had used as he smashed the thing into small pieces. The hounds had gone wild. He and his men had to use branches to keep the animals from ripping the ebony as if it were human flesh.

Dakin passed the sculptured gardens, noting the gardeners hunched along the path, inspecting a plant that grew across the dirt. At least they were doing their jobs, and doing them well. He hated the incompetence, the arrogance, and all of the trouble he had had lately. He would love nothing more than to kill both the bard and the magician with his bare hands.

His retainers would find the bard soon. Judging from the blood-soaked rags Dakin had found in the hut, the bard was in bad shape. He wouldn't be moving very quickly even with his two-day head start.

As Dakin approached the great house, he saw his personal secretary standing before the door. 'What is it?' Dakin asked.

'Milord,' the secretary said, dipping his head. The movement was always a sign of bad news, as if the man expected Dakin to unsheath a sword and behead him immediately. 'You were to meet the Lady Jelwra in Nadaluci this evening.'

Dakin swore softly. The Lady Jelwra was not a person to ignore. She was after his southern lands for their river access. She had already taken the land from Lord Lafa that adjoined Dakin's, claiming that it had belonged to her family for generations.

'I would like a massage and a large meal. Send word to the stable to prepare a different stallion. I exhausted the last.'

'Very good, sir.'

No, it wasn't very good. Dakin pushed past his secretary into the coolness of the hall. He had been planning to stop the Lady Jelwra from usurping Dakin land, but he hadn't known how to go about it. Now he was riding into the meeting exhausted and angry, frustrated from a failed hunt.

He would have to leave the bard until later. But when Dakin found him, he would kill him slowly and painfully. The hounds were too quick. Dakin would think of something that lasted much, much longer.

Chapter 2

Adric sat on a bench in the southeast corner of the courtyard. The sun shone light and thin over the palace's high walls. If he squinted, he could see the gate, and if he stood, he could see the spires of Anda beyond it.

He had been waiting since dawn for Lord Boton. The lord had promised him a trip into the city – Adric's first time ever outside palace lands – and had even showed him his father's seal on the order. The trip felt like a consolation prize. All of the other things he had asked for since he had seen the Enos – a better education, the opportunity to watch his father and the council work – had been met with blank stares and polite smiles. Lord Ewehl had said crossly that no prince before Adric had asked for anything. Adric had replied, equally as cross, that he planned to be different.

The stone bench was cold, and his bottom had grown numb. He had flattened the grass separating the cobblestones with his feet. His fingernails were ragged from chipping at the mortar between the stones in the bench. He wondered how much longer he should wait. Perhaps he had had the day wrong. Perhaps Lord Boton had forgotten him.

Adric stared at the palace walls around him. When he had first arrived at the courtyard, only a few maidservants and a handful of retainers stirred. The windows above him were dark, hinting that the entire palace slept. Now he saw movement through the windows across from him in the west wing, his parents' wing.

With his mother's pregnancy, both of his parents had taken to sleeping late in the morning. Adric used to have breakfast with them. Now he didn't see either of them until dinner time, if then. He spent his days reading in the palace's small library or bothering the grooms in the stables. Once he had tried to follow Lord Boton on his rounds, but the lord gently told Adric he had no place in the farthest recesses of the palace. As Adric watched the palace awaken, he saw the serving children cross the courtyard. Some carried buckets of water on their shoulders. Others ran on some kind of mission. All of them working, all of them doing something important. He wished that just once he could be as useful as they were.

The smell of freshly baked bread filled the courtyard. Adric's stomach rumbled. He had had a small breakfast – four stale biscuits and a soft apple – and he wanted something else. If he went into the kitchen, however, the carriage would arrive. Then Lord Boton would think that Adric no longer wanted to go.

The double doors leading to his parents' wing opened. Two retainers stepped outside and held the doors back. Adric's father emerged, his mother beside him. The sun fell on them, illuminating his father and leaving his mother in shadow. His father's doublet sparkled, and he stood tall and slim. Adric's mother looked small and fragile beside his father. She had one hand tucked in the crook of his arm. The other hand rested on top of her rounded belly. The royal physician had told her that the baby was in danger and that she must spend most of her time in bed. But she had been seeing the herb witches who lived in the kitchen. They assured her that good food and exercise would help the baby more than anything. So Adric's mother walked in the morning and slept in the afternoon. Adric had heard some of the serving girls talk, saying that although his mother ate a lot, she couldn't seem to hold much food. He was forbidden to see her except at the meals she attended, and his father refused to answer questions about her health. Adric worried about her. He wanted a baby brother, someone to play with, but he wanted his mother more.

His father helped her down the single step into the courtyard. She said something and he leaned toward her to hear better. His father cared about his mother. Adric eavesdropped on servants' gossip, since it was his only source of information, and he had heard more than once of a servant's surprise at the king. His father never looked at another woman, unlike the lords of the council, and he banished those who even made such suggestions to scullery work or dungeon duty on the far side of the palace.

As his parents crossed the courtyard, Adric stood up. He brushed the mortar chips from his pants, took a deep breath, and crossed into the sun. His father stopped walking when he saw

Adric.

'What are you doing out this morning, lad?'

Adric felt a little shiver of shock run through his belly. 'I'm waiting for Lord Boton. He promised to take me to Anda.'

'The city?' His mother ran a hand over her face. Deep shadows circled her eyes and made her look older. 'You're too young to go to the city.'

'Your mother's right, lad. You'd best stay here.' His father put a hand protectively over the hand his mother had tucked in the crook of his arm.

Adric swallowed hard. 'But, Father, you signed the order. Lord Boton showed me the document yesterday with your seal.'

His father blinked and stared at the sun. His eyes were small against the lines of his face.

'I thought we agreed that Adric would see the city with you when he was older.' His mother's voice seemed rough on the edge, tinged with panic. She had always been protective of him, saying the oldest child and heir was too valuable to risk.

His father shook his head. 'I'm sorry, lad. I had forgotten. Lord Boton brought the order to me and I did sign it. I think he's old enough, Constance. And with Boton, he certainly doesn't need me.'

The edges of his mother's mouth pinched together. 'I don't want you to go,' she said to Adric.

'I'm the one who asked to go. I haven't been off the grounds, Mama. I would like to see some of the world.'

His father looked down at him. 'Yes. I hear you've been making a bit of a nuisance of yourself, asking questions and wanting to follow the lords.'

Adric clasped his hands behind his back. 'I would like to learn.'

'Learning is something that happens, not something you pursue.'

'Then how did you learn your kingly duties, Father?'

His father's cheeks puffed. 'You have no need to learn *kingly* duties, boy, not as long as I am alive. And I plan to be alive a long, long time.'

'That's not what I meant. I meant – '

'All you need to know to be king is to listen to others and take their good advice. And I am giving you good advice now. Stop making trouble, stop asking so many questions, and stop coveting my job.'

'He's just a boy,' his mother said. She extended a hand to Adric. He took it, feeling the delicate bones of her fingers. 'You don't mean anything, do you, dear? You just want to be like your father.'

Adric almost shook his head. He wanted to be his father's opposite. 'I don't mean to cause trouble,' he said.

'Well, see that you don't cause any more,' his father said. 'Come along, Constance.'

His mother squeezed Adric's hand. 'Be safe in the city. Don't do anything alone.'

'I won't, Mama,' Adric said. His mother's hand slipped through his, and she walked with his father back to the west wing. They fell into shadow, their bodies almost ghostly pale in the dimness. Adric watched until they went back inside, then returned to his bench.

If his father hadn't known of the trip into town, then maybe it wasn't going to happen. But he had seen that look on his father's face before, often in front of a council member at dinner, discussing a policy his father was supposed to have made. Adric clenched his fists. He would not just take the advice of others. He would make his own choices. And if his father didn't want him to learn, Adric would make sure that his father never discovered what Adric was doing. He would learn. He would become one of the wisest men in the kingdom. By the time he was twenty-one, he would be able to give his father advice, just as lords Boton and Ewehl did. And his father would listen.

The bench seemed chillier than it had before. Adric crossed his arms over his chest. The sun had grown brighter now but not warmer. It almost seemed like a winter sun, thin rays without heat, but the winter was long past. His stomach rumbled again, and he wondered if he should give up when he heard the faint clip-clop of horse hooves.

He stood up, then sat back down, not wanting to seem too eager. He had never been to the city, but he knew what it would be like. All the tall, fair people wearing robes similar to those worn by the council, circling the carriage and paying obeisance to their prince. He would lean out the window and wave at them, commanding them to stand up and see him. They would, and he would smile, and then he would get out of the carriage and someone would fix him a spectacular lunch. Word would get back to his father about how well Adric had done in the city, and his father would praise him.

The clip-clop had gotten louder, and behind it Adric could hear the rattle of carriage wheels on stone. His hands had turned cold. He clasped his knees and leaned forward. The carriage rounded the corner, and the air hissed out of him in surprise. It wasn't the blue carriage with the royal insignia painted on the sides, but an unmarked black carriage, the one they used for funeral processions. Four black horses pranced in front of it, their manes caught in black plumes and their tails braided with black ribbon. A groomsman rode in front and two footmen stood in the back. Adric refused to let his disappointment show on his face. That wasn't his carriage. His carriage had still to arrive.

Yet the carriage stopped in front of him. Adric inhaled the scents of horse sweat and leather. The rounded door creaked open, and Lord Ewehl stepped out.

Lord Ewehl was short but so excessively thin that he seemed tall. His skin had sunken into his face, leaving his bone structure jutting prominently. He licked his lips and smiled, but like the sun, his smile had no warmth.

'Are you ready to go to Anda, Highness?'

'Lord Boton was supposed to take me.'

'Lord Boton was called on business. He asked me.'

Adric looked at the carriage and then at the lord. He hated Lord Ewehl, and Lord Boton knew it. Perhaps this was a test to see how much Adric wanted the things he was asking for. If he said no to this trip, he would probably never receive anything else.

'And you chose this carriage?'

'For safety's sake, Highness.'

'Young master!'

Adric turned. One of his mother's maidservants waved at him from the west wing of the courtyard. She picked up her skirts and ran across the uneven stone, her bare feet making slapping noises. When she reached Adric, she curtsied.

'What is this?' Lord Ewehl asked.

Adric took the girl's hand and helped her to her feet. Her skin was rough and already lined, but her hair seemed soft. He wondered if this was one of the women his mother had rescued from the kitchen. The girl glanced at Lord Ewehl, then reached into the folds of her skirt, and brought out a small sheath.

'Your mother asked me to bring this to you, young master, for your trip.'

Adric took the sheath. The leather case was warm. A pearl-studded hilt extended from it. He wrapped his hands around the gems and pulled. A thin knife the length of his forearm emerged.

'She bids you to wear it on this trip, and to be safe.'

'He doesn't need any weapons,' Lord Ewehl said.

The girl glanced at him, and Adric thought he saw something like hatred in her eyes. 'Milady the queen told me not to leave until her son accepted the gift and promised to take it with him.'

Adric undid his belt and slipped the sheath through it. 'Thank my mother,' he said. The small gesture of support warmed him. The girl curtsied again and ran off down the courtyard.

'A weapon might cause you more trouble than you need,' Lord Ewehl said.

'My mother thinks it necessary,' Adric said, 'so I will wear it.'

The lord shrugged, grabbed the bar beside the carriage door, and pulled himself inside. Adric did the same.

The smell of leather was stronger inside the carriage. Two padded seats ran along the front and back walls of the carriage. Lord Ewehl took the front seat. Adric reached back, grabbed the door, and swung it shut. The carriage rocked. Adric sat on the other seat near the far window.

The seat coverings were made of smooth black satin, as were the window curtains. Lord Ewehl tapped on the roof with his fingers, and the carriage lurched forward. Adric hit his head on the wall, sending a wave of pain from his skull down his neck.

'You must rock with the carriage, Highness, or you will get bruised.' Lord Ewehl's lips curved with a trace of amusement. Adric wished Lord Boton sat across from him. Lord Boton would have touched his knee and asked if he was all right.

'What kind of business is Lord Boton doing?' Adric asked. The pain in his head had eased to a dull throb.

'Documents, with your father.'

'My father is with my mother. I just saw them.'

'The work was left over from yesterday. Your father wanted to see them first thing today.'

Adric glanced out the window. They were still inside the palace grounds. 'My father didn't say anything about that when I told him Lord Boton was taking me to Anda.'

'Your father had probably forgotten.'

'Then Lord Boton could have come with me.'

'He does his duty, whether the king remembers what he asked for or not.'

Adric glanced at Ewehl. The lord still had a faint smile on his face. He was lying. Adric had been right about the test, then. He felt a trickle of disappointment that Lord Boton would trick him, test him. Lord Boton had always been the one he could trust. But when he got back, he was sure Lord Boton would tell him all about it, and would praise him for doing well.

Through the window Adric saw the tall, carved stone of the walls pass by him. And then they were outside the palace on a dirt road that curved ahead through rows of large trees. The carriage bumped for a moment, then settled into the ruts that lined the road. The trees outside the window were large. Their leaves and branches formed a canopy above the road, letting only patches of sunlight through. Adric was glad that they were traveling by day. The dark road would be gloomy at night. And even though the trees were young and straight, they reminded him of the whistle-wood trees near the Cache. Those trees had seemed almost alive, as if they could reach out and hold him. These trees lacked that vibrancy, but they still had a presence.

'Do Enos guard these trees?' Adric asked.

'There is a land Enos here, but it is untamed. I believe it works with the Cache Enos. The land here still belongs to the palace. I will let you know when we cross into Lord Demythos' land.'

Adric frowned when he thought of Lord Demythos. The lord wore only black, and when he arrived for the council meetings, he made it a point to give his greetings to Adric. Adric did not know if the lord expected something from him or was simply paying him a courtesy.

Adric's stomach rumbled, and he placed a hand over it. 'How long until we get to the city?'

'Perhaps an hour.'

'Lord Boton said he would tell me what to do once we reach the city.'

Lord Ewehl leaned back and crossed his legs, putting his ankle on his knee. 'Lord Boton makes too much of this. Use common sense, Highness, and you can survive in the city.'

'Is common sense why you chose this carriage?'

The smile slid from Lord Ewehl's face. He tilted his head back and gazed at Adric through hooded eyes. 'I suppose you could say that.'

'I thought we would take my father's carriage, the blue carriage.'

'And announce to the city that the young prince has arrived and is ready to be taken? Not sensible, Highness.'

'You're saying that I'll be in danger in the city?'

'Highness, many people see you as a way to get to your father.'

'Why would they want to get to my father? He's well liked.'

Lord Ewehl chuckled. The sound echoed in the small compartment. 'By the gentry, of course. But as you'll see once we reach the city, many others aren't faring so well by his policies.'

'They're your policies too. You're one of the ones who advises him.'

'So I do. And just because people disagree with the policies does not make them bad.'

'But they threaten my father.'

'No, Highness. They just make certain places unsafe. Which is, I'm sure, why your lady mother gave you that knife.'

The carriage tilted on two wheels as it rounded a corner. Adric grabbed the satin seat and leaned into the curve. The trees were thinning and the road was growing lighter. The rattle of the wheels seemed louder inside, but Adric could barely hear the horses. The carriage itself groaned as it rocked.

'What did the Cache Enos tell you?' Lord Ewehl asked.

Adric felt as if the carriage had stopped moving for a moment. He willed himself to breathe. Someone had been spying on him and had reported to Lord Ewehl. 'I have never seen a Cache Enos.'

'Highness, you saw her a fortnight ago, and ever since you have been hounding us to make you into a "good king."'

'I asked her what would make a good king, and she told me.' Adric licked his lips. They felt dry and cracked.

'Enos never give advice. They prophesy.'

Adric shrugged. 'This one gave me advice.'

'You lie, Highness.'

Adric sat forward. 'You wouldn't talk to my father this way.'

'Your father isn't ten years old.' Lord Ewehl hadn't switched his position, but his body had grown tense. 'What did the Enos say to you?'

'Why is it so important for you to know?'

'The prophecy might be important to the kingdom.'

'Then I will tell my father when I get back.' Adric tightened his fists against his legs. His father bristled at even a slight comment about leadership. Adric couldn't imagine telling his father about the Enos's comments. 'If you're so curious, why don't you ask the Enos yourself?'

'Because I am not a member of your family, Highness. She will not speak to me.'

Adric frowned. 'I thought the Enos were there for us all.'

'They deign to speak to some of us sometimes, but they belong to the land. Only the cities have no Enos protection. And the Enos only speak to those who control the land.'

'You control land. She should speak to you.'

'My own Enos does. The Cache Enos only speak to the royal family. You should know this, Highness.'

'I don't know it!' Adric's voice sounded shrill. 'And when I was with her, I made mistakes too. No one tells me anything. Now do you see why I want to learn? I want to know the things you know and my father knows and what Lord Boton knows. You say common sense will help in the city. I don't even know what common sense is!'

Lord Ewehl finally sat forward. He patted Adric's knee. Adric moved away. 'You will do just fine, Highness. You know more than you think you do.'

Adric looked out the window. The trees had disappeared, replaced by rolling fields lined with hedges. Rows and rows of leafy plants braced against sticks ran perpendicular to the carriage. People knelt beside the plants, picking red balls and placing them in buckets. Adric squinted at some of the plants closest to the road. Tomatoes. He wondered how anything could grow in the drought his father complained of. He stared at the people. They were servants. Their clothes were worn, but none were tattered. Many wore no shirts and revealed sun-darkened skin.

'Lord Demythos' land,' Lord Ewehl said. 'He lets his peasants work unsupervised.'

Lord Ewehl's tone sounded disapproving. But the people looked contented to Adric. They seemed to be working hard and getting a lot done. He sighed and leaned his head against the curtain. 'How much farther?'

'Not much,' Lord Ewehl said.

They rode for the next few miles in silence. Adric watched as the fields eased into hedges and then into trampled grass. Finally, around a corner he saw the spires of Anda, looking tall and spindly against the clear sky.

'We're here,' he said, not caring about the excitement in his voice. Another road merged into the one they were on, and they suddenly found themselves in traffic. Another carriage pulled in ahead of them, and riders along either side. Adric looked at the horseflesh, and decided that it was of poor quality. The riders wore dusty clothes and had sweat trickles on their sunburned faces.

Lord Ewehl leaned his head out the window and looked around. 'Congestion,' he said. 'I hate the city.'

The rumbling of the other carriages mingled with their own, and the thud of the horse hooves grew louder. Voices cried out to one another, and Adric caught only part of the words, nonsense syllables mostly, it seemed to him. A stench grew in the air. He was able to recognize manure and rotted food, but there were other smells equally as foul blended in.

He looked out the window and saw a long wall that encircled buildings. Dozens of horses and carriages were going in and out a gate. The wall and gate were made of wood planks strung together. Adric squinted. Inside, he could see the edges of more buildings made from wood.

As the carriage pulled inside the gate, the noise and smell grew stronger. People, many in rags, their bodies unwashed and coated with dust and dirt, teemed against the carriage. More people, some without hands or with large sores covering their skin, cowered next to the gate. A man on a horse whipped them as he went by. Shouts, calls, whistles, an occasional whinny, and the rattle of carriages built to a cacophony in Adric's head. A man stood on a large rock near one of the buildings, screaming something about the vengeance of the Old Ones. Hands pounded against the carriage, reached for Adric. Voices called for a coin, sir, just one, spare me some money, sir, I haven't eaten in days. Adric wanted to shrink back into the carriage, but he didn't want to miss anything. The city was nothing like he had imagined. It was thriving, alive on its own, and yet frightening at the same time.

The carriage stopped, and Adric had to grip the windowsill to keep from falling. The hands that were reaching suddenly grabbed on, and Adric heard a whistle, crack, and snap of the whip the footmen used to keep ragged people off before he saw the black tip draw blood. Adric gazed across the crowd at the buildings that seemed scattered haphazardly beside the roads. The buildings were top-heavy, their second story hanging out over the first. A woman leaned out an upstairs window and tossed the contents of a slop jar into the street. The liquid splattered people below, and one, a fat man wearing green velvet robes, shook a bejeweled fist at the building. Down the other streets the crowd seemed thinner. The edges of signs blocked his view. Dogs ran through the crowd and he thought he saw a chicken scratching at the dirt.

'Can we get out here?' Adric asked.

'We haven't even reached the central city,' Lord Ewehl said.

'But we've stopped.'

'There must be something in the road ahead. We will start in a moment.'

Adric gazed out the window. His stomach was jumping, and he felt as if he had to move. 'I only have the day,' he said. 'I want to see everything. Let's move.'

He stood up. Lord Ewehl remained sitting. 'I will stay with the carriage. One of the footmen will accompany you. Tell him when you want to go back, that we'll meet in the usual spot in the center of town.'

'The center of town. Okay.'

'Wait.' Lord Ewehl reached into his pocket and pulled out a pouch. 'You'll need this.'

Adric took the pouch. He felt the coins clinking against the cloth. 'Thank you,' he said. He let himself out the door. The sunlight seemed brighter. It was warm here, but the smells seemed less cramped, less closed up. He climbed down the steps into the crowd, and winced as unwashed bodies rubbed against him. He glanced up once to see a footman climbing down from his perch behind the carriage, and then he pushed his way through the crowd to one of the side streets.

As he got outside the throng, he saw merchants pushing carts and calling their wares. One had meats, another fresh fruits. Adric stopped one of the meat carts and bought a chunk of beef, but when he bit into it, the meat tasted rancid. He spat it out and looked for the merchant to complain, but the man had already disappeared. Adric tossed the meat aside, and noted with surprise that a dozen people dove for it.

He kept moving, deciding that he would buy something to eat later. On the corner a troupe of jugglers tossed sticks in the air. They were good, better than some who had come to the palace. Adric saw a merchant toss a coin into a hat one of the jugglers held out; Adric did the same. His coin, gold and shiny, caught the gaze of several bystanders, and they looked at him as if sizing him up. Perhaps they were beginning to realize who he was. He smiled and nodded. A prince should always be kindly to his subjects.

He turned down a side street and had to duck to avoid hitting the base of a sign advertising a cobbler shop. Here the noise was not as loud, but the garbage smell was stronger. A river of waste, spoiled food, and ruined lumps ran in a ditch down the center of the street. Adric sneezed and wondered why they didn't keep the garbage in a central place as they did at the palace. Outside the city, on that patch of trampled grass, would do nicely.

There were fewer people on the streets here. The men wore well-tailored clothes and the women lifted long skirts as they daintily crossed the muck. The signs hung at odd angles, some jutting out into the street, all of them with words and symbols. The cobbler's had a shoe, and the tailor had a needle and thread. Adric was leaning out so that he could see the others when someone grabbed him and shoved him against a wall.

Splinters ran up his back and into his shoulders. A man with a large, running sore under his eye and a mouth half empty of teeth held him by his arms. Adric squirmed. The man's breath smelled like a dead animal.

'I want that pouch of yours, laddie.'

Adric blinked, and then recognized the man as one who had been watching him when he paid the juggler. The man must have followed him. Adric looked for the footman, but saw no one. Fear ran through him then, and a little panic. The man could kill him.

The man reached for Adric's shirt. Adric shoved a knee into the man's groin. As the man let out an ooof of pain, Adric pulled his knife from its sheath.

The man's eyes narrowed. He grabbed Adric's wrist until the knife twisted free. It clattered against the side of the building as it fell. The man yanked the pouch from Adric's pocket, then threw the boy aside. Adric tried to get his footing, but he stumbled and slipped in the muck. He landed, bottom first, in the river of garbage. Water splashed in his mouth and his eyes, burning and tasting foul. He pushed himself up and out, looking for the robber, but the man was gone. Adric walked back to the side of the building. His knife was missing too. His breath hitched in his throat. Lord Ewehl had known this would happen. He had planned to embarrass Adric, and it had worked.

Adric walked back down the side street, past the jugglers and into the crowd. The roadblock was gone. Carriages moved freely down the street. He scanned for the footman and saw no one. The footman knew where the meeting place was. Adric didn't.

He let out a shudder. He was alone. And he was lost.

Chapter 3

Seymour couldn't shake the smell from his nostrils: feces, garbage, human and animal sweat. The city reeked. He had been inside the gate for only a short time and he already hated the place. And the noise was almost as bad as the smells: people screaming at each other; carriages rattling; horses neighing; dogs barking; merchants hawking their wares. Each sound built on the next until they reached a rumbling din that had no substance, only a continual throb in Seymour's head. He felt trapped here, unable to see the sky without something – or someone – blocking his view.

'I don't like it here,' he said. They had walked for hours through the forest. His ears had strained for the sound of Dakin's hounds, and all the time he had thought he would be safe once he reached the city, once he saw the gates of Nadaluci. He hadn't thought that he would be frightened of the city too.

'You have a better idea?' Byron brought his hand down and adjusted his shirt. His face was streaked with dirt and sweat.

A merchant bumped Seymour with his wooden cart. Stepping back, Seymour stumbled against a woman carrying a baby. He stepped up on the wooden platform beside a stable, and leaned against the building as if it provided protection. 'I haven't heard any ideas,' he said.

Byron glanced at Seymour and then looked away. Byron had deep shadows under his eyes and his limp had returned. Seymour had suggested staying in the forest another night, but Byron insisted on coming to the city. He seemed to feel that they would be safer here.

A woman passed, dragging two children along. She crossed into the street ahead of a white horse bearing a retainer. The horse reared and its front hooves narrowly missed the woman. She pushed her children forward as if nothing had happened.

Seymour wanted off the street. He didn't want to get trampled and he didn't want to go deaf. The smell was making him nauseous. 'Don't you know anyone here?'

'I may know some people, Seymour, but I wouldn't know where to find them. I still don't understand why you can't change a few pebbles into gold – '

'They'll change back.'

'We'll be gone.'

Seymour crossed his arms in front of his chest. 'A man only has so much luck, and we might need it later on. I can't guarantee that the spell would work.'

'What's the harm in trying?'

'I don't want to waste my luck on something that will fail,' Seymour snapped. The muscles along his back and shoulders were tight. 'I only have so much luck.'

'Well, I only have so much energy,' Byron said. 'We'll have to stop here. I am not going any farther than Nadaluci – at least for the night.'

Shouts of 'Carriage! Carriage!' rose above the din. People on the street scurried to the side, parting like trees in a windstorm before the large, approaching carriage. Six white horses with gold braided manes and gold trappings pulled the carriage. Two coachmen sat on top and four groomsmen flanked the sides. The carriage itself was white, unblemished by the travel. Four white banners with a blue star in the center flew from each of the groomsmen's stations. A woman gazed out the window, her face veiled by a thin white curtain.

Seymour coughed as dust rose around them. Byron coughed too, but didn't take his gaze from the carriage. Seymour swallowed, barely able to wet his mouth. He was thirsty and hungry as well as tired. 'Where are we going to stay, then?'

The carriage rounded a corner. The flags lingered for a moment, like a hand waving good-bye, before they disappeared. Byron turned. 'We have no choice, Seymour. We stay here.'

People were streaming back into the streets. A beggar limped past, clutching a swollen arm that smelled of pus. Another beggar tugged on Seymour's robe. 'A spare coin, lad? Just one?' Seymour shook him off and turned his back, more in fright than anything else.

'I still don't see how we can stay,' he said. 'We don't have any money, and I really don't want to sleep on the streets.'

Byron ran a hand through his hair. It stuck up in tufts around his forehead. 'I have an idea.'

A merchant in long sheepskin robes tossed a coin at a group of beggars. They dove for the money, pushing, shoving, and fighting among themselves. The merchant laughed and moved on. Seymour shivered. There wasn't even charity here.

'What do you want me to do?' he asked.

'Follow me.' Byron stepped into the road, ignoring the horses much as the woman had. Seymour followed, dodging beggars and manure, wondering if the mud had been caused by rain or horse piss. The stench in the road itself was even thicker than it had been at the roadside. Byron walked quickly and Seymour had to hurry to keep up.

They stopped in front of a row of wooden buildings. Byron glanced at a faded sign advertising an inn. He grinned. He grabbed Seymour's arm and led him away from the door.

'There's a tavern inside that inn,' Byron said. 'I want you to go in and see if there's a merchant or a nobleman of my build. If there is, approach him, make up some kind of story, and find out where his room is. Then come tell me.'

'What kind of story?' Seymour's hands had grown cold. When he was six, he had lied to his father about completing his first spell. His father had demanded to see it, and when Seymour hadn't even known the incantation, his father had punished him by calling a whirlpool from the river and wrapping him in it. Seymour's mother had found it, demanded that his father stop, but by the time he had, Seymour had already been cut in a dozen places by the water's sharpness. He hadn't lied since.

'I don't know what kind of story. Whatever the circumstances demand.'

'What happens if I fail?'

'You won't.'

Seymour wished he was that certain. If he didn't want to attempt a spell, though, Byron's idea was the only chance they had. Seymour grimaced. He couldn't concentrate well enough in the noise to gather his luck web. He glanced at Byron. Byron nodded.

Seymour took a deep breath and walked to the inn door. The door was of deeply carved oak. Seymour pushed and it didn't move. He leaned against it and the door swung open slowly.

The place looked dark and gloomy. Dust motes rose in the light from the door. Then the door shut, cutting out the outside noise as if everyone out there had disappeared. Seymour blinked and saw nothing but darkness. Voices punctuated by laughter reached him. The low tones were a relief after the din of the street. He sneezed once, clearing the outdoors from his nostrils. The inn itself smelled of ale and greasy food.

Seymour's eyes adjusted. Stairs on his left ran up into more darkness. He was standing near the first row of benches. The tavern was crowded. Men huddled around tables, and women in low-cut blouses and skirts ripped just below the knees carried trays covered with mugs. A fire burned in the hearth on the far side. A portly man wearing a grease-stained apron watched everything from a door across the room. Another man sat alone at a small table near the hearth. The only empty chair in the place was beside him.

Seymour pushed his way through the chairs and drinkers, narrowly missing one of the serving girls. She grinned and pressed her breasts against him as she moved forward. Seymour ducked aside and stopped beside the man sitting alone. 'Do you mind if I join you?'

The man grunted his approval. Scars covered his face, and one of his eyes bulged out. Seymour wondered if the man had been in an accident or a lot of fights.

'I was wondering if you could help me,' Seymour said. His heart pounded. This man wouldn't put him in a whirlpool for lying, but the man might add a scar or two to his face.

'Depends,' the man said. He still didn't look up.

The man's tone made Seymour shiver. 'I'm searching for someone.'

'What do I look like, the city guards? Ask the barkeep.'

'You look like a much more observant man than the barkeep.' A true lie, and an automatic one. Seymour flushed. The man finally looked up. Another, newer cut ran just under his hairline, making him seem as if he were perpetually frowning.

'Do I now?' The man took a swig of his ale and wiped his arm across his mouth. 'Who are you looking for?'

'Tall man, slender, very well dressed. I was told he was staying here.' Seymour scanned the room. His eyes had adjusted to the darkness. He saw several men that fit his description.

'You know his name?'

'I know one of his names. He uses many.'

'Hmmm.' The sound was noncommittal, but the man seemed interested. He leaned forward.

Seymour bit his lower lip. He forced himself to continue. 'He travels from place to place under different names. He dresses like a merchant and sometimes like a lord.'

'I might know who you mean,' the man said, shoving his mug aside. 'Why are you looking for him?'

'He steals things.' Seymour wondered at the ease of the lies. They slipped out of him as if he had done it all of his life.

'And you want to get something back?'

Seymour nodded. 'Do you know him?'

'Know him? He's standing right over there.' The man nodded his head toward the far side of the room. A tall lord wearing a satin broad coat and leather pants leaned over a table, holding a coin in his hand. Seymour squinted. The lord seemed shorter than Byron, but just as thin. Seymour hoped that Byron wasn't planning to do anything illegal to this man.

'Where's he staying?' Seymour asked.

'You mean you aren't going to fight him here?'

Fight? Seymour's stomach turned. Of course the man would make that assumption. 'My men are outside. They do that work for me.'

'Count me in for a bit of the take,' the man said. 'I haven't been in a brawl in a long time.'

'Certainly,' Seymour said. He had no intention of seeing this man again, but if Byron was really going to fight the lord, Seymour wanted to have outside help.

'You just yell if you need me.'

'I will.'

The man smiled. The scars disappeared into his face, making his skin seem pockmarked. 'He's staying first door, top of the stairs.'

'Thank you.' Seymour stood up. His knees felt weak. He gripped the chair for a moment, then pushed on. He had done it. He had gotten the information they needed.

He gave the lord in the corner a wide berth, then slipped out the front door. The noise hit him like a wall. The brightness of the sunlight made him squint, and he sneezed twice at the manure-scented road. Byron was squatting beside the building. Three or four beggars sat near him. Despite his ripped clothing, he didn't look a part of them. His bearing was too confident, his skin too clean. Seymour stopped in front of him, and he rose stiffly.

'Well?'

'First door, top of the stairs.'

Byron's dark eyes sparkled. 'Good work, Seymour. Now, go back inside and keep him busy until I come down the stairs.'

'I can't,' Seymour said.

'Why not?'

'I told some guy that I was going to get my men to fight.'

Byron laughed. 'So pick a fight with him if he tries to go upstairs.'

'I can't fight him.'

'I'll be done quickly. You won't have to fight him.' Byron glanced around them. Two of the beggars slept, their heads lolling back against the building. People streamed past: a merchant pulling a steaming cart, a man followed by four children. Byron slipped into the crowd and headed around the row of buildings to the back of the inn. He darted along the roadway and disappeared.

Seymour's hands were shaking. He wanted to be someone else. Or somewhere else. He sighed and went back to the inn. The door seemed heavier than it had before. Inside, the darkness was thick. When Seymour's eyes adjusted, he noticed that the table near the hearth was empty. Some of the tension left his shoulders. The man had disappeared. For a moment Seymour hoped that the lord had disappeared too. Then Seymour saw the tall man sitting in the center of the room, talking with a group of men. The men at the table looked rougher than Lord Dakin's retainers. The men had large, muscular bodies. One man stood out from the others. He was wiry, his arms corded and strong. A long scar ran down the side of his face. They seemed to be discussing something.

After a moment the lord stood up, threw a coin on the table, and headed for the door. Some of the men followed.

Seymour forgot to breathe. He had no plan, no way of stopping the lord. Seymour shot a quick, nervous look at the stairs, but he didn't see Byron. When Seymour turned back toward the tables, the lord was almost beside him.

'. . . get my cloak,' the lord was saying. Seymour had to act fast. There was no time to think of a plan.

He blocked the lord's path. The man seemed taller up close. 'Excuse me, sir,' Seymour said, 'but I have a message for you.'

The lord looked down at him. Seymour felt himself grow cold.

The lord's eyes seemed colorless in the dim light. 'What?'

Seymour swallowed. He remembered the road, the only other gentry he had seen that day. 'Uh, a woman – in a white carriage – she asked me to tell you to meet her. She said – '

'Her name, lad, or you're wasting my time.'

Seymour rubbed his hands together. 'I don't know, sir, but she said it was urgent. She said she'd meet you near her carriage, about a mile south of here.'

The lord hesitated. He turned to the man with the scar running down his face. The scar's ridged edges puckered the man's mouth. 'A white carriage, you said?'

Seymour glanced at the stairs. No Byron. 'Yes, sir. It had four white banners with blue stars in the center.'

'And she asked for me? Why did she send you? Why not one of her retainers?'

Seymour shrugged. 'She said it was important.'

'How did you know where to find me?'

Seymour almost closed his eyes. Lords. What did he know about lords? Nothing except that lords thought of no one but themselves. 'Everyone knows you, sir. We all know where you're staying.'

The lord frowned. 'How convenient for you. This sounds rather odd, lad. Are you sure you're not up to something else?'

'Sir, she did say it was urgent.' Seymour held himself still, forcing himself not to glance at the stairs again. Had Byron left him? 'Please, sir. She's not a lady to keep waiting.'

'That she is not, Lord Kensington,' the other man said. His voice was deep and raspy. 'The Lady Jelwra is a real bitch if something doesn't go her way.'

'Are you sure her carriage displayed white banners with a blue star?' the lord asked.

'Yes, sir. She said you'd know who she was.'

'How did you know who I was and didn't know who she was?'

'I'd only heard people talk about the lady, sir, but I had never seen her before.'

'And you had seen me?'

'Yes, sir. I have often wondered if you needed a magician in your entourage.'

The lord smiled. 'You seem a bit too ragged for my entourage. I take it she is waiting in her carriage?'

Seymour nodded.

The lord tossed him a coin. Seymour caught it, just barely. The lord pushed his way out the front door, the other man trailing behind him. Seymour waited until the door closed before he leaned against the wall. He was going to pass out, he knew it. Deep breaths, deep breaths. Then he would be all right.

Several patrons on their way out glanced at him. The wall was cool but made of rough wood. A sliver stuck into his finger as he pushed against the wall to stand. He pocketed the coin and backed away from the door. He climbed a few stairs, but saw nothing in the darkness. If Byron didn't show up soon, Seymour would sit down. After this tension he might never stand again.

At least he had some money in his pocket. The coin wasn't much, but it would help.

A loud crash at the top of the stairs made Seymour start. He moved out of the way as a tall nobleman bounded down the stairs, a black cape billowing behind him. The man grabbed Seymour's sleeve and tugged fiercely, almost ripping the garment in his haste. 'Come on,' he hissed.

Seymour pulled away. He didn't have the time or energy for more foolishness.

'There you are!' someone shouted from the darkness above. 'I found him for you. Caught him coming out of his room. If you hurry, we can take him on together.'

The man Seymour had talked with earlier ran down the stairs. As he passed Seymour, he said, 'Let's get him.'

The nobleman at the foot of the stairs adjusted the lace on his sleeve, then ran a hand through his thick black hair. He kept his head down.

Seymour frowned. Where was Byron? Something had gone wrong. 'No, wait – '

'You're afraid.' The man spoke loudly in his disgust.

The nobleman glanced up. Seymour's heart seemed to stop. The nobleman looked just like Byron. 'Are you coming or not?' he asked, using his rich voice with authority.

'Ah – yes, milord.' Seymour walked slowly down the stairs. The nobleman had to be Byron. He couldn't be anyone else. Still, he looked comfortable in those clothes, as if they had been tailored for him.

When Seymour reached the bottom of the stairs, Byron handed him a small valise. 'We'll be on our way, then.'

'Hey!' The man leaped down the stairs and blocked their path. His breath whistled in and out between his rotten teeth. 'What's going on here?'

Seymour turned. His entire body was trembling. 'We are going outside. We have people waiting for us. I'll call you if I need you.'

'Oh.' The man stepped out of their way. 'Right.'

Byron grabbed Seymour by the arm and led him out of the inn. The light stabbed Seymour's eyes, and the noise seemed to have grown, throbbing, throbbing, throbbing inside his head.

'We have to move before someone recognizes these clothes,' Byron said.

Beggars surrounded them, crying for money. Seymour tripped as someone jostled him. 'What did you do?' he asked.

'What does it look like I did?' Byron walked faster. He walked along the side of the road, pushing people as he went. 'Let's find a place to stay – far from here.'

'But how – ?'

'Seymour.' Byron stopped. People did not touch him as they passed. Horses avoided him. He seemed to have gained a foot-wide invisible body shield along with the clothes. Seymour couldn't detect any magic, however. 'I stole these, along with an extra change of clothes and quite a bit of money. And I don't want to discuss it. If it bothers you, remember this: you refused to cast that spell.'

Seymour shoved his hands in the pocket of his robe and felt the coin the lord had given him. He had never expected Byron to steal to get them a place to stay. If Seymour had known, he might have tried harder to gather his luck web. It probably wouldn't have worked, but at least he would have had the satisfaction of a failed attempt. He glanced behind them. It seemed as if no one had followed them. 'You look like a lord in those clothes,' he said.

Byron smiled. The tension seemed to flow out of him. 'Do I really?'

'I didn't recognize you.'

'Not at all?'

Seymour shook his head.

'Good.' Byron looked ahead, into the crowd. 'Because that retainer up there is wearing Lord Dakin's colors.'

Chapter 4

Adric walked toward the spires. They looked cold and distant, yet at the same time too large, like the fingers of a giant. His legs ached and he smelled, but no one seemed to notice. The crowd surged forward, and when he thought to look, his traveling companions were always different.

Beside him now, a merchant hurried, his chin up, glancing over the heads to something Adric couldn't see. On Adric's left, a thread of troubadours pushed the wrong way. One hit Adric, jostling him. Their gazes met, then the troubadour looked away. Here on the street, voices milled and rumbled. Occasionally a horse rode through, and Adric dodged as the others did, watching for hooves out of the corner of his eye. When a carriage passed, he stopped and gazed, hoping to see the unmarked black carriage or at least one with an insignia he recognized. But most of the carriages were small and unfamiliar, pulled by two horses and steered by men in simple leather.

As twilight grew, Adric seemed no closer to the spires. He was tired and hungry, but he wouldn't let his fear surface. He knew that Lord Ewehl had to find him. The lord couldn't go back to the palace without Adric.

Someone tugged on his sleeve. Adric whirled, expecting to see one of the footmen. Instead a girl about his own age smiled at him. Her long brown hair straggled around her face. Her skin was thick with dust, and most of her teeth were missing. 'You look lost,' she said.

He could barely hear her over the noise. When the words did reach him, they sent a shudder through him, and for a minute his eyes burned with the threat of tears. He took a deep breath to calm himself.

'Where's you going?'

'To the center of town, the place where the king's carriage

usually waits.' His voice hitched as he spoke. He felt as if he had been alone for weeks instead of hours.

She nodded and took his arm. 'I know where that is.'

Adric trembled. Finally a little bit of hope. The girl led him through the press of bodies to the side of the road. There a small side street angled off into the dimness. It looked like the road he had been attacked on: strangely hung signs, the wooden platform, and haphazardly placed buildings. Only this street had no gutter running down the middle.

'This is a quicker way,' she said. Now that they were away from the noise, Adric could hear a lisp in her speech caused by the lack of teeth. She looked him up and down, taking the lace edge of his sleeve and rubbing it between her fingers. 'Your clothes are nice.'

'They were nicer this morning.'

'It was a bad day for you, then,' she said.

He nodded, not really wanting to chat. He wanted to move, to find the carriage before nightfall.

'It'll cost you a gold piece to get to the center of town.' The girl held out her hand.

Adric stared at her palm for a moment, not understanding her. When he finally realized that she wanted him to pay her, he shook his head. 'I don't have any money,' he said.

The smile left her face and her eyes became flat and hard. 'Lordlings like you always carry money.'

'I was robbed,' he said.

She laughed and snapped her fingers. 'Sure you were,' she said.

Adric opened his mouth to tell her the story when he was tackled from behind. As he landed on the hard-packed dirt, the air whooshed out of his body. Dozens of small hands reached in his clothes, ripping, tearing, searching. His body was cramped and he could barely move. Finally he gasped, filling his lungs. He tried to roll over, but his shoulders were pressed tightly to the ground. A knee dug into the small of his back as the hands moved down to his trousers, cupping and grabbing even his private parts. He screamed and flailed, but he couldn't strike anything. Then the hands disappeared except for the two on his shoulders. The knee pushed harder into his back, sending a dull, throbbing ache around to his belly.

'I thought you said there'd be coins on this one.' A boy's voice, cracking and rough.

'He looked like he would,' the girl said.

'He's no better off than we are.'

Adric pushed against the ground and managed to roll away from the hands and knee. He looked up to see a dozen dirty children looking down on him. 'Look,' he said. 'If we're all in the same position, maybe – '

'You don't know anything,' the tallest boy said. He was the one who had spoken before. His body was stick-thin, and scabs covered his arms and legs. 'Look at you.' He pushed Adric's hip with his foot. 'You're fat and well-dressed, and your hands are soft. You don't know anything.'

He kicked Adric's side. Pain shot up through his chest. Adric tried to get up, but the other children leaped on him, kicking and biting and scratching. He managed to raise his hands to his face as he crumpled back to the ground. Things popped and snapped in his body. His chest burned and he could barely draw breath. A sharp blow landed on his head, and he must have passed out, for when he opened his eyes, it was fully dark and he was alone.

He looked up, his eyelids sticky with tears and blood. The stars shone above him, the same stars as the ones he saw at home. He missed home. He wondered what Lord Ewehl was doing, if the carriage still sat in its appointed spot in the center of town. He had to see.

Adric eased his arms down, feeling sharp stitches of pain in his shoulders and sides. He still couldn't catch his breath, and he could no longer feel his chest. It was as if his chest weren't there at all. His legs throbbed, and he knew he had a long gash near one of his ankles.

He tried to roll over and found that his chest did still exist. The pain was exquisite, so fine-tuned it seemed that if he experienced it long enough, it would send him somewhere else, somewhere better. He toyed with testing the theory, then realized that his mother would worry about him. His mother needed him at home.

Adric managed to sit up, but the movement seemed to take hours. Ahead, he saw a single light burning through open doors, revealing hay, horses, a stable. A boy who was almost a man, whose shoulders were broad but whose body was still child-slim, carried two buckets toward the open door. Water splashed along the sides. Adric licked his lips. He was thirsty and he was tired and he hurt everywhere. If he got a little water, he would be able to make it to the center of town, he knew it.

He tried to stand up, shook, and collapsed on his knees. He didn't care. He crawled, feeling the dirt dig into his palms, his legs. His clothing hung in tatters around him, and in more than one place he thought he felt the stickiness of blood.

As Adric neared the stable, he could smell the richness of hay mingled with horse sweat and manure. Familiar scents, scents of home. Inside, the boy whistled, stopping occasionally to talk to one of the horses. Adric almost crawled in, then hesitated. Everyone else he had met abused him. He didn't dare trust this boy. Adric couldn't take another beating. He swallowed, his Adam's apple bobbling against dryness, and forced himself to think.

He had to get the boy out of the stable without closing the doors. Adric's hand closed around a hard clump of dirt. He tossed it, using all his strength, his arm cracking and tiny shudders of pain jabbing him. The dirt smacked against the far wall of the building beside the stable. Adric leaned forward, his chest burning so badly that he had to concentrate on each breath.

The whistling stopped. The boy appeared at the stable doors, his face half shrouded in shadow. His hair was blond, with pieces of straw sticking out of it, his clothing too small but clean.

Adric grabbed another clump of dirt and, willing himself strength, threw it.

The boy turned at the sound, then walked toward it.

Adric had to move quickly. He crawled along the dirt, keeping his head turned so that he saw the boy.

The inside of the stable was warm. The smell of hay, horses, and manure seemed stronger here. Adric found the nearest pile of hay and burrowed into it. The stiff pieces scratched his already wounded body and the hay dust tickled his nose, but he was warm and he was safe, at least for the moment.

'False scare,' he heard someone say, probably the boy speaking to the horses. The whistling started again, and Adric closed his eyes. His pain throbbed in rhythm with his heart. When the boy left and the light went out, Adric would get himself water, and then he would leave. Until then he would rest.

He sighed once and shivered as hay rubbed against his wounds. The whistling continued and Adric concentrated on it, following the rise and fall of the song until he fell asleep.

Chapter 5

i

Seymour followed Byron's gaze. Through the crowd Seymour caught a glimpse of a familiar brown and tan uniform, and then saw another. He swallowed and pressed his hands together. He hadn't seen that uniform since the day Dakin had led him to the hounds. Seymour had thought the next time he saw it, he would die. That feeling was still very strong. 'What do we do?'

Byron shrugged. 'Risk passing him, I guess. Why don't you wait here? If something happens to me, there's enough money in that valise to take care of you.'

Seymour didn't want to be by himself, especially with stolen merchandise on his arm. 'I can't let you go alone – '

'We have to go separately. Together we'll be too conspicuous. I'll divert his attention and then you run past. We'll meet at that side street down there.' Byron pointed to a street that veered off behind the retainer.

Seymour shook his head, about to protest again, when the cries of 'Carriage! Carriage!' rose. People scurried aside. A woman pushed against Seymour in her haste, knocking him against Byron. She nodded at Byron, her face flushed, 'Sorry, milord,' she said as she passed.

Byron took Seymour's arm and led him to the side of the road just as the white carriage rumbled past. Seymour felt the wind from its wheels, smelled the rich leather of its frame. A young boy stood in the carriage's path, but it didn't slow. A merchant grabbed the child away just in time.

The carriage stopped near Lord Dakin's retainers. The crowd remained near the side of the road, moving forward again but giving the carriage and the retainers a wide berth. The carriage rocked for a moment, and then the door opened and a woman stepped out.

She wore a long white day gown that accented her dark hair and skin. She was tiny, perhaps half Seymour's size. Her hair cascaded down her shoulders in ringlets. She carried a small white fan which she swung like a knife.

Byron took a few steps forward. Seymour followed.

'You are one of Lord Dakin's retainers?' Her voice carried above the noise of the crowd.

'Yes, ma'am.' The retainer bowed and stayed down until she tapped him on the shoulder with her fan.

'Who is she?' Seymour asked.

Byron stared at her. The tension seemed to have returned to his body. 'The Lady Almathea Jelwra. She is one of the richest and most powerful nobles in the kingdom. Her mother used to be on the council.'

'Do you know where Lord Dakin is?' the lady asked.

The retainer stood. 'He plans to be here shortly, ma'am. He had a bit of trouble back at the great house.'

'Trouble?'

'With an execution, ma'am.'

'Those damned dogs again,' she said. 'How barbaric.' She slapped her fan against her palm. 'Tell your master that if he hasn't shown up by this time tomorrow, I shall leave. If I do not see him, I will consider our business concluded and I will so notify the palace.'

'Yes, ma'am.'

The mention of the hounds sent shivers through Seymour. He touched Byron's arm. 'Let's go now, before they notice us.'

Byron's eyes were hooded. Seymour could read no expression on his face. When he spoke, his tone seemed reluctant. 'I suppose we should hurry.'

This time Seymour grabbed Byron's arm, and pulled him past the beggars, minstrels, and merchants lining the streets. Seymour crouched as he moved, hoping to stay hidden in the masses of people. The crowd noise lessened, but he lost track of the conversation behind him. Gentry everywhere, and Lord Dakin coming to the city. They had to get out as quickly as they could.

Once Byron's attention had been diverted from the lady, he moved rapidly. Seymour glanced over his shoulder. The retainers had their backs to Byron and Seymour. The lady was gesturing with her fan, then she began to climb the stairs to her carriage, but stopped when a man approached her.

'Oh no,' Seymour whispered.

'Come on, Seymour,' Byron said.

Seymour nodded. 'We've got to get off this street.'

'That's what I'm trying to do,' Byron said.

'No, you don't understand. Our benefactor is standing over there.'

Byron looked at the carriage and swore under his breath. 'Lord Kensington.' He tapped Seymour on the arm and then loped toward the side street. Seymour had to run to keep up.

The side street was smaller, the road narrower. The smells were less thick here, and the noise dimmer. The crowd seemed different, a bit rougher, filled with people like the one Seymour had encountered the day before.

He looked back at the main road. The lord still spoke with the lady, and the retainers watched. No one had followed. He and Byron were safe.

ii

Afeno huddled in a doorway, watching the street. His stomach ached. He hadn't had a decent meal since Magic left two weeks before. He sighed, wishing he could get enough energy to do some work. But Magic had been his partner. The old man had taught Afeno everything. They worked as a team, Afeno attracting the attention because his young legs could carry him quickly, and Magic taking the money. Only last time Magic had taken the money and had never returned.

A merchant's cart rumbled by, stacked with food. A long, fat sausage hovered on the edge, then toppled into the road. Afeno sprang forward. He pushed his way into the road and dove on the meat, wrapping his arms around the casing when someone hit him in the jaw. Afeno winced. A ragged boy grabbed the sausage and pulled. Afeno pulled back. He wasn't going to let anyone take his meal, especially not some young kid. Afeno twisted his foot around the boy's ankle and yanked. The boy toppled into the dirt, losing his grip on the sausage. Afeno got up, but the boy grabbed his calf. Afeno slipped and fell on his knees. Pain shot through his legs and made his eyes water. Dust got into his mouth and he felt as if he were choking. The boy jumped on top of Afeno and began pounding his back with small fists. Afeno clung to the sausage. If he survived the attack, he would eat again. Eating was worth this.

The kid hit Afeno's ear, and the shooting ache made Afeno roll over. He kneed the boy in the groin and the kid fell over. He heard applause. Afeno glanced up. A group of street fighters and retainers had gathered around them. Coins glinted. They were betting on the fight.

The betting made Afeno even angrier. He hugged the sausage and started to run, but the kid tackled him. Afeno rolled until he faced the kid, then he kicked and bit. The kid pummeled Afeno. Tears were running down the kid's face, leaving tracks in the dirt.

Afeno pushed the kid off with his feet, and ignored the cheering. He gripped the sausage like a sword and as the kid stood up, took a swing. The kid ducked.

Suddenly someone grabbed Afeno by the scruff of the neck. His feet dangled above the ground. He clung to the sausage, wondering if he dared drop it and fight his way free. Damn those fighters. They were in the way.

The kid was still within reach. Afeno kicked him. The person holding Afeno's neck shook him. 'Stop it. Stop it now.'

The man's voice was soft and deep. He didn't yell, but his tone seemed menacing. Another man came from behind and held the kid's shoulders.

'Hey! You got no business here!' one of the fighters yelled. The man was brawny, with arms the size of the sausage. Afeno turned his head from side to side, trying to see his captor.

'Let go of the sausage,' said the man holding Afeno. Afeno held on tighter.

'Let go,' the man said, 'or I'll free it myself.' His grip tightened. The collar of Afeno's ripped shirt dug into his neck. He dropped the sausage. His stomach growled and he felt even more discouraged than he had before. The sausage thumped at the kid's feet.

'You have no right!' the fighter yelled.

'When you address me, you say "sir."' The man lowered Afeno to the ground, but kept a firm grip on his shoulder. Afena turned and saw his captor for the first time. He wore a black cape and pants made from a rich material. Lace decorated his wrists and his collar. But his face was covered with scratches and his skin was too pale. Deep circles ran under his eyes.

'I don't call anybody sir, especially not a lordling in lace and velvet,' said the fighter. The man was big, with thick forearms and a tattoo on his hand. The other fighters closed around him. Afeno wriggled, trying to get free. The sausage wasn't worth being in the middle of this kind of fight. Magic had told him that no one would win with one of these. If Afeno did get away, he would try to grab some of the coins as he ran.

'Pick up your money and go,' the lord said. He pushed back his cape. A fine gold scabbard rested against his hip. The hilt of the sword sparkled with a hundred small jewels, enough to keep Afeno fed for years. 'And give the boys some gold for the insult you paid them.'

'No.' The fighter drew a dagger from his belt. 'But we may let them have some of your riches.'

The lord let go of Afeno's shoulders. Afeno reached for the sausage when the man holding the kid grabbed him. 'You wait.' Afeno glanced at the man. He wore dirty magician's robes, and his face was covered with dust.

'Do you know that the penalty for attacking a gentleman in this city is death?' the lord asked.

The fighter shrugged. 'They'll never know who did it.'

The lord spread his legs to improve his balance. A larger crowd had gathered around them. Afeno thought he recognized a few faces. 'They'll know,' the lord said. 'I've already sent one of my retainers for the mayor's guards.'

The retainers who had been betting with the street fighters backed away. Afeno tried to wrench himself from the magician's grasp. Afeno didn't want to see the mayor's guards. The magician held on tightly. 'Just wait,' he said.

The leader waved his dagger. 'They aren't here yet, lordling.'

He lunged at the lord. Afeno stepped back, into the magician. The lord's sword glinted as it appeared, and with a single clink of metal against metal, the fighter's dagger spun into the crowd. People screamed and hurried out of the way. The lord held the sword at his side and faced the fighters.

'Anyone else?' he asked. The fighters shook their heads. The lord sheathed his sword. 'All right, then. You owe the boys some money.'

The fighters tossed coins at the lord. The money shimmered and sparkled like rain in sunlight. The coins tinkled as they fell. The lord stood and watched; everyone stood and watched. Afeno held himself still. The minute the magician let him go, he would grab as much money as he could.

The fighters turned away and walked down the street. The leader picked up his dagger, rubbed its blade against his trousers, and stuck it in his belt. Then he followed the others.

The lord watched them with a slight smile. As soon as they disappeared, he said, 'Thank you for the help, Seymour.'

The magician's face flushed. 'You could have got us killed.'

'Here.' The lord took Afeno's arm and the kid's. His fingers squeezed into Afeno's flesh. 'Would you pick up the coins and cut the sausage in half?'

'You said that's ours!' Afeno tried to shake himself from the lord's grasp. The grip was too tight – and Afeno was too weak from the last few weeks. His arm would be bruised.

'The sausage is yours,' the lord said. 'But Seymour will divide it for you civilly – unless you want to continue fighting?'

The lord let go of Afeno then. Afeno rubbed his arm. He could try to take everything, but the lord was quick with a sword. Or he could wait until the lord left and steal from the kid. That seemed best.

The magician gathered the coins. Afeno watched closely, trying to see if the magician pocketed any of it. But he just put the money in little piles.

The lord crouched in front of the kid and pulled out a lace handkerchief. He wiped blood away from the kid's nose. The kid let him. Afeno would have pulled away. The kid sniffled a little. He looked too young to be scrounging on his own.

'Tell me what happened,' the lord said.

The kid glanced at Afeno. The kid's brown eyes were large against his face. The kid hadn't eaten well in a long time either.

'Which one of you stole the sausage?'

Afeno had stolen nearly everything he had ever had, but he hadn't stolen that sausage. He and the kid spoke at the same time.

'I didn't – '

'I never – '

'It just – '

'Someone – '

The lord laughed. His laugh seemed to run up and down a scale. 'Who dropped the sausage?'

'It fell off a merchant's cart,' the kid said. 'I grabbed it and he took it from me.'

'I had it first,' Afeno said. 'He was trying to get it from me.'

'So you both reached it at the same time and started fighting over it. Seymour, how much money have you got there?'

'Twenty gold pieces and seven rounds.'

'Rounds.' The lord sounded as if rounds were horrible. Rounds were fine with Afeno. They weren't nearly as much as a gold piece, but they bought food on the street. 'Ten gold pieces each. What are your names, boys?'

'Colin,' the kid said.

Afeno swallowed. He found that he didn't want to lie to the lord. 'Afeno.'

The lord's eyes widened slightly, as if he knew that Afeno hadn't lied. 'You have no family.'

Afeno snorted. His mother had been knifed by one of her clients when Afeno was Colin's age, and he had managed to scramble on his own for a while. Then he had met Magic and they worked together until Magic disappeared with their money. 'No family and no home. I make my way by stealing. Doesn't that worry you?'

'No.' The lord smiled. 'Not since I'm the one who caught you.'

Afeno flushed. His luck had turned poor. He was doing so badly that he didn't notice an obvious mark because he had been fighting for a sausage.

'What about you, Colin?' the lord asked. 'You're alone too.'

Colin's eyes filled with tears. He blinked hard and cleared his throat before he spoke. 'My mother died of fever, and my father met Lord Dakin's hounds. He managed to send me here to an uncle, but my uncle didn't want me.'

The lord nodded. The magician put his hand on the lord's arm. 'No,' the magician whispered.

The lord didn't seem to notice. 'You boys will never survive in this city carrying ten gold pieces.'

'Yes, we will,' Afeno said. He could handle himself. The lord was going to cheat them after all. Afeno should have known better than to trust the man.

'I'll make you an offer,' the lord said, as if Afeno hadn't spoken. 'I'll pay you a copper per day over and above your gold if you travel with us. My friend and I need some companions to do the fetching for us.'

Afeno frowned. Lords had retainers. They didn't need the help of beggar boys. 'What happened to your men?'

The lord grinned. 'I have no men. And I'm no gentleman.'

That explained the cuts on his face. He had stolen the clothes. The whole thing still made no sense, though. Why wasn't he keeping the gold for himself?

'You bluffed the fighters?' Colin asked.

The lord nodded and tugged at the lace on his sleeve.

'In the name of the Old Ones,' Colin said. 'They could have killed you.'

The lord shrugged. Afeno smiled in spite of himself. The lord had courage, even if he did things strangely.

'I'll go with you,' Colin said.

Afeno hesitated. If he went with the lord, he would have food and money. Once he had accumulated enough of both and regained his strength, he could go out on his own again. He didn't want to trust another companion so soon. 'I'll go too,' he said.

iii

The innkeeper gave them his last room. Seymour stopped at the door, while Byron went inside and set down the valise. The room was smaller than the one he had had in Dakin's great house, but cozier. The pallet was wide and thick, and sat on a wooden frame. Large coverlets made the bed almost chest high. A table rested beneath a square window, and a chair leaned against the wall.

'I thought I'd never see a bed again,' Seymour said. He walked inside the room and collapsed on the coverlets. The pallet seemed even softer than the one he had had at the hut. He raised one foot in the air. With the money Byron had stolen that afternoon, he had bought Seymour new clothes and boots. Seymour wasn't used to wearing trousers and the boots were stiff. They aggravated the blisters he had gotten on the walk to town.

He stared at the shiny, torturous boot and pulled it off. Then he repeated the procedure with the other foot. He curled and massaged his toes. 'I may never walk again.'

Byron laughed. 'You'll get used to the boots, Seymour.'

Under his stockings Seymour found two more blisters. 'Maybe.' He glanced up at Byron. 'But I may never get used to you.'

'What do you mean?' Byron's tone was casual, but his body tensed.

'When you address me, you say "sir."'

Byron shrugged. 'Nice line, huh?'

'You meant that when you said it. You know how to use a sword like the gentry, and yet you steal as if you've done that before too. Then you treat fighters with righteous anger when they wager on children.' Seymour propped a pillow against the wall and leaned back. 'Why?'

Byron pulled off his cape and folded it across the chair. Then he sat on the bed, took off his boots, and sighed. 'I slapped an old woman once over a half-eaten piece of meat. She still managed to swallow it before I could grab it, and I was so hungry I could have killed her for it. I saw one of Lord Seritz's men behead a child for picking a gold piece off the street. That's when I decided I didn't owe the nobility anything. If their clothes gave them the license to do what they wanted, then all I needed was a fine outfit.'

'It's not that simple,' Seymour said.

'Isn't it? I don't misuse the clothes, and I don't steal unless I have to. Even then I don't like it.' Byron closed his eyes. Within seconds his breathing was solid and even. Seymour rubbed his feet, finding more blisters. Then he propped himself on an elbow and looked at Byron.

His skin was pale with exhaustion, but the scratches were fading from his face. His fingers were long and slender – magician's hands, Seymour's father would have called them, but Seymour knew that Byron had no magic.

Byron's eyes opened, and for a moment Seymour found himself being appraised in return. Then Byron sat up. 'I can't sleep just yet, Seymour. I think I'll go down and get something to eat. Want to join me?'

Seymour frowned, wondering what Byron had seen. An inept, broken-down magician, too old to have an eighth-level seal, wearing the wrong clothes and a perpetually frightened expression on his face. Now that they were in the city, Byron should have gotten rid of him. Instead he bought Seymour new clothes and talked about traveling to the palace together.

'I'll come down with you,' Seymour said.

Byron smiled and stretched, then stood up. Seymour reached for his boots and slid them over his feet, wincing each time he hit a blister. When he stood, one of the blisters burst, and he limped to the door.

Laughter drifted up from the common room. The hallway smelled of ale and cooked meat. Seymour hadn't realized how hungry he was. He walked down the stairs, gripping the railing the entire way. His feet didn't bend properly in the boots. It felt as if he had strapped thick wood to the bottom of his feet. The trousers felt awkward too. They constricted his waist and rubbed against the inside of his legs. Seymour had worn magician's robes his entire life. The soft shirt and tight trousers – squire's clothing – made him feel like another person.

Only a few people sat in the common room. A table full of local merchants drank and laughed. A serving girl huddled near the hearth. At another table a woman and a man stared at their food as if using it as an excuse not to talk to each other.

Byron sat at a table near the door. Seymour sat across from him and resisted the urge to remove his boots again. Byron smiled sympathetically. Seymour realized that he hadn't seen Byron limp since they stole the clothes.

Byron raised a hand, and the serving girl came to the table. 'We'd like food and some ale,' he said. She nodded. In a few minutes, she returned with two large tankards of ale and plates overflowing with stew. The plates steamed, and the smell of beef and gravy made Seymour's mouth water.

'Too bad we couldn't bring the boys inside,' Byron said.

Seymour glanced up. He hated the thought of traveling with those children. 'We can't trust them in here.'

'Oh, we probably could.' Byron took a sip of his ale. 'I'm just too tired to watch them, that's all.'

The outside door opened, sending chill air inside the room. A thin, balding man dressed in white came in and held the door as the Lady Jelwra and another man walked through. The lady's white gown glimmered in the firelight. The man with her was elderly, and he bobbed as he spoke.

' . . . decision, milady.'

'I don't care,' she said. 'If he doesn't show up tomorrow, I will annex those lands. I have the right to do so. I was trying to be fair.'

The elderly man bobbed again. 'Have patience, milady. The retainer could have been wrong.'

'I certainly hope so. Chasing men with dogs. Barbarous custom. Someone should stop that man before he kills someone he shouldn't.' The lady stopped near the stairs. Her gown swished against the wooden floor. 'I mean it, though, Usci. I will take the lands. It makes no difference to me whether I pay for them or annex them. And Lord Dakin doesn't seem to mind either.'

'Milady.' The elderly man put a hand on her arm. His voice shook slightly. 'If you annex the land, you could have trouble with Lord Dakin.'

'Nonsense. I'll get the king's seal. You know that's both easy and legal. Boton can – ' She stopped and stared at Byron. A slow flush rose in her dark cheeks. Taking a step toward the table, she took a fan from the folds of her skirt. The fan was closed, and she caressed it absently. 'Who might you be, sir?'

Byron stood, took her free hand, and kissed it. He did not release it when he was through. 'Geoffry of Kinsmail, at your service, milady.'

Kinsmail? Seymour pushed his full plate aside. The nerves that had prevented him from eating all day had returned. He had heard of Kinsmail, but the stories were vague and old, like a half-remembered dream.

The Lady Jelwra smiled. The look transformed her face, made her seem little older than the boys they had found on the street. 'Kinsmail does not exist,' she said.

'Beg pardon, milady,' Byron said. 'It did exist once.'

'Indeed?' Her expression remained innocent, but her tone was skeptical. 'You look like a titled man. But you're probably lying to me. You're probably one of Lord Dakin's sons, sent to spy on me.'

Byron smiled in return. He still held her hand. 'Lord Dakin has no sons. And I am no friend of his. He holds the title to Kinsmail land. It seems he annexed it.'

The Lady Jelwra touched Byron's cheek with her fan. 'Lands are lost if the owner doesn't protect them, Sir Geoffry.'

'It's not quite that easy,' he said. 'We have the Enos to think about.'

She pulled her hand away and stepped back. 'I have never had any trouble with an Enos.'

'Not yet. But you're young, milady.'

Seymour clasped his hands tightly. No one talked to gentry like this. If she caught Byron in his lie –

'I'm sure Lord Dakin's Enos does not approve of his dogs,' the lady said.

'I'm sure,' Byron said.

She turned to her elderly companion. 'Does this young man have a claim to Lord Dakin's land?'

'If he is who he says he is,' the man said. 'The Kinsmails and Dakins had one of the few land battles ever recorded in Kilot history. Seventeen men died defending Kinsmail land. They stopped it before it developed into a final time.'

'Mmm.' The lady tilted her head. Her ringlets fell away from her face, revealing diamond studs that ran along the outside edge of her ear. 'Then if I'm successful in my bid against Lord Dakin, I would have to contend with you, Sir Geoffry. That would be ever so much more interesting.'

She gathered her skirts and started up the stairs, her small white shoes clicking on the wood. Byron didn't move. He watched her with the same preoccupied expression Seymour had seen on his face earlier.

She stopped on the fifth stair and looked down at Byron. 'Did I tell you that you look familiar?' She raised her eyebrows and her dark eyes sparkled. 'Perhaps I danced with the Lord of Kinsmail and never even knew it.'

'Perhaps,' Byron said. She walked the rest of the way up the stairs. He didn't move until the creaks stopped in the floorboards above.

Seymour reached for his plate. The food was cool now and he ate it automatically. The meat was chewy and tasteless, the gravy thick with flour. He ate because he didn't want to talk to Byron, didn't want to find out that Byron had been lying to him all along. Byron had been sent to the hounds because he was the Lord of Kinsmail, not because of some peasant uprising. That would explain his ease in the clothing and his understanding of the streets.

Byron's chair groaned as he sat down. He grabbed his plate and began to eat without looking at Seymour.

'You lie well,' Seymour said.

Byron continued eating. He appeared to be swallowing without chewing.

'How did you think of Kinsmail so quickly?' Seymour let the sarcasm creep into his voice. 'I would have been stammering something about shipping or – '

'We'll have to leave in the morning.' Byron ran a hand over his face. 'And I was hoping to buy a lute here.'

'Why so soon?' Seymour asked, surprised by the turn in

conversation.

'Where the Lady Jelwra is, Lord Dakin will soon follow.'

'It's more than that,' Seymour said. 'She isn't sure Dakin will show up.'

'I know.' Byron glanced up the stairs.

'Then why leave?'

'Because,' Byron said softly, 'I don't ever want to see the Lady Jelwra again.'

Chapter 6

Adric's head felt as if it were loose on his neck. His head snapped forward and back. He couldn't get air, his throat was too constricted. Hay filled his nose and he wanted to sneeze.

'Wake up, you little thief!'

His shoulders ached, his whole body ached. He coughed, felt pain deep in his chest. The room was dark, but he didn't want to open his eyes.

'Wake up!' A voice, not the voice of the stable boy, but deeper, harsher, filled with something raw, like anger.

'Be easy, Rogren. He's hurt.' This voice was softer, a woman's voice. Adric wanted to reach to it. It reminded him of his mother.

'He's a thief and he owes me for a night's lodging. Wake up, boy!'

Hands squeezing Adric's shoulders were the cause of the shaking. Adric raised an arm, brushed feebly at the thick forearms that held him.

'He's awake.'

Adric opened his eyes, blinked in the blurry light. The stable seemed grainy, covered with white spots that floated through the air like tears. Three people towered over him, a burly man who smelled of onions, a raw-boned woman with skin as faded as her clothes, and the stable boy, who hung back and watched.

'What are you doing in my stable, boy?'

Adric licked his lips. His throat was very dry. 'The lord – '

'I'm not a lord, lad.'

'Lord Ewehl . . . looking for . . . me?'

The burly man dropped Adric. He fell back into the hay. It poked him, dug into his sores. 'He's not a thief. He's running. Get him out of here, Cassie.'

The woman knelt beside Adric and smoothed the hair from his forehead. Her hands smelled of soap. 'He's hurt.'

'So I can't get any work out of him. And I'll bet he has no money on him either. The night's lodging is lost.'

'We can't just turn him out. I doubt if he can walk.'

'He walked in here, he can walk out.'

Adric tried to push himself up, but the hay kept sliding through his fingers. 'Please,' he said. 'Lord Ewehl – '

'Let him stay,' the woman said. 'He can help me until he's strong enough to help you.'

'He's on the run. And if Lord Ewehl's after him, the palace guard will sweep through here.'

The palace guard. Good. Someone to look for him. Someone to find him. Adric grabbed the woman's wrist. 'Please,' he said again, wishing he could get enough air to say more.

The woman looked at Adric's hand, then at the burly man. 'You were on the run once too, Rogren.'

The burly man grunted and stood up. He prodded Adric with his foot. 'Fix him, then, Cassie, but if he doesn't start earning his way soon, I'll throw him out. You know that.'

The woman watched until the burly man went out the stable doors. Adric coughed. Something to drink would help. 'Water,' he said.

The stable boy dipped a cup in a nearby bucket. Water dripped from the cup's bottom onto Adric's chest. The drops felt cool and soothing. He tried to sit up, but couldn't find the strength. The woman supported his head, and he drank.

The water tasted stale but sweet, so very sweet. Adric coughed, surfaced, and drank some more.

'Can you get me some more water, Milo?' the woman said.

The stable boy disappeared. The woman leaned back and ripped the pocket off her skirt. She dipped the fabric in the water and wiped Adric's face. The water felt cool. 'You have a fever,' she said. 'Someone beat you up pretty badly.'

The woman's hands stopped at Adric's chest. He saw her eyes, then remembered the ornate dove tattoo which the Enos had carved over his left nipple at birth. The sign of his family. He tried to lift his arms to cover it, but could not.

'Milo, come see this.'

The stable boy crouched next to him. Adric closed his eyes. Lord Ewehl said that people would hurt him when they knew who he was, hurt him to hurt his father.

'What do you think it is?' she asked. 'It's not a bruise.'

'It's a marking of some kind.' The boy ran his finger over the tattoo. 'They say nobility does that.'

'Do you think he's a lordling?'

'He's fat enough.' The boy leaned back. 'I'll ask around if you want.'

'No. He'll tell us if he has to.'

Adric felt the panic leave him. She touched him some more, cooling him, soothing him. He was contented to watch her work, wondering how such a washed-out woman could have such a soft and vibrant voice. But he didn't dare be contented. He had to get to the carriage. His mother would be worried.

'Lord Ewehl,' he said.

The woman pushed him back against the hay. 'Just rest now. We'll take care of you.' Adric closed his eyes. He believed her.

Chapter 7

i

Almathea opened the door to her room and stepped inside. What a hovel. A thick, padded bed, a single dingy window, a wardrobe, and two soft chairs were crammed into the small space. If her room was the best the inn had to offer, imagine the hole Sir Geoffry had. She smiled. Sir Geoffry had warm hands and the longest lashes she had ever seen on a man.

The door closed behind her. Usci sat on one of the chairs, his feet curled beneath him like a cup handle.

'So there really was a Kinsmail,' Alma said.

Usci nodded. 'They lost the lands to the Dakins when my grandfather was a boy. I thought all the Kinsmail heirs had died.'

Alma opened the wardrobe. The wooden door squeaked. She pulled out a long satin dressing gown and tossed it on the bed. 'Apparently Lord Dakin thought so too.'

She tugged on her dress, reached behind the neck, and began to unbutton. Usci watched, his expression unchanged. When she had first begun to travel with her mother's old adviser, Alma tried to shock him by changing clothes in front of him, prancing naked around him, and sharing her sexual conquests with him. Usci did not shock. He gave her advice, warned her against standing before windows, and often helped her undress. When her disappointment at his lack of reaction disappeared, she was pleased at the freedom his manner allowed her. She moved in front of him now, and he finished undoing the buttons at the small of her back.

'I doubt that the young man is of Kinsmail,' Usci said.

'He has noble blood.'

'He is good-looking,' Usci said. 'There is a difference.'

Alma shrugged the dress off her shoulders and stepped out of it. Then she took off the slips that gave the gown its fullness. She pulled the dressing gown over her head while Usci picked the garments off the floor.

'He is of noble blood,' she repeated. 'He has the pale look of the northern gentry.'

'Many peasants also have noble blood, milady. And even if he is of Kinsmail, he has no lands. He is little more than a peasant.'

Alma brushed her ringlets, then twirled them around her fingers. 'But a good-looking one, as you pointed out.'

Usci sighed, his arms filled with white skirts. He shook out the dress and hung it in the wardrobe. 'You are here on business, lady. You shouldn't be distracted.'

'Business.' Alma sat on the bed. Its softness gave way under her slight weight. Someone of the king's girth would sink to the floor. 'Lord Dakin doesn't seem to care about those lands his family fought for. If I were here on business, I wouldn't have time to look at Sir Geoffry of Kinsmail. But right now I can look and wonder – '

A knock echoed in the room. Usci closed the wardrobe and walked to the door. Alma put her feet on the bed, tucking them under the folds of her dressing gown. Usci opened the door. In the light flickering from the hallway, she saw a man. But he was too short and broad to be Sir Geoffry.

'The Lady Jelwra?' the man asked.

Usci bowed his head slightly. 'I am her manservant.'

'Lord Dakin has arrived. He begs an hour to clean up and eat, and then he would like to meet with the lady.'

Alma stood, her dressing gown swaying against her feet. 'At this late hour he is lucky if he even sees me.'

'Milady,' Usci said, 'you do owe him the courtesy of a meeting.'

'And he owed me the courtesy of appearing on time. Hunting men with dogs taking precedence over my meeting with him.' She swept to the door, conscious of her bearing and the commanding tone of her voice. The retainer was young, his skin pockmarked, his eyes wide at seeing a lady in her dressing gown. 'Tell your master that I will see him in fifteen minutes, no more. If he does not appear then, I will leave this place in the morning, heading for the palace, and I will not give him an audience. Is that clear?'

The retainer nodded. 'Yes, milady.'

'Then why are you waiting? You are wasting your master's time.'

The retainer bowed slightly, then turned, and hurried down the hall.

Alma sighed. That was almost too easy. She hoped that the confrontation with Lord Dakin would take more energy. Three years ago, when her mother had died on Alma's eighteenth birthday, Alma had decided to increase the size of her estate. She hoped that by the time she was twenty-five, she would be the largest landowner in Kilot, someone whose power and prestige the king could not ignore. She had already acquired two modest holdings, a parcel from Lord Stilez, and most of Lord Lafa's land. She was controlling the river access throughout the center of the country, and the king was already taking notice of her. When she left here, she would go to the palace for another audience, and perhaps some surreptitious advising.

'Go downstairs,' she said to Usci, 'and make sure that Sir Geoffry is not there. I want him out of my way. And keep Lord Dakin busy until I arrive.'

'Yes, milady.' Usci let himself out the door.

Alma opened the wardrobe and stared at the gowns she had brought. She didn't know if she should dress seductively or matronly, be subdued or flamboyant. She almost opted for kittenish, but then decided that her reputation had probably preceded her. She took out a gown that had a high collar, long sleeves, and no lace. Attractive but modest. She smiled to herself, feeling heat flush her cheeks. The battle was about to begin.

ii

Seymour knelt on the floor, his arms resting on the windowsill. The shutters were pushed back, and moonlight flooded the room. Byron slept in the bed beside him. Seymour envied him his ability to rest even amid all the noise. They had come upstairs soon after the Lady Jelwra, and Byron had fallen asleep almost immediately. Seymour had lain on his back, listening to the murmur of voices from the common room downstairs, the laughter of drunks outside his window. He hated the noise, the crowds, and the confinement. He wanted to go back to the country, where things were quiet and moved slower.

If he leaned forward, he could barely see the street below. Two cats started fighting, their screams and hisses rising above the other noise. A drunk kicked them, and they turned on him, crying out as they launched themselves at his legs.

Seymour glanced at Byron. The noise hadn't awakened him. Byron sprawled across the pallet, his arms flung over his head. He snored softly, and occasionally one of his muscles would twitch. Seymour had examined Byron's knees earlier, and except for the aging scabs, the knees had healed.

Byron should have talked to Seymour about the Kinsmail heritage. Seymour would have understood. Perhaps Byron felt that a peasant could only relate to one of his own kind. But to make up the elaborate story about barding, about Rury – Seymour shook his head. He didn't know what to believe. If Byron were truly a Kinsmail, it made no sense to tell the Lady Jelwra. She had no scruples. She would probably tell Lord Dakin about Byron right away because Byron's claim threatened them both. Then Byron would be in even more trouble.

Seymour sighed. He wished he were home, on his soft bed, away from everyone. He could practice his little magicks, take care of himself, and talk to no one. Life had been good there. He wished he had never heard the hounds, had never helped Byron. But Lord Dakin would still have discovered the hut, and Seymour would have had nowhere to go. If he hadn't come into the city with Byron, he wouldn't have known how to take care of himself.

The drunk sat in a doorway, his head against the door jamb, probably passed out. The sounds from the common room had grown stronger. He thought he heard the Lady Jelwra's voice, answered by a man's. Something about that other voice sounded familiar. The hair rose on the back of Seymour's neck. He stood up and went to the door, opening it a crack. Below, a man laughed, a thick, gruff chortle. Semour recognized it. Lord Dakin's laugh.

Seymour's heart beat in his throat. He closed the door quietly and tiptoed to the bed, grabbing Byron's shoulders and shaking him.

'Byron,' he whispered. 'Lord Dakin's downstairs.'

Byron didn't open his eyes. 'It's just a dream.'

'I wasn't asleep,' Seymour said. 'It was Dakin. I heard him.'

Byron stretched. 'Get some sleep, Seymour. This may be the last bed we see for days.'

'He was talking to the Lady Jelwra.'

Byron didn't answer. His breathing sounded even again, as if he had fallen back to sleep.

Seymour grabbed his boots. He was not going to stay here, not if there was even a slight possibility that Lord Dakin was downstairs. This time Byron could save himself from the lord. Byron sighed deeply. Then another wave of laughter rose from the room below. Byron sat up so quickly that Seymour almost dropped his boots.

'That is Dakin!'

'I know,' Seymour said.

'I'm sorry, Seymour. I should have – '

'Don't apologize.' Seymour winced as he pulled on his boots. He grabbed his shirt and slid his arms into it. The material felt sharp and scratchy – new. 'We've got to get out of here. I don't want to see Lord Dakin.'

'He doesn't know we're here.'

'The Lady Jelwra's bound to tell him about you, *Sir Geoffry*. I just want to be out of here before he decides to come up and get rid of the last Lord of Kinsmail.'

'She wouldn't say – '

'You don't know that. And it's my neck you're risking. Now get dressed and let's go.' Seymour was amazed to hear his father's voice come out of his mouth. He had never been commanding before. But then, he had only been this frightened one other time in his life. 'I'll go down first. Then you toss me the valise and follow.'

'What about the boys?'

'What about them?' Seymour had never seen Byron so indecisive. It irritated him.

'I promised that they could come with me.'

Seymour pushed the shutters open farther. He didn't care about the boys. If Byron wanted to risk his life for those children, he could, but this time Seymour was going to look after himself. He straddled the windowsill. 'Just toss me the valise.'

He didn't wait for a reply. He gripped the windowsill tightly and swung his legs outside. The sudden pull on his arms made his shoulders crack. He glanced down. He would have to fall about six feet. He swallowed once, took a deep breath, and let go.

The wind fluttered through his hair and past his face as he fell. His feet hit first, sending a jolt through his body that ran up his spine and caused him to lose his balance. He sat ungraciously in the dust. The cats scattered, but the drunk didn't wake up. The valise landed beside him with a soft thud. Seymour looked up. Byron hung from the window, his cape flapping in the wind. Byron dropped to the ground like a large bird, landed on his feet, and turned to Seymour.

'We're getting those boys,' Byron said.

Seymour stood up, wiping the dust from his new trousers. He picked up the valise. 'Lord Dakin probably has a horse in the stable.'

'If he's inside laughing, he's not going to use it right away.'

'I don't see why we have to risk our lives for two common street urchins.'

Byron's body straightened and his expression grew hard. 'I'm going back for the boys. You can leave without me if you like.'

'And face Lord Dakin alone? No, thank you.'

Byron nodded once, then turned, and walked toward the stable. Seymour followed. The anger and fear made him giddy, and his back ached from the fall. The valise felt heavy in his hands.

The stable stood next to the inn. The stable was an old building; it leaned slightly to one side. As Byron pushed open the door, a horse nickered. Inside, the stable was warm. The smells of hay and leather overlay the animal scents.

Seymour slipped around Byron and looked for the boys. They huddled together on a pile of hay, a stable blanket over them to keep out the night's chill. Byron bent over them to wake them, when Afeno's eyes snapped open.

'We're leaving,' Byron said.

'It's the middle of the night.' Afeno's voice was wary.

Seymour glanced at the door. He could see nothing out there. Suppose Lord Dakin was looking for them already. He would go with the innkeeper to their rooms, find them empty, and come to the stables.

'We had some trouble,' Byron said.

'And you're running from it?'

Seymour turned. The boy would have run, too, if he were facing a similar threat. 'Look, we didn't have to come and get you, but Byron insisted. Now get up and come with us. Every minute you waste hurts us.'

Colin stirred and sat up. He brushed hay from his clothes and his hair. The fear Seymour felt was reflected in the younger boy's face.

Afeno tossed the blanket aside. 'Where are we going?'

'As far from here as possible,' Seymour said.

Afeno stood. He didn't bother to clean the hay off his new clothes. 'Should we take a horse?'

Byron shook his head. 'We'll be easier to spot on horseback. Dakin won't think of looking for two men and two boys.'

'Lord Dakin?' Colin asked. His voice squeaked with fear.

'That's right. He's inside.'

A loud crash outside the stable made them freeze. Seymour thought his heart was going to jump through his chest. Dakin was out there. They wouldn't be able to escape.

Afeno crouched and ran for the door. Byron grabbed at him but missed. Afeno slipped outside. Seymour started to follow, but Byron put a hand on his arm.

'He knows what he's doing,' Byron whispered.

Seymour held his breath. He silently reviewed all the spells he knew. He could draw moisture from the air to make water; he could create a fire by rubbing his hands together; he could make one object appear to be another, but he couldn't make people disappear. His father could do almost anything with his magic. He had a strong luck web and knew how to call the correct spirits. He had been able to memorize anything immediately and would use the spell perfectly each time. But Seymour only knew fifteen spells – and most of them didn't work.

Something cracked outside, and then someone moaned. There was a loud thud. Byron took a step forward, but Seymour shook his head. They didn't dare go out there, not if Lord Dakin was waiting.

Then Afeno peeked his head in the door and beckoned to them. Byron took Colin's arm and led him outside. Seymour followed. The drunk Seymour had seen earlier lay next to his doorway. A stick rested by his side.

'Will he be all right?' Seymour whispered.

Afeno nodded, then turned to Byron, apparently waiting for direction.

'We need to get out of the city as fast as we can,' Byron said. 'And we're heading southeast, away from Lord Dakin's land. You know the way?'

Afeno nodded. He looked both ways before stepping into the road, then signaled that all was clear. Seymour stepped away from the inn, glad to be moving. He could never be far enough away from Lord Dakin.

iii

The houses in the wealthy section of Nadaluci had wide, fenced-in yards. Trees, flowers, and shrubs hid the buildings from view. No one was stirring except Afeno and his three companions.

The street curved and ran uphill. The air smelled of lilacs. Afeno hated the calmness. Cities were supposed to live after dark. But he didn't want to see anyone, and he knew no one would be on the streets in this section of town. Magic had taught him that. 'You tough a rich one in the day,' he used to say, 'because they disappear with the light.'

At the top of the hill, the houses grew more expansive, the lawns lush with greenery. Byron walked solemnly beside Afeno, taking in everything. Seymour stared straight ahead. And Colin kept his head down, as if he weren't worthy of seeing such impressive homes. Their feet shuffled in the dirt, a familiar sound, but Afeno thought he heard something else.

He listened as he walked, hearing the ragged clip of another foot, the off rhythm sound of a person walking too far away to see his quarry. Afeno touched Byron's arm and put a finger to his lips. Byron frowned, listening too, and then he nodded.

Afeno waved Byron ahead and dropped back. The street led out of the city. If this took him longer than he expected, the others would find their way to the east gate.

Afeno half ran to the side of the road. He hid behind a large stone gate corner. The stone was cold against his fingers and his breathing sounded rough in his ears. He took breaths shallowly and listened, hearing the shuffling of Byron and the others grow faint and the single footsteps come closer. He peered around the edge, careful to keep his head in shadow. A retainer in a brown and tan uniform – Lord Dakin's colors – followed the path Byron had left in the road. Afeno swallowed. Retainers never traveled alone. Another had to be with him, guarding against an attack.

Afeno wiped his hands on his pants and thought for a moment. He had never done anything like this alone. Magic had always helped him, thinking up the operation and telling Afeno what to do. Afeno hadn't done well on his own. The last person he had toughed had hit him and knocked him out.

If he and Magic were doing this, one would search for the hidden retainer, while the other attacked this retainer. But Afeno couldn't do both. He had to find the hidden retainer, but he couldn't let this one get away. But he wasn't working alone. Byron had heard the footsteps too. If Afeno couldn't take care of the first retainer, Byron would.

The retainer passed the gate. He moved just quickly enough to keep the group in sight. The other retainer had to be moving too, keeping his companion in view. Afeno waited, breathing soundlessly. The retainer disappeared, and so did the sound of his footsteps. Afeno's body began trembling from staying in the same position too long. Then he heard it, an odd rustle that didn't fit into the hum of the quiet neighborhood. He glanced down the street, seeing nothing, then seeing a movement in the nearby shadows. The retainer stepped out and darted along the edge of the road to duck in behind Afeno's stone post.

They stared at each other for a moment – the retainer's face was chubby and red from too much ale consumed over too many years – and then Afeno rammed forward, shoulder first, into the retainer's stomach. The man fell back against the road, landing with an oof. The man reached for Afeno, knocking him over. They rolled for a minute, Afeno reaching, grabbing for something. He finally found a rock and clubbed the man on the side of the head. The retainer collapsed, his bulk on top of Afeno. Afeno pushed the man away. The man was out. Afeno went through his uniform and found four gold pieces and a dagger. Afeno slid the gold into his boot. Holding the dagger, he went after the other retainer.

Afeno ducked in and out of shadows, using the same method as the man he had knocked out. Within a few minutes he saw the retainer walking steadily in the moonlight. The retainer wasn't as big as his companion, but he moved with an ease that suggested strength. Afeno caught up, then leaped on the man's back from the shadows, and grabbed his mouth. The retainer tried to shake Afeno off, but he held tightly and pulled up on the man's chin. The retainer grabbed for Afeno's wrist, holding it, pulling down. Afeno maintained his grip. He brought the dagger up with his other hand and with one swift, deep, sideways movement he slashed the man's throat.

Warm blood gushed on Afeno's hand as he let go and jumped away. The retainer reached for his throat, making gurgling sounds as he spun. He fell to his knees and then toppled forward, the blood leaving a shiny black pool in the dirt.

Afeno wiped the dagger on the retainer's uniform, then searched the man. He found five gold pieces, a few rounds, a dagger, and a sheathed sword. Afeno removed the sheath and tested the sword. It was too long to wrap around his hip, so he attached it to his waist. Then he stopped.

He had nine gold pieces, more than enough to keep himself for a while, and weapons to defend himself. And he had just proven to himself that he could work alone. He didn't need Byron, didn't need to leave Nadaluci. He slipped the daggers in his boots. He could survive here now, maybe wait for Magic and kill him if he returned.

Afeno turned and started down the hill. The other retainer was beginning to move. Beyond him, Afeno could see the torches still burning in the poorer sections of the city. He had nothing here and no one who cared. When the nine gold pieces ran out, he had no guarantee of additional money. Byron at least would pay him and take him somewhere new, somewhere interesting. Magic would never come back, and even if he did, Afeno wouldn't kill him. He would probably work with him again until the next time Magic cheated him, a few months down the road.

He seemed to be doing circles in the dust. He turned around again and ran past the dead retainer. The blood was running along the side of the street, leaving a black stain in the quiet neighborhood. As Afeno reached the crest of the hill, he could see the others walking slowly in the moonlight. He ran down the street, kicking up stones and dust in his haste, and stopped when he reached them.

Byron glanced over at him and nodded, taking note of the sword and the blood on Afeno's arm.

'What happened?' Seymour asked.

'Two of Lord Dakin's retainers were following us,' Afeno said.

'He knows about us, then.' Seymour's voice shook. 'What are we going to do, Byron?'

'Nothing.' The darkness hid Byron's face. 'They're not following us anymore, are they?'

'No.'

'Good,' he said and continued walking. Afeno felt some of the energy leave him. Byron hadn't even asked for details. Magic had always wanted details. Afeno followed, keeping a small distance between himself and the others. Byron had trusted him to get the job done, and he had. That was enough – for now.

iv

When they reached the gate, dawn painted itself on the horizon. Red and gold wisps of clouds decorated the pale sky. No beggars lined the walls on the east gate, and the sleepy gatekeeper seemed surprised to let through such a tired party on foot.

On this side of the city the forest was thinner. The trees were scraggly and no undergrowth covered the ground between them. Byron kept them on the road. Seymour felt more relaxed now that they were away from the city. The air smelled fresher and the only sounds were familiar – an occasional twitter of a bird, the rummaging of an animal in the trees.

Byron walked beside him, the two boys a pace or two behind. 'What's troubling you, Seymour?' Byron asked. 'You haven't been the same since we entered the city.'

'Nothing.' Seymour trudged forward. He was tired. He hadn't slept in almost two days. He had been frightened and on the move most of the time. He had carried the valise most of the way, too, and his arm was growing tired.

'If we're going to travel together, we need to trust each other,' Byron said.

'Trust?' Seymour let out a chuckle. He concentrated on the trees ahead and the early morning sunlight filtering through the leaves.

'Hmmm.' Byron took the valise from Seymour's hand. Seymour felt as if he had grown ten pounds lighter. 'You think I told the Lady Jelwra the truth, don't you?'

Seymour didn't even nod.

'Well, I didn't. I've been honest with you. My name is Byron and I was Lord Dakin's bard. Before that I was bard to Lord Lafa. A bard must learn everything there is to know about a region. And there is a beautiful song about Kinsmail. The ballad tells the story I told the lady. I was a bit worried when she said I looked familiar. I sang for her often at Lord Lafa's manor.'

Their boots scuffled against the dirt. A bird flew above them, chittering. The sunlight had grown warmer, but the shaded road was still cool. 'Did the hounds chase you off Lord Lafa's land?' The question sounded more sarcastic than Seymour had planned.

'No.' Byron's smile held no warmth. 'Lord Lafa was more

creative. He used my reputation to get rid of me.' He shifted the valise to his other hand. 'I had been in Lord Lafa's service for nearly two years and during that time had had my share of women. I was willing if they were willing, but I was also very careful, if you know what I mean, Seymour.

'One afternoon, Lord Lafa called me into his great room. He sat there with three of his retainers and accused me of impregnating a village girl. The retainers swore they had seen me in her company and they probably had. I liked her, but she wasn't interested in me. I found out why later. She already had a lover. Lord Lafa.

'He wanted me to marry her and claim the child. I refused. He gave me a day to get off his lands and ordered me not to return.'

Seymour glanced at Byron and then at the woods around them. 'I thought this is Lord Lafa's land.'

'If the rumors I have heard are right, this land now belongs to the Lady Jelwra.'

Seymour sighed. He wondered where Byron picked up his information. Seymour felt as if he had lived in darkness his entire life. He wasn't sure he wanted to walk into the light. No one seemed to like Byron, and Seymour wanted to stay out of trouble. 'Was your reputation the only reason Lord Lafa picked you?'

'I told you when you first met me, Seymour, that I'm a troublemaker.' Byron shook his head slightly. 'I was no different then.'

The clip-clop of horses and the rumble of carriage wheels echoed behind them. The carriage was moving rapidly, and Seymour and Byron moved to the side of the road. Seymour glanced back to see if the boys had moved as well. They had.

The driver slowed the carriage as it approached. Seymour recognized the white horses and white banners flying from the carriage corners. His palms grew moist. He didn't want the Lady Jelwra to know where they were. She might send word to Lord Dakin.

The carriage stopped when it reached Byron and Seymour. The Lady Jelwra opened the carriage door. Inside, Seymour could see plush white seats and bright blue trim.

'I'm sure you would rather ride than walk, Sir Geoffry,' the lady said. 'I've never seen a member of the gentry walk before.'

'It's good for the legs,' Byron said, smiling.

'There's room for your companions.'

'Thank you but no.'

Lady Jelwra tilted her head. Sunlight reflected off the diamond studs decorating her ears. 'I didn't tell Lord Dakin about you.'

'Although you were sorely tempted.'

'Although I was sorely tempted.' She laughed, a faint, tinkly sound almost like a wind chime. Seymour thought the laugh did not suit her. 'Don't you trust anyone, Sir Geoffry?'

'I trust quite a few people, milady. You are not one of them.'

Her smile faded to a pout, but her eyes still sparkled. 'I've never had a man turn down a ride with me.'

'Lady,' Byron said, his tone husky, 'someday I will ride with you. But not today. Think of it merely as an opportunity postponed.'

The lady stepped back into the carriage and closed the door. 'I will,' she said, then tapped on the roof with her fan. The driver clucked at the horses and the carriage rode off.

Chapter 8

Adric leaned on his pitchfork. His side ached and he felt so tired. He hated the stable, hated pitching hay. He hadn't had a decent night's sleep since Rogren found him. First the pain was too great, and then, when he was just starting to feel better, Rogren put him to work. Cassie was nice, but she couldn't stand up to Rogren. Adric had barely been able to stand that first day, but he had managed to get some work done.

He sighed and dug his fork into the hay. The stable was clean, and the odors of leather, hay, and tack had faded into the background. He had even become used to the noise.

No one seemed to be looking for him. No guards showed up at the door, no questions on the streets. He tried to send word through retainers and other customers at the stables that he wanted to see the king's people, but no one came. He wanted to go home, but he was afraid to leave here, afraid that Rogren might not take him back. Then he would be out on his own with no protection.

Not that Rogren was much protection. He had beaten Adric one afternoon when he found the boy resting in the hay. Adric's side had hurt much worse after that, but he never slacked off, he always worked.

The stable doors eased open, letting in a sliver of sunlight, and Milo entered, lugging buckets. Water sloshed over the sides of the wooden buckets and left a trail on the floor. Milo set them down and went outside for more. Adric kept working. He knew that Milo was working twice as hard to cover for his own inabilities. And Milo had been patient, teaching Adric how to pitch hay and clean tack.

Milo brought two more buckets inside, then closed the doors. The stable seemed dark without the sun. 'Did you hear?' he asked.

Adric shook his head. Talking left him short of breath and put pressure on his rib cage.

'We have a holiday tomorrow. We are not allowed to work.'

Adric frowned. Rogren wouldn't do that. Rogren insisted on work every day, sunup to sunset. 'Why?'

'The prince is dead.'

Adric felt his heart in his throat. Milo poured one of the buckets into the trough. 'They say he died of some disease,' Milo said. 'There's talk in town that the whole royal family has it and they're all going to die. The royal consort has it and she lost the child she's carrying. So we're going to have to work twice as hard today to enjoy tomorrow.'

'The prince is dead?' Adric repeated. They had stopped looking for him. They thought they couldn't find him, so they declared him dead. And his mother lost the baby. All because of him.

'Haven't you heard the crier? There's about ten of them screaming the news all over town.'

Adric dropped his pitchfork and ran to the door. He knew where the king's guards were now. He had been about to approach them when Rogren brought him back the first time.

'Where are you going?' Milo called.

'I'll be back.' Adric grabbed the stable door and pushed it open. The sunlight blinded him and made him sneeze. In the distance he could hear crier's bells. Milo wasn't lying.

Adric ran down the street to the main thoroughfare, dodging people as he went. His side ached and he could barely breathe, but he kept moving. He had to find the guards, get them to take him home. His father would be angry, but at least his mother would see him. Some of Milo's information was wrong; perhaps the news about the miscarriage was too.

Finally, across the street he saw three retainers dressed in palace gold. He recognized one of the men as the young sword master who gave all of the others lessons. They lolled against a street cart as though they were waiting for someone. Adric took a deep breath, made sure his walk was steady, and walked over to them. 'Ile,' he said. 'Take me home.'

The sword master looked at him. The man's face seemed haggard and his uniform slightly dirty. 'Where's home, laddie, and how did you learn my name?'

'He heard us talking,' one of the other retainers said. He was taller than Ile and thinner. Adric didn't recognize him. 'And now he's going to tell us that he's the prince and we should take him away from all of this.'

'Yes, but – '

All three men laughed. They were mocking him.

'I really am!' Adric said.

'So were the other three we saw this morning.'

'I can prove it!' Adric grabbed his shirt and started to undo the lacing.

'And I can prove you're not,' Ile said. He took Adric's hand and ran his finger along it. 'Calluses. No royalty has calluses, except for sword fighting, which the prince never learned. You've done some heavy work, boy, and you don't have that soft look that comes from easy living.'

'I've been ill,' Adric said. He pulled his shirt open. 'Look, the mark – '

The other retainer pushed him, sending a wave of pain down Adric's side. He tripped, but did not fall. 'Get out of here, lad,' the retainer said. 'The prince is dead. They entombed the body this morning while I was doing watch.'

'They couldn't have,' Adric said. His hands were shaking with panic. 'I've been here.'

The third retainer put a hand on his sword. 'I'm tired of this disrespect.'

Someone touched Adric's arm and he turned. Milo stood beside him, breathing heavily. 'He didn't mean any disrespect,' Milo said. 'He has been very ill with fever and his mind isn't always sound.'

The retainer took his hand off his sword. 'Then take him away before he gets into more trouble.'

Milo put his arm around Adric and led him through the crowds, shielding him, protecting his side. Adric watched a pregnant woman cross the road and thought of his mother. She thought he was dead. Somehow he had to get home. He had to see her, to tell her that he was all right.

Milo stopped when he reached the street leading to Rogren's stables. He laced up Adric's shirt. 'So that's what your mysterious marking means. Why didn't you tell us who you were?'

'I was told not to. They said people might use me against my father.'

Milo smiled. 'Rogren would have. For money. But me and Cassie are all right.'

Adric nodded. He felt tears burning in the back of his eyes. He blinked, trying to make them go away. 'Why do you believe me when they don't?'

Milo's smile faded. He glanced around to see if anyone was listening before he spoke. 'You look different now. You're not a fat lordling. You're slender and as sickly looking as the kids around here. I knew you weren't from the streets when I first saw you. Those clothes we threw away were fine, richer than any I'd ever seen. You didn't know how to use a pitchfork, and it was clear from your injuries that you weren't very successful at defending yourself. And all the questions you asked people who came into the stables. I didn't know who you were, but I knew you were someone important.'

Adric glanced back down the street. He couldn't see the retainers any longer. 'What do I do now?'

'I don't know. But if I were you, I'd get back to that stable before Rogren throws you out.' Milo put his arm around Adric again and began to lead him slowly. 'We can always decide what to do there.'

'You'll help me?'

'I've done crazier things.'

Adric sighed and leaned on Milo. His support felt very, very good.

Chapter 9

Lafa lurched slightly and grabbed for the wall before him. But the wall moved, danced away like people had, moving, constantly moving, and making him dizzy. He swayed a little before regaining his balance. He adjusted his coat and pretended at dignity. *Without dignity a man is nothing,* he had said to Crystal before she died and left him to remember his betrayal in the stink of blood.

His stomach turned. He reached for the wall again and found it this time. The wood's firmness surprised him; he almost expected his hand to pass through it. He took a deep breath to steady himself, and for a moment his vision cleared.

He stood on the street alone, in front of an inn. It was small, dark, something he never would have looked at in the old days. But he belonged there now. His clothes were torn and matted with mud. Passersby glanced at him, then averted their eyes. Someone had spit at him. He remembered now. Someone had spit at him in the last inn. He had stumbled forward in anger, spilling his ale, and the barkeep had thrown him out. People thought he wouldn't remember, but he was cursed with remembrance. The ale couldn't destroy his memory – the memory of Crystal's bloated, blood-spattered body.

Someday he would avenge himself on all of them: the retainers who raped his land; the nobles who manipulated him; the Lady Jelwra, who robbed him; and the peasants, the low-lying filthy scum who treated him as if he were lower than they were. He would get revenge on them all.

He was tired and thirsty. He needed something to drink. He guided himself along the wall with his hands until he found the door. It swung open at his touch and he stumbled inside. Darkness engulfed him, along with the familiar scents of ale and roasted meat. Slowly his sight returned. The inn was almost empty, except for one table – one table and the man who had caused it all.

He wore clean clothes tailored to his form. He reclined in his chair, his long legs stretched before him as he conversed with a smaller man in squire's clothing. Two boys sat beside them, eating quickly. He seemed contented, as if he didn't care that he had killed Crystal, that he had ruined everything.

But he hadn't ruined anything. Lafa knew that. He had known that before he saw Crystal's body and the mess she had made.

Lafa swallowed. The dryness in his throat had grown. If that bard had married Crystal, she wouldn't have come to the manor, and Lafa's wife would not have thrown her out. When Lafa found Crystal, she had already aborted the child. And then she had bled for three days, until she bled dry.

His stomach boiled. He gripped the door frame and shouted, 'Byron the bard, I told you to stay away!'

The bard turned. His dark eyes showed no recognition. Then he nodded, once. 'Lord Lafa.' His voice held pity. 'Would you care to join us?'

The bard's companions looked up from their meal. The squire pulled a chair over.

'No, I would not care to join you.' Lafa was not the equal of peasants and entertainers. He was their master. They seemed to be forgetting that. He weaved toward the bard's table, squinting to see the bard's clothing more closely. Lace accented the bard's slim wrists and he wore a velvet waistcoat. 'I've never seen you look so fine. What did Dakin do for you? Let you marry one of his daughters?'

'He has no daughters.'

Lafa suddenly realized that the bard had no pity for him. The emotion on the other man's face was disgust. Let him feel his disgust. Lafa sat in the chair that the squire had pulled over. The bard hadn't had to watch Crystal die.

Lafa grabbed the wine bottle sitting in the middle of the table and poured himself a glass. The wine was a rich red, the color of Crystal's blood. He had vowed never to drink anything red, but he was so thirsty that he drank until the glass was empty.

The wine was good. It slid gently down his throat. He didn't deserve gentleness. He wanted something harsh. He pushed the glass off the table, enjoying the crash as it shattered against the floor.

All expression left the bard's face. Only his eyes moved, dark, deep, and fathomless. Lafa remembered the look. He had seen it several times, whenever the bard was angry. The man had constantly told Lafa how to run his manor, how to manage his peasants. 'You should leave,' Lafa said, 'before I send my retainers after you.'

The bard leaned back in his chair. His body seemed relaxed, but his eyes seemed blacker, emptier than they had before. 'You have no authority in Coventon, milord. The mayor rules here.'

'Always the smart one, aren't you?' Lafa's hands were shaking. The mayor did control city lands. No wonder that barkeep hadn't apologized when he threw Lafa out. Careless, careless to forget such details. But the bard, this talented peasant, had no right to torment him. 'Wait until you get outside the city.'

'Why? The Lady Jelwra bears me no grudge.'

Lafa gripped the chair. The room was swaying. 'Is she the one dressing you so fine?'

'No, milord. I got these clothes through some good fortune of my own.'

Good fortune. The bard had always had his share of good fortune. Lafa's Enos had said that was because of the silver ring he wore. 'It is an Enos ring,' she said. 'It attracts good luck.'

'Bitch,' Lafa murmured. The Enos had left him when the Lady Jelwra stole his lands. An Enos belonged to the land, not a lord, she had reminded him.

And the Lady Jelwra had snatched the lands from him. He had never guessed such cunning hid behind such a beautiful face.

Lafa pushed himself out of the chair. He was tired of himself. He didn't want to be here. He didn't want to be anywhere. He walked back to the door and stared at the bard. None of this would have happened without the bard. He could still hear the bard's voice, heard it every hour of every day: *She's carrying your bastard, Lafa. You marry her. I won't be responsible for your mistakes.*

Arrogant, insufferable, critical bastard. Lafa was still a lord. He still had power over life and death. He could kill the bard and no one would criticize him for it. The bard's death would be Lafa's vengeance and his salvation. The memories would disappear. Crystal would finally rest in peace.

Chapter 10

Adric gripped the post. His wrists were tied together and braced against a nail. The post seemed like his only friend, his sole support.

The street in front of the stable was empty. The few people who walked past averted their eyes and moved away quickly, as if they knew what they were going to see. The whip snapped in the air before fire burned his back. He bit his lower lip. He wished he had listened to Milo. Milo had told him that Rogren would do this.

'Running away, were you?'

The snap again. Adric tensed as the whip cut into his back.

'Four times now I have the king's guards bringing you back, telling me you're loony.'

The whip wrapped itself around his waist. Adric jerked and splinters jammed into his hands. Out of the corner of his eye, he saw Milo feeding the horses. Milo kept his back turned so that he wouldn't have to look.

'You owe me money, you little thief, and you agreed to work to repay your debts.'

The whip cut across the first welt. A tear trickled down his face, stinging against the scratches in his skin. He hadn't known that his back had so much feeling and could ache so badly.

'Now, are you going to stay, or do I have to sell you to get my money's worth?'

Adric licked his cracked lips. Sell? He closed his eyes and leaned against the post as the whip snapped again. This time the leather dug into his shoulder, and he imagined it searing to the bone.

'Answer me, boy.'

Hadn't he already answered? He couldn't remember. Slowly he parted his lips and whispered, 'Stay.'

The whip cracked again. Adric's back tingled as he waited for the blow to fall.

'I can't hear you.'

The whip whistled through the air and wrapped itself around his still tender rib cage. 'Stay!' Adric screamed. 'I'll stay!'

Milo turned at the sound. His face was white, his eyes luminous and dark. Adric couldn't tell if he had said the right thing. Behind him, leather slapped against the ground. Cloth rustled as Rogren came closer. 'I've been waiting to hear that,' he said.

Rogren rubbed his hand against Adric's torn back. The burning grew until it felt as if his skin were on fire. Milo had disappeared. Adric's knees buckled. Only his tied wrists kept him from falling.

'I want you to work a full day for me tomorrow. From dawn until dusk. No disappearing, no fainting. A full day's work or I'll whip you again. Understand?'

Adric swallowed. His throat was dry. 'Yes,' he said. The word came out as a whisper and he cringed, expecting Rogren to hit him again.

'Good.'

Rogren's knees creaked as he pulled himself up. His footsteps grew fainter until they gradually faded away. Adric closed his eyes. His eyeballs felt thick and swollen. He had never been so in touch with his body. His hands were going numb and a single toe was bent awkwardly in the dust. He tried to remember the feel of silk against his skin, the warmth of the fire in his old room, the richness of the milk he had had for breakfast every morning, but his mind told him such things were not real. They were part of a dream he had conjured to save himself from Rogren, from the pain that seeped into his back and his heart.

The numbness spread through Adric's arms. Had Rogren left him here to die? Adric couldn't remember. He couldn't remember what it was like to be anyone but Adric, the boy with calluses on his fingers.

Hands slid under his arms and someone untied his wrists.

'Slowly. Let him down slowly.'

The voice belonged to Cassie, the healer. Her touch was cool. Perhaps the fire in his back would melt her. He licked his lips to warn her, but speech did not come. The hands eased him down to the ground and he set his cheek in the soft dirt. Up close, the dirt separated into a thousand tiny pieces, and with each breath he arranged those pieces into a new pattern.

'Rogren tore him up good, and he isn't very strong.'

'Hush, Milo. Give me some of that ointment.'

An ant crawled through the dirt. Adric held his breath. The tiny creature climbed over a mound, its feelers waving. Then ice formed on his shoulder and he couldn't stop himself: he gasped and expelled air. The mound crumbled, burying the ant.

'At least he's still alive. Maybe we should notify the king before Rogren kills him.'

'Adric must make his own choices, Milo.'

The ice spread down his back and quenched the fire. The flattened mound stirred. The ant's feelers appeared, then its body, marching across the dirt.

'He can't stay here.'

'He can't survive alone.'

Adric waited until the ant escaped, then breathed again. Pieces of dirt rolled forward and back with each breath.

'What will you do if I leave?'

'I made my choice a long time ago, Milo. Help me carry him inside. I'll tend him there.'

The hands lifted him and he swayed. The ice had stolen his back, but the throbbing in his wrists and cheek told him that he still lived. The sunlight turned into darkness, and a thick mattress replaced the dirt. He closed his eyes. Here he could be safe, away from the post and the snapping air.

Chapter 11

Milord:

I have found the bard. He rests in Coventon, the port off Lafa's lands. A magician and two young boys travel with him. One of the boys is deadly with a knife.

The bard has commissioned a local musician for a lute. While he waits for the instrument, he trains the boys in the art of sword fighting. The bard is proficient. I would not like to face him one-on-one.

His plans are obscure. I have spoken with both lads, and they assure me that the bard heads for the palace. They say he would like to be the king's bard. I don't know if the bard will make it. Lord Lafa has placed a price on his head. Lafa has offered three hundred gold pieces to the man who kills him. Anyone who captures him will get only one hundred gold pieces. Lafa knows that he dare not kill the bard inside the city, but once the bard steps outside the city walls, he will probably die.

The bard does not know of the bounty, or if he does, he doesn't seem to care. Unless you order otherwise, I shall let the bounty hunters kill him. I will step in only if the hunters fail.

I await your reply.

Yours,
Corvo

i

Nica climbed down the spiral stairs from the apartments into the guild shop. The faint odor of the previous night's incense hung in the air. A fire burned in the hearth, illuminating the dark room. The crystals hanging around the door were still, waiting. Pieces of whistle-wood glowed from the shelves.

Xell sat in the chair beneath the shop's only window. He held a cup of tea to his chest as if to protect himself from the morning chill. Thin traces of sunlight played upon his bald head, accented the creases near his eyes.

'The shop is preparing itself for a visitor.'

Nica wound the rest of the way down the stairs. So that was the stillness she felt. She glanced at Xell, wondering if the daily plans would change because a visitor was going to arrive.

'First the luck web,' he said, 'and then we will see.'

The way he touched her thoughts used to unnerve her. Now she accepted it as part of the morning ritual. She sat on a cushion near the hearth. The fire was warm against her back. She concentrated on the feeling, crossed her arms before her face, held her breath, and clenched her fists. Then she chanted softly. The web wrapped itself around her like a lover. She felt warmer, stronger, completed.

Then an unfamiliar vibration whispered in her web. She opened her eyes, cemented the strength gathering, and then, at Xell's nod, reversed it. The layers of the web eased, slipped away, and she was Nica once more.

'This is a guild shop,' Xell said.

'I know.' A small man dressed in a squire's shirt and trousers stood at the door. The crystals around him glowed purple. Eighth level. Low for an adult magician. Nica had passed the eighth level after her first month of training. 'I am a guild member.'

He held out his hand. Xell rose and took it, examining the tattoo on the man's palm. Nica stood up and saw that the tattoo confirmed what the crystals had already told her.

Xell let go of the man's hand. 'Where are you from?'

The man stepped forward. A combination of hearth light and sunlight touched his face, making his features look haggard. His hair was dark and thick, and his green eyes were young. Yet Nica guessed him to be at least in his mid-thirties. 'I'm from Dakin's lands. I'm Seymour, son of Dysik the Great.'

Nica clasped her hand over her wrist to keep herself from shaking. She wished she still had her luck web. Seymour, son of Dysik, magician to Lord Dakin, had met the hounds earlier in the year. A traveler had told her before she went into seclusion.

Xell nodded and extended a hand toward the table near the stairs. 'I worked with Dysik at the palace. Such a talent wasted when the Council of Lords banished him to Dakin's lands.'

Seymour's head snapped back and the haggard look disappeared. He seemed shocked, but Xell's words also seemed to cheer him. Nica knew then that Seymour hadn't known of the banishment. 'He served Lord Dakin faithfully for forty years,' Seymour said.

'And does no longer?'

'He's dead.'

The words hung in the little shop. The purple glow eased out of the crystals, replaced by a slightly pink color that Nica had never seen before. She directed Xell's attention to it and he frowned. 'I'm sorry,' he said. 'We don't get much news from the north.'

He stared at the pink crystals as if he didn't understand them. Seymour looked at the whistle-wood, but did not touch it. Nica waited near the hearth for Xell to invite her into the conversation.

'You do not serve Lord Dakin,' Xell said, his gaze still on the crystals. He turned to Seymour. Nica recognized the expression. Xell was digging into Seymour, examining him, trying to read his aura, his glow.

'Lord Dakin expected me to be the wizard my father was without taking into account my inexperience.' Seymour lowered his head, but not before Nica saw the heightened color in his cheeks.

'And your lack of aptitude.' Xell's words were soft. He had not taken his eyes off Seymour.

Seymour straightened. 'My eighth-level tattoo makes me ineligible for this guild shop?'

Xell shook his head. 'I didn't mean to offend you. Your mother was an herb witch, wasn't she? That too is a noble profession.' Xell pulled back a chair. It scraped against the wooden floor. 'Sit, Seymour. Take some tea with us.'

Seymour looked at the chair, then at Xell, as if measuring him. Finally he walked over and sat down. Xell sat across from him. 'Nica,' he said, 'heat some water for tea.'

Nica dipped some water from their bucket and put it into the pot over the fire. Then she grabbed a handful of bitter-smelling torec tea leaves and sprinkled them at the bottom of the teapot.

'How can we help you?' Xell asked.

'I came to trade spells,' Seymour said. 'I need an offensive and defensive spell that covers four people.'

The water boiled and Nica removed the pot from the hearth. She wished she could see Xell's expression. An eighth-level magician could barely handle parlor tricks.

'What spells can you trade?' Xell asked.

'My father's scent illusion.'

Nica poured the water into the teapot and brought it over to the table. She took three mugs from the shelf behind her and set them in place. Then she sat next to Xell.

'Your father's scent illusion was original. He guarded it like a child. You must have a great need or you wouldn't trade such a spell.'

Seymour ignored Xell's implied question. 'I can already make fire. But I need something else.'

'What mission are you on, my friend?' Xell asked.

This time Seymour could not ignore the question. He looked down at his hands. Nica saw them shake. 'I – I'm traveling to the palace.'

'For whom?'

He glanced up, looking trapped. He sighed and shook his head a little. 'I met up with a bard a few weeks ago. Saved him from Lord Dakin's hounds. We're traveling together.'

A chill ran down Nica's back. 'Lord Dakin's bard?'

Xell did not glance at her, but she felt his displeasure. As his apprentice, she needed his permission to join the conversation.

Seymour didn't seem to notice. 'He was.'

Nica forced herself to take a deep breath. Byron was in Coventon. If only she could see him, thank him, show him how far she had come from the barefoot herb witch he had helped.

A finger touched her mind. Xell wasn't watching her, but she could feel him in her head, feeling her thoughts about Byron. She moved back physically, but the touch remained, cool and a little angry. She didn't care. Byron had saved her life. According to the wisdom of the Old Ones, she and Byron were bound until he owed her his.

'So Byron the bard is in trouble again,' Xell said.

'You know him?'

'I was Lafa's magician during part of Byron's service as bard. Charming man. Odd, though. I never knew what he was about.'

Nica picked up the teapot and poured to keep herself from staring at Xell. She hadn't realized that Xell knew Byron. And that Xell couldn't read him seemed even more surprising. Xell was Enos-trained. He could touch any mind he wanted.

She handed Xell his cup, then handed Seymour his. Finally she poured her own. A bitter licorice smell rose from the liquid. All three magicians put their hands over their cups and rubbed the steam into their tattoos. The Old Wisdom said that torec tea increased the power of any spell cast out of love.

'I don't know him either.' Seymour had turned his hand palm up. His tattoo glowed with the same pinkish color as the crystals had. 'We've traveled together for weeks and I still don't understand him.'

'He learned to close his mind somewhere.'

Nica took her hand off her cup and clenched her fist, letting the steam soak into her palm. The Enos taught magicians to close their minds to protect the less experienced from learning powerful spells. But Byron was not a magician. He didn't carry a magician's blues and purples in his aura, although his aura was strange. It carried the rich reds of the bard, and beneath those lay the white mists of power. She had glimpsed the white on the day he helped her escape from Lord Dakin's retainers.

Xell had also removed his hand from his cup. He sipped his tea, then set the cup down. 'You and Byron are equals. You don't have to be following him.'

Seymour shook his head. 'We're not equals.'

'He has a white aura,' Nica said.

Xell glanced at her. She was part of the conversation now whether he wanted her in it or not. 'I have never seen it,' he said. 'His aura is red.'

'It was white when he helped me.'

'That explains it, then.' Xell took another sip of his tea. He appeared calm, but his stiff movements told Nica that he was annoyed. 'Anyone can have a white aura in moments of crisis, for that is when the most power is used.'

Nica shook her head slightly, not daring to contradict her tutor before a guest. She had met Byron when she was still the village herb witch. A child had been trampled by one of the retainers' stallions. She and Byron had found the boy at the same time. While she treated the child, Byron soothed him. From then on, both she and the child carried a strong loyalty to Byron. Rury had it too. And so, it seemed, did Seymour.

Xell had once told her that true charisma was based in the white mists of power.

Xell's explanation did not seem to satisfy Seymour either. He looked at Nica for the first time. 'You know Byron too?'

'Several months ago, Byron helped me leave Lord Dakin's land just before my brother was captured. I owe – '

'You're Rury's sister.'

'Yes,' she said. She wrapped her hands around her cup. Its sides were warm. 'You know my brother?'

'I knew him.'

Her hands grew cold, even around the warm cup. Rury was dead, then. She had known it, but hadn't wanted to believe it. The dream, the hounds, the blood – she had known since then.

'Byron never said you were a magician.'

She raised her head, grateful for something else to think about. 'He didn't know. I was the village herb witch.'

'You must not tell Byron that you saw her,' Xell said. 'She is in training, in seclusion.'

Nica stood. She took the teapot and poured the tea into a bucket they kept near the back door. Her hands were shaking. Xell didn't have to tell Seymour that. She would have, given time. Xell did not give her enough room to grow on her own.

She leaned her head on the rough wall. She could feel the men looking at her. She didn't care. Rury was dead. Her brother, with his flashing eyes and striking voice. She had always known his ideals would kill him, yet she had never thought she would have to experience his death.

The men talked behind her of spells and magicks. She did not listen. She waited until her trembling slowed before straightening up.

She set the teapot down on the counter and walked back to the table. Xell was looking at Seymour as if Nica had never left. 'Nica,' Xell said, 'get us some parchment.'

Nica reached around the table to the desk near the window. She removed several sheets of parchment, two pens, and two bottles of ink. She set the equipment on the table, then went back to clean the cups. The men bent over the papers, pens scratching as they traded spells. Nica boiled water, rinsed the cups, and then returned to the table. Xell and Seymour traded papers.

'Would you like me to work with you on these?' Xell asked.

Seymour shook his head. 'I think I'll have time to practice on my own.' He set the sheets aside so that the ink could dry. Xell skimmed over the sheet that Seymour had handed him, and seemed satisfied.

'So,' Xell said. 'Where is the bard taking you?'

'To the palace,' Seymour said. 'He wants to be bard to the king.'

Xell leaned back on his chair. 'He's good enough. But before he wanted to be as far from the palace as possible.'

'Perhaps the hounds changed him,' Nica said. 'It has happened before.'

You would forgive Byron anything. The foreign bitterness of the thought startled her. Then she realized that for the first time one of Xell's thoughts touched her.

'The paper is dry,' Seymour said. He gathered up the sheets, holding them as if they would burn him. 'I won't take any more of your time. Thank you for all of your help.'

Xell nodded. 'If you need assistance, please let us know.'

'I will.' Seymour stood and walked toward the door. The crystals' pinkness shone. He let himself out. As the door closed, the pink glow faded, and the crystals were clear again.

Nica sighed a little, wishing she could follow him, wishing she could see Byron.

'It's not wise,' Xell said softly.

'I know.' Nica walked back to the hearth. Chills ran up and down her arms. 'I should let him know that I'm alive. I owe him that much.'

Xell did not move. 'One mistake and you'll destroy your training.'

'Byron's worth that mistake.'

'You think too much of him.'

'No.' The fire's warmth crept up her arms. She felt as if she were being half burned and half frozen. 'You're the one who doesn't understand. He bears the white mists of power. I saw them.'

'And I explained that.' Xell's voice boomed around the room. The crystals jingled. 'I forbid you to see him. You risk too much.'

'We are bound,' she said. 'He saved my life.'

'Leave him alone, Nica.' Xell's anger touched her, but beneath it she felt something else. She took a step toward him, leaving the warmth of the fire.

'You're afraid,' she said with surprise. 'What could Byron do that frightens you so?'

Xell's rigidness snapped. He seemed to melt against his chair. As he stood up, she saw that his arms were shaking. He walked over to her, but did not touch her. 'The white mists of power outside of the palace means war, Nica. The Enos say that when they no longer control the white mists of power, we, the people of Kilot, will destroy the land. And when we destroy the land, the Enos will destroy us.'

'But Byron is Enos-trained. You said so yourself.'

'There's more to it than that.' Xell looked old in the shop's dimness. The flickering firelight crept into the lines of his face, hiding his features in shadow. 'Underneath the palace lies a cache of Enos power so great that only the most powerful Enos guard it. Gerusha discovered the Cache and swore upon it that no war would ever again touch Kilot. The Enos held him and his descendants to that oath. In turn, the Enos hold the key to the royal succession, but otherwise do not interfere in our affairs. It is said that when the Enos begin to interfere in human affairs, the final time has begun.'

Nica frowned. The old legends seemed too vague to her. 'So whoever carries the white mists of power is a member of the royal family.'

'No.' Xell took her hand. His fingers were cold. 'Whoever carries the white mists of power carries with him the power to destroy the entire kingdom.'

ii

The night talked to him. Afeno walked near the ports. The river barges cuddled the docks, their lanterns reflecting orange in the water. Since they had come to Coventon, he had taken to walking the dock area at night, seeing the pickpockets at work, eyeing the whores. Byron kept him busy during the day, but at night Afeno had only Colin to talk to, and the boy was too young to have many stories. Afeno missed the night action. His fingers itched with the urge to dip into a pocket and lift a coin. But Byron had warned him against it, saying that too much was at stake. And for the first time in his life, Afeno had money and no need to steal anything.

He pushed his way through a crowd huddled outside the tavern at the edge of the docks. Inside, he paid a round for an ale he didn't drink and sat at a table near the door. He used to dream about sitting in a tavern and not getting thrown out. Now the barkeep took his money and paid him no notice, as if Afeno had as much right as anyone to come into the tavern. That pleased him.

Three of the whores he had seen outside walked into the tavern and took the table next to his. The acrid odor of sweat mixed with sour perfume wafted over to him. He stuck his nose in his tankard, preferring the bitterness of the ale to the smell of the women.

The woman next to him, a tall redhead with face powder so thick it caught in the lines on her face, slammed five gold pieces on the table. 'I'm buying for everyone!' she said.

Afeno set his tankard down. Whores never gave anything away.

'Where'd ya get the money, Olu?' the barkeep shouted.

'Where do I always get the money?' she asked.

'From Rive. But Rive never buys for anyone.'

The whore smiled. She was missing her two front teeth. 'Not tonight. Tonight he says he's gonna get rich.'

The crowd laughed, but the hum of voices dimmed. Everyone was listening. Afeno leaned forward a little on his chair, hoping that he could find a way to share in the profits too.

'What did he find, a new merchant with a loose purse?'

'Better than that. He knows where Lafa's bounty is staying.' The whore pushed the gold pieces forward. 'Where're the drinks?'

The barkeep began filling mugs of ale. 'We all know where the bounty is staying, Olu, but no one can touch him until he's outside the city.'

The whore shrugged. 'Who's to say how he gets outside the city?'

Afeno frowned, unable to follow the conversation. He had been here night after night, and had heard nothing about a bounty. Men around the room stood up and left their ales.

'Where're you going?' the whore asked. 'I'm buying.'

'Thanks but no thanks,' one of the men said as he pushed his way out the door. 'I'm going to give Rive a little help.'

The whore picked up her gold. 'I didn't tell you this to get you in Rive's way.'

'Rive will probably need our help.'

'Not to pick off a bard,' the whore said.

Afeno froze. His heart suddenly started beating twice as fast.

'A bard that is worth three hundred gold pieces dead is going to be hard to kill.'

Afeno took a deep breath and stood. 'Do you mean the bard who just came into town, the tall, thin, dark one with the fancy clothes?'

Everyone in the bar looked at him. Afeno thought a few people recognized him, but he wasn't sure. The barkeep had stopped pouring the ales. He said gruffly, 'That's the one.'

Someone wanted Byron bad to place a bounty on him. Afeno was shaking. 'I'm down from Dakin's lands. Dakin is paying five hundred gold pieces for him alive.'

'Where did you hear that, boy?' the barkeep asked.

'Nadaluci. It's all over up there.'

The whore stuck her money in her pocket. The men gathered near the door, and the conversations began low, people trying to figure how to get both rewards. Afeno left his ale and slid past the bodies toward the door. He wanted to leave, but most of his money was at the inn with Byron. He owed it to Byron to tell him. But he didn't want to go back. With this many people after him, Byron had no chance of survival. And neither did his companions.

iii

The guild shop was dark except for the embers glowing in the hearth. Nica's hands shook as she laced her cape. She hadn't left the shop since she had become a magician. Xell insisted on total seclusion until she learned her craft well enough to survive on her own.

She had waited until Xell was sleeping before sneaking down the stairs. She would talk to Byron briefly, thank him, let him know that she was safe, and then she would return. Xell wouldn't know until morning, and by then he would be able to do nothing.

A small trickle of fear ran down her back. Her training was all she had, especially now that Rury was dead. But sometimes Xell exaggerated threats. Perhaps he had exaggerated this one.

She crossed her arms before her face, held her breath, and clenched her fists. Her chants were soft. She felt deep relief as her luck web hugged her.

When she opened her eyes and let her arms drop, she heard someone cough. She turned and saw Xell behind her. He was wearing his magician's robes. 'I'm coming with you,' he said.

'I want to do this alone.'

Xell shook his head. 'Lord Lafa put a price on the bard's head. Seeing him alone could be too dangerous for you.'

'I can protect myself.'

'Perhaps. But I doubt that you can protect the bard. If something happens, you'll need my help.'

Nica swallowed. She knew how people reacted to the offer of money, especially people as poor as those who worked on the docks in Coventon. Her magic was untested outside the shop, and yet she was a better magician than Seymour. He would be no help if something happened. 'All right,' she said.

Xell did not smile. He took her arm, then picked up his staff. Another chill tickled her spine. Xell only used his staff for serious magic.

They stepped out of the shop. The night was cold, and the river smelled of fish. No one was on the streets and yet up ahead Nica could hear shouts and cries. She wanted to walk faster, but Xell held her back. He led her through two side streets and around a corner.

And then she saw the crowd. They huddled around an inn. They were carrying torches that illuminated the entire road. Most of the crowd were men, large men, dock handlers and toughs, but a few women stood inside the crowd. They seemed to be waiting. A man leaned out a window. In the flickering light, Nica recognized Seymour's face. He raised his hands and Xell groaned.

'He's got the wrong position!'

Xell raised his staff. The strands of Nica's luck web shimmered as Xell gathered his around himself. He started to chant, but too late. The inn exploded, sending plumes of flame into the sky.

iv

Afeno heard the explosion echo like a crack throughout the city. He was still a mile from the inn. He ran, passing empty docks and emptier streets. He thought he heard shouts up ahead, and he saw flames splash against the sky. Then the fires disappeared and the shouts grew dim. He ran faster, his breathing so loud that he could barely hear his feet pound against the dirt.

When he reached the inn, the street was dark. Small fires burned on the building's face, and the wood was scorched. A large hole gaped in place of the window to Byron's room. The area smelled of sulfur and charred wood.

Afeno ran across the street and through the inn's open door. No one was in the tavern. No one appeared to be in the inn at all. He took the stairs two at a time, rounded the corner, and entered the dark hallway.

The sulfur smell was stronger here, mixed with something else, something rancid. The door to Byron's room stood open, and a thin trickle of light came from inside.

Afeno stepped through the door. Tiny flames burned along the inside of the wall. The pallets were covered with blood. Byron's sword was stuck in the floor at an odd angle. A body lay in the hole where the window used to be. Afeno's heartbeat moved into his throat.

He hurried to the hole and grabbed the body. The rancid smell came from it. Afeno finally recognized it: burned flesh. He pulled the body out of the hole. It was Seymour. His hands and arms were all burns. As Afeno laid him back on the floor, Seymour moaned.

'Seymour!'

Seymour moaned again. His eyelids fluttered. Afeno shook him a little. 'What happened?'

Seymour licked his lips and squinted. 'Afeno?'

'What happened?'

Tears trickled from the corners of Seymour's eyes, but his voice didn't waver. 'Did you find Byron?'

'No. Where is he?'

'They took him. I didn't see – '

'Who?'

'The innkeeper. Some beggars. A hundred people. Byron and Colin fought – ' Seymour coughed. He wheezed for a moment, then took in some air. 'I tried a new spell, but it exploded on me, and I couldn't help – '

'You need an herb witch,' Afeno said. He had to get out of there, out of the stink. He beat the remaining flames out with a blanket. 'I'll be back with an herb witch. Wait here.'

'But Byron – '

'Ten minutes won't help or hurt Byron either way, but it'll help you. Wait here.'

'All right.' Seymour closed his eyes. Afeno ran past the sword, down the stairs, and into the street. The silence was eerie. He could see no one. He hurried through the side streets until he found a sign for an herb witch. He pounded on the door, but heard no answer.

His breath was coming rapidly. Seymour would die without help, and so would Byron. Afeno couldn't spend the entire night looking for an herb witch. He pounded again, louder, and this time the door opened.

The woman was small, elderly, and very sleepy. 'I'll pay you two gold pieces,' Afeno said. 'I have a burned man back at the inn.'

The woman smoothed her hair, turned, and grabbed a pouch. 'Take me there,' she said.

Afeno led her back on the path he had come. She moved too slowly for him; he wanted to pick her up and carry her. Once he reached the inn, he took her upstairs, sneezing at the smell. She knelt beside Seymour and took one of his hands. 'This is bad. Very bad.'

'Can you help him?'

'I can ease his pain. It'll take one with more talent than I to help him.'

'Do what you can,' Afeno said. He couldn't stay in the room. He had to find Byron. Afeno ran down the stairs and into the street. He had originally come from the north and seen nothing, and had found the herb witch to the west and seen nothing. If the crowd had taken him, they had taken him south because east would have meant going around the inn and into a residential district. South led out of town the quickest.

Afeno darted down the nearest side street and saw torches flickering in front of taverns. The taverns were empty, though, and he saw no one else. A half mile down the road, his foot slipped. He looked down and saw a pool of blood the size of the one Dakin's retainer had left in Nadaluci. He swallowed and kept moving. Farther on, he saw a bloody handprint beneath one of the torches on the side of a tavern, and another smudge on a wood post. Then, at the end of the street near the city wall, he saw his own sword resting upright in the dirt.

He walked to the sword slowly. The hilt and the blade were covered with blood. A bloodstained white shirt rested under the sword point. Byron's shirt. Afeno tossed the sword aside and picked up the shirt. The blood was sticky, half dry. He had probably been dead for a couple of hours.

Afeno swallowed, feeling his stomach twist. Byron was probably dead, but Afeno had to find out for sure. He walked through the city gate, into the darkness.

V

Nica shielded her eyes from the flames' glare. She took a step backward, squinted, and saw Byron run out of the burning building, followed by a boy. They faced the crowd for a moment, then the crowd surged forward. She had to do something. She breathed into her luck web, felt its strength.

'Let me,' Xell said.

'No. I owe him.'

'You lack the powers, Nica.'

'Then share yours with me,' she said. She raised her hands, drawing the luck into her fingers. Her power grew stronger, stronger, until it radiated out her hands. She felt another presence, a luck web even stronger, more radiant than her own. She chanted a spell she had only read, then opened her eyes in time to see Byron and the boy disappear.

The crowd lurched forward, not believing the two had disappeared. 'This,' Xell said, and held his staff aloft. Nica grasped the end of the staff, and knew there was another step to the spell. Power jutted forward on a half-lit arc, stopping in the center of the crowd and forming into the Byron who had just vanished. Ropes hung loosely from his wrists and his shirt was torn and bloody.

Someone screamed and the crowd surged forward. The illusion ran, and someone grabbed his white shirt, yanking him backward. A heavyset man stuck a dagger in the fake bard's back.

'Stop that!' a woman yelled. 'You're to kill him outside the city!'

The bard stumbled forward, blood trailing from his back. The crowd followed. Nica watched until they disappeared down a side street. She relaxed her grip on the staff and Xell lowered it, slowly. She cast about in her mind until she found the warmth of Byron and the boy. She raised her arms before her face, chanted for her luck web, to make it stronger, but her reserves were gone. With a soft whisper she reversed the invisibility spell, but when she blinked her eyes, she saw nothing.

'I can't reverse it,' she said to Xell.

'It'll fade in a few hours,' he said. 'Come on, let's go home.'

'I want to see if he's all right.' She ran to the warm place, the place her mind told her housed the bard and the boy. They were a few yards from the inn. She stopped before them, found Byron's shoulder, traced his arm down to his hand, and untied his wrists. Then she stepped away, suddenly afraid to talk to him.

Byron grabbed her hand. Her luck web snapped. Pain as sharp as a thousand glass shards ran through her.

'Who is it?' he asked.

Nica was trembling. Slowly she pushed back her hood.

'Nica!' The pleasure in his voice made her flush.

'The – the invisibility will last another half day. I'm sorry, Byron, but my luck has left me.' She wished that she could see his face.

'You did this?'

'I'm in training. I'm not supposed to see anyone. Please. I should go.' She tried to pull her hand away from him, but he held tightly.

'What were you doing here?'

'I heard you were here. I came to thank you.'

'I should thank you.' His voice was soft.

'We're even now.' Nica pulled her hand free. 'You're all right?'

'I think so,' he said.

'The boy's beside you.'

'Nica – '

'When I'm done training, Byron, I'll find you.' She backed away, then ran down the road. Her body didn't hurt, but she felt pain. He had hurt her, hurt her magic somehow. And Xell had said that seeing someone could destroy her magic forever.

She ran all the way to the guild shop, afraid that the door would not open for her now that her luck web was gone. Xell was waiting outside, holding his staff beside him like a shepherd. He opened the door for her and she went inside.

He had lit candles on all the shelves, just as he had done the night she first arrived. The light reflecting off the crystals blinded her, and she fell to the floor.

'You did very well,' Xell said. 'Your magic will be strong and forceful someday.'

'My web snapped.'

He crouched down beside her and lifted her against him. His touch felt soft, soothing. She closed her eyes and felt him take each strand of her luck web, stitch it together with his own threads, and replace it around her. She leaned against him and he stroked her hair. 'You can't go out again,' he said. 'I can only repair your luck web once.'

She moved away. The web was there, weaker than it had been before but there. She wanted to touch it, to make it stronger, but she knew she dared not.

'Make it disappear,' Xell said, 'and when it returns, it will be stronger.'

Nica wrapped her arms around herself and chanted the web away. But she didn't move after it disappeared. Instead she replayed the pleasure in Byron's voice before she stored the memory in her heart.

Milord:

This bard is more than you portrayed him to be. A great wizard or an Enos or perhaps even an Old One watches over him. Never in my travels have I had such a night as this.

I joined Lafa's bounty hunters on a raid against the bard. After dark, we burst into his room in the inn. He was there, with the magician and one of the boys. Armed only with a sword – no shield or other protection – he held six of us off. His young friend fought and wounded another of the group. Finally, I managed to break past the bard's sword and pinned him against the wall. The entire room exploded. The bard and the boy broke free. The magician was wounded, near dead, but he managed to make them leave. They ran down the stairs and out the door. We followed.

A large crowd waited outside. They captured the bard and boy and held them. They began to take him from the city in accord with Lafa's orders. Somehow – and I and no one else seem to know how – he escaped. I grabbed him for a moment, long enough to run my knife into him, but he kept moving, trailing blood. The boy had disappeared. Then, near the city's edge, I caught him. As I tried to kill him, he vanished as if he had never existed. But my hands were stained with blood.

A great magician has aided him, milord, and that magician is not his own. I have since searched for that magician and the bard and can find neither. But I shall continue my hunt. And when I find him, I will be prepared. No one, *no one*, makes a fool of Corvo and lives.

When you next hear from me, the bard will be dead.

Corvo

Chapter 12

Adric's face dug into the pillow. He was lying on his stomach in a room that smelled of hay and horses. A voice in the back of his head warned him not to move, not to wake up all the way, not to breathe.

'Have you tried to wake him?' Cassie's voice sounded faraway, although he could feel the heat of her body on his arm.

'No, not yet. I was waiting for you.' There was something in Milo's tone that Adric had never heard before. Panic? Fear?

Metal jingled above him, and he felt himself hovering on the edge of wakefulness. An ache started in his back, and he tried to slide back into sleep, but the effort woke him further.

'This was all the money I could find. I'm sorry.'

'That's okay. It'll do. If we need more, I'll take more.'

'Milo! You promised!'

'I never had to protect a prince before. I'll do what I can, Cassie.'

The sheets were smooth and cool, but the pillow was hot against his cheek. The throbbing in his back grew.

He felt Cassie move. The warmth of her body slid down, closer to his stomach. 'I got him as drunk as I could,' she said. 'He passed out a few minutes ago.'

'I thought you were going to use a sleeping potion.'

'I couldn't get out to buy one. He was watching me. I think he suspected something. It was all I could do to get him to drink. I'm a little woozy myself.'

His back felt encased in armor, a crusty shell that held him in place. The throbbing had taken a strange pattern. He blinked once and the throbbing became a burning. Someone was using a hot coal to draw a map on his flesh. He had to sit up, to stop the mapmaking, but sitting up seemed like too much work.

'You can't be woozy.' Milo's voice sounded closer, sharper. 'I need your help.'

'Where are you taking him?'

'I won't tell you unless you come with us.'

'I deserve to know.'

Milo sighed. 'I'll send you a message if we make it.'

The mapmaker set sticks across Adric's back and lit them on fire. The pain shuddered through him, into his stomach, into his legs. Adric gasped and tried to roll over, to put out the fire. Cool hands gripped his arms, forcing him back down.

'Don't move so fast,' Cassie said. 'You'll break the scabs open.'

Her breath smelled of ale, and the ends of her words sounded mushy. Adric opened his eyes, saw Cassie's faded gray dress and, beyond it, the rough wood wall of the stable.

Her hand stayed on his arm. 'I brought a clean shirt and extra ointment. Make sure that you put the ointment on. He'll heal quicker.'

'Okay.'

Adric blinked and turned his head so that he could see Cassie's face. She seemed older than she had before, tired, as if she were about to lose everything. She was looking across him, probably at Milo.

'If the scabs fill with pus and fall off, find an herb witch right away. Pus means that the ointment has failed.'

'But pus is good.'

'Sometimes. Not with this treatment.' Cassie dipped her hand in a jar, then rubbed her hands together. She rose on her knees and caressed his back. Her hands cooled the fire, put out the flame. Tears tickled the edges of Adric's eyes.

'Water?' he whispered.

Cassie looked at him then. Her smile was tender, but a frown still creased her brow. Something sloshed beside him and then Milo came into view, holding a cup. Water dripped off its sides.

'I'm glad you're awake,' Milo said. He crouched beside Adric and put his hands behind Adric's head to help him up.

'Wait until I'm finished,' Casssie said. Her hands touched the base of his spine. The map still burned beneath the coolness, but the feeling seemed faraway. 'All right. Let's help him up first.'

Milo set the cup down and moved out of Adric's range of vision. Adric saw the wall, the choppy splinters in the wood, the rusty nail falling from its peg. Slowly he slid his hands under his shoulders to help himself. Fire threatened his shoulder blades. He waited until the heat faded, then pushed. Milo and Cassie supported him and kept his back straight as he sat up. A sudden dizziness gripped him, and Adric clutched Cassie's arm. The dizziness passed, and he let go, leaving red fingerprints in her skin.

Milo handed Adric the cup. The tin was cool against his fingers. He raised it slowly, almost as if he had forgotten how. His arm shook, and water dripped onto his legs. The cup touched the edge of his lips and he drank, letting the liquid soothe the dryness in the back of his throat.

Cassie glanced at the door. 'You have to get him out of here, Milo,' she said. 'Rogren will wake up in a few hours. He always does.'

Milo nodded. He grabbed a linen shirt that rested on top of a full sack. 'Put this on,' he said to Adric. 'We're leaving.'

The shirt was soft. Adric slipped one arm into a sleeve. The burning threatened with each movement, but he bit his lip and slipped the shirt over his other arm. The material felt good until it touched his back. Then it stuck and clung, eating the coolness and letting in the heat. 'Where are we going?' he asked. His voice sounded raspy.

Cassie laced the shirt. Her fingers were shaking. 'Milo will take care of you. He has food and ointment in that sack.'

Adric shook his head. 'I can't leave the city. They won't find me.'

Milo picked up the sack. 'They're not looking. They think you're dead. We've got to figure out how to prove to them that you're not.'

Adric reached for the cup. His back throbbed, but he forced himself to grip the handle and bring the cup to his lips. He drank the rest of the water, then waited until his heart stopped pounding before speaking. 'What are we going to do?'

'Let me worry about that,' Milo said. 'Come on.'

He held out his hand. Adric took it and stood. The floor was hard, covered with hay and dust. The dizziness returned for a second, but he willed it to go away.

Cassie disappeared behind one of the stalls and returned with one of Rogren's horses. Milo shook his head. 'We can't take that. He'll look for us all the harder.'

She smiled, her eyes a little unfocused. 'Not if the other horses are missing too,' she said.

'Cassie – '

'You'd do the same, Milo.'

'Come with us,' he said. 'Rogren will beat you.'

'Someone has to stay here with Rogren and delay him. I know him better than you do. I'm used to him. I'll stay.'

Adric let go of Milo's hand and stood on his own. The room swayed a little, then steadied itself. Cassie hugged Milo. 'Let me know,' she said. 'Please?'

He nodded and pushed out of the hug. He took Adric's arm, and together they walked out into the night.

Chapter 13

She felt it quivering beneath her bluff, making a fire under the overhang beside the river. It worried about its companions and it was frightened for itself. She had never felt the white mists so close before.

The bluff Enos peered through the young saplings and down the side of the bluff. It was shaped like a large anvil, with the thin portion covering the river like half a bridge. The underside of the overhang was blackened with the smoke of many fires. Travelers camped there, near the water, under the natural protection, and she let them, as long as they did not harm her bluff.

She could smell the smoke, feel the worry of the white mists, but she could see nothing. She decided to tap, to reach into the white mists' mind and see through its eyes. She let her mind slide inside the bluff, crawl through the land, and up into the white mists' mind.

Her mind skidded against wall after wall after wall, falling in an Enos trap, lost inside the white mists. He was *(blocked),* searching for *(blocked)* and hoping, hoping –

She screamed as she surfaced, and from below she heard an echoing scream, male and human, high and powerful. She pulled out of his mind and clung to the edge of her bluff, letting her fingers dig into the soft dirt, feeling the power of the bluff heal her. She was a small Enos with only a small patch of land. The trap set in the white mists' mind had been set by an over-Enos, one who worked with the Cache Enos and the humans, to guard an entire section of land. The bluff Enos had only her bluff, just as her cousin had only the forest, and another cousin only the bend in the river. Their powers were as small as their land. She could have died in the Enos trap, and no one would have ever known.

She scurried down the bluff, weaving through the tree trunks and tall grasses. When she reached the base, she slithered to the patch of large rocks and peered through.

The white mists sat near the fire holding his head. Two boys stood, swords out, facing different directions. Another man, who stank of fire and pain, slept on a pallet, his breathing shallow, his life force thin.

She climbed over the rocks and sat on top of them. The hard surface felt cool and reassuring. She was smaller than the boys, but that did not worry her. She kicked her feet and touched the rim of the white mists' mind.

The white mists looked up. One of the boys followed his gaze and, crouching, pulled a dagger from his boot. He swung his arm back as if to throw the dagger, but the white mists caught the boy's wrist.

'Wait, Afeno,' the white mists said. 'Do nothing until I tell you.'

The white mists' gaze met hers. His eyes were deep and clear. He was Enos-trained and Enos-protected. She was curious but not afraid.

You tapped me. He did not project. He simply allowed her to read the thought in his mind. She scraped along the surface, searching. He was not a magician, then, but a musician and something –

The block stung them both. The white mists grabbed the side of his head. The Enos clung to her rock. The boy's hand tightened on his dagger. When the pain receded, she projected: *Why are you on my bluff?*

We were tired. We wanted shelter so that we could rest.

The man is dying.

The white mists looked at the man on the pallet. He pushed the man's hair off his forehead. The Enos felt the deep affection the white mists felt for the man. *We do not know how to help him.*

The Enos left the white mists' mind, danced across the boys', finding little knowledge and odd skills. She reached into the injured man, blocked the pain, and touched the core of him, tapping and building and reaching deep. Then she left and sat on the rim of the white mists' mind. *He has the knowledge to heal himself.*

If he has that knowledge, he does not know how to use it.

The Enos felt the truth of the statement, knew that such things would change with the morning. She slid down the rock and walked across the river's edge. The dagger boy's body grew tense. The white mists placed a hand on the boy's shoulder. The other boy watched.

She knelt beside the man, took his burned and mangled hands in her own. She spat on his flesh, then rubbed it. The burned skin flaked off and landed in a small pile near the pallet. Pink, healthy skin shone where her hands had touched. She finished his physical wounds and touched his skull, feeling again the core of him and adding a small protection inside.

She finished, bowed to the white mists, and stood, coming only to his waist. 'You may stay while the sun completes half a rotation, and then you must leave. I do not want white mists upon my land. You bring danger with you.'

'Thank you,' the white mists said. 'And thank you for helping Seymour.'

The Enos nodded, recognizing the human need for acknowledgment. As she passed the dagger boy, she touched his arm and said, 'This one must learn that killing is the refuge of a coward.'

Anger, hot and flaming, spun through the boy, and she removed her hand before she got burned. She bowed once more to the white mists, then climbed her rocks, and slid into the trees. She would guard the white mists, see that no blood was shed on her land. Then she would send to the other land Enos to see if they knew of the white mists and why such a danger was present now, after centuries of such calm.

Chapter 14

Adric's cheek rested on the rough wool covering Milo's shoulder. The horse jostled beneath them, and Adric had to hold Milo's waist tightly just to stay on. Grass grew beside the road, and the air smelled of greenery. The silence seemed loud. He could hear his own breathing and the even clopping pace of the horse's hooves.

They had left the city at dawn, both afraid that Rogren was right behind them. Adric sat on his own through that trip, gazing at the spires he had wanted to see so long ago and wishing he were past them. After they hurried through the gate, tiredness overwhelmed him, and he leaned on Milo. Adric couldn't sleep, though. Every time he dozed, he started to slip off, and the scabs on his back would break and pull, jerking him awake.

He gazed ahead and saw people bent over green fields, picking something that grew on small stalks and tossing the something into a bucket. Was the drought over then? He hadn't seen such green in months. The people moved rhythmically: bending, picking, tossing; bending, picking, tossing. Adric's back ached in sympathy. He remembered seeing something similar on his long ride to town so long ago, and not understanding the work involved. He understood now.

He squinted, saw the people more clearly. In the distance, men and older women carried buckets from an unseen stream. Younger women did most of the picking, their slender bodies weighted with babies slung upon their backs. Children crouched on the side rows, looking for plants that had been missed. One little girl stood and watched the horse pass until another child yanked her down.

Adric closed his eyes. The gentle sway of the horse's body rocked him. The wool rubbed against his cheek, scratching him, but he didn't move. He felt the strain against his scabs, the relief as some pulled free, his skin cooled by the flow of blood.

'Milo!' A woman's voice echoed from the field. Adric opened his eyes. The ground seemed closer; the caked dirt looked tired and well used. A woman stood at the edge of the field, waving her arms. 'Milo!'

Milo reined in the horse, and Adric almost lost his balance when the swaying stopped. The woman ran toward them. She lifted her skirts as she stepped up onto the road. 'Milo, why didn't you tell us you were coming? Did you lose your job?'

Milo turned a little, holding Adric's arm so that he wouldn't fall off. 'Mother, I – '

'The only one of us who makes any money and you run away. Did you steal the horse too? It's too fine to be yours.' Her eyes, bright buttons in her sun-leathered face, scanned the horse, Milo, and then found Adric. 'And who is this?'

'Mother, I'll explain when you get home tonight.'

'His back is all bloody.' She circled around them and gripped Adric's shirt. As she lifted it, the scabs ripped off and Adric groaned. 'Someone's whipped him but good. Are you in trouble, Milo? I won't have any trouble in my house.'

Milo's grip on Adric tightened. 'Mother, I said I'll explain later.'

'Who is this boy? He can't stay unless I know who he is.'

Adric licked his lips. 'I'm – '

'He's a friend of mine.' Milo brought his other arm around to steady Adric. 'We worked together. Rogren almost killed him, so we're going off to find something else.'

Milo's mother tugged at her wispy gray hair. 'We'll talk when I get home, Milo. A boy doesn't leave his work because of a whipping.' She gathered her skirts and returned to the field. Milo clucked at the horse.

'Don't you ever tell anyone who you are, you hear me?' he hissed.

'I wasn't – '

'We never talk about it, we never think about it unless it's just you and me. The prince is dead, you got that? He won't live again until you reach that palace. Until then you're my friend. We left Rogren to find our fortune together.'

'Why are you yelling?' Adric clung to Milo's waist. The dizziness had returned. 'I wasn't going to tell her.'

'Because.' Milo leaned forward, balancing his weight. 'If you say who you are, they'll think you're crazy. Out here, they don't whip crazies, they kill them. So if you want to survive, you say nothing.'

'All right.' Adric closed his eyes against the dizziness, but it seemed to grow worse. Every place he went seemed to be worse than the one before. He opened his eyes again as the horse entered a small village. Adric wrinkled his nose at the combined smell of garbage, cooking meat, smoke, and feces. The village was smaller than a city street. The hovels were made of stone with no mortar. Rags filled the larger crevices to prevent cold winds from blowing through. Doors hung ajar because they could not close. Buckets covered with flies sat outside doorways.

In the center of the village, a fire burned in a circle of stones. Dogs ran toward the horse, nipping its heels when they caught it. Milo cursed and swung at them, nearly making Adric lose his balance. The dogs ran away.

He stopped the horse near the fire. The smoke burned Adric's eyes and filled his lungs. He could scarcely breathe. His entire body ached. Milo dismounted. He reached up to help Adric, relaxing his grip as his hands touched Adric's shirt.

'You're bleeding.'

Adric was too tired to say anything. He needed to rest. He let Milo pull him from the horse. Adric's legs were stiff, and his entire body hurt. Milo tied the horse to a post near the fire and half dragged Adric into a nearby hovel.

The hovel smelled of urine and stale food. A thin stream of light trickled in from the door and from the cracks in the stonework. There were no windows. Milo set Adric on a pallet near the door. Adric winced as his body touched straw. The world still moved, even though Adric did not.

'I'll be right back,' Milo said.

Adric reached for him, but Milo disappeared.

Slowly Adric's eyes adjusted to the darkness. He saw two benches, a table, several pallets, and a fireplace. Unemptied slop buckets sat by the door, and the remains of a meal still littered the table's surface.

Itchy spots traveled across his chest. He glanced at his hand and watched a small black bug land on his knuckle. The pallet was infested. He shuddered and tried to roll off, then hesitated when his hands found dirt.

The door banged open. 'Over here,' Milo said.

A woman crouched beside Adric, her skirts covered with mud. 'When was he whipped?'

'Yesterday.'

'Help me get his shirt off.' As she pulled the corner of the garment, pain ran through Adric's back.

'I'll get it,' he said. He made himself sit up and eased the shirt from his shoulders. The fire rekindled in his back. He tossed the shirt aside and lay down again.

'These aren't healing properly,' the woman said. Her finger was light upon Adric's back. 'See the pus? Someone placed salt in the wounds and then used a water treatment. Salt and water together stop the healing.'

'Cassie just used ointment,' Milo said.

'Rogren rubbed my back,' Adric said. 'It burned.'

'He knew what kind of treatment she would use. Damn him.'

'Can you help?' Adric asked.

The woman nodded. 'It will take all day and you will have scars. I have to remove the water and salt, apply some ointment, remove that, and reapply the water treatment. It will be an ugly process.' She turned to Milo. 'You can leave if you want.'

Adric clenched the pallet. He was used to pain. Nothing could be worse than the whipping.

Milo took his hand. 'I'll stay.'

Chapter 15

The road to the palace was empty. They had walked for miles without seeing another person or a single carriage. Seymour gripped the valise tightly. His hands still ached a little, but the pain from his burns was gone. His skin was soft and pink, new as a baby's. He wished he had seen the Enos to thank her.

The road curved under a canopy of trees, threading the light through the leaves. Ahead, he caught glimpses of a long stone wall and behind it, buildings. Byron had said nothing since they reached the forest. He carried his lute against his chest like a shield. His face was white, his lips pursed. Colin and Afeno also walked quietly. It felt as if the group had lost its unity under the bluff near the river.

Seymour switched the valise to his other hand. He wasn't sure he wanted to go to the palace. Ever since they had entered the woods, since he got his first glimpse of the palace walls, he felt as if his heart would pound through his chest. He was a bad magician. His father, one of the best wizards ever, had been banished from this place. Seymour couldn't even cast a spell to protect himself and his friends. The explosion still echoed in his ears, reverberated through his head. Beneath the new pink skin the sensation of fire remained. He had always burned himself with fire spells as a child. He should have realized that his fate as an adult would be no different.

He didn't want to be the king's magician – or anyone's magician – ever again, and he wanted to talk to Byron about that, but Byron had sunk inside himself and didn't seem to hear anything.

The forest smelled of pine mixed with the bitter scent of whistle-wood. Somewhere near here, Seymour remembered, stood the only whistle-wood trees in Kilot. He would like to see them before he left, since most of an upper-level magician's power was based in whistle-wood.

A plan had been forming in his head ever since he had awakened beside the bluff, with the pain gone and Byron's face smiling over his. Seymour would see the group safely to the palace, and then he would go his own way. Where he would go from there he did not know. He only knew that he would leave.

They rounded another corner and the palace wall stood before them. The wall was made of large gray stones, packed with mortar set in an almost circular pattern. A small wood door stood to one side of a large wood gate. Byron stopped and stared as if he had never seen anything like it before. Colin and Afeno stopped beside him.

'What now, sir?' Colin said.

Byron didn't look at him. He walked to the wall, ran his fingers down it, and rested his cheek against the stone. His expression seemed frightened and a little lost. Seymour wondered what it was like to have a dream that would frighten him upon reaching it. He touched Byron's arm.

'Shall we go inside?' he asked.

Byron glanced at him and for a moment didn't seem to recognize him. Then he said, 'I don't know if this is a good idea.'

'The only way to know is to try.'

Byron smiled a little. 'Yes. And what could happen here? No one cares about a simple bard, right, Seymour?'

Seymours hands tingled. Some people cared, but probably not those inside the palace. 'You'll be fine here. You're good enough to play for the king.'

'You've never heard me perform.'

'But I have heard you practice.'

Byron nodded, grabbed his lute, and slung it around his back. Then he knocked on the door. The knock sounded small against the backdrop of the forest. A wind kicked up and danced around them, shaking the trees, and sending a chill down Seymour's back. In the distance he thought he heard singing.

'The whistle-woods,' Byron said. He knocked again.

This time the door opened. An older, heavyset man wearing a gold uniform stared at them. 'Don't need more entertainers,' he said. 'Go ply your wares in town.'

Byron nodded, seemingly willing to let the man close the door. Seymour stepped forward. 'Wait,' he said.

The man glanced at him.

'Byron is one of the best bards in the country. He would like to try his skill before the king.'

'I don't care,' the man said. 'We have several other performing troupes here, and the king is in no mood for entertainment. Go away.'

Seymour's hand trembled. This had been their goal, Byron's goal, and he was saying nothing. All these weeks of preparation, and nothing was coming of it. He couldn't believe Byron's mood or his silence. 'No, we won't leave,' Seymour said. 'I am Seymour, son of Dysik the Great, one of the greatest wizards to perform for the king. His highness unjustly banished my father, and I have come to restore my father's name.'

The guard looked Seymour over, then smiled crookedly. 'I remember your father. He used to give me sweets when I watched the performances.'

'So will you let us inside?' Afeno asked.

'I am under orders not to let in anyone but the gentry on official business.'

'But Byron is gentry,' Seymour said.

Byron's face suddenly came alive – and the expression Seymour thought he read was panic.

'He is Sir Geoffry of Kinsmail. He makes his living barding and needs to petition the king for his lands.'

The guard's smile vanished. 'This is beginning to sound like quite a story.'

'We have many reasons for wanting to see the king,' Byron said. 'We have traveled a long way. We would like to at least spend some time on the grounds.'

The guard sighed, then stood away from the door. 'I am doing this because of your father's kindnesses,' he said to Seymour. 'I expect that you will tell no one when you arrived or who let you in.'

'Thank you,' Seymour said. Byron took a few gold pieces from his pocket and set them in the guard's hand as they passed.

Inside the wall, the chill grew. The palace stood in the distance, a great stone structure that curved in several directions. Beyond it stood a small forest and a hill. Other buildings stood nearby, some made of stone and some of wood. Seymour had been expecting a stink like that in the city, but the air was fresh here. The pine scent had disappeared, but the tang of the whistle-woods filled the breeze. The ground was covered with cobblestones. Thin blades of grass grew beneath the stone. And it was quiet. Retainers crossed the courtyard, intent upon their business. Maidservants ran back and forth, carrying buckets of water or bags of flour. Seymour watched, wondering if the gentry came in a different way, wondering if they saw a different world than he did.

Byron walked around the courtyard, looking up at the buildings and down the narrow corridors that ran between them. Finally he turned around. His cheeks were flushed and his eyes bright. 'We're here, Seymour,' he said. 'We're really here.'

PART TWO

Chapter 16

Firelight danced across the room's smoke-stained walls. Adric sat at the bench, resting his elbows on the table's rough surface. His back itched and he longed to scratch it, but he didn't, knowing that Milo would slap him if he tried.

'Now watch,' Milo said. He tossed a round on the table. The coin spun, catching and reflecting the light. Finally the coin lost its spin, clattered against the table, and stopped. Milo scooped up the coin and put it in his pocket. He sat next to Adric.

'Take the coin from me without me seeing you.'

Adric slid away. 'No!'

'We're not going to be here much longer, Adric, and it's time you learn to take care of yourself. Take the coin.'

Adric shook his head. His back no longer hurt, but the scabs pulled, as if they were trying to come loose. 'No.'

'You have to learn.' Milo took the round out of his pocket and tossed it on the table.

The round, resting flat on the tabletop, no longer seemed sparkly and fresh. It looked worn, the engraving rubbed off by the touch of a thousand hands. Adric remembered the feel of the robber's breath against his face, the fear he had felt as the man held him against the wall.

Milo took the round and twirled it under his fingers. 'Let me explain something to you,' he said. 'We have to eat, and we don't have much money. Where else will we get food if we don't take it ourselves?'

'People will feed us.'

'Even after Rogren, you believe that people will just take us in?' Milo shook his head and took his fingers away from the coin. 'Most of the people who would help us are starving. They can barely feed themselves.'

'But your family – '

'My family is luckier than most. But we still have to leave here soon. You've already eaten twice your share, and they're not used to feeding me either.'

Adric blushed. He glanced around the room, saw again the pallets scattered on the floor, the slop jars against the wall, the precious wood near the fireplace. He had grown used to the place, no longer saw how small and barren it was. 'No one has said anything.'

'You were sick. You needed the food.' Milo picked up the coin and tossed it, then let it clatter on the table. 'We can't expect everyone to be so generous. Nimble fingers are surer.'

The itch on Adric's back seemed to intensify. He longed to rub the skin against the edge of the table, but he knew that would only make the itch worse. He eyed the coin once, then glanced at Milo. He appeared to be looking elsewhere. Adric reached out and Milo grabbed Adric's wrist.

Milo smiled. 'Nice try. But let me tell you something. Stealing is like a bad magician's magic. You need quick fingers and the ability to divert the other person's attention. If you pretend to be doing something else while you're stealing, you won't get caught. Now, try again.'

Milo released his wrist. Adric leaned against the table and watched the flames flicker against the stone of the hearth. He sat like that for a long time, long enough for his shoulders to grow stiff. Out of the corner of his eye he saw the coin, balanced on a crack in the table. Finally he reached, but his fingers closed on nothing. Milo extended his hand. The coin rested on his palm.

'See?' he said. 'You were watching the coin, not me. And you thought I was watching you. You didn't expect me to take it. Diversion is what it is all about. Diversion and quickness.'

Adric sighed. 'So which do I have to learn first?'

Milo flipped the coin into the air, his smile widening into a grin. 'You'll learn them both together.'

Chapter 17

i

Seymour leaned against the wall behind the entertainers' wing of the servants' quarters. The stone was cool against his back, and the cobblestone dug into his bottom, but the sun was hot. He took another bite of a chicken leg, savoring the warm meat. He hadn't eaten in his entire adult life as well as he had in the past two weeks. He licked his fingers, feeling stuffed, and set the half-eaten leg on the ground beside him.

He leaned back and closed his eyes. The sun warmed his face. He had been sleeping a lot too. If only the luxury would last. But he knew that at some point he would be called to perform for the king as the son of Dysik the Great, and then the sham would end.

'Excuse me, friend, but are you finished with that leg?'

He nodded without opening his eyes. He was so close to sleep that he didn't want to disturb himself.

'Wonderful. Do you mind if I join you?'

He did mind, in a distant sort of way. But the voice was female and deep, husky, almost seductive. Women rarely showed an interest in him. They all wanted to meet Byron. Seymour supposed he could open his eyes and answer her question.

She was small, dressed in a blue magician's robe with a woven gold belt that accented her tiny waist. She had braided her long black hair and wrapped it around her head. At first glance she seemed no more than eighteen, but when she smiled, lines crept into the niches around her eyes. She was nearer his own age, thirty or more, although her movements had the vibrancy of youth.

She apparently took his stare for an affirmative, for she sat beside him. The faint odors of musk and incense rose from her. She picked up the leg, ate the remaining flesh off it, and tossed the bone aside. Two dogs sleeping near the doorway woke when the bone clattered against the stone. They ran for it, each grabbing an end, snarling as they tugged. A dainty white cat walked beneath them, as if they didn't exist.

'I've been watching you,' the woman said. Her black eyes reflected silver against the light. 'You have a guild tattoo.'

Seymour rubbed his tattooed palm against his trousers. 'I was sleeping,' he murmured, hoping that she would go away.

'But it's only eighth class. Have you stopped your training?'

The white cat climbed on Seymour's lap and started purring. It was heavier than it looked. He placed his palm on its back and it licked his arm. He pulled away. The contentment he had felt a moment ago was gone. 'Who are you?'

'Vonda of Kerry.'

'The king's magician?'

She shook her head. Light caught silvery strands of hair woven into her braid. 'That's not a position I want. He's gone through fifteen magicians in thirty years.'

Seymour's fingers found a sensitive spot under the cat's chin. Its purring grew louder. His father's banishment had to have occurred before Seymour was born. The king went through the magicians after his father had left. 'Did you ever hear of Dysik the Great?'

She tapped a finger against her lips. Her hands were small and square, like the hands of a child. 'He was before my time. But I've been told that no one could compare with him.'

'By whom?'

She laughed. 'You ask so many questions! And I came over to find out about you.'

'There's nothing to know.' The cat rubbed its head against Seymour's hand. He rubbed back gently. He wanted to go back to sleep. Any questions about him would eventually lead to a discussion of his ineptness, and he wanted to avoid that.

'Nothing? You're traveling with the bard, aren't you? The new one?'

Seymour sighed. So she actually was interested in Byron. As were all the other women who approached Seymour. A few minutes into every conversation, the women would ask if they could meet Byron. 'I arrived with a bard, yes.'

'And you're a magician. Are you on a mission?'

'No.' Seymour scanned the courtyard. The dogs had finished fighting over the bone and rested against the door once again. Sunlight streamed along the cobblestones and accented the shadows against the walls. The courtyard was empty. He and Vonda were alone.

She tilted her head slightly, giving her face a quizzical expression. 'Then you follow the bard?'

'I don't follow anyone. And I can't see that it's your business.' His sharp tone startled the cat. It jumped off his lap and ran across the courtyard. He closed his eyes and waited for Vonda to leave.

'Oh, I see.' Her robes rustled, then he felt her body heat his arm as she leaned against the wall. 'It's a secret mission.'

He glanced at her, unable to tell if she was joking. 'I saved his life and we're traveling together, all right? Do you have more questions, or can I sleep?'

'Just one.' She put a hand on his arm. Her palm was warm and dry. 'Who are you?'

'My name is Seymour.'

'Son of Dysik the Great?'

He blushed. 'What makes you think that?'

'Rumors. The son of Dysik the Great traveling with one of the bard guild's most talented and secretive members.' Her voice lilted with amusement. 'You don't hide your feelings very well, friend Seymour.'

He brought his knees up to his chest and rested his chin on them. The guard was not supposed to have said anything. Now the entire palace was probably talking.

Vonda squeezed his arm. 'Don't worry,' she said. 'Your secret is safe with me.'

'Apparently it's not a secret,' he said. 'And even if it was, how could I trust you? I don't even know who you are.'

'I'm part of Lady Kerry's entertainment troupe. We were going to leave several days ago, but the isolation proclamation trapped us here.'

Seymour glanced at her. He had never heard of the proclamation before. 'We did have some trouble getting past the guard at the gate.'

'Well, it's impossible to leave,' Vonda said.

Seymour relaxed, let his knees down. 'What's going on?'

'I've heard that the king is in mourning.'

'You're a great one for gossip, aren't you?'

She grinned. The lines crossing her face looked as if they were etched by an artist. 'I'm bored.'

'So that's why you came over here.'

'Partly. I was going to offer to train you. But I'm sure the son of Dysik the Great doesn't need any training.'

Seymour let out a small laugh. 'The son of Dysik the Great can't even mind-tap.'

A troupe of jugglers set up in the far end of the courtyard. They tossed balls that flashed red in the sun. 'Didn't your father train you?' Vonda asked.

The sound of the inn explosion rang through his ears, overlaid with his mother's voice yelling at him to iceheal. 'It didn't go very well.'

'Why don't you let me try?'

One of the jugglers dropped a ball. It bounced and rolled toward the side of the building, the juggler chasing, his skin flushed with embarrassment. Seymour understood the feeling. 'I'm thirty-five years old, Vonda, and by anybody's standards, I should be at least fifth class. My last employer thought death was the only way to cure my ineptness.'

'And what about your bard friend?'

'He doesn't say anything.' Byron hadn't even mentioned that horrible explosion in Coventon, although Afeno had said that Byron asked the Enos to heal Seymour. Sometimes Seymour thought it would be easier if they did talk.

'I see.' Vonda picked at the grass growing between the cobblestones. 'Why don't you let me try anyway?'

'No.'

'If the king is in mourning, we're stuck here for weeks. I don't want to sit around.'

Seymour frowned. He had heard nothing about anyone dying. 'What's the king in mourning for?'

'His son died. They say that his air left him and he died.'

A ghost of a memory touched Seymour's mind. 'Fluid in his lungs?'

Vonda shrugged. 'I don't know what the official story was.' She glanced at him. 'You know healing?'

'Some.' His sudden knowledge surprised him. He usually had trouble remembering any spells, even herb witch spells.

'The son of Dysik the Great has a lot of secrets.'

Seymour didn't want to talk anymore. He closed his eyes. 'The son of Dysik the Great is tired.'

'Let me know when you want to start training,' she said. He heard her skirts rustle as she stood to leave. He didn't move. Eventually her footsteps rang over the cobblestones as she left the courtyard.

ii

Milord:

They have entered royal lands. I will wait until an opportune moment and then strike. The Lady Kerry is here with her entertainers and spies. I trust that she too will attempt to kill the bard, but I will be there first. No one uses magic to embarrass Corvo.

I plan to move slowly. I don't know who the bard's powerful magician is, and until I discover that, I will be very cautious. Be assured, my lord, that he will die before the appointed time.

The king, as you know, is in mourning. I have several weeks to work. I will wait one week before putting any plan into action. I hope to hear from you by then.

Corvo

iii

The night was dark and chill. Torches hanging from the walls of the courtyard in the entertainers' quarters only ate at part of the darkness. The rest slipped in shadows across the stone walls, down the stone floors, and into the corners. Seymour leaned against a pile of coats that had been thrown by the wall. He sipped on a tankard of ale and watched the musicians tune their instruments.

The musicians – a horn player, a lute player, a drummer, a fiddler, and a piper – stood at the opposite end of the courtyard from Seymour. They leaned together, planned tunes, and stopped often to tune their instruments. Byron usually played on these nights, sometimes alone, sometimes with the group. This time he had given his lute to Colin, who stood beneath a nearby torch, clutching the lute for dear life.

The music started again, mournful and slow, taking a moment to find its rhythm. The dancers gathered in the middle of the courtyard, the place of the most light and the most shadows. Seymour squinted. He saw Byron, wearing his customary black, holding the hand of a young woman from another troupe. As the music's pace grew, the dancers swung into movement. The women's feet were bare. Their skirts rose above their ankles as they twirled. Seymour could see flashes of thigh in the half-light, and he wondered why he just watched. He should have been out there too, dancing with a woman that he would take to his bed.

The piper began a lilting melody that rose above the rest of the instruments. The dancers whirled to its sound. Patterns formed and disappeared, the steps grew more frenzied and intricate, the music louder and louder. People behind him began clapping, as if the music controlled their hands.

Then the dancers broke apart and joined their audience in clapping to the rhythm. Byron and his partner remained in the middle. He caught her in his arms and twirled her, her skirt rising, displaying her feet and legs to the crowd. Her laughter mingled with the pipes. The music slowed, and they separated, gripping each other's waists as the piper began again. Around they spun, kicking and laughing as they went. The clapping grew louder, the dance grew wilder, until Byron and his partner became a blur of colorful clothes and flesh flying around the cobblestones.

The music rose in pitch, swelled, and stopped. The couple didn't expect the ending. They tried to stop spinning, lost their balance, and fell together against the stones. Byron emerged from the tangle of skirts, then helped the woman up. The musicians started another rollicking number, and she tried to drag him into a dance, but he shook his head and let go of her arm. He grabbed a tankard of ale from Afeno and drank deeply, then handed the tankard back, wiped his mouth with his sleeve, and walked toward Seymour, ignoring the women who tugged his arm.

'Don't you dance, Seymour?' Byron's hair was damp, and his shirt clung to him.

Seymour snuggled against the coats, content in the slight chill. 'I think watching is a lot more relaxing.'

Byron sat next to him, took Seymour's ale, and drank. 'I agree. That was a bit much.'

'You're a good dancer,' Seymour said.

Byron smiled, shook the water out of his hair, and leaned against the coats. 'In my profession you have to be.' He took a deep breath and let it out. 'I'll be so glad when this waiting is over.'

Seymour glanced at him. The torchlight caressed Byron's face, making him look younger. He had never mentioned the long wait before. 'We might be here for a few more weeks.'

Byron didn't move, but Seymour sensed tension rippling through him. 'Where did you hear that?'

'That's the gossip.' Seymour grabbed a coat sleeve and draped it across his arm. He was getting goose bumps. 'They say the king is in mourning. His son died.'

'His son?' Byron sat up. He put a hand on Seymour's leg. Byron's palm was damp and too warm. 'What happened?'

Seymour shook his head. 'I don't know. The woman who told me wasn't too sure. She said that's why we're doing all of this waiting.'

The music grew louder as another fiddler and piper from a different troupe joined in. Nearly everyone was dancing now, clapping, laughing, and shouting. A few of the king's retainers, who always watched the evening entertainment from a distance, allowed women to drag them into the dance.

'No one else seems to be mourning,' Byron said.

Seymour picked up his tankard. The ale was lukewarm and tasted sour. 'It's only a rumor.'

Byron stared at the musicians, all from different troupes, playing together. 'In a few days we'll all be fighting for a place at the king's table,' he said. His voice sounded hollow. 'You've worked up something, haven't you?'

Seymour felt panic rise. The change of subject startled him. 'I have something,' he lied. Maybe he would ask Vonda for help. He had been practicing all of the spells he knew, but they seemed even more hopeless than before. Simple spells that he had been able to perform in the past seemed even more difficult to him. He blamed the explosion. He kept hearing it every time he chanted his luck web.

A man stepped under the torchlight behind the musicians. He wore deep red robes that grabbed the firelight and made it seem brighter. He was bald and his lack of hair made his face seem both old and young at the same time. When he moved his hand, rings glittered.

Seymour finished his ale. He set the tankard aside and stared at the bald man. His presence marked something different. He was not a member of the entertainment troupe, nor was he a magician. He looked almost like gentry, although Seymour had never seen the deep red colors before. The man walked through the clappers at the edge of the crowd. When he reached the inner circle, the retainers stopped dancing. Other dancers, sensing something wrong, stopped too. The musicians brought their instruments down one by one, until a single pipe held and then faded.

Byron leaned forward. 'What is going on?'

Seymour pointed at the bald man. 'That man stopped this.'

'Lord Boton.' Byron burrowed back into the coats, trying to make himself small. 'Maybe there is something to your rumor after all, Seymour.'

The lord was speaking to the retainers. Seymour could hear the deep bass of the lord's voice, but not his words. As he spoke, he moved his hands, and his rings caught the light, sending flashes of glare into the crowd. When he finished speaking, the retainers nodded, then spoke to members of the crowd. One young retainer, his face flushed, leaned over as he passed Byron and Seymour.

'Lord Boton asks that we bed down for the night,' the retainer said.

'What's going on?' Byron asked.

The retainer shrugged. 'I guess we're disturbing the king.'

'We haven't disturbed him before,' Byron said.

'We haven't been this loud before.' Seymour stretched and moved away from the coats. The retainer moved to a small group standing beneath the torches. His voice, asking them to bed down, carried across the wind.

Byron didn't move. He appeared to be watching the lord.

'I'll get Colin and Afeno,' Seymour said, but he didn't leave.

Byron nodded. He waited until the lord left the courtyard, then he stood up. 'The king's son,' he said. 'Interesting.'

iv

The noise in the courtyard faded. The king leaned against his headboard, the blanket warm across his feet. The fire in the hearth had faded, leaving a chill that wouldn't go away. Constance slept beside him, the shadows under her eyes deep. He pushed the hair off her forehead and tucked the blanket around her shoulder. Ever since the death of their son, she had looked gray and old.

He probably didn't look any better himself. He didn't feel any better. For too many nights he hadn't slept and too many mornings he hadn't wanted to wake up. Constance was right. They knew why this was happening, and he had to stop it. He was fifty-five years old, fat, and ill. He would not live much longer.

The headboard dug into his back. He picked up his pillow and adjusted it. The hearth glowed orange, bathing the room in the colors of dawn. If he died without an heir, Kensington would ascend to the throne. Kensington was a good man, but a distant relation. He knew little of the rules that governed the monarchy, and perhaps even lacked the white mists – whatever good that had done the king and his family. The Cache Enos were supposed to protect his family and they had done nothing. The king sighed. He had done nothing either, and he would have to. Should he die without an heir, the council – or the Enos – might not accept Kensington. The nobles – Boton, Ewehl, a few others on the council – might want to seize power themselves. He was certain that was why all ten of his children had died. The succession was in doubt. There would be war.

He slid down in the bed and brought the covers up to his chin. If there was war, the Enos would use the power hidden in the Cache to wipe the humans from the land. Gerusha had set up that pact. Each succeeding monarch had worked to protect it. Now, with Constance drained and his own life force weak, he risked losing what had been built during the centuries.

He had to have an heir, and he had to protect that heir. Constance was not strong enough to bear another loss, and he doubted that he would live until the child reached adulthood. Constance had suggested that another woman, a young woman, become his consort and bear his children. He put his hand on his wife's shoulder. He did not want another woman. He did not want another child.

He cuddled against her back and wrapped his arms around her waist. If only one of his children had lived, he would abdicate power now, let that child make the decisions that he had always hated to make.

'Constance,' he whispered, wishing he had no more worries, wishing he could sleep as she did, wishing that he had the option, the courage, to die in his sleep.

V

The great arched hallway leading into the kitchen was crowded. Seymour stood next to a small suit of armor that crouched expectantly near the wide double doors leading into the banquet hall. The woman next to him, a piper from another troupe, rubbed her hands over her instrument as if trying to warm it. Byron had his back to Seymour. Colin and Afeno peered into the banquet hall. The rich, greasy scent of roast pig was making Seymour nauseous. He stuck his shaking hands into his pockets and closed his eyes.

He should have left as he had planned, when he arrived, after he was sure that Byron was settled. But Byron's moods had fluctuated so rapidly, and his usual confidence seemed to disappear so often, that Seymour didn't want to leave. Besides, he had enjoyed the food and the rest. Now he had to pay for it.

Someone tapped him on the shoulder. He opened his eyes to find Colin beside him. 'You haven't looked yet, Seymour.'

That was right; he hadn't looked. He didn't want to know what he was facing. But he took a deep breath and peered around the corner. Rows of diners sat down two long tables. Another table faced them, and in the center of that table sat the king and his party. The king was a big man with a wide red face. A small woman sat beside him, her graying hair in a bun. The bald man sat a few seats down, next to a man who was so thin he seemed almost skeletal. No one spoke as they ate. The only noise that accompanied the scrape of plates was the music from the Kerry entertainment troupe.

It performed in the box created by the tables. Vonda moved along the head table, performing hand tricks. She had promised not to use any of the tricks that she had taught him, and as far as he could tell, she had kept her word. He wished she had been right about the mourning period. They had been at the palace another week when the king finally opened his hall to entertainers. In that time Seymour had learned one trick fairly well and several poorly. Vonda told him that all he needed to do was relax, but for Seymour, relaxation and magic did not mix.

Byron approached Seymour beside the door. Byron wore his lute over his back. His mouth was drawn thin and his thick brows nearly met over his nose. Small lines had appeared in the corners of his eyes. He did not glance into the banquet hall, and he hadn't spoken a word since they started to wait. His nervousness made Seymour nervous. If Byron was frightened, something would go wrong.

Colin and Afeno had moved away from the door and cleared a small space to practice their juggling act. Byron had been trying to teach them in the few weeks that they had been at the palace, but the boys were unable to work together. Other performers caught stray balls, and one hit the suit of armor, creating a clang that made Seymour's ears ring. Earlier that day, Byron had borrowed jester suits from another troupe, and Seymour was glad that he had. At least the boys' mistakes would look planned.

Seymour moved away from the door and looked at the other troupes. Most seemed bored, although some huddled in small groups, practicing. A thin man stood on the other side of the hallway, watching Byron. Seymour frowned. He thought he had seen the man before. A long scar cut into the man's profile, adding depth to his face.

Seymour leaned against the wall, closed his eyes, and checked his luck web. It still hugged him. Servants pushed through the crowd of entertainers and into the banquet hall, removing plates. Other servants carried trays of cakes into the room. The banquet had already run six courses. Seymour had been standing for two hours. He didn't know how much longer he could wait.

The Kerry troupe's musicians began their closing number, a short ballad composed to honor the king. Byron snapped his fingers. 'This is it,' he whispered.

Seymour's shaking grew. He remembered the explosion, his father's voice calling him a failure, his mother telling him to iceheal, iceheal. The ballad ended and the Kerry troupe hurried in. Vonda followed the last musician into the hall. She touched Seymour's arm and smiled at him. He looked away.

Byron slung his lute into position and walked slowly into the center of the banquet hall. His black clothes added to his slenderness and made him look taller. He stopped before the king's table and hesitated, staring at the monarch. For a moment Seymour thought Byron would forget to bow, but then he did. When he stood, he extended a hand toward the troupe.

Seymour couldn't hear from the doorway, but he could tell from the hand signals when to enter. Colin ran in, purposely tripped, and slid into position next to Byron. The boy stood and bowed before the king. Then Afeno ran toward the head table, his body unusually close to the tables lining the left wall. When he reached the head table, he bowed and slowly rose, extending two bouquets of spoons to the monarch. The king gaped and the diners laughed. Afeno tossed the spoons to Colin, who returned them to their places.

The toss was Seymour's cue. He took a deep breath, feeling a tremble at the base of his stomach. Then he clenched his fists and murmured the words to his fireball spell. A tiny flame appeared in his hand. He tried to ignore it, tried not to see it get big, explode, and eat the night sky, as it had so often in his dreams. The flame grew as he approached the king, the red and orange hues mixing with the air currents like paint on an artist's pallet. When Seymour reached Byron, he whispered another incantation and the flame became a rose.

A gasp echoed through the banquet hall and destroyed his detachment. He felt the heat against his palm, and the rose shattered into a thousand tiny flames that fell to the floor like rain. He was losing control. He tried to stamp out the flames before they reached a table, but some skittered away from him. The diners laughed, thinking it part of the routine, and then they started to applaud.

'Bow,' Byron whispered, and Seymour obeyed automatically. One small flame licked the tablecloth near the king's feet. Seymour rubbed his fingers against his palm, calling the stray flames to himself. They flew to his hands, leaving a piece of charred cloth smoking across from him. Then he felt heat sear his hand. He tried to shake the flames off, and when that didn't work, he called the iceheal spell his mother had taught him so long ago. The flame danced upward, away from the ice that now encased his hand. The crowd watched the flame soar. Seymour whistled for it, knowing that a flame wouldn't come twice in a row, but it did, slowly returning to the ground.

The flame did not settle on Seymour, though; it landed on the main table. Colin turned to the table beside him, grabbed a water pitcher, and tossed water at the flame. The flame hissed as it disappeared, but the water kept flying, finally hitting the thin lord in the face. He sputtered, slid back, and stood as a roar of laughter echoed in the hall. The lord turned, face dripping, to the king, and for the first time the monarch laughed too.

The king gasped for air, then let his laughter die. He clapped his hands. Two servants appeared beside him. 'See to Lord Ewehl.' The servants took linen napkins and started to wipe the lord's face. The lord grabbed the napkins and waved the servants away.

'Young man,' the king said to Byron, 'sing for us. I don't want to laugh anymore.'

Byron nodded to Seymour and the boys. Afeno brought Byron a stool, then the three of them went to the edge of the hall. Byron sat on the stool, his face composed, his body rigid. He placed one foot on the floor and the other on a rung just above. His face was white. Seymour clasped his hands together, wincing as he touched ice. It wasn't over yet. He couldn't relax until Byron was done.

Byron positioned the lute, placing his left hand around the neck and holding his right fingers above the strings. He bowed his head slightly and said, 'I will play whatever your highness desires.'

'A battle song.' The king's smile seemed small and impish on his wide face. 'In keeping with your performance.'

'And what is your favorite battle song, Highness?'

The room grew quiet and so did the hallway. If the bard did not play the song requested, he could be imprisoned for mocking the king. Colin put his hand on Seymour's arm, and Seymour could feel the boy trembling.

The king appraised Byron for a moment, all laughter gone. Then, seemingly assured that Byron was serious, the king nodded. 'I don't know the name of the ballad because I haven't heard it for a long time. The tale it tells is of King Gerusha's victory over the six island kingdoms.'

'A favorite of mine as well, my liege. It has many titles. For this evening, we shall call it "The King's Battle Song."' Byron's long fingers found several chords. His expression softened as he played the melody once through and then he began to sing. His voice was warm and deep and fluid, carrying the words as if to a lover. The song told the history of Gerusha's campaigns and concentrated on the ancient king's heroism. And then Byron sang a verse that Seymour had never heard before:

'Strength, some say, will make a man
and wisdom is his tool
'Twas heart on which Gerusha ran
and compassion led his rule.'

The king stood suddenly, his chair falling behind him. 'Stop, bard,' he said hollowly.

Byron stopped singing, his fingers still poised over the lute strings. He appeared calm as he faced the king, but Seymour could see his left hand trembling.

'Where did you learn that lyric?'

'Which, sire?'

The king's eyes seemed to have sunken into his face. 'The last.'

'An old bard told me them, sire, after I sang the ballad in Lord Dakin's lands. He chastized me for singing the ballad before a mere lord, saying the ballad was written for the royal family, those who would follow in Gerusha's path. And then he told me that I had forgotten a verse and gave me that one.'

'And the bard's name?'

Byron shook his head. 'He would not tell me, sire.'

Seymour wanted to look away but couldn't. Colin had slid closer to him, almost hiding behind him.

A servant picked up the king's chair, but the king did not sit in it. 'That was Adric's favorite verse,' he said softly. 'My oldest son.'

A slight flush rose in Byron's cheeks. 'Sire, I – '

'Don't apologize. You couldn't know. No one remembers him now.' The king ran a thick hand over his face. The woman beside him touched his arm. He put his hand on her shoulder. 'You are very talented, young man. What is your name?'

Byron paused, and when he spoke, his voice came out small. 'Byron, sire.'

'And where are you from, Byron?'

Byron took his hands from the strings and slung the lute over his back. 'I'm late of Lord Dakin's lands.'

'Why didn't he cling to such an adept bard?'

Seymour put his arm around Colin, glad for the warmth. The ice on his hand sent shivers down his back.

'I am quite outspoken, sire,' Byron said, 'and I'm afraid I insulted his pride once too often.'

'Aren't you afraid of insulting me?'

'No, sire.'

'And why not?'

'You are a greater man than Lord Dakin, and therefore harder to insult.'

The king laughed. The sound echoed in the large room. The diners watched but did not join in. 'And you are naive, young man. The greater the man, the quicker his pride is stung. Remember that, Byron of Dakin.'

Byron nodded.

The king helped his lady to her feet. 'I have had enough merriment for one evening. Thank you, young man.' He took a sip from his goblet, then led the lady out of the banquet hall, guards trailing them.

When the king had disappeared, the other diners slid their chairs back and relaxed. Conversation hummed throughout the room. Byron got off the stool. Colin moved away from Seymour. Byron passed them without even looking at them.

Seymour hurried out of the hall and caught up to Byron. The corridor outside the banquet hall was emptying. Byron looked haggard, his back bowed as if his lute weighed twice as much as usual.

'Byron, I'm sorry – '

'What do you have to be sorry about?' Byron's voice sounded older, coarser, with no music in it.

Seymour held out his ice-encased hand. 'I failed. I'm so sorry.'

Byron touched Seymour's shoulder. 'You did well this evening. Everyone thought you were funny. I was the one who failed.'

'But you couldn't have known what the king would choose.'

Byron shook his head. 'I expected to walk in and amaze them all. I imagined them all silent because of my audacity and my talent. And when I finished, I expected the king to stand up and ask me my name, then tell me that he wanted me as his official bard. The king's bard. Such dreams I have. Such silly dreams.'

'You did amaze them,' Seymour said. 'What happened was not your fault.'

Byron smiled, and there was a sadness to it. 'You're a good friend. I'm sorry that I proposed this scheme in the first place.'

'Propose another, and I'll go with you.' The words startled Seymour because he knew they were true.

'They'll probably ask you to stay after tonight. Maybe even be the king's magician.'

'The king has gone through fifteen magicians in thirty years. I value my life too much. I told you once before, I only have so much luck. I think I used most of it against Lord Dakin's hounds.'

'Does that mean you wouldn't stay if they ask?'

'It does.'

Byron shook his head. 'You're a strange one, Seymour.'

'No stranger than you, friend bard,' Seymour said. 'No stranger than you.'

vi

Milord:

He keeps himself guarded constantly. Someone is always around him. I will have to attempt an attack when he is surrounded by people. He performed before the king last night, and the king noticed him. If the bard is dismissed after this recognition, I will have no trouble assassinating him. But if the king decides to keep him on, the bard's death will be noticed. I will send you further communications should events change.

Corvo

vii

Three candles resting on the table sent an orange glow around Seymour's corner of the room. Byron slept near the wall, on his back, his arms flung above his head. Seymour leaned against the wall. The stone was cool and damp. He hated stone buildings, hated their coldness, their dampness. Wood felt warm and friendly, although wood burned so easily.

Seymour's hand tingled as it thawed. A small heart-shaped burn had formed on his palm. He sighed, wishing the ice would disappear faster. He had spent so many nights like this, sitting up in his room, waiting for the ice to melt from his hands. He would burn himself often and his father would always yell to him:

Concentrate, Seymour. Concentrate!

His father's anger always made things worse. Seymour would conjure a fire, his father would yell, Seymour would lose control and the fire would engulf his hand. His father would call his mother, and she would iceheal Seymour. She finally taught Seymour the iceheal spell so that he could do fire spells on his own.

Funny that he hadn't used the iceheal when the room exploded in Coventon.

He should have known better than to trade spells from those magicians. He had a limited repertoire of spells and he didn't dare add to them. He was an eighth-level magician and would never be anything more. When Byron woke up, they would talk about Seymour's abilities and see if together they could find something else for him to do.

The last of the ice chipped away, leaving his palm red and wet. The burn glowed white against the redness. Seymour opened a jar and rubbed some cooling ointment on the burn. He had made the ointment when he started his lessons with Vonda, knowing that he had to be prepared should anything go wrong. The lessons had lulled him; he hadn't made a single mistake. He should have known that everything would fall apart during the performance.

The ointment soothed the burn, making the whiteness seem less fierce. He should have become a healer instead of a magician. Healing was calming, just as magic was violent.

But he was not a healer. He had almost left the iceheal on too long. The last thing he needed was frostbite. But the ice kept the swelling down and kept the burn from going deeper. In a few hours, when the pain started, he would apply the spell again.

Seymour glanced at Byron. He had rolled onto his side, muttering and tossing his head. He looked haggard in the dim light. Seymour would never have been able to fall asleep after such a disappointing evening. But Byron used sleep as healing. Seymour would wait until he was completely exhausted before trying to sleep. By then Byron's tossing would end.

A scratching on the door made Seymour sit up. He knocked the table, causing the candles to flicker. He grabbed the holders to steady the flames. Then he held his breath, waiting to see if the scratching would come again. It did, accompanied by a whisper.

'Seymour? You awake?'

'Who is it?' he whispered back.

'Vonda.'

Seymour felt a flush rise in his cheeks. He didn't want her to see him, didn't want her comments about his performance. But he had already acknowledged his wakefulness, and he couldn't very well turn her away. He got up. The stones were cold against his bare feet. He pulled the heavy oak door open. 'What are you doing here? It's almost dawn.'

'I couldn't get away any sooner.' Vonda slipped inside, her blue robes glimmering gold in the candlelight. Seymour closed the door behind her. 'I came to see how your hand is.'

He put a finger to his lips and nodded toward Byron. She glanced at the sleeping man, then stared. Seymour couldn't see the expression on her face, but he could feel the fascination. He sighed and sat down. He didn't blame her. Byron was the interesting one. He was good-looking and flamboyant, and very much alone. Seymour was alone too, but his features were plain and his manner dull. Now that he had shown what a fool he was to the entire entertainment wing, he didn't blame Vonda for turning her attention to Byron.

'Well?' Vonda whispered.

Seymour looked up, surprised that she was speaking to him. She held out her hand, and it took him a moment to remember what she wanted. He finally turned his hand palm up. She moved a candle closer and crouched, running her finger along the edge of the burn. 'It's not as bad as I suspected,' she said. 'It almost looks like someone icehealed it.'

'I did.'

'Really?' She looked younger in the darkness. The webs around her eyes had disappeared. He wanted to touch her to make sure they were still there.

'My mother taught me how. I used to burn myself a lot.'

'And the ointment that's on there?'

'I made it.'

'Oh.' Her laugh sounded funny. 'Then you don't need this.' She pulled a jar of ointment from her robes. Seymour could smell the mallow leaves, part of a simple child's potion.

He took the jar from her and set it beside him. 'I appreciate it,' he said. 'I'll need it as this heals.'

Her smile was uncertain. She knew as well as he did that her ointment only soothed. The water-based liquid he had placed on his burn would heal it.

'Seymour, I – '

'Shhh,' he murmured. He cupped her elbow with one hand and brought her closer. Her eyes were wide and dark, the silver glow in the center almost gone. He put a finger beneath her chin and tilted her face toward his. Her breath caressed his skin. He leaned forward and brushed her lips with his own, then waited. She did not pull away. Instead she wrapped her arms around his neck and drew him closer. Her body was warm and soft against his. He let his hands slide down her back, and he kissed her again, this time tasting her.

Byron screamed. His cry was high and desperate and ragged. He thrashed on the pallet, striking out against the wall.

Seymour let go of Vonda and hurried to the pallet. He crouched beside Byron, grabbed his shoulders, and eased him away from the wall. Byron grabbed Seymour's wrists so tightly that he cut off the circulation. Byron screamed again, then the scream broke off, and he sat up, his eyes wild and frightened.

'You all right?' Seymour asked. His heart was pounding heavily. Byron had had dreams before, but never like this.

Byron blinked and slowly the fear left his face. He took a deep breath. His entire body was shaking. He let go of Seymour's wrists and the blood came back, making the wrists ache.

'I haven't had that nightmare for years.'

Seymour sat on the edge of the pallet. 'You want to tell me about it? Sometimes they seem less real if you talk about them.'

Byron grabbed a corner of the blanket and rubbed his cheek. The shaking eased. 'I can't.'

Then he looked up and saw Vonda. A mask fell across his face. 'I'm sorry,' he said. 'You have company.'

'Vonda's been training me,' Seymour said. 'Vonda, my friend Byron.'

Vonda approached the pallet. She looked down, her expression as cold and empty as Byron's. 'They say recurring dreams are brought on by past sins.'

'They're probably right.' Byron hadn't moved. 'Vonda of Kerry?'

'The same. And you're Byron now?'

Something flickered across his face, but the expression disappeared too quickly for Seymour to catch. 'That's what I'm called.'

'I thought it was Dasvid.'

'Your memory plays tricks on you, Vonda.' Byron smoothed the blanket, then reclined, resting on one elbow.

'My memory is quite sharp, Byron. I've been watching you since you arrived, wondering what you're doing here. You've learned a lot since you were in Kerry. Even your humility is gone.'

Seymour moved away from them. The air had turned cold, and shivers ran up and down his spine.

Byron smiled, but his eyes held no warmth. 'The humility is bound to return after last night.'

'Ah, yes.' Vonda clenched her small hands in her lap, as if that were the only way she could control them. 'When did you get such an extensive repertoire? And when did you start taking such great risks?'

'Why attack me, Vonda? I never did anything to you.'

Vonda leaned closer, her face almost touching his. 'No. But you nearly killed the Lady Kerry.'

Seymour held his breath.

'I did nothing of the sort.'

'Her daughter died the night you disappeared.'

'Diana?' Byron's mask fell away. 'I had heard she was dead, but I didn't know. I – '

'You what?'

Seymour winced at Vonda's tone. The light hit half of her face, extending her features, making her almost ugly.

'You think I killed her?'

'Who else could it have been?'

Byron's fists were clenched around the blanket. 'I never touched her. She was a friend of mine.'

'She died with your name on her lips.'

'Why didn't you contact me?'

'Because we couldn't find you. You had disappeared.'

'I had to leave.' Byron pulled the blanket tighter. 'If you remember, you were one of the ones who drove me out.'

Vonda brushed her hair away from her face. 'You were dangerous. You still are. I can feel it in the air around you. No one is safe as long as you're alive.'

'So that's why you befriended Seymour? To spy on me?'

Seymour looked away. He called an iceheal, cradled his hand to his chest. He knew it. Vonda being just his friend was too much to ask. Byron was the only person who liked Seymour for himself.

'Don't be ridiculous,' Vonda said. 'I wasn't even sure it was you.'

Byron tossed the blanket aside. He grabbed his trousers and slipped them on, apparently not caring that Vonda saw his nakedness. 'I won't sleep any more tonight. I'll leave you two.' He buttoned up his pants, then grabbed a shirt, and slipped it over his head. 'And Vonda, the night I left, I told Diana something that I had never told anyone else. Maybe you should try to find out who she might have seen, who she might have told.'

'You think you have a secret that people would kill for?'

Byron smiled but said nothing. He let himself out the door and eased it shut behind him. The click echoed in the stillness. Seymour couldn't look at Vonda.

'Did you befriend me to spy on Byron?' Seymour whispered.

She shook her head. 'I was watching you before I noticed him.'

'You mentioned him that first day.'

She came over to him, put her hand on his knee. She was the Vonda he knew again, soft features, warm eyes. 'Byron's different, so much more confident.'

'He just hides his fears better.' Seymour thought back to the night Lord Dakin had appeared in the inn. Byron had panicked that night. He didn't always hide his fears well.

One of the candles guttered, sending dark smoke into the room. 'Seymour,' Vonda said. 'I'm going to tell you something that you can't tell anyone, not even Byron. Can you keep a secret from him?'

Seymour shrugged. He didn't know what he could do right now. Byron didn't trust Vonda and Vonda didn't trust Byron. Seymour trusted them both, and yet he didn't trust either of them. Byron wore many faces and Vonda withheld information.

She bowed her head, her long hair falling like water around her face. 'Tomorrow everyone will learn that I have quit Lady Kerry's troupe. She's leaving me here to watch Byron.'

'Why?'

'To find out who he is, and why he killed Diana.'

Seymour jerked away, letting Vonda's hand fall off his knee. 'He didn't kill her. He said so.'

'I don't believe him.'

'Well, I do!' The cold in Seymour's hand had gone to his bones. He chanted away the iceheal, hoping the ice would melt quickly. 'I don't want to be used in something that would hurt him.'

Vonda frowned. 'Do you follow him, Seymour?'

'He's my friend! Are magicians incapable of simple friendship? Why does everyone ask me that?'

'You defend him so strongly.'

'I'll continue to defend him until he shows me that I can't.' Seymour sighed. He took sides, even against himself. 'Why don't you leave, Vonda?'

She brushed her hair back, stood, and stared at him for a moment. Then she walked to the door. 'I do care about you, Seymour,' she said, and let herself out.

Seymour blew out the candles and crawled onto the pallet. It was still warm from Byron's body. Things were never simple. He always had to make choices. With luck they would leave in a day or so, and he wouldn't be in the middle of Byron and Vonda anymore. He lay down and closed his eyes. He knew that sleep wouldn't come, but he didn't care. He sighed once, and pretended to relax.

viii

The breakfast chamber seemed small with both Boton and Ewehl at the table. The king wished Constance was beside him, but she had said that he would have to start doing business on his own. Sunlight streamed in the floor-to-ceiling windows, illuminating the congealing eggs, the overdone sausage.

'You haven't had a bard in years, my liege,' Ewehl said. 'Why start now?'

The king pushed his plate away. He hated doing business during meals. 'Because I like the man. He's the most talented bard Ive seen for a long time.'

'He upset you during his performance,' Boton said. He had finished his meal. A small drop of egg had landed on his collar.

'The ballad was my choice,' the king said.

'I don't like him.' Ewehl ate another piece of sausage and talked through the food. 'He insulted me in front of the entire hall. He admitted that he was outspoken, and his troupe obviously has no control.'

The king stared at Ewehl. With his dark skin, emaciated face, and beady eyes, the man looked like a snake. 'I haven't laughed that hard in months, Ewehl. I will have the bard and his troupe serve me.'

'Let me suggest a compromise,' Boton said. His voice was deep and soothing. The king found himself nodding before he even realized what Boton had said. Old habits, he reminded himself, and concentrated on the breakfast. 'Hire the bard but not his troupe.'

'No.' Ewehl set down his fork. 'I don't like the man. I don't want him in the palace.'

The king sighed. He didn't want to fight these two. If he was finding it so difficult to fight over a bard, he would have even more trouble when he announced his decision to find a new consort.

The king snapped his fingers. The servant standing by the door hurried to his side. 'Bring the bard to me.'

'I oppose this, sire,' Ewehl said.

'I know.' The king looked at his plate. He had eaten only half of his eggs and one of his sausages. No more meetings over meals. He would waste all of his food.

He snapped his fingers again and two servants removed the plates. Two other servants set cups of tea on the table. Then the door opened and the bard walked in. He wore the same clothes he had worn the night before, and he had his lute slung over his shoulder. Deep shadows ran under his eyes, and his skin looked pale. He seemed almost as tired as Constance. The bard glanced at Boton and Ewehl, and then bowed. 'Highness.'

'I want to make a request,' the king said.

The bard stood and eased his lute into position. 'Anything, sire.'

'Do you travel without your troupe?'

The bard flushed, then ran a hand through his dark hair. 'No.'

The king folded his hands on the table and then leaned forward. 'I have need of a bard but not an entire troupe. You will not perform without them?'

'I will perform without them, sire, but I will not travel without them. I'm responsible for them.'

The king nodded. 'Good. Then we will find jobs around the palace for them. And you will serve me as my bard.'

The bard bowed and rose, his eyes sparkling. 'Thank you, sire.'

'The servant who brought you in will take you to your new quarters.'

The bard bowed again and followed the servant out of the room.

Boton watched him go. 'I don't care for the man much either,' he said. 'Perhaps we can make this a limited appointment.'

'The man is hired.' The king pushed his chair away from the table and stood. 'He is my bard until I say otherwise. Is that understood?'

Both lords nodded. The king strode across the room and let himself into the hallway. It was cooler than the breakfast room. His stomach rumbled, unhappy with the food. He sighed. He didn't have any more strength than he had had thirty years ago. He should have fought then, when he was younger. He had no choice now.

He walked down the hall. He would join Constance. She would soothe him. He wondered if she would do that after the new consort was chosen. He certainly hoped so.

Chapter 18

The canopy of large trees above Milo and Adric covered them with cool shade. High, fluting calls echoed above them, and below, something buzzed and then stopped. Adric took shallow breaths. His back ached, and he wished more than once that Milo had not let the horse free when they arrived in the village.

They were getting closer to the palace. Adric was sweating even though he was cool. Milo wanted to find someone to take them in, but Adric hoped they could get past the guard on their own. They agreed that if someone passed, they would ask for help into the palace. They were posing as brothers looking for work, and indeed, Adric had never felt closer to anyone.

'Shhh.' Milo grabbed Adric's arm. 'I hear something.'

Adric cocked his head. He heard it too – the rhythmic clip-clop of horse hooves. He moved to the side of the road, grass tickling the bottom of his bare feet. Through the trees he could see a single horseman leaning over his mount.

'Remember,' Milo said. Adric nodded. He would not say anything about who he was. He would let Milo do the talking.

The horseman rounded the bend. He was an older man, a guard that Adric had seen but never spoken to. He never traveled alone. Usually he had one or two valets to help him with his equipment.

Milo put one foot into the road and waved. 'Excuse me, sir,' he said.

The guard stopped. 'What?'

'My brother and I are looking for work.'

'Plenty of work in Anda.'

Milo shook his head. 'We've just come from there.'

The guard examined them. His eyes were round, and thick jowls hung around his mouth. 'You're runaways.'

Milo lowered his head. 'Yes, sir.'

'Why would I help runaways? I could turn you in and maybe get a reward.'

'No, please don't!' Adric took a step forward. He couldn't bear to return to Rogren. 'We'll do anything, any kind of work.'

The guard nodded, then clucked to his horse. 'Not interested,' he said.

'Wait!' Adric cried. Milo put his hand on Adric's arm to stop him. 'You need a valet, don't you? You never ride without a valet?'

The guard patted his horse and peered at Adric. 'And how do you know that?'

'We've seen you,' Milo said. His voice shook. 'In Anda.'

'Two peasant boys can't valet.'

'I can,' Adric said. 'I can polish a sword, clean boots, maintain your armor, and take care of your horse.'

'Unusual skills for a peasant lad.'

Milo's grip tightened on Adric's arm. 'We're from town.'

The guard let his reins drop and twisted in the saddle to face the boy. 'What are your names, lads?'

Milo spoke up before Adric could answer. 'I'm Milo, he's Ric. We'd be grateful for the work, sir.'

'Will you run away?' the guard asked.

Milo shook his head. Adric glanced at the palace walls, at home. 'We have no need to,' he said.

Chapter 19

Seymour hurried down the hall. A page had summoned him to sit in on the banquet that evening. The palace had a dozen herb witches, but in the past few weeks the injured and sick had sought out Seymour. His cures seemed to work better than even the court physician's. On this night, a troupe of flame throwers, planning to perform for the king, had lost their herb witch in a carriage accident on the way into the palace. They needed someone to watch and be ready in case they lost control of the flames.

Seymour could do that. He figured fire was his specialty.

But he was already late. He hurried past the suits of armor in the large hallway, turned the corner toward the dining room, and was assaulted by the scents of roast beef, quail, and carrots. His stomach rumbled. He hadn't realized how hungry he was. He crossed into the dining room, his ears automatically adjusting to the low hum of conversation. The tables were set up as they had been the night that he had performed for the king, and they were almost all full. He glanced at the head table. The king sat alone. The chair to his right, normally reserved for his wife, was empty.

'Seymour?'

He turned. Byron was seated at the end of the far table, with the lower retainers. He slid a chair back. Seymour sat down. 'What are you doing here?' Byron asked.

Seymour was still breathing rapidly. It felt good to be beside Byron. They hadn't seen each other for days.

'We have some unprotected flame throwers tonight,' he said. 'I take it you're performing.'

Byron nodded. 'Almost every night. I'm the king's prize showpiece. Everyone tries to see if there's a song I don't know.'

'You're the one who set it up that way,' Seymour said.

'I know.'

A server set a bowl of soup in front of Byron and another in front of Seymour. He picked up his spoon. He hadn't realized that the head table was eating. He glanced up there again. The king was on his second course. Seymour took a spoonful. The soup was cold but sweet. He ate quickly, relieved to put something in his stomach.

'I hate these fruit soups,' Byron said, and switched bowls with Seymour. Byron leaned back in his chair to await the next course. He looked good. He still wore his customary black, but his clothing was silk now. The king had ordered three more lutes for him and kept him well fed. Seymour rarely saw Byron these days because Byron spent his free time sword fighting with Afeno and Colin or learning new ballads. Whenever he had a day to himself, he would disappear, and no one seemed to know where he went.

'I saw Afeno today,' Seymour said when he finished the second bowl of soup. 'His hands are getting nicked from all the sword fighting. What are you training them for?'

'I want them to be good enough to be king's retainers,' Byron said. He sat up as the server set the second course in front of him, a plate full of shells. He pried one open with a knife. 'I hate watching them do kitchen labor.'

'Colin seems happy. He likes the serving work.' A server set a plate in front of Seymour. The shells smelled like fish.

'He's too talented for it.'

Seymour picked up a shell. 'What is this?'

'Oysters.' Byron opened his shell, tilted his head back, and swallowed. Then he set the empty shell aside.

'But they haven't been cooked.'

Byron grinned and took a sip of water. 'I know. You eat them raw.'

Seymour glanced beside him. The retainers already had a stack of shells next to their plates. 'Is this customary?' he asked, thinking he would rather be in the kitchen again, getting his pick of the leftovers.

'The king's trying to impress someone.' Byron picked up another shell. 'But I can't tell who.'

'I noticed a few empty seats when I came in,' Seymour said. He picked up a shell. It was dry and hard.

'There are always two for latecomers.'

'Looks like there are more than two.'

'Yes, it does.' Byron glanced at Seymour's plate. 'You going to eat those, Seymour?'

'What do I eat?'

'Watch.' Byron pried open another shell, loosened the meat, tipped his head back, and swallowed.

'You didn't chew it.'

'No. Half the pleasure is in the swallowing.'

Seymour slid his knife into the shell he was holding. The meat looked grayish in the light. He pried the meat loose, tipped his head back as Byron had done, and felt something slide across his tongue. When it reached the back of his throat, he coughed, then forced himself to swallow. 'Ick.'

'You didn't even taste it,' Byron said.

'It's slimy.'

'You're too fussy.'

Semour handed his still full plate to the nearest server. 'You can have these,' he said. 'Enjoy them.'

Byron laughed. 'I miss you, Seymour. Why don't you visit me more often?'

'I'm not the busy one.' A server stopped beside him. Seymour closed his eyes so that he wouldn't see what the server placed in front of him. It smelled like cooked meat. He opened his eyes. A thick slab of beef covered his plate. He sighed. Normal food.

'I've stopped in to see you a few times,' Byron said. 'You were with Vonda.'

'You could have come in.'

Byron shook his head. He cut into his slice of beef. 'The less I see of her, the better.'

Seymour took a bite of beef. It was tender and succulent, and it washed the sliminess of the oysters away. 'You still haven't told me what happened in Kerry,' he said.

Applause scattered through the banquet hall. Byron turned toward the doors. 'There are your flame throwers.'

Seymour took another bite of beef and turned his chair around. They would have to arrive at the same time as the good food – and as soon as he asked Byron about Kerry.

The flame throwers, dressed in bright red, danced around one another in the center of the room. Each performer held a gray rod. Then, as the rods burst into flames, the performers tossed the brands between them.

Seymour watched the flames shimmer in the air. The scar on his hand tingled. He had gotten so frightened of fire that he let someone else light his hearth at night. He hadn't practiced his magic since the night he performed, and he doubted he ever would again.

'Relax,' Byron said. 'I'll be surprised if they need you.'

Seymour made himself look away from the flames. The room smelled of sulfur and smoke. 'When do you perform?'

Byron shrugged. 'Whenever the king wants me to. Sometimes he doesn't ask at all.'

A flame thrower caught the rods as they flew past him and began to stack them end on end. Seymour watched the tower shiver. If the tower fell, flames would skitter along the floor and set the entire room ablaze. The diners seemed unconcerned. They continued talking and eating as if nothing were going on.

The tower grew until it almost reached the ceiling. Then the flame thrower dismantled the tower rod by rod, tossing the burning brands to his companions. Seymour flinched every time a rod flew through the air. The flame throwers continued their juggling act for a few minutes, bowed, and left the room. The applause that followed them was thin and scattered.

A page tapped Byron on the shoulder. He nodded and grabbed his lute. 'Looks like it's my turn,' he said. 'Someone has to liven up the crowd. Why don't you move to the servers' entrance. You'll get a better view.'

Seymour glanced at the table. A server had removed his plate. Seymour got up and pushed his chair in. The servers' entrance was a small door near the head table. Seymour leaned against the wall just beyond the door. He wasn't the only one standing. Other performers, entertainers, and servers lined the walls. The scar-faced man that Seymour had seen the night of their performance stood a few feet away. Seymour had seen the man around the palace a few times, always watching Byron.

Byron pulled his stool into the center of the hall. He leaned against it as he had that first night, one foot resting on a rung. 'Requests, sire?' he asked.

The king shook his head. Byron tuned the lute, then began a light ballad, filled with running chords and bawdy verses. The hall grew quiet.

Vonda stood across the hall. She hadn't seen Seymour. She was staring at Byron, her hands to her temples, her eyes glazed.

Seymour recognized the expression. He had seen it on his father's face when he mind-tapped. She was trying to tap Byron.

The music continued, but Byron stopped singing. His fingers still found the chords and he swayed to the beat. A frown creased his forehead, and Seymour remembered what Afeno had said about the bluff Enos. She had come from the woods, she and Byron had stared at each other, and after she had healed Seymour, they spoke as if they were continuing a conversation. Byron knew how to tap as well. And if he knew how to tap, he knew how to block a tap.

Seymour no longer wanted to be in the hall. His duty was done; he could leave. He pushed off the wall, when the main doors into the hall opened. Two pages held the door and bowed as the Lady Jelwra walked in. She paused, making sure she had the king's gaze, and then curtsied. Her long white dress accented her dark skin, and she wore pearls in her dark hair.

Seymour sank back against the wall, feeling its chill against his shirt. He had to stay now, to see what she would say when she saw Byron. If she revealed him as Geoffry of Kinsmail, and if the king got angry, Seymour would run, find Colin and Afeno, and get them ready to flee the palace as soon as Byron left the banquet hall.

The lady walked behind the diners, greeting those she knew. She acted as if the music provided a backdrop for her entrance. Byron did not turn, but Seymour could tell he was aware of the change in the room. Vonda let her hands fall to her side, the tap apparently unsuccessful.

The lady stopped when she saw Seymour. She chucked her fan under his chin. The wood edges scratched. He couldn't bow as he should have for fear that the fan would dig farther into his soft skin. 'Is your master here?' she asked, her words barely audible above Byron's music.

'I have no master, milady.'

Her smile challenged him. He hated the way it failed to light her eyes. 'Not even the king?'

Seymour blushed, but kept his voice level. 'Besides the king.'

She removed the fan and turned away from Seymour as if he no longer existed, leaving the scent of roses behind her. She rounded the corner to the king's table, patting Lord Boton on the shoulder as she passed. Seymour rubbed his chin and recited a simple heal spell. The scratches stopped itching.

Byron bent over his lute and switched to a lazy instrumental that he often played when trying to calm himself. The battle with Vonda must have been a difficult one. Seymour wished he could signal Byron to warn him about the Lady Jelwra, but even as he stepped out to catch Byron's eye, the lady approached the king.

The ballad broke. Byron's fingers fumbled along the strings. The king had taken the lady's hand, but stopped to look at his bard. Byron recovered with a bridge into a sad ballad. The lady sat beside the king and whispered something without taking her gaze from Byron.

Seymour shoved his hands into his pockets. His palms were sweating but his fingers were cold. He didn't want to leave the palace. He had never been this happy before. He wished she had never appeared. He wanted to go to the king and deny everything she had told him.

Byron finished the ballad with a plaintive note that hung in the air before fading. The applause was warm, but Byron didn't acknowledge it. The lady had not taken her gaze from him, and the king noted her intent stare.

'Byron, play something for Alma.' The king had taken her small hand in his.

Byron lifted his head and met the lady's gaze. Something in his expression made Seymour even colder. Byron got down from the stool and bowed before the head table, his attention on the lady.

'Byron?' The Lady Jelwra's voice was low and mocking. The king looked sharply at her, and Lord Ewehl sat up straighter in his chair.

'Yes, milady.' The lordly posture Byron had had when he first met her had disappeared. He leaned back against the stool, relaxed but deferential.

'My new bard, Alma, the one that I told you about.' The king's voice carried in the quiet room.

'The one who knows every ballad ever written?'

Byron shook his head. His fingers toyed with the strings. 'Not every ballad, milady, but most. I'll play whatever you wish to hear.'

The lady tilted her head. She smiled the same smile she had used with Seymour. 'Do you know any ballads about the Lord of Kinsmail?'

Seymour clenched his fists in his pockets. His fingernails dug into his skin. The scar-faced man grinned as if something amused him.

'Certainly, milady,' Byron said. 'There are several. Is there one in particular that interests you?'

'A ballad about Sir Geoffry, the last Lord of Kinsmail, would interest me greatly.'

Seymour closed his eyes. She was teasing them.

'To my knowledge, milady, there is but one song about the last Lord of Kinsmail, and it does not mention him by name. It runs like this . . . ' Byron strummed a few chords, then sang a song about battles and wars, about a man who had lost everything and still lived for the day he would get his home again.

When he finished, he let the music die before speaking. 'Is that the ballad you meant?'

The king was frowning and the hall was silent. Seymour knew what they were thinking: the Lady Jelwra had stumped the bard. If she said that he had sung the wrong ballad, she would ruin Byron as quickly as if she exposed him as the Lord of Kinsmail.

The lady shrugged and pulled her hand from the king's. 'I had no particular ballad in mind. I had simply heard a legend about the last Lord of Kinsmail, and I wondered if there was a ballad that retold it. Thank you, sir bard.'

Applause began somewhere near Seymour, then scattered around the room. Byron bowed his head, acknowledging it. When it had finished, he turned to the lady. 'Is there something else you would like to hear?'

She studied his face, then shook her head. 'Oh, something about deception and lies and love.'

'Your wish, milady.' Byron ran his fingers across the strings and began a ballad about a ladylee who had disguised herself as a servant to gain entrance into the king's chambers. The song was funny and as the diners laughed Seymour let himself relax. Maybe she wouldn't say anything. Maybe she would extract a price for her silence. Or maybe she didn't care about a bard.

When Byron finished, the king stood. He hadn't smiled since the lady had arrived, and now his face looked gray and tired. Byron slung his lute across his back and got off the stool.

'Stay, Byron,' the king said. 'This will only take a minute. I'll want you to play when I'm through.'

Byron sat back down. The king put his hand on the Lady Jelwra's shoulder. She rested her cheek on his hand, then looked up at the crowd.

'With the death of my son,' the king said, 'I have no heir. My Lady Constance is too old to bear another child and has graciously offered to step down from her rightful place at my side so that I might become a father again. I am announcing to you all that I am looking for a lady or ladylee to help us through this troubled time. And I will, in two weeks' time, hold a festival to choose her.'

The king let go of Alma's shoulder. 'I only offer the chance to mother the heir to the throne, and cannot offer my companionship. That belongs, by right, to the Lady Constance.'

The king sat down. The Lady Jelwra tried to take his hand, but he moved away from her. Lord Boton whispered to Lord Ewehl, and then they left, followed by members of the council.

Seymour looked at Byron. He should have begun a song immediately, but he was staring at his lute as if he had never seen it before. The silence seemed heavy.

'Play,' the Lady Jelwra said.

Byron's hands moved across the strings, but the song sounded flat. He did not sing for a long time. When he finally began lyrics, his words seemed sad and slow.

The king gulped an entire tankard of ale. The Lady Jelwra whispered to him, but he did not respond. After Byron had finished two songs, the king left. Byron sang one more ballad, one that spoke of love betrayed, and the hall was quiet until he was through.

Chapter 20

The palace grounds seemed darker, older, more careworn. A serving woman walked by, her feet bare, the edges of her skirt ragged. Adric had never noticed poverty at the palace before. He scurried along the cobblestones, almost skipping. Milo had to run to keep up.

The guard, Butante, had shown them to their quarters, leaving his dirty clothing and sword behind. Then he had gone on to a meeting, and Adric had grabbed Milo's sleeve, forcing him out onto the palace grounds. If he didn't go to his father immediately, everyone would wonder why he had waited and might even use that against him.

He stopped in front of the west wing door and glanced around before trying it. The door was locked.

'I don't like this,' Milo whispered.

'We have to try,' Adric said. He led Milo across the courtyard, past the bench on which Adric had sat that long last morning. He touched the stones, barely able to remember their coldness and his own anticipation. He had so much to tell his mother – and he hoped his father would do something about Rogren. He knew that they would help Milo's family. Anyone who had saved a member of the royal family had to be rewarded.

They reached the main doors, which stood open. The palace interior smelled musty. A guard standing just inside the door put a hand on Adric's shoulder as he entered.

'What's your business, lad?'

By now he had learned. He understood that he no longer looked like the prince and that people would not recognize him. His lie was ready. 'We're Butante's new valets. He sent us to get something he had left in the audience room.'

'The king is in the audience room. You can't go in there.'

'All right,' Adric said. 'At least let me tell Butante. He's waiting in the west wing. I'd like to show my brother so he knows how to find his way there later.'

The guard grunted his assent. Adric circled in the great room, staring at the marble floor, the high, vaulted ceiling. He was home! He hurried down the corridor to the west wing, then veered down a side corridor that he knew led to the audience chamber. The corridor was narrow, filled with paintings Adric had never looked at, and performers' closets that he used to hide in. Milo struggled beside him.

'Do you know where you're going?' Milo asked.

Adric nodded. 'I lived here my whole life.'

He glanced at Milo, saw how his friend seemed to look smaller here, almost faded. He put his arm around Milo. 'Don't worry,' Adric said. 'Once I tell my father what happened, he'll let me treat you like my brother, like I want to.'

Milo bit his lower lip. His shoulders were tense.

They rounded a corner and Adric saw the edge of a stairway. He took a deep breath. He was almost there.

Footsteps rang in the hall above and voices murmured softly. Adric started up the stairs before recognizing whom he heard. Lord Ewehl, the man who had left him. The lord stood at the top of the stairs, talking with a retainer. Then the lord started down the steps, his dark robes flowing behind him. Adric turned his face and tried to run past.

'Just a minute, lad.' The lord grabbed Adric's shoulder. 'Where are you going?'

'I have a message, sir,' Adric said, his head still lowered. The lord put a bony finger beneath Adric's chin and forced his head up. When their eyes met, the lord gasped.

He turned to the retainer at the top of the stairs. 'Get the guards. Tell them there are intruders in the palace. Hurry!'

The retainer ran down the corridor. Adric wrenched himself from Lord Ewehl's grasp and tried to pass him, but the lord reached out. His arm hit Adric and pushed the boy backward. Milo grabbed Adric's shirt, trying to prevent his fall, but Adric couldn't get his balance. They tumbled down the stone stairway, Adric protecting his head with his arms. The sharp edges of the stairs opened the remaining scabs on Adric's back. He sprawled at the staircase bottom, unable to get his breath.

Lord Ewehl hurried toward him, his dagger down. Adric

pushed away along the floor, but the lord grabbed his shirt and pulled him to his feet. Milo leapt on the lord from behind. The lord let go of Adric. Adric took two steps toward Ewehl as the lord swung Milo off his back. Adric reached for Ewehl's arm and missed. The lord's dagger swung past, followed by a thud and a groan. Adric turned, saw Milo stumble forward, the dagger in his back.

Adric attacked the lord, pounding him and forcing him against the stairs. The lord raised his hands to protect his face. Adric kicked him in the stomach. The lord's feet snagged on the stairs and he fell backward, his head smacking against the stone.

Milo leaned against the wall. Above them, Adric heard footsteps. He put his arm around Milo's waist and dragged him into a nearby performers' closet, slamming the door behind them.

The closet was dark and smelled of greasepaint. The light filtering through the cracks in the door illuminated a lute, juggling clubs, and a magician's robe. Adric spread the robe out like a pallet and helped Milo onto it. Milo grabbed his wrist.

'Adric . . .'

Adric covered his friend's hand. 'I'm going to get help.'

'No.' Milo's voice sounded weak. 'That man, he'll kill you.'

'I'll be all right.'

'No, Adric, please . . .'

Adric pried his wrist free from Milo's fingers as the doorknob rattled. Adric backed away until he cringed against the damp stone wall. The door swung open. A tall, slender man dressed in black filled the doorway. The light against his back hid his face in shadows.

The man closed the door. Adric decided to take a chance. He stepped forward. 'Please,' he whispered. 'Help me. My friend is dying.'

The man knelt beside Milo and placed his hand over Milo's face.

'I'm sorry.' The man's voice was deep and melodic. 'But I'm afraid that your friend is already dead.'

PART THREE

Chapter 21

i

To the Lady Kerry:

I had difficulty tapping Dasvid's mind. He has a forceful brain, perhaps trained to resist probes by an Enos. I attempted the tap during the king's announcement banquet. My tap did not reveal the mental picture which Dasvid carries of himself, but I did learn that he refers to himself as Byron. He struggled against me through most of the tap, but I was able to get a brief picture just after the king's announcement.

In that flash I learned that Dasvid feared for a young boy who appeared half starved and abused. The fear had a direct relationship to the announcement. The child's identity and relationship to Dasvid are unknown.

The Lady Jelwra's unannounced appearance at the banquet also disturbed Dasvid. She appeared startled by his presence as well. She hinted that his name might not be Byron, and she made references to the last Lord of Kinsmail. The reference disturbed Dasvid's companion, Seymour.

Dasvid has become a favorite of the king's. The relationship seems quite strong. No direct attack on Dasvid is possible at this time.

You might not be the only one who wants the bard dead, milady. Corvo, the assassin whom Lord Ewehl paid to kill Lord Demythos a decade ago, is here at the palace. He won't tell me who he's working for and, of course, I can't tap him. I will keep an eye on him, though.

Please obtain information relating to the last Lord of Kinsmail. I will attempt another tap and maintain surveillance. I suggest no action be taken against Dasvid at this time.

Vonda

ii

Almathea removed the diamonds from her ears, set them on her dressing table, and inserted pearls. She glanced in the mirror: her face looked fat in the wavy glass. The dressing room was too small and claustrophobic. The edges of her skirt hit the wardrobe as she moved.

She glanced into the sitting room. The overstuffed furniture scattered around the walls looked uncomfortable, but no more uncomfortable than Vonda. She still waited, her hands folded in her lap. She looked like a spider, fat and contented, waiting for the kill. Alma had been wondering why Vonda was there. Alma had no designs on Kerry land, and she had never spoken with the Lady Kerry.

Alma sighed and returned to her mirror. She had already kept Vonda waiting almost an hour. The message had to be important for Vonda to wait that long. Alma brushed her long, dark hair and pulled it away from her face. Then she wound a strand of pearls among the curls and stepped back, surveying herself. It would have to do. She had only so much to work with – her hair was coarse and too thick, her face dark and plain – and too little time. The king's announcement had surprised her, as it had surprised the other gentry, and she wanted to make sure the king saw no one else at his festival.

She smoothed her hair one more time and pulled the door open. Vonda glanced up. Her skin formed little webs around her eyes and the corners of her mouth.

'Well, Vonda,' Alma said, 'what is this thing that is so important?' She continued standing so that Vonda had to look up. Upstart servants had to be kept at a disadvantage.

'I'm pleased that you agreed to see me, milady.' Vonda's voice was soft, like the rustle of parchment. 'I have come to discuss the king's bard.'

Alma moved her head slightly. The pearls in her hair clicked. Vonda had been watching the night before; Alma remembered that. Time to put the spider lady on the defensive. 'Is he your lover?' Alma asked.

Vonda smiled. The look was cold. 'Of course not, milady. I'm here on business.'

'Indeed.' Alma walked to the sideboard and poured herself a glass of water. She did not offer Vonda one.

'The Lady Kerry believes that the bard is not who he claims to be. You too seem to know something about the man. I was wondering if you would like to share your information.'

Alma swirled the water in the glass as if it were full of wine. Then she took a sip, savoring the taste, and leaned against the chair across from Vonda. 'What interest does the Lady Kerry have in this?'

'A personal one.'

Alma sighed, as if she were bored. In fact, she was even more interested. She loved secrets and gossip. Her power had its base in the kind of knowledge she picked up from others. Now that she knew Lady Kerry also had suspicions and an involvement with Sir Geoffry, Alma would search for the information on her own.

'I'm afraid I can't help you,' Alma said. 'The man looks familiar, but I don't know where I have seen him before.'

'Beg pardon.' Vonda bowed her head a little, keeping her gaze on Alma. 'But I do not believe you, milady.'

'The Lady Kerry lets you talk like that? Interesting the manner of different gentry.' Alma took another sip of her water and stood. 'You may leave.'

Vonda bowed her head again and scurried around the chairs. When she reached the door, she stopped. 'I hope you consider the request, lady.'

Alma smiled and waited until the door closed before setting the glass down carefully. Impertinent witch, calling Alma a liar and asking for help in the same meeting. Alma adjusted her skirts, checked the mirror once more, and let herself out of her suite.

The corridor was cool. A retainer standing near her door bowed his head at her. She ignored him. Sir Geoffry was the puzzle. She hadn't expected him at the palace and she certainly hadn't expected to see him performing for the king. Perhaps Geoffry believed that once he had the king's favor, he could petition for his lands. Bad plan, of course. The king now saw Geoffry as lower class, and no amount of history could change that.

She turned down the corridor to the audience chamber, lifting her skirts as she climbed the small flight of stairs. The doors to the chamber were open. Retainers stood against the walls like statues, swords and banners crossed above their heads. Strange decorations; she did not like them. The king sat on a large chair on the dais, and Geoffry stood before him, hands clasped behind his back. Geoffry wore a linen shirt and breeches instead of his usual black. The clothing accented his slender frame and made him look younger.

Alma stepped inside and curtsied, making certain her attention was on the king. The man was too fat and smelled of sweat and ale.

She supposed that if she became the new consort, she would have to do all of the work, with the king on his back and his stomach in the way. She frowned, wishing there was another way to become part of the royal family in Kilot.

'Alma!' The king sounded pleased. He stood up and extended his hand to her. She rose, nodded once at Geoffry, and climbed the stairs to the dais.

'I hope I'm not disturbing anything.' She glanced at Geoffry. He was not looking at her; his gaze was on the king.

'No, no,' the king said. 'We'll be finishing shortly. Did you have something to discuss?'

'Only lunch.' Alma smiled. 'I'll just wait in a corner until you're finished.'

'We could quit now. Lunch sounds excellent.'

Lunch did not sound excellent. Alma wanted to know why Geoffry was talking to the king, and she didn't dare ask. She didn't want the king to know how curious she was about things. He knew that she was intelligent and that she could be difficult, but he didn't have to know that she was determined to make her own power base in the kingdom. 'I'll just take a chair and wait until you're through,' she said.

She walked to the back of the dais and sat on one of the wood chairs near some velvet curtains. They brushed against her back and the chair seemed stiff, uncomfortable. From her vantage point, she could see Geoffry's face, but not the king's.

The king sighed and sat back in his chair. 'Finish, bard,' he said.

'I have told you about the conditions in the countryside,' the bard said. He leaned on one knee, the other leg straight down the stairs. He was as close to the king as he could be without being disrespectful. 'I'm worried about an uprising. The wheat crop failures are costing many peasants their livelihood. People are starving, and the gentry is doing nothing. On Lord Dakin's land – '

'I don't care about Dakin,' the king snapped. 'What do you want from me?'

Alma clasped her hands in her lap, wishing that she had been present for the beginning of the conversation. She wondered what crop failures had to do with Geoffry's land claim.

'Sire, I checked with the store master. You have enough food here to feed an entire army under siege for three years. You can afford to share it, and it might ease tensions in the countryside.'

'I see no reason to feed peasants.'

Neither did Alma. And she could see no reason for Geoffry's request. The man was crazy. He should have been petitioning for his lands rather than speaking for the unwashed.

'The common folk keep this country alive, Highness,' Byron said. 'The gentry live off the land, but the peasantry work it. Without them we would have nothing. Right now, neither the gentry nor the kingdom itself does anything for the peasantry – '

'I have heard enough!' The king pounded his fists on the chair and the entire dais rumbled.

Alma suppressed a smile. She had never seen the king mad before. He looked like a red-faced, roaring bulldog – the small, yapping kind her mother used to keep. The retainers along the walls stood at attention and stared at the dais. Geoffry took the remaining steps in two leaps. He crouched before the king.

'You'll listen to me, sire, because if you don't, it could mean the end of the realm as you know it. Not one of you pays any attention to the peasantry. The beautiful Lady Jelwra over there wants land and power. Lords Ewehl and Boton want to run the kindom their way. The council spends more time exchanging land than doing any real work. When governing is done, it is done for the landed, not for the people who work the land. I've traveled through the realm, sire. I know its people. And, believe me, you had better start working with them instead of ignoring them.'

The king didn't move. Alma's urge to smile had disappeared as well. She didn't like Geoffry's assessment of her, nor did she like the way he asserted that assessment to the king.

'You think these isolated incidents will become a mass uprising,' the king said. His anger seemed to have disappeared.

'I know it, sire. Kilot's history shows it. The Dakins took their lands because the Kinsmails, who controlled it, failed to care for their peasants after a major fire swept through the forest up there. The first Dakins helped the peasants and the peasants helped them. The present Lord Dakin has forgotten the lessons his family learned. If his heirs manage the estate as he has, Dakin will not control that land much longer.'

'But attack the king?' The king was clenching his fists so tightly his knuckles turned white.

'Sire.' Geoffry's voice softened. 'Have you forgotten what happened to Queen Glerek two hundred years ago? She abused her peasants. Her laws forced them into starvation and forced the crop failures. If it weren't for the Enos working to protect the land, she would have died in an uprising.'

The king sighed. 'I have made no laws hurting the peasants.'

'You have made no laws to help them either, sire. And they are starving.'

The king looked at Geoffry. His cheeks were flushed and his eyes glowed. Alma wondered if passion always made his face seem so alive.

'I must discuss this with Lord Boton,' the king said.

Geoffry's smile did not reach his eyes. 'Don't you ever make decisions on your own, sire?'

'You are an impertinent young man!'

Geoffry nodded. 'I'm glad we agree on something, Highness.'

The silence seemed long. Alma resisted the urge to squirm in her chair. Then the king chuckled. 'You did warn me about that, didn't you?'

'Several times.'

'And I warned you that I didn't take criticism well.'

'But only once.'

The king's chuckle grew into a laugh. The guards relaxed, and so did Alma. She didn't want anything to happen to Geoffry, and she didn't want anything to interfere with her own plans. 'And so what do you suggest, sir bard?'

'Feed them, sire. And let them petition you with their grievances.'

'Petition me? Those people in these chambers? I wouldn't know what – '

'Sire, this chamber was built for that purpose. And if you don't want to accept petitions, assign another to sit in your place.'

'You're lucky that I like you, bard, and that you have good ideas.' The king waved his hand in dismissal. 'I will consider your grievance my own way. And tonight you will sing for me so well that I will forget your impertinence.'

Geoffry bowed. 'Thank you, sire.' And without a single glance at Alma, he left the audience chamber.

Alma stood and put her hand on the king's shoulder. He was tense. She stared at the doors, wishing she could see through them and see Geoffry. He never did what she expected. He was one of the few people she had ever met who she couldn't read. Usci was another. She wished he were here instead of home, tending to her business. He might understand the bard. Perhaps she would send for him.

The king patted her hand as Lord Boton stepped through the curtains in the back. Alma had suspected there were listening chambers, but she was surprised that the king would reveal them to her.

'What do you think, Boton?' the king asked.

'The bard has a point, sire. He knows the lands better than we do, and several gentry have reported trouble with their people. I'll look into the matter. But I would also have someone watch that bard. He reminds me too much of Lord Demythos.'

Demythos. Alma squinted. Her mother believed that Demythos had been murdered because of his unpopular and outspoken views.

'You know, Boton,' the king said softly, 'there are still times when I miss that man.'

'He tried to run your kingdom.'

The king looked directly at Boton. 'So have others.'

Lord Boton's eyes widened. Alma felt a shiver run down her back. The king seemed shrewder today than he ever had before. She wondered, if she became consort, whether he would prove as malleable as she had hoped.

'Demythos was a good man. He thought of others before himself.' The king smiled. 'You're right, Boton. The bard does remind me of Demythos.'

Lord Boton frowned. The king took Alma's hand off his shoulder and stood. 'Alma and I are going to lunch.' He led her down the stairs and tucked her hand into his arm. His body seemed almost too warm. He leaned his head near hers. 'I see you so rarely, Alma, and I do miss your mother so. She was the heart of the council.'

Alma nodded. She had heard that before. Too bad her mother was not the heart of Jelwra. Her father had run the lands, and had raised Alma. She would never give as much away as her mother had.

'I would love to discuss the bard's proposition over lunch,' she said, turning the conversation from her mother. If the king liked the former lady of Jelwra, he would not like Almathea.

The king patted her hand and walked her slowly out of the audience chamber. 'I no longer discuss business over meals,' he said. 'Ruins the digestion.'

As if anything ruined the king's digestion. Alma did not sigh, but she made a silent vow. She would never, ever have a meal alone with the king again – at least not until she became consort.

iii

To the Lady Kerry:

Dasvid shocked the palace by confronting the king over the crop failures. Surprisingly, the king listened to him. The king and the council examined the situation and decided to allot five pounds of food per family as long as the wheat disease continues. Dasvid has also been promoted to the king's representative to the underclasses. He is to hear their petitions and to bring valid claims before the king. Dasvid seems to enjoy the job. He spends most of the day listening to the petitions and his evenings entertaining the king.

The king's fascination with Dasvid is unusual. Most entertainers would have been banished for their impertinence, yet Dasvid is still a favorite. He seems to have no outside contacts. His only real friends are his traveling companions, the magician Seymour and the boys Colin and Afeno.

As you requested, I met with the Lady Jelwra. Dasvid fascinates her as well. Mentally, she refers to him as Sir Geoffry. Although my tap of her mind was abortive, I learned that she has not known him long and is not clear about his identity. She is also planning something to do with the king, but the idea was nebulous and unfocused because it had nothing to do with our conversation. During our meeting the Lady Jelwra protected Dasvid from my questions. I do not know why.

Vonda

iv

Alma finished buttoning her day dress and looped the braids around her head. She set the remaining pins on her dressing table. The room was a mess without Usci, but she didn't want any of the palace serving people inside. The dressing room was hers, sloppy as it was, and she didn't want anyone snooping.

She sighed and checked her appearance one final time in the wavy mirror. She hated hunting, thought it both boring and barbarous, but right now she couldn't refuse any invitation of the king's. She liked the way he looked at her when he thought no one else was looking, the way his eyes gleamed, as if he were thinking that he could make love to her and she would be useful to him.

She could make love to him too. It would take a little imagination and a lot of fantasizing, but she would be able to hold him and please him – and have a child with him. And she was glad that she wouldn't have his full attention. The king would feel affection for her, but the Lady Constance would take care of the love. Alma would love her children, and she would love the kingdom, and she would love her power.

And until she had those things, she would do what the king asked.

She grabbed a fan and her small whip and let herself into the hallway. The hallway was dark, the faded portraits staring at her as if they were laughing. She touched her hair, sorry she had agreed to the hunt, sorry that she had agreed to be up at dawn. As consort, she would lie in bed until noon and stay up until dawn: those were civilized hours. She gathered her skirts and headed toward the stables, her leather shoes scuffling against the stone floor.

A door opened in front of her, and she had to step back to keep from walking into it. Sir Geoffry emerged and, seeing her, took her arm. His touch was warm and gentle. 'Are you all right, milady?'

She stepped around the door and peered inside. She had noticed the doors lining the corridor, but thought they led to serving closets. Geoffry's had a lute, juggling equipment, a table, and a desk. 'Do you always open doors with such enthusiasm?'

'When I know that I will stop a beautiful lady, I do.'

'Such a silver tongue, Geoffry.'

He frowned. 'I wish you wouldn't call me that, lady. My name is Byron.'

'Really?' Alma smiled at him. 'Or will your name change again if I see you in a different part of Kilot?'

His grip tightened on her arm, and he led her into the little room. The air was stuffy and hot, but smelled faintly of soap and leather, like Geoffry. He closed the door. Alma leaned against the desk, unwilling to sit unless he did. 'You haven't told me,' she said. 'Is Byron your real name?'

The laughter had left his face. His eyes were hard and black. 'I don't plan to tell you, milady. You know enough already. I wanted to make it clear to you that if you decide to reveal what you know about me, I will reveal what I know about you.'

Alma tilted her head a little. She took a deeper breath, and forced herself to stay calm. More important men than Geoffry had threatened her, although she had never expected it of him. Something she had done worried him. 'And what do you know about me, Sir Geoffry?'

'I know how you've been expanding your lands. I doubt even lords Boton and Ewehl know the details. Your recent council defeat won't take away all the lands you stole from Lafa, not if you can provide the documents with the king's seal. And we both know that you have those. Too bad you can't use your mother's key to the document room to get the deed to Kilot itself. You'll have to sleep with the king for that.'

The edge of the desk dug into Alma's thighs. Her palms were sweating. She thought no one knew that her mother had had an extra key to the documents room. Lord Boton kept the kingdom records in that room as well as the king's seal. It had been so easy to transfer Lafa's land, forge the king's signature, and seal the document. And she had done it long before Geoffry came to the palace. 'I assume you want more from me than silence,' she said.

He leaned against the wall and crossed his arms in front of his chest. 'The lady becomes cold when she feels threatened.' He smiled. 'We're not enemies, Alma. In fact, I think we can work well together.'

'Either you would like my help in the documents room, or you too would like to sleep with the king to gain a kingdom.'

Geoffry laughed. The warm, melodious sound filled the small room and made Alma shiver. 'Neither, lady. I just want the title that I'm due.'

'Why don't you approach the king and ask for it? You're in his favor now.'

He sat on the cot. The wood groaned. 'It's not that simple.' His hand rested beside him, almost inviting her. She noted the movement, but ignored it. After a moment he sighed. 'Lady, if you do plan to vie for the king's offer, watch yourself. Lord Ewehl has spies all over the castle, as does the Lady Kerry. I believe Lord Kensington is receiving regular reports as well. Those in power will do anything to retain that power. Even murder.'

'You sound like such an expert, Geoffry. And you've only been here a few months.'

'Byron, lady.' He rested on one elbow and looked up at her. His body was smooth and strong, the shoulders wide and hips narrow. She wanted to touch him, but she had to hunt with the king. Her future had to come before her passions.

She stood, knowing she had to leave the room before she took Geoffry's silent invitation. 'I'll keep your secret, sir bard. But don't expect me to keep it at my own expense.'

He gazed at her over his shoulder. 'I never expect more from people than they are capable of.'

Alma longed to smack him with her whip and wipe the confident expression from his face. Instead she let herself out of the room and slammed the door behind her. She hurried down the corridor, afraid that she was already late.

Geoffry knew too much. He was a gatherer of information as she was, and that made him dangerous. He knew so much about her, and she knew nothing of him. It was time she learned.

The stables were at the back of the palace, near the forest that housed the Cache and the whistle-wood trees. Alma opened the side door leading to the stables. The wind was strong, the air cool. Her braids slapped against her face, and her skirts twisted around her ankles. The groomsmen held two mounts. Lords Boton and Ewehl already sat on theirs, as did Lord Kensington. Alma smiled at him, unaware that he was at the palace and angry that she hadn't known it. Geoffry had known. He had warned her about Kensington.

'Lord Kensington,' she said. 'You didn't join us at dinner last evening.'

'I arrived late, milady.'

She took one of the groomsmen's hands and swung into the sidesaddle, arranging her skirts so that they flowed along the horse. He probably had arrived as quickly as he could after he found out about the king's announcement. Should the king die without an heir, Kensington would inherit the throne.

In the distance a wail rose and echoed. A shiver ran down Alma's back. She had heard the whistle-wood trees before, but they always frightened her. 'Where is his highness?'

'Here, Alma.' The king emerged from the stable. His breeches were too tight, revealing every roll of fat in his thighs. She thought of Geoffry's legs, tight and muscular, and forced herself to concentrate on something else. 'I'm pleased that you could join us this morning.'

'I'm surprised at the sport,' Alma said. 'My Enos refuses such bloodletting on Jelwra land.'

'The Cache Enos don't mind, if someone eats the fox we kill.' The king waved his hand at the stable master. 'Free the fox.'

The master turned and opened a small cage. Something red and black flashed out, disappearing among the trees.

'And the hounds.'

A group of five dogs, barking and yipping, ran from the stable, following the same path as the fox. The men clucked at their horses and the mounts galloped after the dogs. Alma did the same, her mare barely able to keep up. She didn't mind. The sport sickened her. If people were going to kill something, they should get their own hands bloody, rather than letting animals do the work for them.

The king glanced back at her once and waved. She waved too and smiled as prettily as she could. The forest was dark, and the whistle-woods moaned, as if in sympathy for the poor fox. Brambles grew in the underbrush, and Alma steered her mare beside the trees, hoping that her skirt would catch. It took more than one try, but finally she heard a small ripping sound.

'Highness,' she called, but the king didn't notice. Gallant old fool, she thought to herself. At least the groomsmen would see the rip and support her reason for leaving the chase. She leaned forward on the sidesaddle, gripping her horse with one hand and trying to free her skirt with the other.

She heard the sound of a single horse galloping back toward her. A fat, bejeweled hand flipped her skirt free. She looked up, expecting to thank the king, and saw Lord Boton smiling at her.

'I feared you lost, milady.'

'And so did I, milord.' She didn't like the fact that Boton had been watching for her.

'You rode too close to the trees.'

'I'm not used to riding in such an enclosed area. The Jelwra land isn't as wild.' The tree moan grew higher, almost a shriek. Alma took her skirt from Lord Boton's hands.

'Then let me accompany you back to the palace,' he said. 'The others are far ahead and would be hard to find.'

'Thank you, milord.' Alma turned her mare around and rode beside the lord. The shriek of the trees was dying back.

'I'm glad that I can talk with you, lady,' he said. 'I oppose your attempts at becoming the king's consort.'

'I expect that, milord. I threaten your power.'

'And you threaten a system that has worked since long before you were born – '

'And a system that provided you with more lands than you can manage. I have watched you, milord. You pretend to advise the king, but the interests you watch out for are your own. Of course you will oppose me. I'm too strong for you.'

'You're not as powerful as you think you are, milady.'

'And neither are you, Lord Boton.' Alma clucked at her horse and galloped toward the stables, leaving the lord behind her. She smiled, feeling the game begin. Power was the sport she enjoyed. And Lord Boton would make the sport interesting, and so would Lord Ewehl. She was smarter than both of them, and she knew more about them than they knew about her.

As she got closer to the palace, she heard shouts coming from the side gate. She swung her horse around to see what was causing the noise.

Several guards had gathered in a small alcove near the stables. They held an old, large peasant man. He wore a ripped shirt and tattered pants. His face was fleshy and jowled. Geoffry stood on the steps leading into the palace, watching the fat man as if he were about to kill him.

'You have no right to hold me!' the fat man shouted. He twisted against the guards' arms, glanced around for help, and finally saw Alma. 'Help me, lady! I came here for assistance and that man won't let me see the king.'

Alma glanced at Geoffry. He hadn't moved. He didn't seem to notice her. 'He decides who is worthy of seeing the king,' she said. 'I have no jurisdiction in this matter.'

'You have some jurisdiction, milady,' one of the guards said. 'He drew a knife on the bard, and the bard refuses to do anything about it.'

'Is that true?' Alma asked. Geoffry still hadn't looked at her, but the man spoke:

'He insulted me.'

'That's no reason to attack a representative of the king. What had you planned to do about this, Byron?' She could not get the edge of irony out of her voice when she said his name.

Geoffry finally looked at her. A long, bloody gash ran down his left cheek. 'The peasant is no threat to me. Let him continue his wretched life away from the palace.'

Something else had happened here, something she didn't understand. A peasant who attacked the gentry – or a representative of the gentry – had to be imprisoned or executed to show others that such behavior was forbidden. Perhaps Geoffry didn't know that. 'Arrest the man,' Alma said. 'Let the king decide what to do with him.'

'But lady, you haven't heard my case!'

Alma brought her horse up close to him and looked down at him. His face was florid, his eyes piggy. He smelled of ale, onions, and stale sweat. 'I heard enough. You wanted to let the king decide your fate. He will.'

'Bitch!' the man screamed. The guards dragged him off. Alma dismounted and gave her reins to one of the guards. Then she sent another for an herb witch. She climbed the stairs to Geoffry and touched the blood on his face. The whistle-woods moaned.

'I wish you hadn't done that, lady,' he said.

'And why not? Peasants do not threaten gentry. It is the law and it keeps us safe.'

'I am trying to establish among the lower classes that the king believes in justice for everyone. If someone comes here with a petition and gets arrested, where's the justice?'

'They have to know they can't attack you.'

'He wasn't held properly.'

Alma wiped the blood on her skirt. 'Then ask the king to release him.' She turned, but Geoffry grabbed her arm. His grip was so tight that it hurt.

'Milady,' he said. 'I think you of all people should realize that sometimes power is best served by not being exercised.'

'Where did you learn about power, bard?'

'The powerless always know about power.' He scanned her face, his gaze finally stopping at her lips. He wanted to kiss her, she could feel it. She leaned into him, wanting to kiss him too, then remembered Lord Boton at the stables.

'If the powerless know that much, then the peasant should understand why I arrested him,' she said. She wrenched her arm free and ran up the stairs. He was distracting her and she didn't need distractions. She had to concentrate on the king. The king, not Geoffry.

V

To the Lady Kerry:

Dasvid refused to accompany the king on a hunt this morning, preferring instead to hear petitions. He is a good listener usually, letting most who come leave feeling as if they were heard. This morning, however, a man entered who angered Dasvid almost immediately. The man introduced himself as Rogren, an innkeeper. Dasvid's entire manner became rigid. He asked the man to state his complaint. The man said he had stable boys who had run away and were seen heading to the palace. He wanted permission to search for them. Dasvid asked what the man would do if the boys were returned to him. The man said he would whip them. Dasvid said that he had heard that the man had whipped his boys unnecessarily. The man denied it. Dasvid also accused him of not letting a healer treat the whipped boys, even though the man lived with a healer. Again the man denied it. Then Dasvid asked the man how many boys had run away from him over the years. The man claimed a dozen or more. Dasvid denied the man's petition, citing that the man's treatment of his stable boys was cruel. The man offered to change his behavior. Dasvid ordered him to hire new boys and to have the boys report to Dasvid in three months. The man claimed that Dasvid was being unfair. Dasvid asked the man to leave.

The man pulled a knife from his tunic and flung it at Dasvid. The knife grazed Dasvid's cheek. He stood up and told the man that his petition was permanently denied. The man ran toward Dasvid, but the guards caught the man and dragged him outside. Dasvid followed. The Lady Jelwra was returning from a hunt, saw the incident, and demanded the man's arrest. Her actions angered Dasvid.

I found this affair curious, milady. Dasvid knew of this Rogren and clearly hated him. I will see if I can get permission to go into the palace dungeon to see what this man knows of Dasvid.

Also this morning, Dasvid met the Lady Jelwra in the performing closet that he uses as an office. They were in there for some time. The door was too thick to listen through, and I could not find a nearby chamber. The lady did leave disheveled and angry. Shall I warn her about the fate of Dasvid's lovers?

Like you, no one here has heard of Geoffry of Kinsmail. But the Lady Jelwra did anger Dasvid this morning by referring to him as Geoffry. Have the Kinsmails any connection with your family? Is there some reason why a lordling pretender to Lord Dakin's lands would kill the Ladylee Diana?

Vonda

vi

The king's gardens smelled of roses. Red, yellow, white, and pink roses decorated the walkway, hidden by high hedges. Benches lined the path. Alma didn't have to be told that roses were the Lady Constance's favorite flower.

The king led Alma to a bench in the center of the garden. Huge hedges surrounded them and roses twined at their feet. Here in the small alcove, the smell of roses and pine was almost overwhelming.

He placed his hand on top of hers. His palm was cold and clammy. 'Alma,' he said, 'I am very fond of you.'

She threaded her fingers through his. 'And I of you, sire.'

'And if I had my way, there would be no festival at all. Do you understand me?'

She did, but she wanted him to be clear about what he meant. She leaned over, grabbed the edge of a half-opened rose, and inhaled its fragrance. 'I'm not certain, sire.'

He sighed. 'I'm going to choose you as my consort, even though Boton and Ewehl do not want me to. They believe you are too strong. I think you are just strong enough. You are like the bard said you are, eager for lands and power. I probably won't live to see our child to adulthood, and I need someone strong to guard him. I believe that most, if not all of my children, were murdered. You will be ruthless enough to protect the child's land and power. You can do what I could not.'

'Not the most flattering reasons for being chosen as consort,' Alma said. She smiled. 'But I do understand, and I am glad there will be no pretense between us. I know of your love for the Lady Constance, and I will respect it. I will also guard any children we have as ruthlessly as I guard everything I own.'

The king squeezed her hand. 'That is all that we need,' he said. 'So, will you go along with this charade for another week, and then become my consort? We need each other, Alma.'

His eyes were half shaded with fatigue and his skin was full of lines. He seemed almost gray. For the first time Alma saw the strain he worked under, and she was pleased that she would be able to ease it. 'Yes,' she said. 'I will wait.'

The king slipped his arms around her and hugged her to him. His arms were soft, his hold gentle. She found, to her surprise, that the crook of his shoulder was a comfortable place to be. Being his consort would not be as bad a task as she had feared.

He kissed the top of her head and then he let her go. She leaned back and saw his face. His eyes were rimmed with tears.

'I won't try to take the Lady Constance's place,' she said.

He nodded and patted her hand. 'Would you mind walking back on your own?' he asked. 'I would like a few minutes alone.'

She ran her hand along his cheek and stood. She hadn't realized before what a gentle man the king was. She would make this easy for him. She would be the strong one. 'I will see you at dinner, my liege,' she said.

She wandered down the path. The encounter with the king left her feeling tired. She should have been ecstatic, finally achieving, within a few short years of her mother's death, the goals she had set for herself. But in the garden the game seemed like something other than a game. The king had a heritage to uphold, so he had to take another woman, even though he didn't want her. And all of his children, murdered. Alma frowned. She remembered her mother speaking about such things and being shushed by her father. And she remembered the miscarriages, her mother's offer of another, better herb witch, and the palace's refusal. With the death of this last son, the king had a reason to be despondent.

Laughter floated across the bushes, children's laughter. A shiver ran down Alma's back. She never thought of children at the palace. She rounded a corner and saw that the door to the gate was open. On the walk outside sat dozens of children. Their clothing was ragged, their feet bare and their skin dirty. Geoffry sat in the middle of them, cross-legged, his lute around his shoulder. He began a ballad, and the children sang with him. Their voices were scratchy and out of tune, but he didn't seem to notice. Alma had never seen him smile like that, eyes sparkling with a pure enjoyment. He ducked and leaned toward the children, calling them by name and flirting with them as he never did before the king.

When the song ended, they all clapped. Geoffry set down his lute and clapped with them, and then the laughter started again.

'Does anyone dance?' he shouted.

Childlike heads shook in unison. Alma stopped at the edge of the gate, leaned on the wall, and watched them.

'Dancing is easy,' Geoffry said. 'If I were a head shorter, I would show you how. Colin, why don't you grab a lady and show these ragamuffins how to enjoy music.'

Alma glanced for Geoffry's companions, and finally found the one, Colin, sitting at the edge of the crowd. He was watching her. When he caught her eye, he smiled and stood up. He stepped over the children and stopped in the center, next to Geoffry. Colin took the lute and sat down.

'You show them,' he said, 'and I'll play. You're much better at dancing than I am.'

Geoffry reached for the lute. 'I also have more experience with a lute.'

'Yes,' Colin said. 'But there's a lady behind you who already knows how to dance, and I'm not worthy of being her partner.'

Geoffry turned and stopped when he saw Alma. She held her breath, half expecting the pleasure to leave his face. It did not. He bowed in front of her and extended his hand. 'May I have this dance, milady?'

The children were watching them. Dozens of expectant eyes. Alma glanced over her shoulder, but did not see the king. She took Geoffry's hand. It was warm, dry. Colin played a simple, lilting melody. She stepped closer to Geoffry. He put a hand around her back, and her heart beat a little faster. He danced easily, gracefully, leading her as if he had danced his entire life. She whirled with him, finding his rhythm easily. Her fingers found the soft hair brushing his collar. The muscles in his back rippled, and his gaze never left hers. He smelled of warmth and sunshine.

He smiled, his lips slightly parted. He was inclining his head toward hers when something whizzed past her shoulder. He threw her to the ground, and she scraped her elbows. The children screamed and ran. Geoffry pulled his sword and crouched. Colin dropped the lute and pulled his sword. Alma grabbed the dagger she hid in the waist of her dress. She stood and glanced around. An arrow shivered in the gate where she had been standing a moment before.

Geoffry put a finger to his lips. He walked to the gate and examined the arrow. Another whizzed by, narrowly missing his head. He ducked, grabbed Alma's hand, and tugged her away from the garden.

'Colin,' Geoffry cried. 'Report this to the guards. I'm getting the lady out of here.'

'No,' Alma said, 'report to the king. To the king only.'

She followed Geoffry down the path and to the cobblestone courtyard. No arrows whizzed past, and she sensed they were alone. They passed retainers, servers, and a group of jugglers practicing against the wall. Geoffry led her to a door on the far side of the palace and pushed her inside. The corridor was small and dark, filled with clothing, equipment, and children. It had the faint smell of greasy food. Alma had never seen anything like it. Her breath was coming rapidly, but she felt as if she could run another few miles.

'Where are you taking me?' she asked.

'To my quarters,' he said. 'We can talk there.' He pushed open a small wood door and bent over as he entered. Alma did the same. His room smelled like the performers' closet had – of soap and leather. A pallet rested on the floor, next to a rough wood table and a few chairs. A magician's robe hung against the wall, and two lutes leaned beside it. He closed the door, leaned on it, and stared at her. Then he reached out and cupped her face with his hand.

'Are you all right, Alma?' he asked.

The warmth in his voice made her shiver. She ran her hands up the silk of his shirt, wanting to touch him. He slipped his hand beneath her hair and tilted her face forward. His lips met hers hesitantly. She pulled him toward her and opened his mouth, tasting him.

His hands slid down her neck, to her sides, finding her breasts and caressing them, sending little shudders of pleasure through her. Then he reached the back of her dress and unbuttoned it as his lips followed the path his hands had made. The dress fell, followed by the undergarments. She reached for the hem of his shirt to undress him, but he grabbed her wrists.

'Let me love you, Alma,' he whispered. He put his arm behind her back and led her to the pallet. She lay on the coarse blanket and reached for him. He took her hands and held them beside her, kissing her breasts, her stomach, working his way down. Her imprisonment frustrated her and she rolled over, trapping him beneath her. She untied his pants and pulled them off him. She rubbed the inside of her thigh against him, and he moaned, reaching for her. But she pinned his hands to his side and smiled at the urgency on his face as she slowly, ever so slowly, eased her body onto his.

Once she felt him inside her, she sat still. He gazed at her through half-open eyes. 'You're beautiful,' he murmured. She leaned over and kissed him. Then she released his hands.

He pulled her against him, and they moved, together. Their kisses, caresses became wild. She could feel his warmth inside her. The brush of his lips against her neck made her want more of him. She forced him deeper inside her and shuddered as an orgasm pulsed through her. He stopped moving, bringing his head up to watch her. His mouth was bruised, his eyes light brown, his hair covering his cheekbones. She reached for him again, and this time they rolled across the floor, touching, kissing, biting. Her hair fell loose, and he poured it over them like fine wine. His arms drew tighter around her, and they climaxed together.

'Oh, Alma,' he groaned, and buried his face in her hair. She held him, still shuddering, not wanting him to move. His weight felt good. She closed her eyes and ran her hands up his arm. A laugh bubbled inside her.

'You're still wearing your shirt.'

He lifted his head, looked down at himself, and laughed with her. 'You're beautiful,' he said again, and kissed her.

A knock on the door made them freeze.

'Byron, it's Colin. I have to talk to you.'

The knob turned.

'Not now, Colin,' Geoffry said. His breath caressed Alma's cheek.

'Byron, it's important. I couldn't see the king and – '

'Not now, Colin. I'll meet you outside in a few minutes.'

'Byron – '

'Go away, Colin. I'll meet you outside.'

The door handle clicked as the boy released it. Geoffry didn't move until the boy's footsteps disappeared down the hall. Then Geoffry let go of Alma and helped her up.

'This is no place for you, milady.' His tone was soft. He brushed her off and helped her with her clothing. Then he finished dressing himself, his expression somber.

'I didn't mean to do that – ' he began.

She leaned over and kissed him. 'Never explain,' she said. 'And never apologize.'

He grinned. 'I'm not sorry for what happened. But I did bring you here with honorable intentions. I just wanted to talk.'

Alma sat on one of the wood chairs. Her body felt lethargic and good. 'So talk.'

He sat beside her. 'Those weren't stray arrows, you know.'

'I know. I expect they belong to someone employed by lords Boton and Ewehl.'

Geoffry frowned. 'Boton and Ewehl?'

'They think I'm going to be the king's next consort.'

'And are you?'

Too late she realized that he had been thinking something else about the attack. If she had listened, she would have found out instead of revealing her secrets to him. 'I'm afraid I am,' she said.

He stood up and walked to the door, waiting there with his back to her. 'Then I am sorry for what I did, Almathea.'

'For what we did.'

He shook his head. 'I did. I was hoping to petition the king during the festival. After that I had hoped – '

'Petition the king?'

He sighed and faced her again. 'It doesn't matter, Alma.'

'Petition him for your lands, Geoffry?'

'My name is not Geoffry and I have no lands!' His sharp words echoed in the tiny room. He extended a hand and helped her to her feet. 'I've been lying to you, Alma. Maybe I am what I appear to be, a simple bard trying to survive.'

'No.' Her heart was pounding. The lethargy was gone. 'You handle yourself like a lord.'

'Let me put this to you simply, milady. I am a bard. Bards know legends and stories. Bards are good mimics who live among gentry. Bards are also good thieves. I stole those clothes you met me in. And I made up Lord Geoffry of Kinsmail.'

'You're lying.'

'Not now I'm not.'

They stared at each other, breathing as heavily as they had when they were making love. 'There is no Geoffry of Kinsmail?' she asked.

'No.'

'Then who are you?'

'Does it matter, milady? I am not the king.' The bitterness in his tone shook her. And it didn't matter who he was, whether he was gentry or not. She would become the king's consort and could not have a relationship with any other man without the king's permission.

'Then I am the one who must apologize,' she said. She put her hand on the doorknob. It was cool to the touch. 'I let myself get carried away.'

'Alma.' He spoke her name as if it were a caress. 'Be careful. Boton and Ewehl are the most dangerous enemies you can have. If you need help, come to me. They watch the king continually.'

'I will, Geoffry,' she said and left the room.

Chapter 22

i

To the Lady Kerry:

I have met with the peasant Rogren. He claims that he has never seen Dasvid before and knows nothing of him. I believe this Rogren. He had no reason to lie to me.

I look forward to seeing you in less than a week. The palace has been abuzz with the news of the king's new consort. Unless matters change, it looks as if the Lady Jelwra will hold that position.

Vonda

ii

Alma poured herself a glass of water, and sat on the window seat overlooking the courtyard. She wished that the day of the festival would hurry. Since her meeting with the king and her afternoon with Geoffry, she had not appeared throughout the palace. The king, when told of the attack, had frowned and told her to keep to her rooms. He placed two guards outside her door. She agreed, because she had wanted to think.

She reclined against the satin cushions. Vonda the spider lady was due. She had requested a meeting. Alma had already turned her away twice. Alma was now getting so bored that she decided seeing Vonda was better than seeing no one at all. She sipped the water, letting its coolness caress her throat. After seeing what spirits had done to her father, she drank nothing but water. She had a cool head and a sharp mind, and planned to keep them, even late at night.

A knock echoed on her door, and then it opened. Vonda scurried in, curtsied, and took the chair across from Alma without being asked.

'Please sit down,' Alma said, letting sarcasm into her voice. Vonda did not even apologize. She leaned forward.

'I have some information for you, milady.'

Alma glanced down at the courtyard. Geoffry walked past, talking with his boy Afeno. She sighed as she watched him, remembering the gentleness of his hands upon her body. 'What information?' she asked without turning around.

'It is about the bard,' Vonda said. 'And I am afraid it will cost you some money.'

Geoffry disappeared at the edge of the courtyard. Alma turned. 'If you won't speak freely, leave. The Lady Kerry pays you for information. I will not.'

'Not even if the information can save your life?'

Alma smiled. 'I doubt that you would have such information. I will not pay you for anything, Vonda. You may leave.'

Vonda stood up. When she had almost reached the door, Alma said, 'I hear that Lady Kerry arrives at the end of the week. When she gets here, I think I will tell her that her spy tries to sell information to other gentry. I don't think that the news will please her.'

'You wouldn't, lady.'

Alma set her empty water glass down. 'Never attempt to blackmail a person without first understanding how ruthless that person is. Your life is based on secrets and on your security with Lady Kerry. Mine is based upon my own wit and knowledge. I have nothing to lose in this interchange, Vonda. You do.'

'You want me to tell you what I know.'

Alma shrugged. 'If you don't, I will talk to the Lady Kerry. If you do, I will show you my thanks by keeping silent. If I don't find out, I will merely have wasted an hour talking to you. If I do, you will have saved your position with the Lady Kerry.'

Vonda leaned against the door. 'You don't like me, do you, lady?'

'My opinions about peasants are not important. If you have nothing to say, leave me alone.'

Vonda sighed and took a step forward. 'Milady, I have known the bard for a long time. Ten years ago he worked for the Lady Kerry, and he left after murdering the Ladylee Diana.'

'Geoffry?'

Vonda took another step into the room. 'Yes, Geoffry or Byron or Dasvid, as he was known then. After Lord Demythos' death, the bard came to us, saying he had been an apprentice to Lord

Demythos' bard. There was no way to prove it. The lord's bard had died in the same "accident" which had killed the lord. Later, I discovered that no one remembered Dasvid on Demythos' land or in his manor.'

'What reason would Geoffry have to lie?'

'I don't know, milady. But Lady Kerry took him in. He was handsome even then, but not nearly as talented. He knew a few ballads, but he was a quick study. Any time a wandering bard came through, Dasvid learned the bard's entire repertoire. He also earned the attention of the ladylee. That was when I grew suspicious. I was afraid that he would entice her somehow, become her lover so that when she became Lady of Kerry, he would be her consort – or her favorite, depending on how she interpreted class laws. As you know, he could easily pass for gentry.

'So I began the search for his past. He hadn't any. His life seemed to begin the moment he showed up at Kerry Manor. Lady Kerry confronted him. He repeated his story, but I did a mind tap. Somewhere he learned to block mind taps and he has gotten good at it, but he was younger then and I could touch the fringes of his emotions. He was lying and he was frightened, although I didn't know why. After he left, I told the Lady Kerry and she decided to revoke his bard's license and send him away. I wanted him imprisoned, but she said there was no reason.

'After his meeting with the Lady Kerry, Dasvid went to see the ladylee. The guards reported a quarrel, although they couldn't hear what was said. When we reached the ladylee, she had been stabbed to death. Dasvid had vanished.'

Alma had not known the story. She was pleased to have information about Geoffry, but she didn't let the pleasure show. 'You don't know that he killed the ladylee.'

'He was the last to enter her chambers. I think he knew we were going to get rid of him and thought she was in on it. No one else had access to her that night. He thought she had betrayed him and he murdered her.'

Alma glanced back out into the courtyard. 'And what has this to do with me?'

'Milady.' Vonda's voice was smooth. 'After you had sex with the bard, you told him that you were going to be the king's consort. What deeper betrayal is that?'

Alma clenched the fist nearest the window. Vonda had been watching. And now she would try to blackmail Alma to keep the information quiet. Geoffry wouldn't talk – if the king knew that Geoffry had slept with his future consort, Geoffry would die. Alma wouldn't have to pay the spider lady anything. And Alma wouldn't let the woman know how much she had angered her. 'If he was going to kill me, he would have done it then.'

'And leave you in his chambers? I doubt it. He's too intelligent for that. There has already been an attempt on your life. He could simply stage a successful one, and the attention would fall on lords Boton and Ewehl. The king is already using Dasvid for an adviser; Dasvid would rise in the ranks. By killing you, lady, he would increase his position in the palace.'

The argument made a crazy sort of sense. Alma turned back to Vonda. The woman sat on the chair, looking as if she belonged. 'Why are you telling me this?' Alma asked.

Vonda's bright eyes glowed. 'Because, milady, I want you to help us catch him.'

iii

To the Lady Kerry:

We may have a possible ally in the Lady Jelwra. I will set up a meeting between the two of you after the king's festival. I believe she will be consort then and will have enough power to help us get rid of Dasvid.

Vonda

iv

Alma had spent the last three hours dressing. She had never taken so long on her looks before. But if the king planned to name her consort, she planned to look the part. She wanted the council to think her feminine and pretty, and forget her scheming in the past. She wanted everyone to believe that she would be a puppet, little Alma content to raise the royal brats.

She would surprise the kingdom later.

Her hands shook as she buttoned the remaining seed pearls on the front of her gown. She had added some color to her dusky cheeks and some kohl around her eyes. She had wrapped her hair around the top of her head, letting small strands curl around her face. She wore a small cap around her topknot, and inside, she stuck the small dagger she had used to defend herself the day she had been with the king. She tied another dagger to the inside of her thigh. Most of the gentry, hundreds of unrecognizable servants and performers would be at the festival. She needed to be prepared for anything.

A rap on the door startled her. She let herself out of the small dressing room into the sitting room. 'Yes?' she called.

'Milady, the king would like you downstairs before the dancing begins.'

So much for her grand entrance. He probably wanted to choose her for the first dance. 'Thank you,' she said. 'Tell his majesty that I will be there shortly.'

She went back into the dressing room and looked in the full-length mirror. Her long, heavy white skirt hid the dagger. And as she moved her head from side to side, she couldn't see the smaller dagger hidden in her hair. She was ready.

Three servants accompanied her down the hallway to the ballroom. The rumble of voices greeted her, along with the smell of wine and baked bread. The room was full. Servants lined the walls. Lords wore their house colors and their women did the same. The available ladies huddled in a corner. Lady Kerry stood to one side, holding a fluted glass filled with wine. She was older than Alma remembered, and smaller. Toward the back of the room, three string players and a harpsichordist consulted about music. The bard – she could no longer think of him as Geoffry – his lute across his back, stood beside the king. Both wore black, and both watched as she stood in the door.

Alma made the servants open the doors wider. She opened her fan and held it in front of her face. The page announced her: *the Lady Almathea Jelwra*, and the room grew silent. The young ladies in the corner seemed to eye her with jealousy, and the lords with approval. Lady Kerry's expression was cool. Alma did not look at either the bard or the king.

She curtsied, extending a hand. Someone took it, and she stood, finding herself face-to-face with the king. He waved at the musicians to begin and slid an arm around her waist. He led her onto the floor. His steps were tired and slightly off; within a moment she was leading. No one else danced. Everyone else watched them. As she whirled, she saw the bard's eyes dark and sad, oversized in his pale face.

'It's a good crowd,' Alma said.

'They love a party.' The king sounded tired. The black suited him, and his mood.

'Is the Lady Constance here?'

He shook his head. 'She thought it best to wait in our rooms. She didn't want to detract from the new consort.'

It sounded as if the Lady Constance would cause no trouble at all. Alma was pleased. Her position as consort would be an easy one.

The music finally ended. The king bowed before her and kissed her hand. She curtsied once again, and as she stood, he cried, 'Let the dancing begin!'

Then he let go of Alma's hand and found Lord Seritz's daughter, leading her to the floor. Alma walked to the side, ignoring the couples who walked past her, hand in hand. A single man leaning against the wall watched her. A jagged scar ran down one side of his face, making him look as if he were perpetually smiling. Alma felt the dagger against her leg, reassured by its weight. She walked up to the man. His body didn't move as she approached, but his eyes did.

'Who are you with?' Alma asked.

'My name is Corvo, lady.' His voice was raspy, barely audible above the music.

'That, sir, is not the answer to my question. I want to know who you're with.'

A tall, slender man wearing black had stepped beside her. She turned, thinking it was the bard. Lord Kensington smiled down at her. 'May I have this dance, milady?'

'In a minute,' she said. The scarred man bothered her, and she would get rid of him if she didn't discover who he was.

'I don't want to wait, Alma,' Lord Kensington said. 'This might be my only chance this evening.' The lord slipped her into his arms and danced her out onto the floor. 'The king let the entire crowd know of his interest in you.'

'Nonsense, milord. He wanted to start the dances with a woman he knew. The Lady Constance refuses to attend the ceremonies, saying that they belong to the new consort.' The music blurred in her head and she was getting dizzy. She saw the bard sitting on a stool near the musicians. 'What is the bard doing here?'

Kensington glanced at the bard and frowned. 'Bards always record their liege's triumphs.'

Something in his voice made Alma look at him. 'A triumph for the king would not be a triumph for you, would it, milord? If he dies without issue, you're next in line.'

'Alma, your forthrightness has always astonished me.' He tightened his grip on her back. 'I don't want to be king. I don't relish being a puppet.'

'But you could change the system.'

'Changing the system is like trying to stop Lord Boton's schemes. It's impossible. I would remember that when you become consort.'

'I don't think you give up as easily as you make it sound,' Alma said. The music stopped and she pulled away from him. 'Thank you for the dance, milord.'

'Always a pleasure, milady.'

She turned and found herself facing Lord Dakin. His lady, looking heavy and tired, clung to his arm. He didn't see Alma. He walked toward the king. Alma followed. She wanted to let Dakin know that she hadn't forgotten him.

A hand grabbed her arm. She wrenched herself free. Lord Lafa swayed before her, his clothing rumpled, smelling of ale. 'You look pretty, lady. Did you use the money from my lands to buy all those clothes?'

'Let me by, milord,' Alma said, pushing past him. She went around a number of people and reached the king just as Lord Dakin reached him. The lord did not acknowledge her presence, and she realized then that he was ignoring her. The king took Alma's arm and tucked it in his. Lord Dakin turned to say something to his lady, froze, and then turned red. Alma followed his gaze. He was staring at the bard.

'What's he doing here?' Dakin cried. 'I ordered him killed!'

The lord's words echoed throughout the ballroom. Conversation stopped and everyone turned. The bard stood up and nodded at Lord Dakin. The lord let go of his lady, pushed past a throng of young lords, and stopped in front of the bard.

'How did you avoid my hounds? What sort of sorcery do you practice?'

'Good evening, milord.' The bard clutched his lute to his side.

His voice was calm. 'It 's nice to see you looking fit.'

Alma glanced around the room. Most of the gentry were watching. Seymour, the bard's toady magician friend, stood near the door, his face white and his eyes wide.

'I ordered this man put to death!' Dakin's voice rose. 'Guards, arrest him!'

The guards didn't move. The king squeezed Alma's hand and led her over to the two men. He smiled at them, and Alma thought he seemed more amused than alarmed by Lord Dakin's outburst. 'Lord Dakin,' the king said, 'I would like you to meet my bard, Byron.'

Lord Dakin's flush grew even darker. 'Sire, this man is dangerous. Lafa expelled him from his lands, and I ordered his execution. You are not safe with him here.'

'What did he do?' the king asked.

'He started a peasant uprising.'

A low murmur ran through the room. 'He squelched one here,' the king said. 'And I believe he said that your actions caused that uprising on your lands.'

'He lies!' Dakin said.

The bard watched the two men. Alma watched the bard. He had lied to her about Geoffry of Kinsmail. He had stolen the clothing he wore. And yet he had seemed passionate when he had spoken to the king. Bards were great actors, the bard had said, but what goal would he have achieved by forcing the king to feed his peasants?

'He has been honest with me,' the king said. 'And he is now a member of my household, under my protection. If you have a quarrel with him, you may petition me. Tonight we are having a celebration. Byron, since you have become the center of such controversy, why don't you play for us?'

The bard smiled. He picked up his lute, nodded once to the king. He began a light ballad, and worked his way through the gentry, flirting slightly with the ladies, encouraging the lords to dance to his melody. The music had toe-tapping lilt and seemed almost richer than the dance music the musicians had played. A few of the bolder lordlings swung a lady into their arms, and the bard left a circle of dancers in his wake.

He passed the king again, but did not look at Alma. She felt that if she let go of the king, the bard would stop playing and take her into his arms, dance with her before the entire crowd.

Someone screamed behind her. The bard whirled, catching the blade of a dagger in his lute. Alma dropped the king's arm and reached into her hair, searching for the assassin. A knife glinted as it whizzed toward her. As she dove away, she heard a grunt.

A woman screamed and then another, and soon the entire hall was filled with shouts and cries.

The king fell onto the dance floor. He clutched at the knife in his breast. Alma gripped her own dagger tightly and waited. The lords toward the back had encircled someone. The bard dropped his lute and hurried toward the king. Alma waited another minute, then crouched beside the king.

His eyes were open and empty. His hands, which had been moving a moment before, had fallen to his sides. The bard touched the king's face, his fingers shaking. The bard felt for breath and then closed the king's eyes.

Alma took the king's hand and clutched it against her breast. His skin was still warm. She shouldn't have been holding him. The Lady Constance should have been beside him in his final moments; his final thoughts should have been of her.

'Calm down!' Lord Kensington's voice rose above the din. 'Calm down! We must remain calm! Someone, close the doors!'

The doors slammed as the guards obeyed. The screaming had died down, and everyone turned toward Lord Kensington. Guards dragged the assassin to him. A chill ran down Alma's back. She had spoken to the assassin earlier. The man Corvo who had refused to answer her questions. The scar running along the side of his face was livid.

Lord Kensington ignored the assassin. 'How is he?' he asked Alma.

'He's dead,' she said. The words didn't seem real. He had promised her a world she wanted. He had danced with her only a moment before. Her mother had died slowly – and her father had killed himself with drink for years. Death happened slowly, not in the space of a heartbeat.

Kensington nodded. He bowed his head for a moment, and everyone else in the room did as well. Alma glanced through her eyelashes at the bard. He had stood up. Kensington sighed. 'As the king's closest relative, I will have to take his duties. Unless there is any objection, I will act as king until the council officially approves my claim.'

The bard snapped his fingers. His young companions, Colin and Afeno, flanked him. Seymour hurried forward from the other side of the room. 'There is an objection,' the bard said.

Alma let the king's hand go, and she stood. The bard looked as tall as Kensington, and more powerful.

'What do you dispute, bard?' Kensington asked, his tone barely civil.

'I claim the throne.'

Alma took a quick breath and heard others around her do the same. Kensington laughed. 'By what right?'

'By right of birth.' The bard pulled open his silk shirt. He had a red tattoo carved over his left nipple. 'Send a guard for the Enos.'

'It's a false claim,' Kensington said. 'All of the king's children are dead.'

'Not all,' said the bard. 'Send for the Enos.'

'Guards, arrest the usurper!' The guards took a step toward the bard. Colin and Afeno pulled out their swords.

Alma frowned. The bard's claim could be true. It would explain his secretiveness, his unwillingness to discuss himself, and his bitterness when he had learned that she was going to be the king's next consort. Still gripping her dagger, she stepped between Kensington and the bard.

'He has the right of law, Lord Kensington,' she said. 'Only an Enos can verify a tattoo claim.'

Kensington's eyes narrowed. 'Send for the Enos,' he said. Two guards left the room. The boys kept out their swords. Alma clutched her dagger. The bard did not move as they all waited.

Alma glanced at the king. He looked silly on the floor, as if he had fallen asleep and no one had bothered to move him. She had grown fond of him. Then she glanced at the bard. If his claims were true, he would need help running the kingdom. And he was young and attractive, and she was already unable to keep herself from touching him.

The main doors opened, and the crowd parted to let an Enos pass. She was small and hidden in her robes. She looked like a young child coming down to say good night to her parents. When she reached the center of the room, she knelt before the king and touched the dagger in his breast.

'The blood,' she whispered. And then she turned to Kensington. 'You allowed blood.'

He was pale. 'This man has made a claim to the throne.'

The Enos stood and faced the bard. She touched her temples. The bard reached out and grabbed Seymour's shoulder. The bard's knuckles turned white, and sweat trickled down his face. The Enos put her hands down, and the bard took a step backward and would have fallen if Seymour hadn't caught his arm.

'State your name,' the Enos said. Her voice rasped. Alma had to concentrate to understand her.

'Abington Byron Adric of Kilot,' the bard said.

Alma studied him, looking for traces of the king in his face. Young Adric had died of some disease when she was a very small girl.

The Enos took the bard's hand and faced the crowd. 'The tattoo is of the king's house. It has the proper strokes and aging marks. His claim is valid. Kneel before your next king.'

Alma glanced around the room. Lord Dakin had gone pale. Lady Kerry slapped her fan against her leg. Lord Boton didn't move, but Lord Ewehl took tiny steps backward, as if he were trying to leave the room.

'This man is no heir to the throne!' Kensington said. He turned to the crowd. 'You would take the word of a simple Enos? The bard probably set this up!'

'It is the law,' Alma said. Her voice shook. 'The Enos makes the determination. You know that, Lord Kensington.'

'And Lord Ewehl can testify that I did not die of illness, can't you, milord?' the bard said.

Ewehl stopped moving.

'The small scar on his temple is my gift,' said the bard. 'It happened months after I "died." Shall I tell them of the incident, milord? How you discovered that I lived and tried to kill me again? If it weren't for Lord Demythos, you would have.'

Ewehl turned and tried to run through the crowd. The guards caught him and brought him forward. His entire body shook. Lord Ewehl's reaction, more than the Enos's verification, made Alma believe the bard's claim.

'What would you have me do?' Ewehl asked.

'Tell them what happened.'

Lord Kensington crossed his arms before his chest. His expression had changed from one of anger to disbelief. Ewehl bowed his head. 'The young prince disappeared on a trip to Anda and we waited – '

'The truth, Ewehl,' the bard said.

'I'm telling the truth.'

'I can strip you of your lands and remove you from the council. Unlike my father, I know the laws.'

Ewehl closed his eyes. 'It was determined that young Adric asked too many questions and would not be a good ruler – '

'By whom?'

' – would not listen to our advice – '

'Our?'

'I will not implicate others!' Ewehl snapped. 'Let them implicate themselves.'

'Go on,' Lord Kensington said.

'He wanted to see Anda. We thought, since the Lady Constance was again pregnant, that he would simply disappear in town. We thought that he wouldn't survive. We waited weeks before announcing his death. But several months later, I was walking in the palace when I saw him on the staircase, heading toward the king's chambers. I tried to stop him when I was attacked by another boy. In self-defense I – '

'Who lies now?' the bard asked. 'You tried to kill me and Milo protected me.'

' – I stabbed the other and ran for the guards. By the time I returned, the boys were gone. A trail of blood led to one of the closets and there we found the body of the friend, but the prince had again vanished. We searched for him, found nothing, and assumed he was dead.'

'Lord Demythos took me in, hid me, and cared for me,' the bard said. 'He made sure that no one would hurt me.'

'And then someone assassinated Lord Demythos,' said Alma. 'My mother spoke of it. She was afraid that someone was after all the gentry.'

'You have admitted to treason, Ewehl,' Lord Boton said.

Ewehl glanced at Lord Boton, and for a moment neither of them moved. Then Lord Boton stepped forward and examined the bard as if he were a serf on auction. 'You look nothing like the king or the Lady Constance. And Adric was a fat, lazy lad. I don't discount the Enos's testimony, but I won't accept you as my liege until you answer a few questions.'

'Ask them, milord.' The bard stood, hands clasped behind his back.

'You have been here for months. Why didn't you tell the king who you were?'

'Lord Ewehl just admitted that he and his friend tried twice to murder me. I decided that this time I would not return to the palace before I could defend myself – and I decided that before I identified myself, I would gain the king's trust. As you learned earlier, I had. I was going to speak with him this week, but he put off the appointment.'

So that was what he had meant by petition, not for his lands but for his title. Alma glanced at him. If he had spoken to the king before the festival, the celebrations would not have been held and she would not have become consort. She would have lost the kingdom before she had a chance to save herself.

'Why didn't you confide in any of the gentry?' Lord Boton asked.

'I did,' the bard said. His voice was bitter. 'Lord Demythos protected me for years. I was with him on that hunt. His death was no accident.'

'The questions are not necessary,' said the Enos. 'This man's claim is valid. The Old Ones have studied his movements. He wears the white mists and he bears the tattoo. When he drops his shields, his mind carries the memories of a prince's life. I challenge any magician to tap and then dispute my words.'

'I will not be ruled by a liar and a thief!' Lord Dakin cried.

'Why not?' the bard asked, looking at him. 'I was, just recently.'

'Or a murderer,' added the Lady Kerry. 'He killed my daughter, Diana. Who's to say he didn't murder the king?'

'The pretender shed the king's blood,' the Enos said. Alma frowned and glanced at Kensington. No one else seemed to have heard.

'I did not murder Diana or the king, milady,' the bard said. He raised his voice. 'Think once, all of you! It would be easier for me to have the king's acceptance and approval than it would to take over after his death. Now my rule will be questioned every step. If my father had lived, I would have had his blessing. No. It suited a handful of others to do away with the king before he sired another child.'

He surveyed the hall. 'Will the council members, the gentry, and my cousin Kensington accept me? Or will I have to fight for my rightful claim?'

Kensington spat on the ground at the bard's feet. 'I shall die before I accept you as ruler of this land.'

The bard met Kensington's gaze. 'Reconsider, milord. I don't want to be your enemy.'

Kensington shook his head. 'You will never rule me.'

The Enos crouched between them, clutching her head and lowering herself to the ground.

'Then leave, milord,' the bard said. 'But let me give you a piece of advice. If you want to assassinate me, do it yourself. Don't hire an assassin to throw your daggers for you.'

Kensington reached for the bard, but Afeno grabbed his hand. The boy threw the lord back against one of the guards.

'As for the rest of you,' the bard said, still looking at Kensington, 'those who agree with Lord Kensington may leave with him. But should there be a battle and should I win, I will remember every one of you.'

The Enos huddled on the floor, her arms wrapped around her head. Alma reached down to touch her, to see if she were all right, but the Enos shook off Alma's hands.

'We're not through yet, bard,' Kensington said.

'I realize that, cousin.'

Kensington turned and pushed his way through the crowd. Lord Dakin, Lady Kerry, Lord Lafa, and a few gentry that Alma didn't recognize followed. The others glanced at the door, then glanced at the bard.

'If you choose to remain,' the bard said, 'I want you to swear your obedience to me as your liege lord. I need public evidence of your trust.'

The door's slam echoed in the large room. No one moved. Alma took a deep breath. She had no liking for Kensington and he had none for her. The bard was her best choice. She knelt in front of him.

'On the word of the Enos,' she said, 'I accept you as my liege lord.'

The bard offered her his hand and she stood up. He smiled slightly, and then she stepped aside. One by one, the remaining gentry came forward and knelt before the bard. Alma watched for a moment, then crouched beside the Enos. The old woman seemed to have withdrawn into herself. The Enos was whispering and it took a moment before Alma understood what the woman was saying.

'The blood,' the Enos was saying. 'I am so sorry, Old Ones, to have started the blood.'

PART FOUR

Chapter 23

The dressing room was small and smelled of Diana's perfume. Kensington removed his cape. It was getting stuffy, and his back was crammed against the dressing table. He wondered what was keeping Diana. She should have returned by now.

He shifted his weight on the small stool and peered through the slit the Lady Kerry had carved in all the dressing-room doors. Diana's room was small, two windows on either side, the curtains blowing in with the night breezes. A lamp guttered on the wall above his door. Paper rustled on her bedside table and a book fluttered open. Her bed was high and ruffled, the quilt handmade. A dressing gown hung on a peg and shoes were scattered on the floor. Hardly the meeting place for a woman and her lover.

He rolled the papers in his hands. He would catch her with her lover, prove to her that the man was a liar and a class-jumper. Then the lord would show her the papers and take them to Lady Kerry. Diana didn't dare say no to him again. She would be his consort one way or another.

He let the papers rest in his lap. They revealed nothing; that was the beauty of them. The youth had hidden most of his past. The spies were unable to verify his story. Members of the estate remembered him, but said that few on the grounds knew of his presence. Too bad Demythos was dead. It would have been nice to reveal his secrets too.

The outer door squeaked as it opened. Kensington froze. He knew that the ladylee would not come into her dressing room – not if the bard was with her – but he was frightened anyway. He leaned against the slit carved above the door.

Diana was alone. She closed the shutters with one hand and pulled the pins from her red hair with the other. Then she unbuttoned her gown and let it fall to the floor. She was slender and much more finely formed than he had thought. He felt a tightening in his groin. He would have her. And she would enjoy it.

She put on the dressing gown and tied it around her waist. A knock sounded on the door, and she paused.

'Yes?'

'Milady, the bard insists on seeing you. He says he will not go away until you speak with him.'

Diana smoothed her hair. 'Let him in,' she said.

Diana's lover pushed the door open. His lute hit the door frame, sending a ghostly chord through the room. His face was pale and his eyes seemed too wide and dark. He slammed the door and Diana jumped. 'You could have been honest with me,' he said.

'What do you mean?'

'I just had an audience with your precious mother and her spying magician – '

'Vonda?'

'Vonda. They couldn't find anyone who saw me on Lord Demythos' estate, so they are calling me a liar and a class-climber. I'm dangerous and to be thrown off this land after they revoke my bard's license.'

'Dasvid, I'm sorry, I – '

'Don't pretend, milady. I thought we were friends. I thought you trusted me. I had even thought one day you would help me.'

'Help you?'

'But no. You and your mother send out an Enos-trained spy to check out my background and judge me before you hear why so many on Demythos' estate never saw me. And then you threaten to take away my bard's license, the only thing that stands between me and starvation. The only thing, Diana.'

Diana reached out for him. She was trembling. 'I didn't know, Dasvid. Honest I didn't. Please believe me.'

He watched her hand, then took it, and pulled her to him, burying his face in her hair. 'I'm sorry, Diana, I'm just so frightened.'

'You have no reason to be frightened, Dasvid.' She spoke to him as though she were speaking to a child. 'I'll help you.'

Her long fingers stroked the bard's neck. Kensington touched himself, felt his arousal build. She would touch him like that soon.

The bard took her hands and pushed her away. 'I'm sorry, milady. I shouldn't have done that.'

Kensington frowned, then realized the bard was referring to the hug. So the bard and the ladylee were not lovers. A shiver ran through the lord. That changed everything.

'No, Dasvid, it's all right.' Diana sat on the edge of the bed. She patted a spot beside her. He hesitated for a moment, and then sat, keeping a distance between them. 'Explain this to me.'

'I can't, milady.'

'You barge in here, accuse me of plotting your ruin with my mother, say Vonda – who is a very able mind-tapper – believes that you are dangerous, and you say you were going to ask for my help.' Diana touched his arm. 'You owe me an explanation.'

The bard sighed. He covered her hand with his own. 'I owe you one. I can't give it to you.'

'Don't you trust me?'

'It's not a matter of trust. It's a matter of safety, yours and mine.'

'Did Lord Demythos help you in this manner?'

The bard nodded.

'And did he die because of it?'

The bard started. Diana smiled. 'I'll pry it out of you one way or another, Dasvid. You may as well tell me.'

The bard glanced around the room. Kensington held his breath. It seemed as if the bard could see him through the slit in the door. 'Are we alone?'

'Yes.'

The bard didn't stop looking. Diana let go of his arm. 'Do you want me to prove it to you?'

Kensington glanced around the dressing room. He was too large to hide under the table, and he couldn't get into the wardrobe without someone hearing. If she found him, he would have to try the original plan. With the Lady Kerry already mistrusting the bard, the plan might work.

'No, that's all right,' the bard said.

Kensington let his breath out slowly.

'Milady, this story is hard to tell. I doubt that you will believe me.'

'Let me decide what to believe,' Diana said.

The bard stood up and turned his back to the lord. He swung his lute around, examined the instrument's side, and then laid it across the bed. He unlaced his shirt. Diana watched him, a flush building in her cheeks. The bard pulled the shirt off and threw it on top of the lute. His back was marked with deep welts, left by improperly healed whippings.

'Do you recognize the crest?' the bard asked.

Diana reached up and touched the bard's chest. 'It's the king's familial crest,' she said. 'What does it mean?'

'It means that I'm the king's son.'

Kensington pressed against the slit. He could see nothing but the bard's back.

'The crest could be forged.'

'It's not. If an Enos was here, I'd prove it to you. It's not forged, Diana.'

'But how do you know?'

'I spent my first decade in the palace.'

'Then your name is not Dasvid.'

'It's Adric. Or it was. Lord Demythos called me by my second name for so many years, I answer to it much quicker. Byron, milady.'

'Byron,' Diana whispered.

Kensington whispered the name too. Abington Byron Adric of Kilot. He remembered when the boy was born. The crest tattooed on his chest had a dove on it, and the Enos had used a small dab of permanent red dye to decorate the tail feathers. Several years before, the child had disappeared, and after months of half-hearted searching, he had been given up for lost. The palace had made up some story and decided the boy was dead. The palace couldn't ignore him any longer. Prince Adric had been the eldest.

The bard picked up his shirt and turned to put it on. Kensington saw the tail feathers, the red spreading across the design as the Enos had predicted it would. Diana gasped.

'The scars. What – ?'

The bard shrugged on his shirt. 'I was whipped several years ago, milady, and then improperly treated. That's one reason why I'm reluctant to be on my own again.'

'Then you were planning to tell me this.'

He laced the shirt. 'When the time was right. I still need some type of protector until I figure out how to reach my father. I tried once and was nearly killed.'

'Why would someone want to kill you?'

'I don't know. They attacked me when I was a boy, when they could have manipulated me. Sometimes I even think my father was behind it.'

Diana touched his arm and pulled him back to the bed. 'You're telling me the truth, aren't you?'

'It would be stupid to lie about something like this.' He picked up his lute and slung it over his back. Then he kissed her cheek and stood up. 'I'm going to go now, Diana. It's better not to stay too long.'

'Dasvid – '

The bard smiled. She smiled too.

'I'll help in any way I can. Stay here. We'll get you back to the palace.'

He shook his head. 'No. Your mother doesn't trust me. And I don't trust her. If word got back to the palace, we might all die.'

'Wait.' Diana pulled a small silver ring from her hand. 'My Enos gave this to me. She said it brought good luck.'

'No, Diana, I can't.'

She pressed the ring into his hand. 'I can't help you because I'm not Lady Kerry yet. But as soon as I am, I'll contact you. I'll stay in touch – '

'No.' The bard slipped the ring onto his finger. 'No, don't contact me until you're lady. This is dangerous, Diana, and someone will kill to keep me away from the throne. You're the only friend I have right now. I don't want anything to happen to you.'

'Where are you going to go?'

He shrugged. 'I don't know. But I'll be all right.'

Diana grabbed a sheet of parchment from her bedside table. 'There is something I can do. Just wait.' She opened a drawer and pulled out a pen and inkpot. She dipped the pen and began to write. 'Will you use the same name?'

'I hadn't thought about it – '

'All right. You're Byron again.' She handed him the parchment. 'It'll get you in anywhere. No one will need to know if your license has been revoked or not.'

The bard took the parchment. 'It may be years, you know,' he said.

'I know,' she said. 'Now go before my mother makes good her threats.'

The bard ran his finger along her cheek. 'Thank you,' he whispered and let himself out. Diana leaned against the bed frame. A tear glistened in the lamplight. She wiped a hand over her cheek.

Kensington clutched the papers. They were worthless now. He had to think. He had only a few servants with him at Kerry. By the time he sent someone to find the bard, it might be too late. He would have to risk losing the man. If it weren't for the ladylee, he would go himself.

Diana walked to the dressing room. She glanced about, saw the dress, and picked it up. He pushed open the door, grabbed her, and covered her mouth. Her cheeks were damp. 'Don't scream, milady,' he said. 'We have a lot to discuss.'

She nodded and he let her go. She moved away from him. 'What are you doing here? How long have you been here?'

'Long enough to possess a few secrets. Very interesting lover you have there, Diana.' Kensington smiled at her. This might be easier than he thought.

'He's not my lover.'

'No? And who's going to believe that? He was in your chamber for a long time.'

Diana stared at him. 'What do you want, milord?'

'I think we should strike a bargain, milady. In return for my silence about your relationship with a bard, you will become my consort. Sound fair?'

Diana laughed. 'I've refused you three times, milord. What makes you think that I'll accept you under threat?'

Kensington leaned against the wall. 'I heard every word uttered in this room. All I have to do is send a messenger to the palace. Does the bard mean anything to you? You're the only one who holds his secret. How will he feel when he learns that you've betrayed him?'

Diana whirled, slid her hand under her pillow, and pulled out a dagger. She pushed Kensington and shoved the dagger against his breastbone. 'I don't like to be threatened,' she said.

'So you believe the bard.' He kept his voice calm. He liked the way she touched him, how close she was to him. Her perfume smelled better mingled with her scent.

'What I believe doesn't matter. But if what he says is true, you would be killing him.'

Kensington looked at the dagger. Diana's hand was trembling. 'What are you going to do?'

She opened her mouth, drew in breath, and Kensington thought she was going to scream. He grabbed her wrist. She pulled away from him and tried to plunge the dagger into his chest. He sidestepped. The dagger hit the wall and stuck. He lunged for the hilt, knocking her hand away. Diana reached for the blade as he pulled the dagger from the wall. She hit him, knocking him off balance. Her hand covered his and they fell to the floor. She had him pinned. She tried to pry the dagger from his hand. In a moment she would scream and the guards would catch him. He wrenched his arm free and shoved the dagger forward. It thunked as it slid between her ribs.

Diana's eyes widened. As he let go of the hilt, her hands found it. She tried to pull it out, but her fingers kept slipping. She fell back against the bed, blood spreading along her dressing gown. Her hands slid off the dagger. He touched her face, but her eyes were empty.

He crawled over to her and hugged her against him, stroking her hair. Diana. He wanted her as badly as he wanted the land. He closed his eyes and forced himself to think. The bard was the last one seen leaving the room. If Kensington left another way, they would blame the bard. He was already under suspicion.

Another way. The window. He kissed Diana's head and leaned her back against the bed. Then he hurried to the window and pulled back the shutters. The wind blew in, chilling him. He leaned out. The drop was long, but he was tall.

He hefted himself onto the stone ledge. He gripped the edge tightly and lowered himself to his full length. Then he took a deep breath and let go. The fall seemed to last forever. Finally his feet hit the mud – the soft, soft mud that cushioned his fall.

PART FIVE

Chapter 24

i

The air was still, but the whistle-wood trees moaned. Their cries echoed deep in the earth, warning of the final time, warning of blood. The sound throbbed across Kilot, to the dwelling of each Enos. Dakin's Enos sidled up to the riverbank and listened. Jelwra's Enos stopped a conversation with Usci in mid-sentence and put her ear to the ground. The bluff Enos, sleeping beneath one of the young trees, let the cries seep into her dreams, filling her mind with blood and white mists.

They all stood, they all responded, they all headed for the Cache, knowing they had to arrive before the final time started, before the bloodletting began. The Old Ones were calling, and time traveled in circles in the mind. The earth cried for blood, was filled with blood, would fill with blood, unless the bloodlust ended before it even began.

ii

Byron entered the audience chamber before dawn. The room was empty. He had been up all night, thinking, consolidating his power with his friends. And now he had to take action, even though he wasn't ready.

The chamber felt long that morning, narrower than usual. The swords decorating the walls seemed ominous, more a warning than decoration. Byron climbed the stairs and stopped before the dais. The king's chair was wider than the others, covered with hand-carved animals and scenes from Kilot's history. The chair was his now. As a child he used to sit in that chair, feet dangling above the floor, and imagine how he would rule Kilot. Then, when he lived on the streets, he used to remember those moments and think them part of a long, cruel dream. His younger self might have thought that the dream was over now; he knew that it had merely changed.

The polished wood was smooth and warm to the touch. Yesterday his father had sat here, listening to lords Boton and Ewehl, and probably thinking of the upcoming festival and a life that included Almathea. If Byron had spoken to him yesterday, the king might still be alive. But the king was dead, and the assassin wouldn't admit who hired him. The Enos said Kensington had started the bloodshed, but she could have been referring to other bloodshed, the attempts on Byron's life.

The squeak of the chamber door echoed in the morning stillness. Byron whirled, his hand on his sword. Afeno smiled a funny little half smile and waved. Byron smiled back. So much for ceremony. But he and Afeno were friends, not king and subject, and Byron never wanted that to change.

Byron let his hand relax and he sat on the chair. The carvings dug into his back and buttocks, and he wondered how his father had managed to spend all day there. 'Did you find Lord Boton?'

'Colin's bringing him,' Afeno said.

The door opened once more, and Colin entered, followed by Boton. The lord still wore the clothes he had worn the evening before. They looked crumpled and stained. The deep circles under the lord's eyes made Byron realize that Boton hadn't gotten any sleep either.

'You sent for me, sire?' Boton spat out the title as if he wanted his mouth free of it.

Byron stretched his legs out across the dais and crossed his feet at the ankles, pretending a relaxation he did not feel. 'I did. We have a lot to discuss, and I thought it best that we talk in private. Take a chair, Boton.'

Boton grabbed a chair behind Byron and pulled it closer. Alma had sat in that chair when Byron petitioned his father to feed the peasantry. Byron sighed. He would redecorate the audience chamber, remove the memories of his father from the room. 'Boton,' he said. 'You swore your allegiance to me last night. Do you intend to maintain that oath?'

'Yes, sire.' Boton clenched his ringed fingers together. The metal scraped as he twisted his hands. 'I would like to serve you as I served your father. Perhaps I can be of even more assistance to you since you are unfamiliar with the ways of the palace.'

A shiver ran down Byron's back. He remembered that tone from his childhood, Boton wheedling to get what Boton wanted. 'I don't plan to be the puppet my father was.'

Boton flushed. 'Are you accusing me – ?'

'Don't be so defensive, milord.' Byron smiled. He had gotten the desired reaction. 'Right now I don't know whom I can trust and whom I can't. I'm speaking to you now, alone, because as a child I felt closer to you than I did to my own parents. I want your assessment of the current situation. Tell me, what would you do if you were in my place?'

Boton leaned forward, resting his elbows on his knees, his clasped hands extended before him. He had obviously been thinking of this. 'I would bury your father with full rites and then make a proclamation to the people that I am king. Then I would secure my power. I would inform the guards that they would lose their lives if they did not serve me. I would threaten the gentry with land loss if they did not support me. And I would surround myself with people that I trust, as you have done, sire.'

Byron almost shook his head. Boton was testing his power, seeing if he could manipulate the newest king. Pity. The child in Byron, the Adric part of him, had hoped that Boton had been a pawn, like the king. But Boton was as manipulative as Ewehl, and had probably helped plan Adric's death.

'I have confined Lord Ewehl to his quarters,' Byron said. 'I would like you to begin an investigation into Ewehl's past actions. I want a daily report on the things you have learned. You will work with the Lady Kerry's former magician, Vonda. She's Enos-trained and can mind-tap.'

'But, sire, I already have duties.'

'Yes, I know,' Byron extended his hand. 'Give me your keys for a moment, will you?'

Boton handed Byron a ring of keys. The metal was warm from Boton's skin. Byron turned the ring over in his hands. The documents room key was not on the ring. 'Are these all of your keys?'

Boton nodded.

'That's too bad.' Byron stared at the ring. 'When I was a child, I went to see the Cache Enos. She predicted that I would be able to trust a man carrying an ornate gold key. I remembered that you carried a lot of keys, so I thought that man was you. Perhaps she meant Lord Demythos.'

Boton dug into a pocket at the side of his robe. He pulled out a thin, gold key with scrollwork on the handle. Byron took the key from Boton's hand. 'This is it,' Byron said, and pocketed the key. 'Colin, will you escort Lord Boton back to his room?'

'But my keys – '

'You'll have no further use for them.' Byron enjoyed the edge of panic in Boton's voice. 'I am relieving you of your responsibilities. The investigation of Lord Ewehl should take up all of your time.'

'But, sire, a king never carries keys.'

Byron smiled. 'I take it this was one of the palace rules you were going to inform me about. I had an unorthodox upbringing, milord. I tend to break rules.'

Colin approached the stairs. 'I'm to escort you, milord.'

Boton stood, glanced hesitantly at Byron, and then walked down the stairs.

'Colin, after you have accompanied Lord Boton to his chambers, stop at Lord Ewehl's rooms and bring me his keys as well.'

'All right, Byron,' Colin said. He put his hands behind his back. 'Are you ready, milord?'

Boton said nothing. He raised his chin as he left the room, but he seemed a little more crumpled, a little more tired. Byron knew that he couldn't believe Boton's defeated look. The man had ties that no one knew about. He was someone to watch, to guard against, at all times. As they passed Afeno, Byron saw Afeno's hand reach out. Boton left the room and Afeno dropped another set of keys on the ground.

'Thank you, Afeno,' Byron said. Afeno left his post near the door and walked up the stairs. He gave Byron the keys. The ring was heavy and nearly solid with keys of all shapes and sizes.

'You just made an enemy, you know,' Afeno said.

Byron shook his head. 'I merely confirmed one. He was an enemy a long time ago.'

A knock on the door startled them both. Afeno grabbed his sword and hurried down the stairs. The door swung open to reveal two of the guards. Byron stood, body stiff, ready to defend himself if he had to. The guards bowed.

'State your business, gentlemen,' Byron said.

The guards rose. One of them looked familiar. Byron frowned, but couldn't place the man's face. 'Sire,' the familiar one said. 'This is Cifin, and I am Ile. We felt we had to talk with you.'

Ile. Ile. He remembered Ile around the palace – and once outside, when Byron had run away from Rogren for the first time. Ile had not believed that Byron was prince. An old, old anger shuddered through him. He placed a hand on the table to steady himself.

'Lords Kensington, Dakin, and Lafa have left the grounds, sire, as has the Lady Kerry. Their servants are gone too. A handful of their retainers stayed, sire, because they said they remembered you. Lord Dakin's people especially. They said you helped them in the past.'

Ile was trembling.

'Go on,' Byron said.

'The lords plan an uprising, sire. I have heard it from a couple of different sources. They're going back to their lands to raise an army.'

The chill at the base of Byron's spine grew stronger. 'Why are you telling me this?'

'Sire.' Ile stepped forward, head bowed. 'I taught you how to hold a sword, remember? And I watched you teaching the boys and I wondered who you were. And then last night, when you told about how you survived after they left you in Anda, I kept thinking about this thin little boy who came to us, swearing he was the prince and saying he could prove it. That was you, wasn't it?'

Byron nodded.

'I didn't believe you, sire. If I had, I might have saved a few lives. Your father wouldn't have died last night.'

Byron walked down the stairs. Afeno still clutched his sword, and Byron trusted the boy for protection. Byron stopped in front of Ile. The man smelled of sweat. 'You don't know that. They might have tried something else. If I had stayed here, maybe Lord Ewehl and his people really would have killed me.'

'That's kindness, sire, but I figure I owe you.'

Byron nodded. He understood such debts.

'Sire.' The other man, Cifin, spoke, Byron turned. 'I came because I'm captain of the guards. I wanted to let you know that the guards are behind you, every one. We've seen what's been happening here over the past decade or more, and we've seen you working with the peasantry. We'll support you over Lord Kensington and we'll help you should you have any trouble with the council.'

Byron smiled. 'I'm trying to take care of the council. Ewehl's locked up and I have just confiscated Boton's keys. I will run this kingdom my own way.'

The captain nodded, as if Byron's words relieved him. 'Sire, if this does come to war, I don't know how much support you will get. You will have mine, but none of the men have ever fought before. They may not last through it.'

'I know.' Byron suppressed a sigh. He had thought on that all night. Kilot had not seen war since Gerusha. Most people had no idea what kind of hardships they would experience. Byron didn't know either. He hoped that the rumors of Kensington's uprising were just talk. 'Drill the men. Have them participate in exercises and set up teams so that they can practice. If something does happen, they will at least be mentally prepared.' And mental preparedness was half of the battle. He knew. He had not been prepared for his father's death.

'And don't forget,' he said. 'Kensington's people have never fought either. Whoever has the most confidence will surely have an advantage.'

The men nodded. Colin slipped back in the door and stared at the men. Afeno leaned over, explaining the situation.

'I will help you as best I can,' Byron said. He held out his hands. The men clasped them. 'I value your support, and I thank you for coming to see me.'

They bowed and then left the room. Byron was about to walk back up to the dais when he saw a movement outside the door, a flash of dark hair and white clothing, and heard the rustle of shoes against stone. 'Alma?'

She peeked around the corner, looking shy and coy for the first time since he had known her. She stopped in front of the door and curtsied. He walked over to her, took her hand, and helped her stand.

She smelled of jasmine and her hair shone. But she too had shadows under her eyes, and he wondered if she actually mourned for his father. Then he shook away the thought. Alma probably mourned for the lost land, the lost opportunity. 'Colin, Afeno,' he said, 'leave us.'

'But – '

'Leave us. If I'm dead when you return, kill the Lady Jelwra.'

Colin frowned and left the room. Afeno stopped in front of

Alma. 'I don't trust you, milady. If you hurt Byron, I'll do more than kill you. I'll make sure that your death is very slow, very painful, and very humiliating.'

Alma didn't flinch. She smiled a little and looked at Byron. 'Such loyalty,' she said.

Afeno nodded at Byron, then followed Colin out of the chamber, closing the doors with a flourish. Byron took Alma's hands and led her to the dais.

'You don't know that you can trust me,' she said. 'They really should have stayed.'

He sat on the bench beside the table, spurning his father's chair, and bid her to do the same. 'You're too power-hungry to murder me at this stage,' he said.

'Your descriptions of me are not flattering.' She brushed him as she sat down. Her skin was soft, and he longed to hold her.

'Why did you make love to me when you thought I was a bard, Alma?'

Her eyes widened slightly. She obviously hadn't expected him to ask that question. 'I thought you were a lord.'

'And how do you feel now that you know who I am?'

'A bit confused.' She smiled. 'Although now I know why you refused to let me remove your shirt.'

He ignored her attempt at humor. He had been debating this move all night. Seymour hated Alma and didn't trust her. Neither did Afeno. But sometimes trust was not the most important thing. Power was. Alma understood power. And Byron thought he understood Alma. 'You planned to become my father's consort.'

Something like fear flickered across her face, and her body grew tense. Byron noted her reaction and finished his thought. 'Would you consider being my consort instead?'

She didn't mask her relief and he wondered at it. What had she expected? 'Why?'

'You heard Lord Boton last night. I must secure my power quickly. An heir, or the promise of one, would help.'

'You have no children?'

He shook his head. She looked almost plain this morning. He preferred her this way. The flirt that had emerged around the king had angered him.

'Why me?' she asked.

'Several reasons. I have no lands, just the royal property, which is worthless – '

'I will not sign my lands over to you,' she said.

He smiled. 'I didn't ask you to. Just listen. Our heir would get the royal lands and your lands, building a nice power base for the child. It would not guarantee me power, but it would assure our child of it.

'Second, I'm not sure how long I'll live. With Kensington rising and my strange circumstances, I don't know if I'll have a year as king. If you're pregnant, Alma, you will have the throne. I know you'll survive. You're ruthless in a way that I am not. If you aren't pregnant, you will have the trappings of power around you and you will give my cousin a fight. I don't want him to rule. I've watched him over the years. He would be like me; he would rule. Only he has a cruelness in him, an anger that could destroy this land.

'And finally, Alma – ' Byron hesitated. He wasn't sure how vulnerable he wanted to be with her. 'You fascinate me. I want you beside me, not opposing me.'

'You are like your father,' she said. Her voice was soft. 'No talk of love and tender things, just my strength and how much I will add to the kingdom.'

'Does that disappoint you?'

She smiled and shook her head, but her eyes seemed cold. He leaned down and kissed her slowly, then the kiss built. They clung to each other and he could feel the passion growing as it had before. He let her go before he made love to her there in the audience chamber.

A flush had risen along her neck into her cheeks. The coolness had left her eyes and he could see the fire in them, burning for him as much as he burned for her. 'All right,' she said. 'I'll stand beside you and be your strength.'

'My consort?'

'Your consort, and your queen.'

He took her hands, but did not kiss her. Her words seemed to add to the heaviness he was feeling. He should have felt more happiness: he had the woman he wanted, the position he wanted. But nothing happened the way he wanted. He had needed his father's blessing and the years to learn the kingdom again. Now he was alone, beside a woman who would betray him if she had to, leading people who weren't sure if he had a right to rule them.

iii

The bluff Enos followed the moans of the Old Ones along the river and down into the Cache. She had never left her bluff before, found the world outside little different but stronger, as if other Enos built their magic into their lands. The Cache itself was dark and cold, the entrance half hidden behind rocks near the river-bank. Humans never saw the entrance. Only the moaning of the Old Ones led Enos to it.

Under the ground, glowing rocks replaced the Old Ones' moans. She followed a winding, dirt-covered path down, down, down into greater dampness and darkness. The rocks' light only made the darkness seem more oppressive. She wondered how Enos could live down here, away from the open air and the touch of green things. She shuddered and remembered her dreams of blood.

A rush of warm air filled the tunnel, and as she rounded a corner, an Enos stood in her path. She stopped. She hadn't seen one of her kind in generations. She had been alone on the bluff, watching human travelers, speaking to only a few, the last the white mists.

The other Enos stood before her, hidden under a robe, her hands wizened and old. *I am Zcava. Are you named?*

The bluff Enos touched her fingers to her forehead. The voice had entered her mind: she hadn't entered its. So strange. So foreign. The bluff Enos thought back to a time when she had spoken with others. They had called her something then. The word came slowly. *I am Ikaner, the bluff Enos. What is this that I have come for?*

Zcava turned, her robe sweeping the dirt. *Follow me.* She ducked through a side passage. Ikaner followed. The air had grown warmer and humid, smelling of roots and wet dirt. The light grew brighter and she squinted, then stepped into a large cavern.

The rock walls stood higher than her bluff. Thick bits of rock broke from the ceiling and the floor, but the entire ceiling glowed with a sunlike light. Trees and underbrush grew around the rock pillars. Flowers and vegetables stood off to the side. She had known that the Cache Enos guarded the Old Wisdom, but she didn't know that wisdom gave light to darkness and taught things to grow without sunlight. Her gifts were tiny. She only maintained growth, made sure that the sunlight filtered into the leaves, guided the water to roots. She didn't know that the Enos could create such things from nothing.

It took a moment before she saw the other Enos scattered among the rocks and trees. Most were examining the floor, as she wanted to, to discover the source of the growth. None of the Enos were young. All had wrinkled skin and balding heads. Their bodies had shrunk and, like aging trees, looked as if a sharp wind would uproot them. She hadn't realized how old they were, how long they had been guarding the land. The thought made her tired, and she sat on a moss-covered rock.

Why am I here? she repeated.

A thousand thoughts answered her, none the same. But in each reverberation she saw white mists mixed with blood. She frowned, remembering the white mists. He had seemed kind. He had loved his friend and had not hurt her bluff.

What has he done? she asked.

We shall wait for the others. That response was strong, and she recognized Zcava's presence. Such a serious thing for the Old Ones to call the Enos from their lands. She wondered if she would be allowed to return to the grove, to the sacred place where she had sprung, as a seedling, from her father's branches.

No answers came to that thought. The others had stopped listening and she liked that better. She was used to the silence of her own mind. The humid air clung to her, and she missed the breezes of her bluff. She leaned against the wall and sighed, wishing that she could go home. But she was bound by her upbringing and training to listen to the Old Ones, to hear their proposal.

Her world was finally changing, and she wasn't sure she liked it.

iv

Byron stood at the door leading to the west wing, his parents' wing. He remembered nights lingering in that wide hallway, hoping that his parents would include him in their special time, hoping they would notice him.

They never had.

He pushed the door open and stepped into the wing. It smelled of leather and perfume – his father's and mother's scents. Alma said she had seen his mother the night before and had told her the news, thinking she needed to speak to someone the king trusted, not Boton and Ewehl. Alma had stayed up all night with his mother, holding her and listening to her cry.

Byron hadn't thought of the woman until Alma mentioned her.

His footsteps echoed as he walked down the hallway. A door stood open and he glanced inside. His parents' bedchamber. A large bed stood against the wall, dwarfing the room. A hearth faced it, and chairs and a table stood near the window.

His mother sat in a rocker against the far wall. She wore a shawl and she stared across the bed at the rippled window glass. Byron looked at her. She was smaller than he remembered, and her face had fallen in on itself, as if grief had crippled her. That look was beginning when he left. It had grown and softened her, made her into an old and tired woman. She had borne ten children. All had died. Then her husband died, and her eldest child came back from the grave.

He knocked on the door. She did not turn. He walked inside and knelt on the woven rug beside her chair. The yarn dug into his knees.

She took his arm and tugged on it. 'A king does not kneel before anyone,' she said. Her voice still had the richness he remembered. It had melody, as his did, only her melody was sadness.

'I will always kneel before you,' he said.

She took his face in her hands, turned it from side to side as if it were a vase she was deciding to buy. 'They speak the truth, then. You don't look like either of us, but your eyes are my father's. May I see the marking?'

He unlaced his shirt. She pushed the material aside, her palm dry on his skin. 'The red did bleed,' she whispered. 'The Enos said it would.'

She took her hand off him and he felt a lack. He wanted to ask her to hold him, to welcome him home, but he said nothing.

'I would have sent word long ago,' Byron said, 'but Lord Demythos did not think it wise.'

'Demythos was a good man. He used to tell me not to worry so. Now I know why.' She gazed over his head, at the windows and the hunting grounds beyond. The sun touched the tops of the trees, making their leaves a pale green. 'Adric?'

He started at the name. She said it as she used to when she was angry with him: the tone cold, the word crisp.

'Did you kill him?'

'I was singing at the time.'

'You know what I'm asking you.'

She had to know. Kensington was the only other one with a motive. She had probably spent the entire night wondering if her son had killed her husband. 'I did not hire the assassin, Mother. I was planning to speak to my father before the ball, but he postponed it. I wanted to earn his trust before revealing myself.'

'Alma said that,' she said. She looked at him, her eyes suddenly alive. He remembered the look, remembered wondering as a child if she could see what he thought. 'I do believe you.'

Her tone told him that he was dismissed. He kissed her hand and stood, wishing that she would hug him, just once, and tell him that she had missed him and was sorry to lose him. But she couldn't. Her eldest son had died when he was ten and was placed in the crypt long ago. She had ridden in the black carriage that had borne him on his last journey and she had mourned him over two decades before. Whatever she had felt rested in the crypt with the body of an unknown boy, the one she believed to be her son.

He left the room, knowing that to her, he was neither ghost nor relative, merely a usurper who had watched the man she loved die.

He leaned against the wall outside the wing. He had never been welcome there. He never would be. He bowed his head and walked, feeling like a stranger in the place his heart had always called home.

V

Ikaner sat on a little niche high above the cavern floor. She didn't move even as more Enos arrived. This place reminded her of her bluff, and she didn't want to leave it until she was allowed to go home.

The Enos filled the cavern, making it seem as if it were growing Enos instead of plants. The thought struck an old memory in her and she leaned back, touching the trunk of a young tree. It burned her fingers, and she saw the holes twisting in the wood. Whistle-wood. They were preparing a new cycle. Young seedlings would fall from the young trees, and Enos would begin again. She wondered if the souls of the Old Ones would remain outside in the old trees until the trees died, or if the Cache Enos would transplant the younger trees into the grove at the correct time.

The thought made her sad. There were still generations before the seedlings would mingle with the spit of their mothers to form new Enos, and generations more for the young Enos to gain wisdom. But here, in this cavern, Ikaner saw the future – and the end of her own life.

Time travels in circles, she reminded herself, and the ending was always the beginning. She had already died on one part of the circle and she had just been born on another. She could not deny herself either experience or the circle would break.

Enos! Gather! Zcava stood in the center of the cavern, her arms spread. Her robe had fallen back, revealing her shrunken body and almost fleshless bones. Ikaner moved closer to the edge, but did not climb down. Other Enos crawled forward into a circle. Their minds clamored at her, but she did not listen.

The Old Ones have brought us here. The white mists is in the palace again and the humans talk of war. We have heard of Enos helping humans and we hear of blood on the earth, hundreds of lives bleeding into the soil. The Old Ones are afraid that the final time will begin.

Ikaner clutched the damp earth. It was not her earth, but contact with the dirt and greenery made her feel stronger.

I saw the white mists when he came across my land, she tapped to them all. *I healed his companion because he requested it. His mind is protected with Enos traps, but he seemed to be a good man and to love the earth.*

I placed the traps in his mind, Zcava said, *and I led him on this path. He came to me, seeking prophecy. The Old Ones asked that I warn him and I did. The warnings started the blood – the humans tried to kill him. I went to the land of Demythos and trained the white mists after he had survived attacks upon him. He knows violence and anger. I am afraid that he will coat the land with it.*

I too helped him. Ikaner looked across the cavern, saw another Enos leaning against a tree, her fingers clutched around her staff. *The lord of my land, Dakin, coats the land with blood, has dogs eat people that he does not like. I cannot protest, for the animals use the remains as food. But I feared the blood of the white mists. A human magician tried to help and I boosted his spell. For that I ask the Old Ones' forgiveness.*

Voices clamored in Ikaner's head. She shielded against them, rubbed her fingers against her temples.

The dogs fit the prophecy! Zcava's presence rose above the others, penetrating Ikaner's shields. *So far the white mists has followed the prophecy to the end. If he completes the last stage, the blood will flow upon the land, it will grow hungry for blood, and we must kill them to feed our grasses, our fields, our trees. The Old Ones have called us because the last stage of the prophecy begins. When the last stage is fulfilled, we must return to our lands and begin the deaths. I am sorry, Enos, but time travels in circles and we are bound.*

Ikaner thought of her land, its love for water and sun. Traces of bloodlust had remained in the soil when she arrived on the bluff. It had frightened her, that land memory, made her hungry in a way that sent slivers of pain through her. She liked the touch of the human, liked the way the injured man had felt when she healed him, liked the love lodged in the white mists' heart.

The white mists is trapped by the prophecy? Ikaner asked.

As are we all.

The Old Ones should allow change. Trees withered and died, the land grew green, then brown. Change was part of living. Ikaner leaned against the sapling whistle-wood and wondered at the cruelty of the Old Ones and the blood upon the lands.

Chapter 25

i

The suite smelled musty. Dust motes rose in the air, although Byron had ordered the rooms completely cleaned. Fresh linen covered the bed in the back room, and the coverings had been removed from the furniture. A servant brought in the last of Alma's clothes and hung them in the large wardrobe. Byron's two outfits hung in the other wardrobe. Alma said she would have tailors come to make him more clothes.

Alma sat before a mirror in the dressing room. She wore a skimpy white shift and leaned her head to the side as she combed her long dark hair. Byron caressed the smooth skin on her shoulder. 'You're cold,' he murmured.

She took his hand and kissed the palm. 'Do you want to warm me up?'

He touched a finger to her lips and then pulled away, his body trembling. He would love more than anything to stay here with her, to consecrate the room and begin their life together. But their first action as a couple would not be lovemaking; it would be participating in his father's funeral.

Byron lifted a curl from her back and kissed her neck. She smelled of roses and her own warm musk. He sighed. 'Get changed, Alma. We have to be ready for the service.'

She set down her brush. 'You're worried about this gathering, aren't you?'

'Lord Kensington's coach arrived an hour ago.'

'You think he'll challenge you?'

Byron shrugged. 'I don't know, but I want to concentrate on him right now. You and I have time to concentrate on each other this evening. Now change. I want you at my side in the mausoleum.'

Alma turned back to the mirror. Her reflection was distorted, her eyes too wide, her chin too narrow. 'Impertinent bard,' she said, 'ordering ladies about.'

Smiling, Byron left the dressing room and crossed the suite to his own room. He pulled open the wardrobe and stared in at the two outfits hanging there. Not elegant enough for a king, but they would have to do. He removed the silk shirt and matching trousers and tossed them over a chair. Then he stripped, staring for a moment at his body.

The last time he had lived here as a member of the royal family, he had been fat and out of shape. He was trim now, almost too lean, with more scars than a man ought to have. Once he had been frightened of being like his father; in apppearance at least, he had nothing to fear.

He did, however, have to watch his back. The gentry were frightened of an active monarch in Kilot. This afternoon they would discover that he had already consolidated some power by making Alma his consort. He should have waited until the mourning period for his father had ended, but Byron had to move quickly. Most of the gentry would be at the services. Byron had to use the time well.

He slipped on his clothes and brushed his hair, making sure he took as much time as he could. Alma and his mother were to ride around the grounds in the black carriage as part of the mourning ritual. He should have gone with them, but he couldn't bring himself to climb into that carriage again. He would wait and say good-bye to his father in the mausoleum itself.

He glanced around the room and saw his lute. He touched it, wishing he could bring it. But this afternoon he had to be a monarch, not a bard. Moving without the lute on his back made him feel naked somehow.

He let himself out of the dressing room. The suite smelled of Alma's perfume and when he looked in her dressing room, he noted that she had left. She was a good choice for him. Her strength would help him, and maybe, after a time, the attraction they felt for each other would grow into something. He smiled, feeling a sadness. The Enos had said to him in another life, in another time: *You came to find out if you would be loved.* Then he had said no. Now he would probably say yes.

He opened the door and let himself into the hallway. Two guards stood beside the door and nodded at him as he passed. He walked down the stairs and felt the jitters grow in his stomach.

A ruler is loved differently, Highness.

And right now he wasn't loved at all. He would go into that chamber and participate in a ritual before people who hated and mistrusted him. And some who had tried to kill him.

He pushed open the double doors out of the north wing and stepped outside. The air was chill and fresh. A slight wind made the whistle-woods moan. He blinked at the brightness of the sunshine. To his right, carriages lined up in the courtyard. He recognized Lord Lafa's and Lord Dakin's. Everyone had come to see what Byron's future would bring. He shivered once. He wasn't sure he wanted to find out.

The mausoleum was a gray stone building half hidden by the palace walls. It was long and rectangular. The roof rose in spirals around the edges. A large round chimney stood in the center of the roof, to release the smoke from the bier.

The guards outside the mausoleum bowed when they saw him, then pushed the door open wide to admit him.

The mausoleum smelled damp. Thousands of candles burned along the walls and beside the pews. A hundred people faced forward staring at the bier and the large crypt beyond. Gentry that Byron had met and some that he hadn't waited for the ceremonies to begin. The stone room was cold, and each movement echoed in the stillness. His mother and Alma stood to the side, waiting for him.

His father's body rested on the bier. He looked smaller, as if death had diminished him. Three large circles, one inside the other, enclosed the bier. Each circle represented an Old One, and each contained symbolic significance. The circles predicted the next monarch's future.

Alma handed Byron a burnstick and took his arm. Her hands were cold. Her hair shone and her gown was simple and chaste, no low-cut bodice, no lace on the collars. Byron glanced at his mother. She was hunched and she trembled as she moved. Her face was hidden by a thick veil, but occasionally the candlelight would reflect her tears. She leaned on Alma for a moment, then stood and led the procession down to the bier.

The crowd stood as his mother passed. Byron waited until she had almost reached the Flame of Life, then he and Alma started down. He clutched his burnstick tightly. The gentry watched them, and he heard a ripple of whispers as people realized what

Alma's presence meant. He could sense the shock, feel the discomfort. It did not please him like he thought it would. He just wanted the ceremony to end.

His mother dipped her burnstick into the Flame of Life. The flame turned blue as the burnstick caught. His mother then brought the flame to the center of her consort's bier, lighting the Circle of Remembrance. As the flame encircled the bier, she leaned over and kissed her husband for the last time. Then she took her place behind the bier, standing to the side of the door to the crypt.

Byron approached the Flame of Life. It generated little heat, but he could smell a wisp of smoke. He stuck his burnstick into the flame and watched as it turned blue. Through the fire, he saw Lord Lafa. The lord appeared sober, and seemed as majestic as he had when Byron first met him. The lord was watching Alma, and his gaze was filled with hatred. Byron made himself look away. He carried his burnstick to the bier and lit the Circle of Power, canonizing his father's past and establishing his own control. As the flames engulfed the circle, he took his place beside his mother.

Lord Kensington sat in the first row. He showed no surprise at Alma's presence, and did not seem to resent Byron's participation in the ceremony. The lord's lack of emotion made Byron tense. He had believed that even Kensington would have enough respect for the dead to wait until last rites had ended before challenging the new monarch.

Alma carried the flaming burnstick to the last circle, the Circle of the Future. She as consort guarded the future of the kingdom in her womb. If Byron had had a child, that child would have been lighting the circle. As she lowered her burnstick to it, a small draft caught the flame and it flickered. The gentry gasped. Byron twisted his ring. If the last circle didn't burn, custom decreed that he had no future. He would die before his rule truly began.

Alma's burnstick went out. Small sparks flew in all directions. She was forbidden by law to return to the Flame of Life. Her gaze caught Byron's, and he thought he saw fear in her eyes. He wished he could go to her. Whether or not the superstitions of the bier were true, they would affect his support among the gentry. A small smile made its way across Kensington's face, and Byron felt a chill run down his back. He should have checked the burnsticks before the ceremony. Kensington could have had his magicians treat the sticks.

Alma waited for the circle to light. As she stepped away, a whoosh echoed, and the far corner of the circle erupted into blue flame. Byron felt some of the tension flow from him. The bier had sent a sign: he and his descendants had a chance to continue ruling in Kilot, but the chance, like the flame that spread around the circle, was slim.

Alma took her place beside Byron and slipped her hand through his arm. She was trembling. She too knew that the sign boded ill for their future. Fear flashed through Byron. If Alma thought she had no chance of surviving with him, she might turn against him. He slid his hand over hers, wishing that he could reassure her.

His mother bowed to the figure on the bier, then walked into the crypt itself. Byron bowed and followed, as did Alma. The crypt seemed even colder than the outer room had, and had a damp, musty odor. They stopped at the cornerstone on which his father would lie and placed the burnsticks into the small circular holes carved for them. Byron looked past the monarchs into the side reserved for the royal family and noted that one crypt near the end was empty. He squinted to read the inscription and started when he realized that it had been his. He wondered who had rested on the bier in his place.

The three of them left the crypt and returned to the great room. They again bowed to the dead monarch, circled the flames, and walked up the aisle. Byron could hear the rumbling as the first row of gentry made their respects to the bier.

He followed his mother out of the mausoleum and into the dying sunlight. They would have a half hour before the death banquet. His mother continued toward the palace, Alma behind her. Byron stopped and gazed at the mausoleum. Smoke rose from the curved chimney on the roof. He would see that smoke for another month or more, until the flames completed their circles and his father was laid to rest with his ancestors.

For weeks people in the palace had watched the smoke rise from a burial that was supposed to have been his. Byron shuddered. No wonder so many of them found it hard to accept him.

He entered the palace as he had left it, through the north entrance. He hurried up the stairs and pulled open the door to his chamber, half expecting Alma to be waiting for him. The outer room was empty. He opened all the doors in the inner chambers. The musty odor had returned and dampened the smell of Alma's perfume. All of the rooms were empty. For a moment he thought of trying to find her, then rejected the idea. He would see her at the banquet. They could talk after that.

He grabbed his lute and walked to a chair in the main room. The instrument felt warm to his touch, like a living thing. He tuned it, then played a random series of chords. The sounds filled the chamber, made the empty feeling disappear. He hadn't realized until he heard that most of his chords were in a minor key how much the lighting of the Circle of the Future had frightened him.

His fingers found the melody of a lullaby and he let the notes echo. He rocked back and forth, feeling himself gather strength. Soon he would have to face the gentry in the banquet hall. Afeno was angry at him for going ahead with the death banquet in traditional form.

The traditional form followed the pattern of the bier: the monarch and his family sat in the center, with the past council members in the inner ring, present council members in the middle ring, and the rest of the guests in the outer ring. Guards were stationed outside the room, so as not to hear any state secrets that could emerge in impromptu eulogies. Afeno had pointed out that Byron was trapped and a single dagger could find him easily. But Byron was gambling that Lord Kensington was too smart to attempt that assassination. If Byron did die, the lord would first have to be tried for treason before he could take over.

A knock on the door made his heart leap. He knew it wasn't Alma – she would have come in – but he found himself hoping for her anyway. He set down his lute and pulled the door open. A page stood in the doorway. 'The guests are ready, sire,' he said.

He thanked the child and closed the door behind him. Then, flanked by two guards, he walked down the long, narrow hallway leading to the banquet room. Alma stood outside, her back to Byron. She was talking with a retainer wearing blue and gold. Kensington's colors. Byron closed his eyes. Already it had begun.

The retainer looked over Alma's shoulders and saw Byron. The retainer made a quick bow to Alma and disappeared before Byron reached them. He extended his arm to Alma. 'What was that?' he asked.

'Lord Kensington wanted to express his regrets,' she said, 'but did not think he should approach you. I told his retainer that I would pass on the words.'

Byron nodded. The conversation had seemed too involved for that. And if Kensington had felt that way, he could have told Alma himself. Byron would investigate further when he was alone with her. 'Ready?' he asked.

The guards pulled the doors open, and Byron and Alma made their entrance. They eased their way through the openings in the circles, greeting the gentry as they passed. Lord Dakin refused to return the greeting. Lord Kensington and Lady Kerry sat on opposite sides of the circle and ignored Byron's nod.

Byron and Alma took their seats beside Byron's mother. Dishes with cold soup were already in place. No one spoke, according to custom, and the hall filled with the sound of clanking dishes. Byron's shoulders were tense. He could feel a headache building along his neck. He wanted to turn, to survey the guests, but knew that he couldn't show any signs of nervousness. He ate the vegetable stew and mutton and dessert slowly, concentrating on his food. The hair on the back of his neck rose. He heard a movement behind him, and then his mother stood.

For a moment he didn't understand what was happening. Then he realized that she was about to give her eulogy – tradition demanded that she go first. Byron was not allowed to speak about his predecessor, a way of preventing the new king from defining the old. Only the old king's friends, relatives, staff, and council members could eulogize him.

His mother lifted the veil from her face. Her eyes seemed dull, as if the tears had washed the color away. 'I have lost five sons and four daughters.' She spoke softly. Some of the gentry in the back circle leaned forward in order to hear. 'And as one son returns to me from the dead, I lose the person who helped me go on living. I don't plan to die soon, but I know I no longer have a life. Yet I will not speak of the past, but of the future – my son's future and my future through him.

'When Adric was a child, his free-thinking ways frightened most of us. It's clear that he continues to act for himself, that his survival has depended upon his quick mind. My son has survived against great odds, and I believe that he is the stronger for it.

'I have never spoken out on policy before, but it is my right as consort and as the new ruler's mother to do so now. Kilot has not seen a war for hundreds of years. Our land's island status has protected us from invaders, and we have had peace within.

Emotions flared the night my consort died and Adric surprised all of us. That night could be forgotten and forgiven. If this split between the royal house is not mended, Kilot could be divided. The outer island circles will break off from us and we'll lose our protection. I will urge now, while my consort's body lies encircled on the bier, that you support this man who is my son.'

His mother pulled her veil over her face and sat down. Byron did not look at her. He stared straight ahead and listened to the silence that engulfed them. He had his mother's support, and yet he felt the undercurrent of blame in her words. If he had kept silent about his identity, the kingdom would have remained at peace.

Loneliness encircled him like the flames encircled the bier. He wished Seymour could give him a potion to heal the melancholy that was filling him. But there were no herb-witch cures for his ailments. He had to struggle and fight on his own, alone, for a cause no one else seemed to believe in. He watched as a lord stood in the back to speak. All his life Byron had wanted to come back here, to sit in his rightful place, and to use the knowledge he had learned during the years of hardship. But nothing was as he had imagined it, and he wondered if happiness was as much a myth as the tale-tellers said Gerusha was.

ii

A whisper of smoke carried in the breeze. The whistle-woods moaned. Each cry was different, distinctive: one had a bass tone, another a touch of treble. Ikaner stood in the grove, reaching for the souls of the Old Ones. She was finding nothing against the ground except for a strange sense of nostalgia. She had seeded here, and in the caves the Enos had brought her to flower, before wiping her mind and tying her soul to her bluff. The training had settled well. She wanted to go home, to sit on the bluff, and feel the river wind touch her face, without hearing her ancestors cry from the trees that imprisoned them.

Yes? The voice rose with the cry of the trees, and at first Ikaner wasn't sure she heard it.

I have come to ask a question. Her thoughts felt as if they echoed in silence, as if no one heard. She couldn't project into a mind as she was used to, and the ground felt as if it forced the thoughts to bounce back, into the wind. Strands of her thinning hair brushed across her face, and she pushed them back.

Speak.

I have met the white mists. He has strengths.

He threatens the land with blood.

No. Ikaner glanced around her. The trees appeared to be glowing, as if from an internal heat. *Humans have fought before. We threaten the land.*

If the humans pollute the land with blood, we destroy the humans. It is our agreement from long past.

The winds rose, making the shrieks louder. Ikaner could barely hear her own thoughts. *But if we add human blood to the land, we too pollute the land.*

We follow the prophecy.

She whirled in the wind, seeing if another Enos stood near her. She was alone in the trees. She shivered. The wind had become chill. *You make the prophecy.*

She heard no response. The trees wailed and then the wind died. The silence pushed against her ears, making her feel as if a great pressure had left her body. She felt strange here. She wanted to go home to her bluff, and think about growing trees and directing sunlight. She wanted to be the bluff Enos again instead of Ikaner, one of many.

You make the prophecy, she thought again, but the thoughts seemed to echo in her mind, trapped, as she imagined human thoughts to be. She stepped out of the grove into the sunlight, and knew she was alone.

iii

The laces on Byron's shirt flapped against his chest. Seymour stood inside the door to the royal apartments as if he could go no farther. Byron leaned against a chair and rubbed a hand against his face. His skin smelled of Alma.

'I will do what I want,' he said, 'and that's the end of it.'

Seymour glanced at the door leading to the bedchamber where Alma still slept. 'That's not the end of it, Byron. When you die, we all die for supporting you. It's not your life anymore, don't you understand that?'

Byron grabbed the laces and finished threading them. 'It never was my life,' he said.

'Kensington will kill you if you meet alone. At least put a guard in there with you.'

'Afeno will be behind the panel.' Byron had discovered the listening panel in the audience chamber, a place he suspected that Boton and Ewehl had used often.

'And he won't be able to get out in time to save you.'

Byron shrugged. 'If I die, I die.' He picked up his lute and slung it over his back. 'Maybe we'll all be better off.'

'Don't ever say that,' Seymour said. 'Don't ever.'

The bedroom door opened and Alma leaned against it. Her long black hair flowed down her back. She had put on a white dressing gown that seemed to reveal more than it covered. 'You'll wake the entire kingdom.'

Seymour looked at her, then looked away. She crossed her arms over her chest. Byron smiled at her with a warmth he didn't feel. 'Good morning, Alma.'

She didn't smile back. 'If you're going to see Kensington, you're a fool.'

'It's my affair.'

'It's our affair. I agree with Seymour, for once. You'll jeopardize everything.'

'He asked for the meeting, and I'm going to give him another chance. The last thing I want to do is fight him.' Byron could feel the strain in his back and shoulders. If only he could relax. 'I think fighting him would be worse than my death.'

'Well, I don't,' Seymour said. 'You'll leave the kingdom to Kensington, who obviously cares for no one but himself – or it'll go to the lady over here, who has shown her potential for abusing power as well. Or have you forgotten, now that you're her lover, that she stole land from Lafa using the king's seal?'

Alma stepped into the room. Her skirts swayed and she seemed to be taller. 'What I did is none of your business.'

'Stop it,' Byron said. 'I'm going to see Kensington, and that's all there is to it.' He pushed past Seymour and let himself into the hallway, slamming the door behind him. The guards looked straight ahead, as if pretending that they heard nothing. Byron walked down the hall, hearing his footsteps ring out against the stone floor.

They were right. He was taking a risk by meeting Kensington alone in the audience chamber. But Byron wanted to see if he could prevent the kingdom from splitting further.

He passed the performers' closets, passed the portraits of his ancestors, and climbed the stairs where Milo had died. The door to the audience chamber stood open, and inside, he saw Kensington sitting on the king's chair. A little chill ran through Byron. Kensington was going to play power games.

The best way to win was to do the unexpected. Byron bounded down the stairs to a performer's closet and grabbed a stool. Then he carried it into the audience chamber, and set the stool on the floor near the stairs. He swung his lute around from his back. The instrument made him feel whole. He tuned it, watching Kensington from the corner of his eyes.

The lord looked haggard. His face seemed even thinner and shadows dwelt beneath his eyes. He templed his fingers and tapped them against his chin. 'We have a meeting,' he said.

Byron ignored him and finished the ballad that he had been playing. Then he rested one arm on his knee and another on his lute. 'Lord Kensington,' he said as if he were sitting on the royal chair instead of Kensington. 'You wished to see me?'

'I've come to make a deal with you, bard.'

'A deal, milord?'

Kensington leaned back in the chair, trying to appear relaxed. 'You know that your support from the gentry is weak. If I win even one battle, they will gather around me. I sense that neither of us wants a war. The Lady Constance made it clear that she didn't either. And I think I know a way to prevent one.'

Byron did not move. 'Go on.'

'Since the Enos confirmed you, there is no doubt that you have a right to the throne. But being an heir does not make you a good ruler. You have not been trained in the art of leading; your past makes you almost unworthy to deal in the courts of Kilot. The gentry know this and that is why their support of you is weak.'

Kensington's analysis of the gentry was accurate. Most of them perceived Byron as Kensington did, a peasant who by accident of birth now ruled the kingdom. None of them knew about all the years of preparation under Lord Demythos.

'I propose this,' Kensington said. 'I shall become regent – not king – and all of the affairs of state shall be in my hands. You will sit on the Council of Lords and retain your honorary title. Keep the Lady Jelwra as consort. She's a good choice for you. Then when your eldest child comes of age, I will step aside. Although you will not rule, your child will. This plan will ensure gentry support and will keep Kilot from dividing.'

Byron clutched the neck of the lute. The plan sounded good and if Byron and Kensington had had a different history, Byron might have considered it. But Kensington had tried to kill him, and none of Byron's brothers and sisters had lived. He had no guarantees that his own children would live either.

But if he agreed to the plan, Kilot would remain at peace. He thought of the blue flame guttering out, and the sparks that flew, finally igniting the last circle. Alma was the key. And Seymour was right. She craved power as much as Kensington did. With Alma as his consort and Kensington as regent, Byron would probably die. Alma would do anything to ensure her position of power – even murder.

'And if I don't agree?' Byron asked.

'I have gathered an army and I will begin its training. I'm afraid you leave me no choice but to take this kingdom by force.'

'Why do you want the throne, Kensington? There was never any power here in the past.'

Kensington gripped the arms of the chair. He looked diminished there, as if the office were too big for him. 'You aren't going to agree, are you?'

'No.' Byron spoke softly, not taking his gaze from Kensington's. 'There are too many factors against me. I don't know if Alma will remain my consort should I agree or if my children will live or whether I will live, for that matter.'

'And if I gave you my word?'

Byron twisted his ring, wondering if it had ever brought anyone good luck. 'You are right. The gentry is worried about my lack of experience. But I'm worried about yours.'

'Mine?' Kensington stood and walked around the chair. 'I've been at the palace most of my life. I run a huge estate. I know more about these things than you ever could.'

'Perhaps.' Byron smiled. 'But have you ever gone without food? Been beaten because you were unable to perform a simple task? Have you ever lived in a miserable one-room hovel full of lice and ticks and disease?'

'No.' Kensington grimaced. 'And I can't see that it matters.'

'It does matter. Although the gentry have the money in this

kingdom, they do not have the numbers. Have you thought, milord, that for the third season the wheat crop has failed? The soothsayers predict another drought. People are starving. Healthy people will allow a ruler to ignore them. Dying people have nothing to lose. They will overthrow our system and throw the land into chaos. I think I could prevent an uprising and protect Kilot, while making the peasantry feel as if they are part of the government. Could you?'

'I don't want them in government.'

Byron strummed a chord on his lute. The notes echoed in the room.

'You won't reconsider?' Kensington asked.

'No.'

Kensington took a deep breath and walked down the stairs. When he was across from Byron, Byron stopped him. 'Milord. I answered your questions. Now answer mine. Why do you want to rule Kilot?'

Kensington frowned, glanced at the chair, but did not move. 'For years,' he said, 'the system has been falling apart. It worked for a long time. The council made the decisions and the king enacted them with his seal. Then, a few generations ago, council members stopped caring for Kilot. They figured out that they could gain themselves. They revised documents and land surveys, and increased their own holdings. They redistributed funds to injure the gentry not in power. My own father took lands from Lord Styler's mother when she failed to keep her seat on the council. I plan to change the system, become a strong ruler and abolish the Council of Lords until things are under control.'

'Noble goals,' Byron said. 'Why kill to achieve them?'

'I didn't kill your siblings.'

'I was referring to me.'

'I didn't send you out to die. That was Ewehl.'

'I know.' Byron slipped his lute across his back. 'But you knew my mother was having difficult pregnancies and that my brother was dying of a wasting disease. Everyone with access to the royal doctors knew that. I've thought about it for a long time, and all I know is this: you were at Kerry when Lady Kerry banished me. You were in three cities that I was in, and in all three I narrowly escaped a murder attempt. You were on Dakin's land a few weeks before the hunt. And you were at the palace during the two attempts on my life. We are going to fight each other, cousin. I will not arrest you here because that would not ensure my throne. I simply want to know how you knew who I was and why you decided to kill me.'

Kensington had turned pale. 'I – it started after the Ladylee Diana's death. The Lady Kerry wanted you dead and I agreed to help. When I learned who you were, that didn't change things. A murderer shouldn't sit on Kilot's throne.'

'Then you don't qualify either,' Byron said. He looked at his hands. The calluses on his fingertips were flat. 'I could have used you. We want some of the same things. But I can't trust you, milord. Not now.'

'My offer still stands.'

'I'm sorry.' Byron stood. 'The audience is over.'

Kensington stared at him for a moment, then turned, and left the room. Byron stood in the silence, clenching his fists and wondering why he felt as if the fire along the bier had gone out.

iv

Ikaner walked on the patterned stone, hands shaking, head bent. She had never been on human land. She couldn't feel the earth. The stone covering the grass was dead, as was the stone forming the walls. Her feet had no contact. She felt completely alone.

Off to her side, men with weapons shot at trees. As the arrows pierced the trees, she felt little thuds of pain that echoed even through the dead stone. The white mists was not like that, she reminded herself. The white mists respected her land, respected her bluff. He had affection for the people around him.

People stared at her as they passed. She should ask one of them where she could find the white mists, but she could not remember the human word for him. She had planned on following the land, but the dead stones blocked most feeling. She had followed the feeling to the dead stones and then felt nothing.

She glanced around at the stone walls, the stone benches, the dead stone surrounding her, and she hesitated. She had to warn the white mists. The only way he could save himself and save the land was to know what he risked. Her trees had seemed alien with the bloodlust. She had felt them looking toward her, smelling her fluids, searching for blood. She had almost forgotten that feeling until the meetings. Until the talk of blood-filled land began again.

A hand touched her arm. She jumped. No one had ever snuck up on her before. She had always listened through the ground. She turned and saw herself facing Zcava.

The white mists can solve this himself. Zcava's expression was stern, her grip on Ikaner's arm tight.

He doesn't know about the prophecy. If he knew, he would not fight.

He has a prophecy of his own. The final test is tonight. If he fails that, he doesn't need to know about the blood on the land. His destiny is sealed. Zcava pulled on Ikaner's arm. *Come with me.*

I must see him.

Zcava let go of Ikaner. *If you see him, you shall die and your bluff will burn and fall into the river.*

You threaten me.

I speak the truth. The Enos may not interfere in the lives of humans.

You prophesied to the white mists. You blocked his mind.

Zcava nodded. *With permission of the Old Ones. The Old Ones do not want you to interfere.*

Why not? Ikaner was motionless. The humans walked around them as if they did not exist.

Because you are a bluff Enos and your place is on a piece of land overlooking the river. Zcava bowed her head. Her hood hid her face. *Come back with me.*

Ikaner felt blind on the dead stone. She could not find the white mists on her own, and she did not know if she wanted to lose her bluff. Suffering the bloodlust might be better than having no bluff at all. She glanced around one final time, hoping to see the white mists enshrouding a human shape. But she saw human shapes with faded colors, prancing and sparking, and that was all.

Zcava had started back to the Cache. Ikaner followed.

V

Byron leaned against a fence post, feeling the cold stone dig into his back and buttocks. He wore a simple linen shirt and black trousers, the most comfortable outfit that the tailor had made him so far. The other clothes were too formal, too regal for him.

A group of archers huddled on the patch of grass just ahead of him, shooting arrows at targets drawn on the trees. Ile instructed them, setting up different formations, demanding that the archers shoot while moving.

Byron rested an elbow on his knee. Something about these practice maneuvers made him uneasy. The entire situation made him uneasy. Something was wrong. He felt as if an old ballad was nagging at the back of his brain, but he couldn't remember the melody. He had forgotten an important piece of information, and the more he concentrated on it, the more it eluded him.

A rider broke through the trees. His horse was lathered, and his clothes were ripped and dirt-covered. He stopped and spoke briefly to Ile, who pointed to Byron.

The rider nodded and rode toward the fence. Byron stood. The rider reined up, and Byron caught the scents of sweat, leather, and horseflesh.

'The guardsman told me that you could help me, sir,' the man said.

'Sir' not 'sire.' Byron frowned. 'What did he tell you?'

'That you were in charge here, sir, and I need your help. I need to find the Lady Jelwra immediately.' The rider reached into his breast pocket and removed a packet. His fingers partly covered the seal, but Byron recognized Lord Kensington's colors embedded in the wax.

'What business do you have with the Lady Jelwra?' Byron asked. His heart pounded against his chest.

'I have to deliver this to her.'

'I'll take it.' Byron extended his hand for the packet and smiled slightly. He tried to keep the sarcasm from his voice. 'I'm her bard.'

'I'm sorry, sir bard,' the rider said, 'but I'm to put this in her hands and no one else's.'

'She is in the palace garden.' Byron pointed the way. The rider thanked him, clucked at his horse, and rode off. Byron turned and followed. He walked slowly, hoping that the rider would leave before he arrived. Part of him didn't want to know what the rest of him was certain of. Perhaps if he had told the rider that he was king –

But no. The rider would probably have galloped off, leaving everyone even more suspicious. Byron's feet clanged on the flagstones. He let himself in the north wing and climbed the stairs to the second floor. Then he hurried down the twisting hallway to the second-floor library, which overlooked the gardens.

The books smelled musty and old. Dust covered the floor. No

one had been in the room in years. Byron walked through the stacks to the rays of light at the far end. He used to love this room, used to spend hours here when he should have been learning to ride, or learning sword play. Lord Demythos had had a library, but it hadn't compared with this one.

Byron stopped in front of the windows, put his hand on the edge, and looked down. Alma sat on a bench and thumbed through the papers. She was smiling at the rider, who stood before her. A servant stood behind her and she turned to him. He handed her a sheet of parchment, and a pen and inkwell. Alma scrawled on the parchment, then sealed the letter, and handed it to the rider. He slipped the parchment into his breast pocket, nodded at something she said, something that Byron could not hear, and mounted the horse. Alma watched as the rider rode away. Then she too left the garden.

Byron gripped the edge of the windowsill until his fingers went numb. He had hoped that he could trust Alma. He had thought that she cared about him enough to work with him instead of against him. But everyone he had ever trusted had failed him in some way. Diana must have told Kensington about him. Lord Boton had sent him to his death. His father had never cared, and his mother no longer wanted him.

Rulers are loved differently, the Enos had said.

Byron's smile was thin. Rulers weren't loved at all.

Chapter 26

i

The land screamed. Ikaner sat up. The cavern was dark; the fire stones had gone out. Her hands felt hot, as if something were burning her palms. She lifted her hands from the earth and the feeling disappeared. But the land screams, the churning, the pain continued. And through it she could feel the drip-drip-drip of blood.

The other Enos awoke, their thoughts crowding her mind. *What is it? – My land! My land – Stop her. She cannot leave – The blood is necessary. We must use the blood –*

Ikaner shut out their voices and huddled. Outside, the whistle-woods moaned, but the moans rose and sounded almost like human laughter. The young trees beside her swayed in an imaginary breeze. The blood seemed to flow underground on a path to the new trees. The whistle-wood moans felt more underground than aboveground.

Ikaner felt through the earth, found the blood flow, and traced it back to a field not far from her bluff. More blood drip-drip-dripped into the land, and human cries mingled with all of the others. She could feel death, the moment that the blood stopped flowing in a number of different places. But the fresh blood carried the pain beneath the whistle-woods and the whistle-woods grew excited. Beside her, the young trees swayed. The warmth of their bark radiated at her like a fire.

Then the human screaming stopped. The blood stopped dripping into the land. The flow continued, and the land touched its pollution, encircled it as if it were something to be explored.

Ikaner shivered. The bloodlust had begun.

ii

The dawn was golden. Byron watched the morning-touched rays illuminate the green leaves in the garden. He shivered. The night had been cool and his clothes were damp. A wind rose with the sun, ruffling his hair and sending a chill through him. In the distance the whistle-woods began their moans again.

The whistle-woods had cried all night, although he had not, until this point, felt a breeze. The sound had frightened him, but he hadn't gone inside. He couldn't face Alma, couldn't bear to question her about her messenger. And he couldn't sleep next to her without touching her. She would have touched him back, and the passion would have flowed between them, and he would have hated her for using her body to lie to him, and hated himself for letting her.

He stood and stretched. The bones in his back cracked with stiffness. The guard who had also spent the night in the garden smiled wearily. Byron nodded to him and then walked toward the palace's east wing.

He hadn't planned to see Seymour, at least not consciously. But he found himself in front of Seymour's door before even considering where he had gone. Byron knocked once. The sound echoed in the stillness, and then he remembered that it was just dawn. He turned to leave, hoping he hadn't awakened anyone. The door swung open, and Seymour faced him, his hair tousled and his eyes sleep-filled. He wore a pair of breeches loosely tied at the waist.

'Byron?'

'I'm sorry, Seymour, I didn't mean to wake you.'

'It's all right. Something happen?'

'No. I just wanted to talk. Go back to bed.'

Seymour ran a hand through his hair, managing to mess it more. 'I'm awake now. Just wait. Let me get dressed.'

Byron nodded. He leaned against the wall. He was tired. It would have been nice to go into the room and sit while Seymour dressed. The door opened again and Seymour came out. As the door closed, Byron caught a glimpse of another figure on the pallet. Vonda.

'You look awful,' Seymour said. 'Where have you been?'

'In the garden. Thinking.'

'What about?'

Byron glanced around the corridor. The doors looked thinner here, as if the oak were less solid in the east wing than they were in the north wing. 'Let's walk,' he said.

They went out into the courtyard. The sunlight had crossed the top of the east wall, casting cool shadows on the gray stone. Byron wanted to talk about Alma, but he couldn't bring himself to say anything.

'I've been thinking about how to approach this fight with Kensington,' he said. 'I don't want to attack him. And yet I don't want him to strike first.'

'If he attacks first, he commits treason.'

'And may lose the support of the gentry.' Byron sighed. He wanted to go back to the garden, where it was warmer. 'But we risk losing lives.'

'Either way we lose lives,' Seymour said.

Byron shook his head. 'Not if we don't fight.'

'We have to fight,' Seymour said. 'We don't want Kensington as king. Byron, you – '

'I want to keep my power without loss of life.' Byron spoke softly.

'It's too late for that now. We have troops all around the palace. Before dawn, two hundred of them went out to the fields by Anda for a special training exercise – '

'Alma opposed that.' Byron felt a chill run down his back. Alma knew too much about policy.

'She still asleep?'

'Probably,' Byron said. He turned away from the mention of Alma. 'We could recall the men. Perhaps try to negotiate with Kensington further.'

'We had our chance at negotiation,' Seymour said. 'You won't agree to Kensington's terms, and he won't tolerate you as monarch.'

He stopped speaking and stared ahead. Byron followed his gaze. A thin column of men straggled into the palace gate. They were dirt-covered and many were bleeding. Most sat down as the gate closed behind them. Byron ran toward them, his heart pounding in his throat. Seymour ran beside him. The troops had collapsed in shadow, and as Byron left the sunlight, he felt as if the world had grown colder.

The men wore the tattered remains of clothes. They smelled of powder and burnt flesh, of blood and fear-stained sweat. Byron sent a guard for the healers. Seymour crouched beside the nearest man and unwrapped the bandage around the man's arm.

Ile leaned against the gate. Blood trickled down the side of his face, but his wounds looked superficial. Byron went to him.

'What happened?' he asked.

Ile reached out. His hands were covered with blood. 'I'm sorry,' he whispered.

Byron took the bloody hands, felt the stickiness coat his own palms. 'What happened?'

'We were setting up – maneuvers, like we talked about – and then everything was – they were shooting at us, arrows, flaming arrows, some hand-to-hand. The ground was burning.'

'The two hundred? You were with the two hundred men near Anda this morning?'

'Yes, sire. Kensington's men were waiting for us. They had his colors.'

Byron glanced around him. The other healers had arrived and were applying ointments, ripping away clothes, cauterizing wounds. The smell of burning flesh grew stronger. 'There's only twenty-five men here. Where are the others?'

Tears filled Ile's eyes and ran down his cheeks, mixing with the blood until they fell to the ground in long red drops. Byron tightened his grip on Ile's hands.

'Where are the others?'

'We had to leave them,' Ile said. 'I think they were all dead.'

'Think?'

Ile nodded. 'We brought a few of the bad ones with us, but they collapsed on the way. There wasn't any movement on that field. None.'

'None.' Byron was numb. Two hundred men. He let Ile go. A healer carrying bandages passed him, and he grabbed her.

'Sire?'

'This man. Help this man.' He propelled her toward Ile. His hands left bloody prints on her arm.

The woman wouldn't move. 'Sire? It's Nica.'

'Nica?' Her features came into focus. Wide eyes. Innocent eyes. Not like Alma's eyes. He touched Nica's cheek. 'Nica? I didn't know you were here.'

'I came to help you.'

The smear his finger left on her face looked like Ile's bloody tears. 'It's too late to help me,' Byron said. He pushed past her, but she caught his arm.

'Sire. Byron.'

Her voice was soft, affectionate when she used his name. He had loved her once. Thought he loved her once. Before Alma. Always before Almathea.

Nica shook him. 'Byron, please. Listen to me. I came here to warn you.'

'Warn me?' He tried to concentrate on her words. 'There's no need to warn me. The worst has already happened.'

'No. You've got to stop this fighting or the Enos will destroy us all. Do you understand me? The Enos said – '

'I know what the Enos said.' The words still echoed in his mind. *They train you to be ruled, as your father is ruled, as your grandfather was ruled before him.* He grabbed Nica's wrists and pulled her hands from him. 'I have to think.'

'But, Byron – '

'Help them, Nica.' He put a hand to his face. His palm smelled of iron, of blood. 'I cannot.'

iii

Ikaner dug into the ground, ignoring the heat, the burning against her fingers. The young trees beside her shuddered and moaned. There was no wind inside the cavern, but the air smelled fetid. She touched the trees and felt a sickness: youth overcome by something more powerful, something forcing its way into the sap. Her fingers blistered as she dug, the heat almost unbearable. No one paid any attention to her. She had blocked the other Enos out. They were below, arguing about the white mists, planning destruction of the humans, trying to decide if the humans should destroy themselves.

Finally she found the trickle of blood. It whispered to her, the words faint and sing-song: *When I am a sapling, you will move me into the sun. The air will be young again, and I will be warm. I will bend with the wind and live forever.*

She wanted to pull up the young trees and move them, plant them outside in the air. She grabbed the base of the nearest sapling. Beneath her burned palm, the tree screamed.

She backed away and almost fell off the edge. The hum of Enos voices in her mind stopped. She turned, and they were looking at her. *Come here,* she said.

They stared at her and then stood as a unit. She crawled back to the blood. The tree was still screaming, the blood coursing to the young tree's roots. She shoved a rock between the blood and the tree. The blood boiled against the rock, tried to surge over it. The tree's screams eased to a moan.

You cannot stop us, the blood whispered. *We are stronger.*

Ikaner said nothing. She was an Enos. She protected land. She would protect the trees as she had protected her bluff – with her life, if she had to.

iv

The blade glittered. Byron saw his reflection in it. The image wavered and faded, colors blurred against the light. It seemed to have found him, this dagger, and now it would not let him go. He liked the way it sparkled.

The door was heavy, but he opened it anyway. The guards let him do anything. So different from before. Never had he had such freedom. He closed the door gently, waiting for the snick of the latch. The main room was dark and he carried no light. He waited until the darkness faded into gray shapes.

The door to the bedroom was open. Light cracked around the edges, white light for a woman who wore nothing else. Inside the chamber she slept, her hair sprawled along the pillow. In sleep she was plain, young. The moonlight caressed her: she wore nothing else.

Her chest rose and fell with each breath. Her ribs were etched lightly under her skin. He could count them if he wanted to. He eased the blanket down, revealing her small, pert breasts. He didn't want to mar such perfection, but two hundred men – the blood of two hundred men already stained her hands.

The dagger rose and his arm followed, waiting over the delicately etched bones, beneath the tiny breasts. Then it came down and the moonlight caught the blade, bathing it with white light. His ring, Diana's ring, flashed, and an Enos's voice echoed in the room:

A knife glistens in the darkness. A simple silver ring adorns the hand which guides the weapon on its deadly path, the path which seals the darkness forever.

He whirled but could not see her, this hidden Enos who spoke with the voice of prophecy. He was alone, with the white lady, in the moonlight.

Chapter 27

i

The Enos crouched around the blood, watched it surge against the rock. Finally it quit and burrowed into the ground, going underneath.

Saplings and sunlight, it whispered. *Move us.* The voice in her head made Ikaner shiver.

Zcava touched the stain on the rock. *It is the Old Ones. They go for their new home.*

Behind her the young tree screamed.

They kill the tree! An Enos reached for the tree, as if to save it. Zcava grabbed her hand.

It is the way.

Enos do not kill trees. Ikaner dug for the blood again. She could feel the pollutant in the land, the thirst rising from the grove beyond the Cache. *Enos help the land survive. The Old Ones will kill this grove.*

To save themselves. Zcava pushed Ikaner away. *We cannot survive without the Old Ones.*

Enos die for their trees. How can the Old Ones ask the trees to die for them?

We need the Old Ones. They are our wisdom.

Ikaner leaned back. That was why she was not allowed to stop the white mists. He was supposed to kill. The humans were supposed to die so that the Old Ones could live. They would travel on a river of blood to the young trees, replace the sap, remove the young tree souls, and live. *So many lives,* Ikaner thought.

We need the Old Ones, Zcava repeated.

Even if the white mists did not kill, we would need human blood? The land beneath Ikaner grew more and more thirsty. The trickle of blood did not flow, but she could feel land tendrils spreading, searching for more blood.

The white mists will kill. The humans will die. So the Old Ones have prophesied.

The trickle had disappeared under the ground. The young tree had stopped screaming. Ikaner felt it, felt its life force weak against the blood. She grabbed the tree, added her strength to its sap. The bark burned her fingers, the whistle-wood screeched, blood spurted from the hole beneath the rock. The little tree shuddered and clung to her in fear.

Enos died for their trees. She sat before the small grove. No one defended it, no one guarded it. The young tree's branches held her close. She had become their Enos, and she would protect them.

ii

Byron sat at the top of the stairs, his back against the wall. One foot rested on the step below, the other leg extended before him. His eyes were closed, his breathing ragged. He still clutched the dagger.

'Byron?'

He opened his eyes. Seymour sat on the second step. He looked worried. 'I was looking all over for you. Where have you been?'

Byron felt as if he were climbing out of a heavy sleep. His eyes were scratchy and dry, his throat parched. 'Thinking.'

'Well, I'll give you more to think about. Kensington's men ambushed our archers just outside the palace.'

'Another slaughter?' His voice worked slowly, the melody gone. He felt empty inside.

'No. We turned the ambush around. We lost a handful, but Kensington lost almost everybody.' Seymour smiled. 'We are going to succeed.'

Seymour's pleasure sent shivers through Byron. 'How many?'

'We lost about ten.'

He wasn't communicating well. His mind was sluggish. 'How many did Kensington lose?'

'Hundred or so. I don't know.' Seymour frowned. 'That upsets you?'

'Yes.' Byron dropped his head onto his arms. Alma hadn't known about that maneuver. She hadn't known at all. He sighed. 'I've made a decision.' His voice sounded hollow inside his arms. 'Let Lord Kensington know I want to negotiate peace terms.'

'Negotiate? But we're winning!'

'We're all losing, all of us.' Byron made himself stand. He was dizzy. He put a hand out to steady himself. The wall felt damp. 'Come with me. We can talk about it.'

Their footsteps echoed in the corridor. The guards standing outside Byron's door nodded when they saw him. He handed one of them the dagger. 'Keep this,' he said. 'I don't want to see it again.' Then he let himself in the door and froze. Alma sat on a cushion, her fingers toying with his lute. The notes she plucked were jagged and toneless.

'I've been waiting for you,' she said. 'You haven't been here for two nights.'

He couldn't look at her. All he could see was her face as it had been on the pillow, bathed in moonlight. Fear surged through him again. He had snapped and nearly killed her.

'Byron? Are you all right?' Seymour put a supporting arm behind his back and led him to a cushion.

Byron nodded. The weakness passed. 'I haven't slept.' He waved away Seymour's concern and forced himself to look at Alma. 'Why do you want to see me?'

'There's a leak here in the palace.' She threw a packet at him.

'What is this?'

'I placed a spy in Kensington's camp.'

Byron picked up the packet. The papers were light. He recognized Kensington's seal. 'A spy?'

'Well, no one else seemed to know what they were doing.' She shrugged. 'I'm sorry about the first attack, but I didn't know about the ambush. The spy didn't warn me. But this time I sent word to your archers and they were ready.'

Byron closed his eyes. 'You say there's a leak here.'

'Oh, don't worry. I found it.' Alma sounded smug. Byron forced himself to look at her.

'Who is it?'

An empty smile played at her lips. 'Why don't I let Seymour tell you?'

'Me?' Seymour's voice rose. 'I don't know anything about a spy.'

'No?'

Byron forced himself to concentrate. 'Seymour? Why should Seymour know?'

'Because he's the spy. He and Vonda, the spider lady.'

Seymour? Seymour a spy? Byron shook his head. How could he

believe that Alma betrayed him and not believe that Seymour would? 'Is that true, Seymour?'

'No!' He knelt beside Byron.

Alma watched them. She set down the lute, and ghost chords echoed in its belly. 'Then tell me how Vonda knew of the battle this morning. A battle I didn't even know about.'

The color drained out of Seymour's face. 'How do you know Vonda knew?'

'I saw her leave early. My spy says she's been bringing Lord Kensington regular reports.'

'Oh no.' Seymour sat heavily. 'I told her so much because I trusted her. You can kill me, Byron. You have every right to.'

Byron put his arm around Seymour and hugged him close. He remembered Seymour's burned hands, the stench of burned skin, his gratitude that he would no longer have to perform. This fight was Byron's. His friends had suffered enough. 'There's been enough death.'

Alma snorted. 'I would pick my confidants more carefully, Byron.'

'Leave him alone, Alma.' The dizziness returned. Byron felt the strain weaken him. 'I need sleep.'

He knew now what he should do. It was the only way. 'Send that dispatch, Seymour, to Kensington.'

'What dispatch?' Alma asked.

'Peace terms.'

'We're giving in?' Her body tensed. Not with displeasure but with anger.

'No,' Byron said. 'We're trying something new.'

iii

The blood flowed and she squeezed it out of the trees. Other Enos joined her, and soon the cavern was splattered with whispering, flowing blood. *Soon there'll be too much to fight*, Zcava had told them. She was going to wait until Ikaner and her Enos were too tired, and then she would help the Old Ones find their way into the trees, into the future.

Ikaner thought of her bluff, the warm river breeze, trees unthreatened by death. She wanted to see it once more. Zcava was right: there had been more blood in the morning. She knew that once the Enos joined the fight the blood would flow like her river and it would drown the young whistle-woods.

The young whistle-wood voices were soft, and they dreamed of music, of combining tones, of nurturing seedlings, and creating Enos. Every creature had dreams, even the Old Ones. But the Old Ones dreamed of survival and youth, something they had had. The whistle-woods dreamed of new things: of their future.

Ikaner had no future. She left the others to guard the trees. She had to stop the Old Ones before the blood began to flow again.

Enos die for their land.

She wished she could see her bluff one more time.

iv

Byron's chambers felt cold. He had been cold since the night he had spent in the garden. He leaned against one of the chairs, Alma beside him, and watched Seymour. The guards behind them were silent.

'And finally, he wants to know if you're afraid to put your terms on paper.' Seymour looked up from the dispatch. 'Well?'

Byron smiled. 'Of course not. Get a scribe to take a message.'

One of the guards left the room. Alma's hand caressed his arm. She was worried about him. So was Seymour. They hadn't left him since the night he snapped. He wasn't going to break now. He wouldn't let himself. His violence would be directed against the one it should have been directed against in the first place: Kensington.

A scribe came into the room, bowed, and took his place beside Byron. The man was old, his skin puckered against his bones. 'Sire?'

'I want you to pen a dispatch.'

The scribe set out his pen, inkwell, paper, and wax. Byron set the seal on the table. As soon as the scribe was ready, he began:

'Kensington: My terms are simple. I propose a one-on-one fight between the two of us. The victor becomes king. Meet me tonight in the field near Anda – the field where you slaughtered my men. Bring witnesses and the weapon of your choice. Before I fight, however, I will need your oath that the fighting between our houses will end.'

'You're insane,' Seymour said. 'Byron, if you lose, everything will be wasted. Everything.'

Byron signed the parchment and watched as the scribe sealed it. Then he placed the seal back into his pouch. 'No, Seymour. If I win at the cost of hundreds of lives, what have I gained? A kingdom where the people and the gentry hate me. If I win on my own merits, I'm free to rule as I please.'

'And if Kensington wins?'

'I'll be put to death, of course. Alma will survive, she always does. Your friend Vonda will save you, and the kingdom will go on as before.'

'You're afraid, aren't you?' Alma asked. Her voice purred against her throat and her hand had left his arm. 'Afraid you aren't worthy of other people's lives.'

Byron didn't move. He wasn't worth other people's lives. 'This is my fight,' he said. 'It's yours because you chose to enter and Seymour's because I involved him in it. But the two hundred peasants who died this week had no argument with Kensington. Neither had their families. Now what do all those people do? I'm not in the business of making paupers. I will secure my throne or die trying. It's cowardly to let others do my fighting for me.'

'Why didn't you kill Kensington the night the king died?'

'Because I had hoped he would eventually support me.'

'Byron – '

'I am not going to discuss this anymore,' Byron said. He got up and left the room. The hallway seemed even cooler, but he felt more relaxed. He had made his choice. He would have no more blood on his hands.

V

Ikaner's hands throbbed. The blisters had popped, letting pus run down her arms. She held the burning torch away from the trees and touched the bark of the old, bowed whistle-woods. No tree spoke back to her, no life flowed through it. These whistle-woods had been dead longer than she had been alive.

We are your wisdom.

The blood will save us.

If you kill us, the Enos will die.

Ikaner felt the strength of the voices in her head, the whispering hush-hush of their logic. *Enos die for their trees,* she thought.

Enos cannot live without us. We grow you, nurture you.

But we fertilize our own seedlings. The heat from the torch seared her hand. Nothing lived in these trees, but the act she was about to commit seemed unspeakable. She thought of the seedlings, the young trees, and the land, licking blood and absorbing bloodlust. She thought of her bluff, and then she swung the torch around and shoved it inside the whistle hole of the nearest tree. The bark caught, but the tree did not scream. She lit the next tree and the next, and then something grabbed her mind, tried to force her out of it. She put up shields and winced as they broke, shattered, taking portions of her mind with them. The Old Ones were flowing to her, trying to become part of her.

She did not touch the next tree she set aflame. The smoke smelled of dead things and the air grew hotter. She lit another tree and another, until the entire grove burned. Voices clamored in her mind. She sank to the ground, clutching her head. She could feel them holding her, their souls older than hers, stronger, and she so tired from saving the trees. Her mind faded, and she crawled through the fire, the smoke to the outside.

And stopped. The bloodlust hushed through her veins: the lies of the Old Ones, dead at the time of the last lust, caused by a white mist the humans called Gerusha. The Old Ones had killed trees then, had tainted the land, and waited until they grew stronger. More Old Ones now, and they hated Enos, hated trees, wanted only their own power.

She grabbed a dead whistlewood and held it, the shards of her mind gathering into one final picture. The fire seared her clothing, dug into her skin, and she saw her bluff as she had first seen it, leaning over the river, the grasses bending with a light breeze, young trees – her children – calling to her. The water had been cool and fresh, the trees gentle. She had rested among the grasses. She had rested among the grasses – and decided that she wanted to die there.

She reached through the ground for her bluff. It felt her, she knew, across the distance, wrapped itself around her, and as her consciousness flickered against the power of the Old Ones, it promised her it would hold her as she had held it, helping her die so that they could all live.

vi

The field stood under the gray skies. Hundreds of feet had churned the dry earth. Here and there Byron could still see the imprint of a body, but the blood had soaked into the dirt long before. He paced the length of the field, feeling no fear. The calmness that had come with his decision stayed with him. If he didn't win, it didn't matter. No one else would die.

Kensington had not yet arrived. He had chosen swords for the fight, and Byron had then specified no shields or armor. He wanted it to end quickly.

Seymour stood beside Alma at the edge of the field. Alma's eyes were bright with fear and excitement, a small dagger hidden in her hair. Byron had smiled as he watched her insert it that morning. She would survive. She was the strongest of all of them.

Colin waited apart from the others. Byron had refused to let him bring a lute, although composing was Colin's last test before he could become a bard. Byron did not want this battle to be glorified in song.

A handful of guards stood behind the boy, prepared to whisk Byron's friends to safety should anything go wrong. Afeno stood with his arms behind his back, watching, waiting. If the guards did not come through, Afeno would.

A page ran across the field to him. 'Horses! From the north.'

Byron glanced across the barren land, catching Kensington's flag in a cloud of dust. He walked slowly back to his people and waited.

Kensington dismounted across the field. His supporters did the same. Seymour walked over to them, his face set. He was to get Kensington's oath in writing. When he reached the lord's entourage, he stopped. Byron frowned. Vonda stood beside Kensington. Seymour glanced quickly at her, then turned his back on her. Kensington handed Seymour a piece of parchment which Seymour read. Then, nodding, Seymour returned.

Byron walked to the center of the field, his feet sinking in the dry earth. As Kensington approached, Byron extended his hand. 'Good luck, milord,' he said.

Kensington stared at the hand in surprise. Finally he took it in his own and shook. 'And to you.'

The observers gathered around them, leaving just enough room for the battle. The two men separated, pulled their swords, and circled each other for a moment. Byron's eyes were on Kensington's, his concentration high. He could feel his muscles tense with anticipation.

Kensington lunged. Byron parried, and steel crashed against steel. Kensington backed away and Byron followed, the swords meeting at each thrust. Kensington's sword broke free. Byron attempted to flip it loose but failed, losing his balance. Kensington lunged for Byron's open side. Byron whirled as Kensington's blade swished past him.

'Very good, milord,' he murmured, recovering himself. Kensington smiled, his blade cutting through the air. Byron's blade met it and again they were at a stalemate.

Then Byron broke away. Kensington thrust, his right hand tight around his sword, his left open. Byron suddenly realized that Kensington had never fought without a shield or a dagger in his left hand. Parrying, Byron worked his way toward Kensington's left. Kensington continued to circle and thrust, like a cat toying with a mouse. Byron's right arm was getting tired, the muscles heavy, but he felt a curious exhilaration. Out of the corner of his eye he could see Alma, her brow creased with concentration. Her concern pleased him and he again turned his full attention on Kensington.

The lord attempted an inward thrust, but Byron moved out of the way. He plunged his sword into the opening left by Kensington's maneuver and felt a shudder run through him as the blade pierced Kensington's side. Kensington clutched the wound while he backed away. Byron followed, enjoying the sight of blood on Kensington's hand. Kensington thrust twice, Byron parrying. Then Byron lunged again. This time Kensington anticipated the action and the swords clashed. They moved close to each other, like two dancers.

Kensington whirled, catching Byron off guard. The lord's sword hit the bard's arm with an amazing force. Byron winced as the blade slit through the skin, suddenly angry that he had allowed himself to be hit. He attacked, slashing viciously. Kensington, unable to parry the rapid blows, dodged and then again attempted an inward thrust.

Byron's sword hit Kensington's. His weapon flew across the field. The force of the blow snapped Byron's blade and he tossed away the hilt. Kensington threw himself at Byron. The wind left

Byron's body as his back hit the dirt. Kensington's hands were about his neck, squeezing tightly. Byron gripped the lord's wrists, attempting to pry the man away. His lungs burned with lack of oxygen. Near panic, he brought up his knees and used the strength of his legs to roll over.

As Kensington hit the ground, he grunted but did not loosen his grip. Byron brought a knee against Kensington's groin and for a brief instant felt the hands about his neck go slack. He took a gulp of air and pushed Kensington away. Byron got up, breathing heavily, unwilling to grapple in the dirt like a child.

A second later, Kensington was on his feet, a dagger in his hand. Byron heard the spectators gasp. Swords were the agreed-upon weapons. He couldn't see past that knife, wanting to kill the man. Byron swung a fist at Kensington, but Kensington ducked and slashed. The knife slid across Byron's stomach. He staggered from the blow. Kensington lunged again and fear made Byron dodge.

He grabbed Kensington's wrist and pulled him to the ground, trying to knock the dagger free. Kensington struggled, but Byron held on for a moment. Then he let go and stood up. A look of confusion crossed Kensington's face. As he pulled himself to his feet, Byron kicked the knife, knocking it from Kensington's hand. It soared straight above them, and they forgot each each in their scramble to catch the dagger. Kensington's hand closed around the blade, but the pain made him release it. Byron caught the hilt, then grabbed Kensington's shirt, and tossed him back into the dirt. Byron put the blade to Kensington's throat, digging the sharp edge in ever so slightly.

'Do you concede? Or do I have to kill you?' Byron asked. Kensington pushed Byron, but the bard retained his position. He pressed harder against Kensington's throat. The spectators leaned closer.

Kensington's eyes glittered. 'Concede,' he said, his voice harsh from the blade's pressure. 'I concede.'

Byron tossed the knife point down into the ground and helped Kensington to his feet. Kensington rubbed his neck. Byron walked toward Seymour, feeling dizzy with the loss of blood, knowing he was near collapse. Then he heard the thunk of a blade piercing skin. He turned to see Kensington fall face forward in the dry earth, Alma's dagger in his back.

Byron's anger returned, banishing his weakness. 'Almathea!'

Alma caught the anger in his tone. Her dark eyes flashed with a light of their own. She took a few steps forward and flipped Kensington over, not noticing as his blood stained her white gown. In his hand, the lord held his dagger.

'He was going to stab you in the back,' she said. 'Should I have waited to see if you noticed?'

Byron ignored her sarcasm. He dropped to his knees beside Kensington. The lord smiled and let go of the dagger. Byron took his free hand.

'Seymour.'

Seymour and Vonda both came over and propped Kensington on his side. Kensington's breath came in gasps. They began to work on his back when the lord's grip on Byron's hand tightened. Fear shot through Kensington's face and his breath rattled in his throat. After a moment Byron reached up and closed Kensington's eyes.

Byron stood, feeling another wave of dizziness flow through him. He steadied himself and then turned to Almathea. She was staring at him, her chin jutting out slightly. He had never seen her looking so beautiful.

'Almathea,' he said, extending his hand. 'Come here.'

She took his hand and he pulled her into his arms. Her touch was light, careful of his wounds. He didn't know how long they stood there, his face buried in her hair, his arms encircling her small frame, but he needed her support to prevent his collapse. She had supported him from the moment she saw him. Perhaps that meant she loved him. Perhaps she only saw that her future was best with him.

But it didn't matter. He had what he wanted now. He wasn't going to lose it.

Epilogue

The grove still smelled of burned trees. Byron stood at the edge and watched the Enos crouch over the land. They cleared the burnt earth, watered it and fertilized it, as if they expected it to grow again. He would miss the whistle-woods. They had touched his childhood.

The Enos came to him, her head bowed. She looked like Lord Demythos' Enos, but he wasn't sure. 'I'm sorry about the whistle-woods,' he said.

She held out a hand to him. Burns scraped along the palm, removing skin, revealing a substance beneath that looked like wood. *Come.*

He took her hand and followed her to the mouth of the Cache. 'I can't,' he said when he realized that she wanted him to go in. 'It's forbidden.'

Things change. He thought he felt a touch of sadness and fear mingled with the words in his mind. The Enos led him inside the Cache.

The air was cold and damp. Glowing rocks led them to a cavern. The air inside was humid and the light intense. An indoor garden greeted him.

Come.

He followed the Enos up a footpath and saw before him a grove of thin saplings. Whistle-woods. She must have heard his thought.

Our future. And again he felt that rill of fear.

He nodded, pleased to see the trees. He wished he could show Alma, but knew that he would never be allowed inside the Cache again.

The Enos took his arm and led him to the center of the grove. He sat on a rock, smelling the tangy scent of the whistle-woods.

'No prophecy?' he asked the Enos before him.

She bowed her head, then reached and touched his temples.

Slides moved in his mind, the barriers she had set up decades before. He felt her pull them from him.

The old ways are gone with the Old Ones. The future is dark, and we make our own choices now. Her fingers left his temples. *Peace between us?*

Byron nodded, wondering if there had ever been any strife. *Yes,* he thought, knowing that thoughts meant more to the Enos than spoken words. *There will be peace between us always.*

Peace. The word seemed to echo through his head, as if it were spoken by hundreds of different voices. He leaned back in the whistle-wood grove, felt the trees touch him.

Our future, he thought and smiled. He finally believed he had one.

ABOUT THE AUTHOR

Kristine Kathryn Rusch's short fiction has appeared in *Aboriginal SF, Amazing Stories, Isaac Asimov's Science Fiction Magazine, The Magazine of Fantasy and Science Fiction*, and many other magazines. Her work has been nominated for both Nebula and Hugo Awards and reprinted in *The Year's Best Fantasy, The World's Best Science Fiction* 1989 and *The Year's Best Science Fiction*. She won the John W. Campbell Award for the Best New Writer. Along with her partner, Dean Wesley Smith, she won a World Fantasy Award for her work on *Pulphouse: The Hardback Magazine*. She is the editor of *The Magazine of Fantasy and Science Fiction*.